Thailand Joy

a novel by

David Young

Thailand Joy

ISBN 974-243-104-3
First printing 2002
© 2002 by Editions Duang Kamol, Ltd.
Text by : David Young
Published by : Editions Duang Kamol

Printed in Thailand by :
Editions Duang Kamol, Ltd.
212 Ngamwongwan Rd.,
Kwaeng Tungsonghong, Laksi,
Bangkok 10210
Tel. 0-258-9957, 0-2580-9959, 0-25809910, 0-2591-0359-60
Fax 0-25809910
e-mail : edk@dk.co.th
http://www.dk.co.th

Other books
by

DAVID YOUNG

ೞ൞

THE SCRIBE

2

ผู้ชายเปรียบเหมือนช้างเท้าหน้า
ผู้หญิงเปรียบเหมือนช้างเท้าหลัง

Men are the front legs of an elephant
Women are the back two

(Thai proverb)

Part One

1

Jakkrit Kittikorn was drunk again. He spent the afternoon wandering the dirt roads of his village, singing songs, shouting to his neighbors, and frightening schoolchildren. Many of the schoolchildren were used to him by now, but there were still some younger ones who were spooked by his rambling and roving. Jakkrit didn't mean any harm. He just wanted to warn them about the tiger that lived in the nearby wood. Or was it a giant lizard? Yes, a giant lizard with fangs the size of butcher's knives. Bah! If they didn't want to listen, let them be eaten! It served them right! *Som num na!*

Night came. Most of the villagers had already returned to their homes. Save for a row of unsightly townhouses, the houses of the village were all similar in appearance. They were wooden and stood almost ten feet off the earth, supported by heavy stilts.

Their roofs were slanted to keep the rain from leaking in. In front of the houses sat much smaller homes, resting on a single pole, and decorated with garlands. Anyone passing by would see tiny figurines placed inside. These were spirit houses, and they kept misfortune at bay by providing a place for restless ghosts to reside. Some of the more elaborate spirit houses, like the ones in front of the Jerriporn or Apichak homes, served doubly as a Keep Away sign for drunks like Jakkrit, who had neither home nor spirit house to protect him from misfortune.

And so he sang. He sang old songs that he had learned in school. He sang songs that he had learned from his mother. Love songs, work songs, children's songs. Jakkrit knew them all by heart, and his drunkenness made the lyrics sound sweet. He was much too drunk to speculate just where he had taken his wrong turn in life, and even if he had the clarity of mind, the past was better off left buried in song. Soon, however, he was thirsty again. He remembered that Prapeut's shop stayed open late and started to walk for the hundredth time through the village. Of course, he had no money in his pockets, but maybe Prapeut would be good hearted enough to give him a drop on credit. Stingy old Prapeut had never been known to do this in the past, why should he bother changing his ways tonight? Because he was Jakkrit's last hope, that's why.

Walking was difficult. The darkness had blotted out the road before him and the voices of trees rubbing their bamboo trunks in the wind gave him the idea that someone was trying to sneak up from behind and steal his soul. Perhaps it was the ghostly hag that Phii Tannawan claimed he saw stalking the rice fields, though Jakkrit hadn't a clue as to why a ghostly hag might be hanging around this village. Stealing souls around here was like a pickpocket fishing for empty wallets. Move on, ghostly hag. Move on or bring me a bottle, thought Jakkrit.

*

Everyone in the village knew Jakkrit. Jakkrit knew everyone in the village. From the corner boys who drove women to the market on their motorcycles to the crazy widow who lived alone with her unknown riches, everyone. He was one of those people who seemed to have been around forever, despite his young age, and would go on forever just the same way. How he ate was a mystery. Where he slept was a mystery. He was a tall man with long, skinny legs that he often tripped over after too much to drink. His face, though not unpleasant to look at, had unfortunately aged far beyond his years and gave him a certain grimness that was uncommon for someone in their late twenties. Thus, when drunkenness turned him into a buffoon, it was hard to know whether one should laugh or be afraid of him. Generally, the villagers tended to ignore him.

The drunk man's foot hit a stone and he fell down somewhere in the dark. A warm paralysis overtook him as he lay on his back in the dirt. A million stars shone above him. Damned if he could recall a song about the stars. All he had was a song about the moon.

"Duang jaan wan pen roi den bun na paa..."

and that was all he could remember. He was out of songs. Never! He was never out of songs! From somewhere in the distance came the sound of Tannawan's ghostly hag. On second thought, it was just a television. A man and a woman were having an argument in a popular soap opera.

"You've got lipstick on your cheek!" screamed an actress.

"I have not!"

"It's that servant girl of ours, isn't it?"

"She's not a servant girl - she's a princess!"

Jakkrit opened his mouth and let out a few nonsensical words. Then he lifted his hands from the dusty ground and pressed them to his face. So many stars! Jakkrit had a song for every one of them. Just give him a moment to think.

The television program cut to a commercial. It was an advertisement for soap. Jakkrit had seen the commercial many times, though just where was impossible to remember. It was for a special kind of soap that got rid of BACTERIA. Jakkrit smiled and kicked up more of the dust on the road. The commercial had a short jingle in English. It went like this:

Clean and Happy
Clean and Happy
Bye Bye Bac-tee-ree-ahh!

A song for a star. Jakkrit began to sing. Only the cl of clean came out as a cr, like in cream. The p's sounded like b's and the multi-syllable 'bacteria' was so garbled, even Jakkrit didn't know what he was saying.

Whoosh! The light and noise of a thousand angry fireflies suddenly descended upon him. Jakkrit sat up, swatting his chest and ears.

"Jakkrit, you fool!" said a voice. It was Phii Apichak and his swollen boat wife, coming home from their *gooey teeo* restaurant in town. Phii Apichak drove a motorcycle and wore a green army helmet on his head. He had a greasy face with plenty of boils that were the result of standing over a steaming tub of pork broth for years on end. His wife sat in a rusted sidecar, her strong, beefy arms holding various pots and pans that rattled against one another each time she shifted her weight.

"Mao!" she declared. "Drunk!"

"You'd better get out of the road," said Apichak. "I almost ran over you!"

"Cream and Habby," said Jakkrit.

Apichak's wife shook her head. *"Mao."*

"I'll say it one more time. Get out of the road!"

Apichak pointed a pink scalded finger away from the road, in case there was any doubt about which direction he meant. Jakkrit responded by waving his hand in the air.

"Bye bye."

Apichak had had enough. He revved the engine and steered around the drunk man's body. His wife looked down at him as they passed. Her face had run the same gauntlet as her husband's but had somehow survived the assault of grease and sweat. Instead, it was her ill temper that made her so unbearable to gaze upon.

"Mao," she declared again, and disappeared in the night.

Darkness at last. The sounds of the night were now only voices from the television soap opera. Jakkrit lay back down. Where were his friends who knew so many of the old songs? His friends were gone. They had all left for the city to find work. Jakkrit closed his eyes and tried to think. Thinking was difficult. The commercial jingle was stuck in his mind as though someone had plugged a cassette tape into the back of his head. Clean and happy, clean and happy. He couldn't sing it. He could only hear it.

Then there was another sound, another light. There was no mistaking this noise. Jakkrit opened his eyes. It was Nongluck, coming home from her job at the hair salon in town. Nongluck wasn't just any hairstylist. She was a beauty expert. She knew the right kind of shampoo to use, the right kind of conditioner, all that. She did fingernails, toes, and waxed off unwanted hair. She had even read a book once and could tell people what season they were; hot, rainy, or cool. Jakkrit might have asked her to marry him a long time ago, or had he only thought about it? Nongluck was very pretty. If he had asked, he couldn't remember what her answer had been, though he guessed it was no. He did remember which season she told him he was. He was the hot season.

Nongluck drove her brother's car, an old Japanese model that often broke down. Jakkrit wondered if she might stop and sing a song beneath the stars with him. What happened next happened so fast, he didn't have a chance to consider how inappropriate it would be stopping a pretty lady to sing with him, especially when he could only think of a commercial jingle for soap. It happened when the noise and the light of Nongluck's brother's car were at their loudest and brightest. Jakkrit felt something press down on his long legs. There was a loud snap, two loud snaps come to think of it, and an even blacker blackness, punctured by the fingertips of a bone white skeleton. The sound of the car disappeared around a bend as Jakkrit watched still another visitor emerge from the dark.

It was an old woman.

It was the hag that Tannawan had spoken of! The one he claimed gutted his chickens and ate their intestines. And laughing, you should hear her, hee hee hee! The hag hobbled close to Jakkrit and bent down over his legs. Her hair was matted and smelled of dung heaps. Jakkrit tried to say "Go away, hag!" but his fear wouldn't allow it. The hag took something from him and scuttled away like a wounded insect. Jakkrit felt his muscles go weak and he closed his eyes.

There it was, his song for the stars. One had come to him at last.

It went like this.

2

It was five o'clock in the morning when Prapeut decided to go outside his house and break up pieces of concrete with a sledgehammer. The noise awoke his daughter, Mantana, who at first thought the walls were falling down around her. She stayed in bed until a cock began to crow, then sat up, deciding the whole venture was useless. She had been dreaming about her mother and wondered if she called out her name in her sleep. Why else would her father be hammering concrete at five in the morning?

Mantana sat up in bed and sighed. She was a remarkably beautiful girl, having retained every bit of her childhood radiance, brought into a new light by young womanhood. Her hair was dark, her eyes only a fraction of a shade lighter and bore an intensity that constantly made those near her wonder what she was thinking, when most of the time, she wasn't thinking anything at all. Despite the fact that everyone she met commented upon her beauty, Mantana always considered herself rather plain. She was convinced the beauty that others saw was only a shadow of her mother's that had been passed on to her. Now *there* was the real beauty.

Mantana swung her feet over the side of the bed and set them on the cool wooden floor. She looked at her toes and imagined each one to be a separate little body with a toenail for a face. She wondered what they would talk about if they had mouths. Would they be sore about having to sleep so close together like the Duangdao family whose house burnt down last month? Would they wish they could live in nice shoes and curse her when she walked around barefoot? Mantana thought about her toes a little while longer, then stopped thinking about them altogether. Today was a very important day for her and she shouldn't be thinking of silly things like toes. Besides, she wasn't nine as she was when her mother died. She was nineteen. Old enough to work.

In fact, she had worked ever since she could remember. She helped father with his store. She washed clothes for two families in the village. She sold lottery tickets on the side. Mantana worked, but what was her money compared to that of the Jerriporn boys, Aze and Art, who had each gone to a university and found jobs in Bangkok? Within six months, Khun Jerriporn and his wife had the money to buy a new car, a new television, and a satellite that didn't work yet, but certainly looked impressive on the roof of their house.

And what about the widow Amnuay? Where her money came from might be a mystery to some, but Mantana remembered the old stories, and couldn't mention her name without shaking her head and cursing her lot. The widow Amnuay had torn down her old house and built a new one in its place; an ugly, modern residence with bars upon the windows and a surrounding brick wall with shards of broken glass sticking out of the upper row. The place reminded Mantana of a prison. Whenever a delivery truck from the appliance store in town rambled past her father's store, there was never a doubt about where it was headed. The widow Amnuay had made another purchase. At times like this it was best to find work to do and avoid her father's eyes. She knew as the whole village knew that Prapeut would never have a new car or a new house or a new satellite that didn't work. He would only have a daughter. Work, bills, debts, one big mortgage and two empty pockets. And the sight of the widow Amnuay's latest purchase always threw him into the blackest of moods. He began by cursing himself, then moved on to Mantana, then his wife, who he cursed for dying. He made threats that ranged from selling Mantana to the highest bidder to taking up with the widow and sharing in her suspicious wealth. No matter what his threat might be, it was always scandalous and shocking.

After this day, however, things might be a little easier for him. This was the day Mantana left for Bangkok.

Mantana sighed and turned her eyes to the photograph of her mother that sat on a table next to her bed. It was a color photo, but taken so long ago that the yellows and greens now seemed painted on with a timeworn brush. The colors dated the picture. No modern camera would ever produce a photo like this. Still, it was the only photograph Mantana had of her. What the camera hadn't captured was made up for by the memories she kept inside her. She had once been a strong woman who held on to her customs and beliefs the way one might hold a lantern in a dark cave. They guided her, but it was her own eyes, her own feet that led her through the days. At least until the cancer came to take her life.

How she missed her.

Outside, the hammering stopped. Mantana opened a set of doors and climbed out of the room in which she and her father slept. Down below was an addition to the house that Prapeut had built after his wife died. The room had a concrete floor, brick walls, and a flat, tin roof that amplified the sound of raindrops until they were as loud as Chinese firecrackers. The inside of the room was about as cheerful as the sight of the widow Amnuay's jailhouse. Once upon a time, her father had planned to build a whole new house, and used to brag to his family about what it would look like. Spacious and cool, made with the finest wood. Two bedrooms, and a living room where the three of them could lie about and eat and watch television. When he saw that it would only be the two of them continuing on in this life, he threw away his plans and built the ugly, concrete floored room instead.

"Joy!" came her father's voice from outside.

"Yes," she answered. "I woke up when you started hammering."

"Coffee?"

"I'm making it now."

The door opened. Her father stood there, smoking a cigarette. His heavily lidded eyes looked at nothing in particular, yet at the same time seemed to be involved in the deepest concentration. These were the eyes that her mother told her she inherited. Thus, it wasn't without some personal interest that made her wonder at the hint of nastiness she and she alone seemed to notice in them. She never considered her father an evil man, but he did have his moments of wickedness. Like the times he refused to give her money for schoolbooks or the times he called her worthless. If these were truly the eyes that were passed on to his daughter, did they include the rotten part of his soul as well?

These days however, Mantana noticed her father had little time or desire to be rotten. His hair always seemed a little bit grayer than it did the day before, his face a little rougher. He didn't suffer from lines and wrinkles any more than a stone left to bake in the sun withered beneath the heat. The flesh on his face only grew harder, more resilient to change, and more silent in emotion. As he stood in the doorway, Mantana guessed that he had something on his mind, though she knew it was pointless to ask. Her father rarely responded to questions. Ask him what day it was and he'd point to the horizon, then walk off while the inquirer searched to see what he was pointing at.

Still, this was the big day. The day she was leaving and even though she had reminded him about it for the past week and a half, he hadn't said whether he approved or not. He only grunted and went off to do some chore that didn't need to be done. Her father's work was construction. The store he owned only brought in a small sum of money that kept them from starving when work was scarce. Work had been scarce lately, and this was how he kept himself from thinking about his debts. Mantana was afraid to bring up her decision, but was forced to because she knew he wouldn't.

"I'm leaving today, father," she said. "I'm leaving on the eleven o'clock bus."

He took a long drag on his cigarette, then flicked it to the ground.

"Phii Nongluck said I could ride with her to the beauty parlor in town. The bus station isn't far."

Outside, Min the dog wandered up to the door and sniffed her father's shoes. Min was a wretched thing that had lost all its fur to some canine disease. The dog's skin looked raw and painful. It was the kind of mutt that wouldn't get much more than a name in its lifetime. Prapeut kicked it in the snout and sent it yelping away. Mantana ignored the act of cruelty and lifted a coffee mug from a plastic rack to wipe clean with her shirttail. She waited patiently for her father to speak, but when she looked up, saw that he no longer stood in the doorway. There was only the sun now, rising above the trees, promising another hot, dry day. Mantana set the cup down and sighed.

Bang, went the hammer against the concrete.

*

By ten in the morning, Mantana was packed and ready to go. She carried a single black bag stuffed with clothes and toiletries. In her front pocket was three hundred baht that she had kept from selling lottery tickets. She normally handed the money over to her father to help pay for the mortgage on the house. The mortgage was already three years old. It had been taken out to pay some business loans, so her father said. Mantana suspected that the business consisted of throwing dice and laying down cards. A business her father was never very good at.

Speaking of her father, just what was he doing, fluttering about the house? Normally, he would have finished his chores by now and left to open the shop. Only today, he was still working outside, doing this and that, but nothing of importance. When Mantana left the house, he had taken the front wheel off a rusted out wheelbarrow and was scraping it with a knife. She stood watching him in the morning sun and noticed his neck and shoulders wet with sweat. In his back pocket was a blue handkerchief. Mantana bowed her head. The color of her father's handkerchief was the same color as the hospital sheets on the bed in which her mother died. It was odd that these memories were so strongly with her today. Normally, she didn't think of her mother's death, and when she did, she certainly didn't show any emotion over it. Now, she suddenly felt like crying. She supposed that the most difficult things to forget about that day were her mother's words to her. They came after Prapeut had left the room to look for a nurse because his wife was in pain, and Mantana stood watching over her in the seventh bed of a room full of beds, all of them vacant except hers. Why was it suddenly her mother's turn to be sick? Surely there were others who deserved to be in that bed besides her. Others who didn't take care of themselves and didn't have a family to take care of as well. It was such a big, empty room, without even a picture on the wall. There was only a television mounted on the wall, facing her mother. The television wasn't turned on and

Mantana remembered wishing that it was; because nothing terrible or serious can happen in the middle of a game show or soap opera, can it? Suddenly, mother set a hand upon hers. The skin was cold but her voice was calm and clear.

"Take care of your father, Joy. See that he doesn't get old without two or three things to show for himself."

Later, she found out that it was an extra fifty baht per day to have a nurse turn the television on. Prapeut would have done it but his wife insisted that dying was already expensive enough. So the television was kept off and Mantana's mother passed away to the sounds of car horns and parking guard whistles outside the hospital window. And her blue sheets were the same color as the handkerchief that stuck out of her father's back pocket as he worked beneath the morning sun.

"I've arranged for Phii Kum to wash your clothes," said Mantana, swallowing her thoughts. "Just be sure to put your dirty things in the basket."

He continued to scrape without looking at her.

"And I've written down the address where I'll be staying. I'll be sharing a room with Darunee."

"I don't know Darunee."

"Of course you know Darunee."

"Bring me a screwdriver," he said.

"Which screwdriver?"

"The one inside."

Mantana set her bag down and went back into the room. There was a worktable against one wall, littered with screws, bolts, and nails. Every time she had tried to organize the little pieces, her father would scatter them on the table, looking for one particular sized screw, bolt, or nail. The only thing that stayed in place was her father's gun, an unlicensed .38 that was locked in the top drawer. Beneath the table was a metal box where he kept most of his tools. She tried there first.

"Do you want a big one or a little one?" she hollered from underneath the table, and shooed a gecko lizard clinging tight to the wall.

A loud crash from above caused her to jump. Something had hit the roof! Something big! Maybe it was a suitcase of money that had fallen out of an airplane. Maybe it was a meteor. Mantana knew about meteors. She had learned about them in school. She forgot about the hammer and ran outside to look. Her father was looking too. He was out of breath and his eyes looked like tiny jewels in cracked tamarinds.

"What was that?"

No answer. Never an answer. Her father simply shrugged his shoulders and walked off in the direction of his shop. Mantana stepped back and stood on her toes to see what had landed on the roof. It was something black with a piece of metal that reflected the sunlight. She gave a slight gasp and looked for her bag. Her bag was gone. Her bag was on the roof.

Mantana went to the back of the house and carried a wooden ladder to the front. Up she went, and in a few minutes her bag was back down on the ground. Darunee's father had probably acted this way on the day his daughter left, too. But now that Darunee was sending home five hundred, sometimes a thousand baht at the end of each pay period, Mantana was sure he no longer minded her absence. Mantana's father would feel the same, once he had two or three things to show for himself. Maybe she'd even strike it rich there, like a celebrity contestant on a television game show. But weren't celebrity contestants already rich, before they went on game shows to win money? Yes, they were filthy rich, and this thought only depressed her.

After putting the ladder back where it belonged, she placed her hands together and faced the house she grew up in. "*Sa wat dee ka,*" she said with a bow, then dusted off her bag and ran to the road. Maybe it was better this way, without a good-bye. Besides, she would be back to visit soon.

Nongluck's great big Japanese car was already stirring up the dust at the end of the driveway.

3

Phii Nongluck had been married and divorced all before she was twenty-one.

It remained a source of gossip in the village as to why she never bothered with it again. Certainly not because men didn't find her attractive. They did. Her hair was dyed a light brown, and she wore it in two long braids that hung down past her shoulders. She still had the face of a teenager though she was nearly thirty. Some of her older customers chided that her beauty would fade in a few years and it would be impossible to find a husband. Nongluck only laughed and told them she already found a husband once and that if she weren't worried, they shouldn't be either. Fortunately, she escaped most of the dirty lies that housewives liked to spread. Probably because she cut hair so well, and always stocked the latest magazines for customers to read beneath the dryers.

"Did you hear the news?" asked Nongluck on the way to

town. "Some bandits came into the village last night. They ran into Jakkrit and broke both of his legs."

"That's terrible,"

"He was drunk," said Nongluck.

Mantana nodded her head, though she couldn't tell whether her friend meant it as an observation or a condemnation. She always considered Jakkrit friendly, despite a certain bleakness in his eyes that, like her father, made one wonder where the root of his thoughts lay. Mantana had only spoken with him when he came to her father's shop to buy lippovitamin energy drinks, the kind that drove a person mad if he drank too many of them. He was usually polite, except for the time he told her a wild bear had escaped from the zoo and was hiding in the woods just outside town. Zoo? What zoo? Maybe not from the zoo, said Jakkrit, but it was there and it liked to eat little girls just the same. But Mantana was not a little girl anymore, was she? Jakkrit's bear story had made her laugh. She didn't think he was drunk at the time, but looking back, supposed that he was.

"So you've got a job in Bangkok," said Nongluck.

"Yes. Do you remember Darunee? Her nickname is Som."

"Her older sister moved to Bangkok three years ago. We were good friends. I don't know what happened to her."

"Well, Darunee went too. She's working in a department store near Sanam Luang. I told her to write if a position became available."

"And she wrote. What kind of job is it?"

"I think I'll be a salesgirl. Maybe a cashier. Som didn't say."

Nongluck cast her eyes upon Mantana and appeared to scrutinize her.

"Being a salesgirl or a cashier is all right for now," said Nongluck, in a motherly tone, "But you should keep your eyes open."

"What do you mean?"

"You and Som didn't get any further than *mathiyom* six. No

one will give you a good job unless you know someone or have a special skill that few others have."

"Like cooking?"

"No, not cooking. Anyone can cook. I mean being able to use a computer or speak a foreign language."

Nongluck passed a slow moving bulldozer and jerked back into her lane.

"Just don't forget that money isn't made for men," she said. "If you've got a good brain, there'll be some for you, too."

The exit to town was approaching in the distance. Already, the fields and trees were disappearing, with enormous piles of scrap metal and half finished buildings taking their places. Giant concrete pipes lay scattered around an empty field. They had been there for as long as Mantana could remember. Even so, the sight of them always prompted her to wonder what their original purpose was for. They must have cost money, she thought. Someone must have paid to have them delivered to this particular spot. Nongluck made an illegal U-turn and nearly ran a motorcyclist off the road as she swerved for the exit.

"I just hope I'm able to send some of what I make to my father," said Mantana.

"How is he?"

Mantana heard her question, but answered another one, the one inside of her, instead. "It's so unfair that the people who work hard all their lives have to grow old without any of the things they've wanted over the years. Just once, I'd like to take my father shopping and let him pick out anything in the store. Tools, clothes, a fishing pole; anything!"

"Money doesn't always mean happiness," said Nongluck. "And you'll often find that most of the things people buy aren't necessarily the things they want. Look at the widow Amnuay."

"Let's not talk about her. I'll only get upset."

They drove for a while in silence. Outside, a half dozen

skinny buffaloes grazed at the base of a billboard. A wind-torn sign fluttered from the sign's metal grating: **ADVERTISE HERE.**

"You know, Joy, if all else fails, you should think about finding yourself a rich husband. A rich *foreign* husband. Bangkok would certainly be the place to look."

Mantana looked at her friend to see if she were serious. "What foreigner would want me for a wife? He wouldn't be able to understand me."

"You'd be surprised. Some men don't want a wife for conversation. They only want to be taken care of."

"What kind of life would that be?"

"Better than most."

"That's a funny thing for you to say."

Nongluck shot her a warning look. The warning was not to mention the past. "Just make sure you've got a safety net," she said.

"You mean money."

"I mean money without anyone whispering behind your back. You've got to be able to hold your head up when you walk down the street."

Mantana knew all this and didn't want to discuss it anymore. Who was Nongluck to lecture her? Where was her storehouse of money and skill and rich foreign husbands? She could barely keep her car on the road! Mantana switched on the radio and found a song that made her think of a village boy she once had a crush on. She turned the volume up so that neither of them could talk. It was a love song with a chorus that went:

> *Love has come*
> *Come into my heart*
> *And loneliness can't touch me now*

Mantana tried to sing along but stopped just short of the second verse.

It didn't sound so good to her now.

*

It wasn't the first time Mantana had been to Bangkok. When her mother was alive, the three of them had often come to make merit at the temples. Once, they had even gone to an amusement park, despite her father's complaints, and Mantana rode her first roller coaster. Back then, the city was a grand and exciting place to visit, seen from her child's eyes. She remembered tall buildings, wonderful movie houses, and modern hairstyles on beautiful women. Now, the buildings all appeared to be up for sale. The movie houses had been taken over by Hollywood, and the clothes and hairstyles were modern only in the sense that they tried to copy the American actors and actresses. What was once grand now seemed sold out. What was once exciting now had a layer of filth upon it.

The bus ride was long, and the electric fans did not rotate as they were supposed to. Mantana arrived at the Mor Chit Bus Terminal late in the day. She got off the blue cross-country bus and got on a red city bus. There were so many people, it was difficult to hang on to her bag whenever the driver stopped to let someone on or off. A tall, thin boy was constantly squeezing past her, shaking a metal cylinder of coins and collecting fares where he could. When a seat opened, only the nearest and fastest were allowed to sit. No one seemed to notice Mantana and her heavy bag. She felt hot and nauseous when she finally got off, and had been holding her pee for so long, she didn't have to go anymore. It made her wonder if she had sweated it out through her skin and, if so, did she smell bad like so many others on the bus?

The name of the store was Rim Ping. The store sold cosmetics, clothes, household goods, televisions, radios, and shoes. On the second floor was a movie theater, in the basement, a grocery store and food court. Mantana walked through the aisles, looking at the salesgirls and imagining herself in their places. They wore white blouses with green vests and matching green skirts. There were plastic nametags on their vests with HELLO, and their names printed in English. Mantana read some of the names as she walked. There was a Nut, a Nok, a Pop, and a Tik. She walked to a glass counter and looked at the hundred shades of fingernail polish before noticing a woman watching her with a salesgirl's indifference.

"Can I help you?" asked the salesgirl. Her nametag said 'Kul.'

"Do you know Miss Darunee? Her nickname is Som. I'm supposed to meet her here about a job."

The woman repeated the name and appeared to be thinking. There was so much make-up on her cheeks and neck that her skin looked as if it could be peeled off to reveal a whole new face underneath.

"Do you know which department she works in?"

"No," said Mantana.

"Hmm. I'm sorry. I don't know anyone here named Darunee or Som."

Mantana went up the escalators to the cinema. No, no one knew of an employee named Darunee or Som. She couldn't be at another store; this was the only Rim Ping Department Store in Bangkok. Maybe the food court? Mantana went downstairs and walked by the small restaurants and drink stands. Men and women stood in chef's hats selling *gooey teeo, pad thai, hoy tawt, kao pad,* and *kao moo daeng.* The sight of food made her ravenously hungry, and she realized that she hadn't eaten a thing since she left her village. She moved to the coupon booth and waited in a small crowd of men and women who kept stepping in front of her to buy coupons. At last, she made it to the window and pushed a twenty baht bill through the opening in the glass before nearly losing her place again.

"Twenty, please," she said.

The girl in the booth looked up at her. What do you know, it was Darunee.

"Joy!" she said happily. "You made it!"

Mantana explained how she had looked for her all over the store. The people behind her started to push forward.

"I have a break in fifteen minutes," said Darunee. "Sit down over there and wait for me. We'll have lunch together."

Mantana did as her friend instructed. Would that be her job as well? Sitting in a booth, collecting money and handing out the correct amount of food coupons? She hoped not.

It didn't look like much fun.

4

The employees of Rim Ping were each allowed a dormitory room in a building no more than twenty minutes away. Long-term employees of ten years or more were given a room of their own on the fourth floor. The rest had to share. Each room contained a ratty mattress, a standing wardrobe assembled from metal pipes and plastic, and a small table that was too low to pull a chair up to. The walls had originally been painted white but had turned yellow over the years, and in some spots, black. The worst part for Mantana, however, was the window. It was not so much a window as it was a hole in the wall with bars. Behind the bars sat a tightly woven wire screen with a thousand dead insects stuck in the tiny grating. It might as well have been a spider's nest for all the good it did as a window.

"It's not very nice," said Darunee, "but it's free."

Mantana set her bag down on the skinny bed and looked around. A stuffed Winnie the Pooh bear, brown with age, served as the only pillow. On the wall above the mattress hung a poster of a little *farang* boy and a little *farang* girl dressed in expensive outfits. They were standing in a field of grass and looking down at a flower in the little *farang* girl's hand. Below the pair was written:

LOVE IS THE NATURAL RHYTHM

Love is the natural rhythm. Mantana had no idea what it meant.

"How is everyone in the village?" asked Darunee.

"Jakkrit had his legs broken by bandits."

"I don't care about Jakkrit. What else?"

Mantana thought for a moment. "I still see your mother when she comes to the shop."

"What about Khun Suwit? Do you ever see Khun Suwit?"

Khun Suwit lived with his wife and daughter. Everyone in town knew it, and Darunee ought to know it too.

"I saw him drinking with Jakkrit one day."

"But he wasn't attacked by bandits, was he?" she asked, a hint of worry in her voice.

"Not that I know of."

Mantana started to unpack her things. She was so tired she felt she could lie down and fall asleep the moment she closed her eyes.

"I'm glad you're here, Joy. The last girl I had to live with was a pig. She'd bring food home only to watch it go bad. And if I threw anything away, she'd yell at me and tell me to replace it."

"What happened to her?"

"I think she went to work in a go-go bar. She once told me she would be better off as a prostitute."

"Was she pretty?"

"She was fat."

Mantana laid out a towel from her bag and dug further in for a bar of soap.

"How much is our salary?" she asked.

"Three thousand a month. Three thousand five if you don't take the room."

Mantana looked at her. "I thought you said the room was free."

"It is," said Darunee. "Three thousand is the regular pay. The extra five hundred is a bonus if you provide your own living space."

"So the room is five hundred baht per month."

"No, it's free."

Mantana didn't feel like arguing. She stood and walked down the hall to the bathroom. Two girls with skeletal eyes watched her pass by from the open door of their room. For as bad as her living space was, it was a paradise compared to the bathroom. The first thing that struck her was the incredible stink, almost as if an animal had died within the pipes and its rotting smell continued to drift up through the sink and toilet. The lower half of the door had rotted away, and a square piece of metal had been hammered in to replace it. Small insects with black wings hovered in the air and clung tightly to the walls. The floor was wet, and a discarded slipper sat collecting an oily film beneath the sink.

Five hundred baht per month, she thought, and closed the door.

*

Darunee was the same age as Mantana. She had grown up in the same village and attended the same schools. She had done poorly in almost every subject, but no one really noticed because Darunee was so cute. Always smiling, always sunny. By the time she was sixteen, she was a beautiful young lady sought out by all the boys her age. Darunee had no time for them. She had started an affair with the affluent and notorious Khun Suwit, who was twice her age and already married to a woman in town. Her trysts were a secret from everyone except Mantana, who often used to tell her "Leave him alone! You don't want to be a *mia nawy!* You don't want to be a minor wife!" But Darunee only laughed and showed her some new piece of jewelry that Khun Suwit had bought for her.

One day, Darunee showed Mantana her stomach. Sure enough, there was a child inside. Mantana went with Darunee to a doctor in town and Darunee had to sell all of her jewelry to pay for what the doctor did to her. Darunee was sick for weeks. She lost so much blood, her skin turned white and she could only eat rice soup. If that wasn't enough for poor Darunee, Khun Suwit discovered that she had sold all his gifts and left her with two black eyes to remember him by. Darunee wasn't so beautiful after that. Mantana knew there was more to the story, but didn't dare ask. She had heard that Darunee's mother discovered the truth behind her illness and beat her daughter's legs so badly that she couldn't wear skirts for a month. There were rumors that Darunee had been ordered to leave, and rumors that she could no longer set foot outside her house. Whatever the truth might have been, it was in the past now and had no bearing on the present. Besides, what good was the past when it brought only sadness to mind?

The next day, Mantana reported for work at seven o'clock in the morning. She filled out some papers and signed her name to a document in which she agreed to a fifty per cent reduction of the first two months salary. The fifty percent she wouldn't receive covered a job security deposit in case she stole anything or made a mess of her apartment. Fortunately, she was allowed to start right away. She was given a green vest and a green skirt. She had a name tag that said HELLO on it. For the first week, she worked downstairs in baggage check with another girl her age named Pusadee. Pusadee was a plain-looking girl with a flat, northeastern nose. Before she had a chance to get to know her, however, she was relocated to a food coupon booth. Both positions were startlingly unpleasant, but the Coupon booth was a little bit better, only because a plastic screen kept her separated from the impatient horde of customers.

During the third week of work, she was moved to the information counter.

"You're very lucky to work information," Darunee told her, back in their tiny room. "All you have to do is sit."

"Yes, but the time goes so slow there, I sometimes think the clocks are moving backwards."

"You'll get used to it."

Darunee was right. Mantana sat. She sat from eight until eleven thirty in the morning, and again from half past twelve until five o'clock with a fifteen-minute break at three. She had a microphone and a list of things to say. She wasn't allowed to say anything that wasn't on the list. She read promotions, sales, food court menu items, and the names of movies that were playing in the upstairs cinema. Occasionally, one of the painted salesgirls would hand her a slip of paper and she'd have to request the owner of a certain automobile to move his or her vehicle. When she wasn't speaking into the microphone, she was giving directions to the toilet. She was telling people when the store closed. She was answering the phone. It seemed everyone in the store considered Information to be a *sabai sabai* position. Calm, easy, all you do is sit! Thus, small side jobs were often given to her. Price tag these pantyhose, rubber-stamp these forms, you're new here, aren't you? Then take the staples out of the left corner of these documents and restaple them in the right.

Darunee was half right. Mantana sat, but she never got used to it.

*

The only excitement came when one of the plainclothes security guards caught someone trying to steal. The criminals were mostly teenage girls who had tried to remove price tags from cheap items and stick them over price tags of expensive items. Nearly all broke into uncontrollable sobs when they were escorted away. Mantana felt sorry for the thieves, but she was glad they were caught. Nothing in life was free, or even cheaper than the retail price for that matter. Sometimes, however, she watched an old man or woman, older than her father, being led to the manager's office and she secretly wished they had gotten away with their wrongdoing.

In the afternoon, she ate lunch with Darunee and Pusadee.

"I saw another shoplifter get caught today," said Mantana. "A girl this time; younger than I. The guard took her upstairs and came down again without her. Then the girl came down an hour and a half later and left the store. She looked upset, but she didn't go to jail."

Darunee and Pusadee continued eating. Mantana looked at each of them.

"Do you know why?" she asked.

"Why what?" said Darunee.

"Why some shoplifters go to jail and others are allowed to walk free."

"The manager has a kind heart."

"No," said Pusadee. "He gives the criminals an opportunity to bribe him. If they can't pay, they're off to jail."

"Don't believe her, Joy. Khun Nemit is a nice man."

This time, Pusadee looked up from her plate of food.

"Why? Because he gave you a job?"

"No. Because he's always smiling. And he talks to me."

"What does he say?" asked Mantana.

"Well, he asks my name a lot and asks whether I'm new here. But that's only because there are so many employees. He says other things, too. 'Keep smiling.' 'No one likes a sad face.' 'Turn that rainbow upside down.' Things like that."

"He's told me that anyone can wear a uniform, but only I

can wear a smile," said Mantana.

"He says that crap to everyone," said Pusadee. "I just wonder what he says to the sweet faced thieves who are locked in his office."

"What do you mean?" said Mantana.

"Maybe nothing," said Pusadee. She glanced to her left and met the eyes of a made-up salesgirl, sitting at a nearby table. She turned away quickly and took a cautious sip of water. "Whatever goes on in that office of his," she whispered over her food, "just remember that you didn't hear it from me."

*

On another of those long afternoons, the salesgirl named Kul from the Miss Lovely Cosmetics stand wandered over to chat with Mantana. Kul was older, with sketched in eyebrows that made her look like a vampire. Mantana didn't like to look at her, but welcomed the opportunity to make new friends. Kul asked where she was living, and how she liked it. Then the information phone rang, and it was for Kul.

"Oh," she said. "I have to wait on a customer. Can I leave this here? I'll be right back for it."

Kul set a small paper bag on the information desk and hurried off. Mantana laid it aside and didn't think of it again until closing time, when she realized Kul must have forgotten about it. She called the Miss Lovely desk to remind her.

"I'm going out front to wait for my ride," said Kul. "Would you mind giving it to me there?"

No, Mantana didn't mind, and even though the security guard hadn't bothered to search her bags like he usually did upon leaving the store, there wasn't a reason in the world to think anything more of it. Sure, if only Kul the vampire salesgirl didn't stop by and leave another small bag with her the very next day! This time,

Mantana didn't set it aside. The bag was stapled shut, but she had become an expert at removing staples. Inside were bottles of fingernail polish, lipsticks, eye shadows, and an expensive skin whitening cream made by the Miss Lovely Company. Mantana quickly closed the bag and resealed it. A thief! She chewed on a fingernail, wondering what to do.

On her next fifteen-minute break, she told Darunee what had happened. And what was happening now.

"If anyone catches me with the bag," she said, "They'll think *I'm* stealing."

Darunee mulled over the situation. Her eyebrows formed two wavy lines on her forehead. Finally, she spoke.

"Don't tell Khun Nemit. Kul's worked here for a long time. You could create a lot of hard feelings if she lost face in front of everyone."

"But I could lose my job!"

"Just give the bag back to her before she leaves the store," said Darunee. "Act like you never opened it."

Mantana looked at her friend. "Would you do it for me? "

"Hm," she said. "If I do it, she'll think you know something."

"I *do* know something!"

"Yes. It's better if you give the bag back to her."

And so, at exactly ten minutes before the store closed that evening, Mantana carried the bag to the Miss Lovely Cosmetics counter and set it upon the glass case. Kul looked at her, looked at the bag, and looked again at Mantana. Her eyebrows were arched more than ever.

"Here's your bag," she said.

"I'm sure to forget it, Nong Joy. You'd better give it to me outside. Just like last night."

Mantana already had a lie prepared. "I have to stay late tonight and type something for Khun Nemit. I won't be leaving when you do."

Kul watched her with blood hungry eyes. *"Really?"* she said.

Mantana smiled nervously and backed away. That wasn't so hard now, was it? Oh, yes it was! She knew that Kul knew that she knew - and she had the feeling this was something that wouldn't just go away on its own.

That didn't stop her from wishing it would, and paying respect to every Buddha in sight on her long walk home.

5

The next day, the store manager, Khun Nemit, strolled by the information desk in a light blue suit and matching tie. Although it has not been pointed out before, it should be noted that the size of this man was something of a peculiarity. Khun Nemit was an incredibly small person. It was but a matter of inches that kept him from being mistaken for a little boy or a big doll. His hair reminded one of a mannequin's; hard and black and heavily oiled in one direction. Two heavy lines ran from the sides of his nostrils to the corners of his mouth. He swung his arms as he walked and maintained an ear-to-ear grin that grew even bigger when he saw Mantana.

"Good Morning, Joy!" he said in English.

Mantana knew that *Khun* was a way of saying 'you' and called back to him, "Good morning, You Nemit!"

Somehow, it didn't sound right to her.

Two things happened to Mantana that morning that would forever change her working environment, and consequently her life. The first thing that happened was this. The Rose Petal Cosmetics girl, whose nickname was Pop, brought a bag to the information desk and left it there with Mantana. The second thing that happened was very similar to the first. The Sunnyday Cosmetics girl, Tik, brought a bag to the information desk and left it there too. And what did both girls say to her with poisonous smiles?

"Give it to me outside, after work."

While the first bag threw poor Mantana into a panic, the second reduced her to tears. Why were they doing this? What did they want?

Then a voice, "Joy! What's wrong?" It was Pusadee and her wide, *Isan* nose.

"I have to see You Nemit!"

"Who?"

"*Khun* Nemit! Could you keep an eye on information for me?"

"I've never worked information."

"Just tell people where the bathrooms are!"

Mantana's mind felt like a dammed up river as she rushed to the second floor. She opened the door marked EMPLOYEES ONLY and went down a short hallway to the manager's office. The door was already open. Khun Nemit sat at a large desk with the telephone to his ear. When he saw Mantana standing in the doorway, he said something quietly into the receiver and put the phone down.

"Joy!" he said. "What's the matter, child?"

"Excuse me, sir,"

"You're crying! Please, come in. Close the door."

Khun Nemit stood and unnecessarily moved one of the large wooden chairs for her to sit down in. Watching him lift it was like watching a child struggle with a piece of furniture that weighed more than his muscles could handle. Mantana closed the door and wiped a hot tear from her cheek.

"Who made you cry?" he asked, slightly out of breath.

The thought of speaking their names caused her to choke on her words.

"They're - they're thieves!"

"Of course they are."

"They bring bags to me!"

"Yes, they do."

"I know what's inside!"

"I'm sure."

"I won't help them! I won't!"

"No, dear. No help for the wicked. Now, calm down and tell me all about it."

There was another knock at the door. Khun Nemit straightened his necktie and patted Mantana's shoulder as he moved to answer it.

"Yes? What is it?"

"Sir, excuse me sir, these were found behind the information counter."

Mantana turned in her chair. It was the security guard, handing over the two bags that Pop and Tik had left with her and a third she didn't recognize. Impossible! Impossible! The dammed up river suddenly burst free, and a thousand strange species of fish came rushing out, swimming in every direction. Khun Nemit thanked the guard and closed the door. He walked slowly past her chair and emptied each bag's contents onto his desk. There were Rose Petal products, Sunnyday products, and Miss Lovely products, hidden inside the third.

"Joy," said Khun Nemit in a less friendly tone. "What can you tell me about these bags?"

Mantana breathed deeply. Tears would get her nowhere. She cleared her throat and told the entire story. Khun Nemit listened with his arms folded across his chest. His suit didn't seem made for such a pose, and the material stretched tightly across his back and shoulders. It was only when she finished that he relaxed and moved back behind his desk.

"That's quite a story," he said. "What you're telling me is that all my salesgirls are crooks."

"I don't know if all your salesgirls are involved, sir. I only know that Kul, Pop, Tik, and quite possibly the security guard are trying to make me look like a criminal."

"I'm no detective," said Khun Nemit, "But it seems to me that if those girls you mentioned have the security guard working for them, it would be much easier to steal the merchandise themselves. Why would they entrust it to you?"

"I don't know, sir."

"You don't know?"

"Maybe they want me to be fired."

"And why would they want that? Surely, none of them are jealous of your position."

Mantana didn't answer. Maybe some people had an innate badness in them that caused them to do mean things. This was what she thought, but couldn't just blurt out something like that. Khun Nemit folded his hands and sighed deeply. He began to speak about store policy and the reliability of his employees. He spoke about how rare it was to find his trust violated. Finally, he named names and personally vouched for each girl's honesty, based upon their long-standing employment and personal relationship with him. He even stated that the salesgirls all had previous opportunities to steal large sums of money from him, and didn't. Why would they risk their careers over a few bottles of fingernail polish and skin whitening lotion?

"And the security guard," he said as Mantana wept silently, "is my nephew. Why would he -"

Mantana didn't know. She just didn't know. The room

became terribly small all of a sudden. Khun Nemit sat watching Mantana, who had lowered her head and wasn't looking at anything. When he spoke again, his voice sounded like some unidentified reptile, calling from a dark forest.

"Of course, this doesn't mean I believe you're guilty."

Mantana waited for him to finish.

"I suppose that if you could somehow convince me of your loyalty to the store - your loyalty to me -"

Without raising her eyes, Mantana was aware of Khun Nemit's movements. She knew that he stood and bent those funny little legs of his as he came around to her side of the desk. She could see without seeing Khun Nemit twist his mouth and suck at a piece of rice lodged in a back tooth. And she could feel his eyes upon her, specifically the part of the neck that her shoulder-length hair didn't cover.

He touched her.

Mantana jumped from the chair and stood, shaking and afraid. Khun Nemit held up his hands and made a 'tsk tsk tsk' sound by clicking his tongue against the roof of his mouth. He cocked his head, smiled his smile, then walked over to the office door and inserted a key that locked it.

"Don't be frightened, Joy," he said. "You want to keep your job, don't you? You want those salesgirls to stop harassing you, don't you?" He came a step closer with each 'don't you.' "You want your friends to keep their jobs too, *don't you?*"

Mantana felt his small hands on her waist. The first rule she was taught in life was to respect her elders. There were other rules, never stated directly, but there in the books and classrooms and TV programs just the same. Rules about how men were strong and women were fragile. Rules about how men were smart and a smart woman followed her man. Rules about how men were like the front legs of an elephant and women were to be regarded as the hindquarters. Mantana didn't know whether she believed in these rules. She could easily beat up boys as a child and was always twice as smart. But hadn't her mother once told her that the inside of a durian fruit was yellow because everyone agreed that it was? A person could go crazy calling durian fruit a different color every day of the week. Some things just were, and that was that. Only it wasn't the color of durian fruit or the rules of being a woman that occupied her thoughts as she backed up against her boss's desk. Logic was as far away as her village. In fact, it was something quite unlike logic that punched the keys and rang up one indisputable truth for Mantana: a stranger in a blue suit was unbuttoning her blouse and touching her where no man, not even her father, had touched her before.

"So young," he whispered, licking his lips, "so beautiful."

Mantana's hand fumbled through the cosmetics that littered the desktop. She could hear some of the vials roll off and hit the floor. The small hands upon her suddenly lifted and pushed, just enough, until she found herself sitting on top of the desk. The next few moments seemed to last a lifetime. Mantana watched the little man's head lower itself toward her middle, while his fingers drew her skirt back. She said the word *stop* but didn't recognize the voice as her own. The man looked up with his ugly grin. Mantana's hand found the telephone. She lifted the receiver and saw his eyes dart to the left.

"Who are you going to call?" he asked. "Who's going to risk being fired for a farmer's daughter from the North?"

Actually, Mantana had not considered calling anyone. She brought the receiver down and got him on the forehead. His face registered a look of bewilderment. Mantana hit him again. This time, he made a funny noise and jumped to his feet. He held his head and stepped backwards toward the door. You can't leave, thought Mantana. I have to leave. She looked for something else to hit him with when he suddenly dropped to his knees and said something that chilled her to the bone:

"I can't see you anymore, Nong Joy,"

and fell, face down, upon the floor. A pair of glasses shot from his coat pocket and skidded to her feet. Mantana picked them up. One of the lenses was cracked. She gasped and thought for a moment that her entire body might explode with fear. Only now there was silence. Now there was just a pair of broken glasses. She stepped over her boss's body and tried to open the office door. It was locked. She turned and looked down at the little man. Despite the inches, he really did look like a big doll in a blue suit. Only now, some of his hair had become unglued and it appeared as if a set of dark claws were sticking out of his skull. Mantana trembled. She cried, sweated, and felt as though she were going to throw up but somehow, somehow, guided her hand into his pockets, first his coat, then, with some maneuvering, his pants. The keys were in his right front pocket. She balanced herself by placing her left hand upon his shoulder, and wiggled in deeper, until she felt them with the tips of her fingers.

Then he moved. More than moved; he was having a seizure of some sort. His arms and legs kicked and jerked like a frantic wind-up toy that had fallen on its side. Mantana tried to back away, but her hand was caught in his front pocket, and she screamed each time his body rose and fell. Finally, she placed her two feet against him and pushed. There was a small rip as the material gave way and her hand was free, keys and all. The force of her push rolled Khun Nemit onto his back. Oh! Oh! The sight of that face! If there were ever a time when Mantana did not believe that a wretched spirit could hide beneath a person's skin and make that person do nothing but evil deeds, then that time was over. The way Khun Nemit was twisting and screwing up his face convinced Mantana that there could only be a demon, quite possibly two, battling it out inside his head. Be gone! Shoo! But she couldn't tear her eyes away. Especially when Khun Nemit opened his and looked right at her.

Was he awake? Was he *dead*?

Mantana forced herself to blink. She unlocked the door and ran. She ran past the cinema, down the stairs, through the crowd of customers and salesgirls, and out the front doors. Maybe she heard her name being called, maybe not. What did it matter now? Whichever evil spirits resided in Khun Nemit's head had gotten a good long look at her. Now, misfortune knew her name, too.

She might just as well try hiding from the sun.

6

Mantana did not tell Darunee where she was going in the note that she left, mostly because she didn't know herself. She did warn her not to trust the salesgirls and promised to visit when she was out of danger. Then, bag in hand, she got on a bus and rode it as far from the department store as it would take her.

She spent a large part of the day riding the bus.

By late afternoon, dark clouds had gathered and the air seemed ready to pop. Mantana got off before the rain began and went inside a public market where women with heavy arms sat behind tables of vegetables, staring dully into space. Mantana continued walking. Her senses told her the meat section was straight ahead so she veered to the right to avoid passing through it. Markets always seemed to her to have erupted out of someone's bad dream. The voices and smoke and traces of blood in the air were so nearly tangible, it could only be a deranged version of the world she knew as real. It wasn't necessarily a bad feeling. A part of her even enjoyed the vileness, though not a part she would ever admit to. She stopped out of habit to price a batch of fresh eggs and found them to be twice as expensive as the eggs in her village. Bangkok!

An old beggar woman's cup touched her arm. Mantana turned and looked at her. The woman's hair was gray and thin, and her face reminded her of a folded piece of cardboard. There was a dirty baby boy wrapped in cloth and tied to her back. Denizens of the market. Mantana dropped a five baht coin in her cup. The woman bowed her head and moved on, pushing her cup, blind to the faces, as most were blind in return. Only the baby on her back looked around with wide and curious eyes. Mantana watched them disappear, then counted the change in her pocket. She no longer had enough for *kao phad* without breaking her remaining hundred baht bill. She would have to eat *gooey teeo*.

The restaurant section of the market was located in back. Each stall had four or five tables before it where people sat hunched over their noodles and soup. The air was brown and moved in slow, thick lines until a rotating fan caught and dispersed it. Mantana read each restaurant's menu board as she walked. She stopped before one of the larger stalls and read a yellow sign taped to a faded wooden advertisement:

HELP WANTED. CONTACT MR. CHAI.

Mantana went to a table close to the plastic display case of vegetables and packaged noodles. A young girl with a long ponytail and dirty white apron set a metal drinking cup of ice water in front of her. She couldn't have been more than nine years old. Mantana asked for a bowl of soup and a job. The girl nodded and called into the kitchen. Minutes later, a large man with a fat mustache and black-framed glasses appeared. Mantana waiied politely.

"Uh," he said, thoughtlessly setting his fingertips together. "You want to know about the job?"

"Yes."

"Dishwashing."

"Can I start right away?"

"You could, but we're closing in three hours. Come back tomorrow at seven a.m. if you're serious."

"Why wouldn't I be serious?"

The man let out a laugh and clapped his hands together. "I'm Mr. Chai," he said.

"Joy."

The young girl returned with Mantana's order and placed it next to her water. There wasn't any silverware on the table. Mr. Chai placed a hand on the girl's shoulder.

"This is Newt," he said. "She's a bank manager."

"Really?"

"Not yet. She's still in training. You can ask her to add any amount of money together, and she'll have the answer for you like that!"

Mr. Chai snapped his fingers together to show how fast she could add amounts of money together.

"Newt," he said, "What's fifty plus fifty?"

"One hundred," said the girl.

"Sixty-three and thirty-seven?"

"One hundred."

"Eighty take away thirty, multiplied by four and divided by two?"

"One hundred."

"You see?" said Mr. Chai, "A bank manager."

Mantana laughed as he instructed the girl to fetch a plastic basket of forks and spoons. As she dug into her food, the nightmare of the morning sank further and further into the distance, as though it happened yesterday or the day before. When she finished, she thanked Mr. Chai and asked whether he knew of an inexpensive hotel nearby. Her bag was painfully obvious.

"Where's your home?" he asked.

Mantana told him the name of her village and the town it was near.

"That's far. What's seventy-three and twenty-seven?"

"One hundred?"

"OK. You're smart enough to follow directions. Walk out of here and turn left. Go straight ahead until you reach Soi Nine. Not far down Soi Nine is a place called MR Apartments. Go in and tell the receptionist that you're starting work with me tomorrow and you've got no money to pay for a room. I'm right, aren't I?"

"I've got a little bit."

"Put it in a bank. Better yet, don't put it in a bank. You never know with banks these days. Just don't forget to tell the receptionist that you're a good friend."

"And she'll believe me?"

Mr. Chai called for the girl. She came to him with a serious look on her face.

"I'll give you one of my daughter's ears to take with you as proof."

Newt squealed and covered her ears with her dirty hands. Mantana laughed for the second time that day. The market might have been a coarse pocket of reality, but it was here, she believed, that the true gems of society were found.

"You'll have to try it my way," he said. "Be here at seven o'clock tomorrow morning. You can begin work then. I'm sure you want to know how much I'm going to pay you. Think of the lowest amount you'll work for and cut it in half. That's the best I can do."

Mantana tried to pay for her meal. Mr. Chai told her he'd take it out of her pay. She said goodbye to Newt, lifted her bag, and walked out of the market. It was a relief to be out of there. She remembered Mr. Chai's directions and turned left at the main road. A sign told her where she was. Soi Thirty-Six. Thirty-Six! Mr. Chai forgot to tell her that the apartment building was over twenty city blocks away. Tuk-tuks and taxicabs sped by but what good were they to a poor girl from the North? She was down to her last one hundred baht, and the whole city might as well know. It would be nothing but long hours, low pay, and *gooey teeo* from now until - *when?* When did poverty end? Mantana knew the answer. Poverty never ended, at least not honestly.

Just then, the sky opened up and sent down large drops of rain that splattered on the sidewalk and against her shoulders. Bangkok rain. It stank, thought Mantana.

She spotted a sign and moved quickly past a pair of garbage pickers, into one of the sois. There was a small hotel with dirty plastic letters nailed to the outside wall in both Thai and Chinese. ROOM FOR RENT. It looked like the kind of place a traveler or a vagabond could stay for under a hundred baht a night. Mantana thought about her remaining money. As long as she had it, she would be wondering how to save it, or how to spend it. But once it was gone, her life would be given over to chance. She closed her eyes and saw the evil ghost of misfortune that lived inside of Khun Nemit. It had seen her, sure. It even knew her name. But wasn't it better to face evil ghosts than run from them? She could have convinced herself of anything that allowed her to go in and take a room.

Mantana opened the glass doors and went in. She saw two women standing at a reception desk talking to another behind the counter. The women closest to her wore short skirts and thick coats of lipstick. They differed from the department store salesgirls only in that they didn't immediately try to sell her something.

Mantana approached the counter under their watchful eyes.

"Do you have a room?" she asked.

"How many nights?" asked the bony receptionist.

"Just one."

"Oh, I'm sorry," she said with a smile. "We're full."

"Then why -" Mantana caught the eyes of a lipstick girl

and didn't finish. "Do you mind if I sit in the lobby and wait for the rain to stop?"

"That's for guests only," said the receptionist, "There's a coffee shop through those doors. If you order something, you can wait there."

Mantana moved her bag from her right shoulder to her left. She turned and walked away from the counter but couldn't decide whether to go into the coffee shop or out the door. She stopped walking. For a moment, there was only the sound of the falling rain, outside. She took a step and felt her leg twist in an odd direction. Her bag fell from her shoulder and landed on the ground with a crash. Then she, Mantana, followed it down.

Both of the lipstick girls screamed and rushed to her side. Their shoes made the sound of a three-legged horse trying to gallop around a racetrack.

"Are you all right?" asked one of them.

"I think so."

Mantana sat up and looked around. The girl who had spoken held up a black cube made of sawdust and plastic. It was the heel of Mantana's left shoe.

"Do you have another pair?" she asked.

It wasn't just the lips, Mantana realized. The girl's entire face was covered in make-up. Her cheeks were painted pink. Her eyebrows had been drawn in with a pencil. Even her eyelashes were too long to be real.

"No," said Mantana. "These are my only pair."

"Well, you aren't going anywhere until you have them fixed. What's your name?"

"Joy."

"What are you doing, wandering the streets, Joy?"

"I was looking for a job."

The woman glanced at her friend. Mantana couldn't read what was in her eyes but she felt that the other somehow could.

"Did you find one?" asked her friend.

"I'm going to wash dishes at a *gooey teeo* restaurant in the market."

Both women let out silly laughs. Her job, her heel, her poverty; Mantana was embarrassed. She took off her broken shoe and held it in her hand. Maybe it was this, maybe it wasn't, but when she spoke again, the words surprised even her.

"I killed my boss this morning and ran away before I could receive my salary."

The women stopped laughing.

"What did you say?"

"I'm sorry," said Mantana, still looking at her broken heel. "I'm very tired."

They helped her to her feet and started to walk. She still had on one shoe, and her balance was off. She leaned against the girls for support.

"I think you'd better follow us," one of them said.

And that was how Mantana didn't have to go back out in the rain.

7

It was a shame that Mantana did not have a chance to tell Mr. Chai that she wouldn't be taking him up on his job offer. He had been so kind! But the lipstick girls, Ning and Peung, had made another offer and the next morning found Mantana in a pair of borrowed shoes, heading in a very different direction. The girls had been very understanding once they heard her tale of woe and comforted her by saying that the store manager "probably wasn't dead" and would by any account be "too afraid to go to the police." They gave her a blanket and let her sleep on the floor of their room. And now they were taking her to meet their boss and see about getting her a proper job. Mantana considered herself very lucky to have found such friends.

Of the two, Ning was definitely the friendlier. She was twenty-seven, with a round face that stopped just short of being babyish and fat. Her hair was cut to look as if it were constantly being blown forward yet coated with enough gel to keep it away from her eyes. She had long, thin limbs, and two scars on her left wrist she got from a motorcycle accident that occurred when she was young.

Peung didn't speak much and maintained an impatient, somewhat annoyed expression upon her face. Ning pointed out that men found Peung sexier than she but a smile and some conversation would have put Mantana more at ease around her.

"Now remember, Joy," said Ning, in the back of a cab, "Don't act shy around the boss. Smile and pretend to have a lot of energy."

"What's the boss's name?"

"Khun Rangsan. He's very nice. It's his wife you have to watch out for."

The cab arrived at the address that Ning had given. It was a restaurant with blue windows and white letters that spelled the words COWBOY RODEO NIGHT around a cartoon cowboy on a bucking horse. Below this, in Thai, was written FOOD AND DRINKS, BEAUTIFUL GIRLS, LOVELY VOICES. Peung paid the driver while Ning lit a cigarette on the sidewalk. She could almost pass for a movie star in her short purple dress and cat eye sunglasses. Peung was equally attractive in black jeans and a tight red number cut above her naval. Mantana felt awkward and childish standing in the shade of the restaurant awning with them.

"Do you smoke?" asked Ning.

"No," said Mantana.

"Good for you. It's a terrible habit. I wish I could quit."

Ning lit the end of her cigarette and held the pack out for Peung. They both looked very sophisticated with cigarettes between their lips.

"Could I try one?" said Mantana.

"Sure!"

Ning handed over her already lit one and took another from the pack. Mantana noticed that it was her last one.

"Oh, never mind," she said.

"No, no, go ahead," said Ning.

"But it's your last one."

"Don't worry. I'll buy more."

Ning watched Mantana take a long exaggerated puff. A ball of smoke emerged from her lips, and she gagged on what was left in her lungs. She held out the cigarette as she doubled over, coughing. The girls both let out their silly laughs and helped her straighten up.

"You've still got too much of the countryside in your lungs," said Peung.

Ning took the smoking butt from her fingers and set it back between her own lips.

"You'll get used to it," she said. "You just need to inhale more often."

"I thought you said it was a terrible habit."

"It is," said Ning, taking another drag, "But who likes to smoke alone?"

*

The restaurant was twice as big as it looked from outside. At first, Mantana thought there were at least eighty tables, but later found out there were only fifty-five. Three round columns covered in fake tree bark divided the front of the restaurant from the back and made it clear which tables were for watching the show and which were for maintaining a low profile. Long fluorescent lights hung above the seating area, each one hidden behind a screen of colorful, tightly strung plastic beads. The biggest one of all hung just in front of the stage. Streams of tinsel radiated from it like cheap sunlight, held to the ceiling by staples and tacks. The stage itself rose about four feet from the floor and ran the entire length of the back wall. There must have been fifty colored lights along the outer rim and another twenty-five or more on the ceiling. A large electronic keyboard sat dead center while giant speakers piled one on top of the other stood menacingly at each corner. The curtains that covered the performers entrance and exit were lime green. Reflective stars were pinned to the folds. The back curtain was pink, with a Happy New Year banner strung across it, though the new year was already six months old.

The restaurant was empty except for a technician replacing bulbs from the top of a ladder. Peung wished the two of them luck and left to attend to some business of her own. Mantana walked close to Ning, still feeling nauseous from the cigarette.

"How can you be sure I'll be hired?" she asked.

"Because you're young and pretty."

"But I've never danced before."

"Don't worry. Peung and I will show you the routines."

"You're both being so nice to me."

"If you're ready to go on by seven p.m. tonight, Peung and I each get a four hundred baht finder's fee."

Mantana stopped walking. "Did you say *tonight*?"

Ning gave her a sideways glance. "You did say you wanted to make some money, didn't you?"

"Yes, but that gives me less than a day to learn all the routines."

"Joy," she said, "The audience doesn't care if you can dance or not. The women come to hear the music and the men -" Ning ran her eyes up and down Mantana's body. "The men don't care about your dancing either."

The door to Khun Rangsan's office was open. Ning led the way. A man was kneeling behind a large wooden desk, and didn't appear until the sound of a metal door clicked shut. Probably the safe, thought Mantana. Khun Rangsan was older than she expected. His hair still retained its original blackness, though streaks of gray could be seen at his temples. A pair of round glasses sat at the end of his nose. There was something birdlike about the man, noticeable in his gestures and manners. He seemed nervous, but nervous with a plan, as though he were listening for the worm hidden beneath the ground, waiting to make his move and pluck it up. Ning and Mantana waiied him upon entering.

"*Sawadee, sawadee,*" said Khun Rangsan, almost whispering his words. "Please sit down."

"Khun Rangsan, this is Joy. She wants to be a dancer."

The man-bird adjusted his glasses and looked at her.

"Hm. Can you sing?"

"Oh yes!" said Ning. "She's got a lovely voice. She's just a little shy. I'm sure that after a few numbers, she'll get over her stage fright and be completely at ease with a microphone."

"Do you have any experience?"

Ning reached over and pinched Mantana's cheeks with her thumb and index finger. "Look at this face! And this body! You won't find a girl this beautiful outside of a modeling agency!"

"But can she sing?"

Ning released Mantana's face and slapped her on the knee. "Sing!"

"What?"

"What do you know? You know *Ruen Pae*, don't you?"

"Yes."

"Well then, let's hear it!"

Mantana looked at Khun Rangsan. Khun Rangsan looked at Mantana. The office grew terribly quiet. Mantana cleared her throat and sang. Her voice sounded flat. She was very nervous. Then, in a moment of inspiration, Ning placed a hand over her eyes, blocking the light and the faces.

"Don't think!" she whispered. "Sing!"

At first, Mantana didn't understand her newfound friend's idea, and found it impossible to take her advice and not think. She did her best, however, and let her mind drift back to her village. She thought of a lonely day at her father's shop, watching the lazy dogs stretch out in the shade of a bamboo tree, then leaning upon her elbows, waiting for a cool wind to blow. These were the times when she would sing to herself, and this was the voice that came to her in Khun Rangsan's office.

She sang the song from start to finish. It was only after the last note had faded from her lips that Ning removed her hand.

"Do you think you could do that with your eyes open?" asked Khun Rangsan.

Mantana smiled. "I think so, sir."

Ning clapped her hands and held them to her breast. She would get her four hundred baht finder's fee after all.

A strange cry came from outside. The smile on Khun Rangsan's face disappeared faster than if he had bitten into a sour mango.

"Ning," he said, "If you'd escort Joy to the rehearsal room and show her a few dance routines, I think we can -"

He never got to finish his sentence.

"MISTAH RANGSAN KA-AH!" said a voice so shrill, Mantana's hands instinctively moved to cover her ears. Luckily, the voice came from outside the office door. Any closer and she wondered if the sound would cause Khun Rangsan's glasses to shatter in their round eye frames.

Mantana looked at Ning, who seemed to be holding back a grin.

"Yes, Bew?"

The voice went on in a strange, broken English, quieter now, but still in the pitch of two balloons being rubbed together.

"Mistah Rangsan, do your eyes close?"

Khun Rangsan sighed and answered in Thai. "Yes, Bew. They're closed."

"Do you have another with you?"

"Yes, Bew."

"Oh! Oh, oh! You close your eyes, too!"

Mantana closed her eyes. She heard a light thud as something was placed on the floor behind her. There was much fumbling with electronic equipment, cursing, silence, then music. Mantana recognized the song. It was a love song from a popular American movie with an out-of-place disco beat added to the background.

"Okay!" said the voice, "Open your eyes!"

Mantana turned in her seat. A man stood in the center of the office. He was at least six feet tall, from the bottom of his white spiked heels to the top of his fiery red wig.

"Hello! My name is Bew Beautiful. How are you? I fine, thank you!"

Bew was dressed in a sparkling blue gown with long, white gloves. There was a string of pearls around his neck. He had shaved off his body hair and covered his face and neck in the make-up base Mantana knew from the salesgirls at the department store, the kind that made one's skin resemble a kind of temple stone that neither absorbed nor reflected the light. On top of this, Bew had colored his feminine face in exaggerated shades of pink and rose. His eyebrows were drawn in lightly, the right one curiously higher than the left. Mantana watched his face and she watched his hips and feet. All that was Bew moved in rhythm to the music.

"Hi!" he crooned once again, flicking back his rose-colored hair. "I am Bew! Please call me Beautiful! OK? I think."

Bew spun around on one heel and lip-synched the song lyrics into an invisible microphone. His face might have shown great emotion if it weren't so difficult to tell where the make-up ended and the features began. In between verses, he waved to his audience. Only Ning waved back. Khun Rangsan kept his hands folded before them.

"I love you!" he cried in English.

"Don't stop your heart!"

"I keep you forever!"

Mantana didn't know what he was talking about. She had the feeling he didn't either.

After some more dancing, some of it quite lewd, the song ended. For the grand finale, Bew squatted low to the floor and hid his face behind his hands, careful not to smear his make-up.

"Bew," said Khun Rangsan, "That's enough, Bew."

Bew jumped. His red wig jumped with him. "Clean and happy!" He twirled to the cassette player and pressed the stop button. Then he moved cartoonish and catlike across the room to stand between Ning and Mantana.

"Hello!" he said, smiling down at them. "My name is Beautiful. What's your name? Oh, me too."

"Bew, where did you get that dress?" asked Khun Rangsan.

"Mistah Rangsan, *Ka!* Tonight Bew sing a song Titanic, OK? Yes, I think."

"Has my wife -"

"Wife you say sing a song Titanic."

Mantana reached to feel the material of Bew's gown. He hissed and slapped her hand.

"Bew," said Khun Rangsan, wearily, "I've told you one hundred times before. We have enough female dancers. What we need are men. Do you understand?"

"Bew understand but Bew not a man. Bew have these!"

He pointed to his chest, which bulged, however lopsided, with breasts.

"You didn't have them yesterday," observed Khun Rangsan.

Mantana pinched a small fold of his gown. It really was a lovely dress. Bew let out a squeal and slapped her hand again. Then he slapped the arm of her chair, once, twice, and a third time.

"*Mao!*" he said. "You a *mao!*"

"Come on, Joy," said Ning. "We'd better start rehearsing."

Mantana waiied Khun Rangsan and thanked him again.

"Good bye Bew," she said. "I'll see you tonight."
"Bzz bzz bzz!" said Bew.
The two girls were laughing as they walked out of the office.

8

The restaurant was not at all like the cafes and coffee shops her father used to haunt in the years after her mother died. Those places, located on the outskirts of towns and villages, always frightened her with their dark windows and suspicious characters hanging around the parking lot in the middle of the afternoon. This locale seemed much more inviting to her, like a place she might see on television.

From behind the backstage curtain, Mantana could watch the restaurant tables fill, one by one. Unsmiling waitresses led families, couples, and groups of anywhere from five to fifteen businessmen to their appropriate seats. The waitresses wore traditional northeastern outfits, a black sarong with a colorful design at its base, cut just below the knees. A sash was wrapped around the left shoulder and tied at the opposite waist. The girls were young and wore their outfits lazily. Their noses gave them away as

Bangkok girls, playing dress up for thirty-five hundred baht per month. Enough to eat and pay for their cellphones, thought Mantana.

From seven until ten there would be nonstop singing, nonstop dancing. There would be three costume changes. There would be music and lights. There would be a twenty-minute break, and the whole thing would begin again.

The restaurant employed forty girls in all, Mantana included. Last week, there had only been thirty-five. The week before, twenty-eight. Whatever the number of girls, they were split into two groups that danced and sang in rotating shifts. Tonight, there would be a dancing line of fifteen girls that would change every thirty minutes. The girls who weren't dancing were free to do as they wished, provided they didn't miss their turns at the microphone. Each girl was required to sing at least one, but no more than three, songs. The more a girl sang, the better chance she had of receiving garlands from admiring customers. And if a girl sang well, a fifty, a hundred, even a five hundred baht bill might be pinned to the wreath.

The girls who were not singing roamed the floor, looking for a customer to sit with. Becoming friendly with customers meant a big tip at the end of the night. And if a girl were lucky, a customer might come back with even bigger tips. According to Ning, Peung once received two gold rings from a man who claimed he wanted to marry her. When he stopped coming, she sold the rings to a pawn shop and made a nice profit.

"You a new girl, yes?"

The voice snapped Mantana out of her trance. It was Bew Beautiful, no longer dressed as a woman, but suited up for the show. Bew was one of only two male performers, even though he shared the girls' dressing room and sat down to pee.

"My name is Velour. Fee ee ewl oh your aah, Velour."

Mantana understood his English, but attempted none of her own.

"I thought your name was Bew."

"Oh! Oh no! Look!"

He waved a long-fingered hand before his suit as if anxious to introduce himself. It was a red suit, studded with small, plastic diamonds that glittered in the light. The wig was gone, and his eyebrows had been carefully sculpted into two masculine lines. His black hair lay slicked back over his ears.

"It green," he said. "Yes?"

Mantana knew her colors. "It's red."

"Oh!" Bew unbuttoned the front of his suit and opened it. He was wearing a green fishnet bra flat against his thin chest. "Is green, yes? Yes. Time I wearing a green this, I am Velour. Time I wear a pink this, I am Margarita."

"When are you Bew?"

"Time I wear a no this!" he said and cooed loudly as he squeezed the empty cups of his bra. He hurried off, probably with nowhere to go, but too loopy to sit still.

Mantana adjusted the neckline of her outfit. It was a silver number with long sleeves and white fringe hanging wherever the material ended. Outfits were provided by the restaurant. The sight of them hanging on a rack in plastic bags did little to calm Mantana's nerves. Three of the five different outfits she would sooner or later be required to wear consisted of little more than a miniskirt and halter top. The rest were one-piece bathing suits. The rack stood in a room opposite a long mirror with a row of tables pushed against the wall beneath it. Girls sat in the narrow space putting on make-up and fixing their hair. Mantana had been introduced to almost everyone, but was too restless to remember their names. She had a suspicion hers had been forgotten as well.

Fortunately, there was Ning. She spent the afternoon showing Mantana what to do and helped to arrange the line-up so that she would be between Peung and herself. As it turned out, there were no actual dance steps. There was merely a tambourine that Ning banged against her hip. One shake of the tambourine meant turn left, two, turn right. In between shakes, she was to try to do what everyone else was doing.

Ning was wearing a silver outfit too. She had painted her eyelids blue and reminded Mantana of a sexy space girl. All that was missing, thought Mantana, was a pair of antennae sprouting from her orange hair.

Ning found her backstage and gave her a pill to calm her nerves. Mantana put it in her pocket to discard when Ning wasn't looking.

"We won't have to go on first," she said. "Watch the other girls for a few numbers. Get a feel for where to stand and when to switch routines. And don't forget to smile, even when you're unsure of what to do next. Smile and follow whatever Peung and I are doing. Have you decided what songs you'll sing yet?"

"I wanted to ask you about that."

"The best performers sing *Luk Thung*," said Ning. "They're the ones who end up with the most wreaths at the end of the night. Most of the girls play it safe by memorizing what's popular and easy. They don't even try to sing those Isan songs."

Mantana knew all about *Luk Thung*. It was a style of music straight from the heart of the rice fields and villages of the Northeast. Mastering a *Luk Thung* song was no easy feat. It required the control and manipulation of one's voice box to produce a sound that waved, warbled, and echoed onto itself. To an untrained ear, *Luk Thung* sounded like a broken record. To the men and women of Thailand, however, a *Luk Thung* song seemed to reach back into a collective memory that may or may not have been real. Memories of a time when life was uncomplicated and one's fate was bound to the land. There were no automobiles in a *Luk Thung* song. No cities, or cellphones or video games imported from Japan. There was only harmony with nature, the love of one's family, and the joy of being drunk among friends. Bew was good and the audience thought so too. At the end of *Sang Nang*, which he performed under a blue spotlight, the line-up of dancers parted and moved off stage. Bew / Velour introduced the next singer.

"That's who we're dancing for," said Ning. "Are you ready?"

"I think so."

Peung and the three other girls who were part of the next dancing order got into line ahead of them and waited silently for their cue.

The next singer was a woman. She slunk to the microphone from the opposite side of the stage wearing a dress that looked like a giant spider had woven a black web around her body with the threads thickening around her breast and middle. From where Mantana stood, it was difficult to see her face, but she could tell by the applause and whistles of the audience that she must be a very beautiful woman.

"Who's that?" asked Mantana.

"That's your boss. Your other boss. She's Khun Rangsan's wife. She's beautiful, but she's a bitch when she's angry. Try not to cross her path."

At the side of the stage, a young boy hit a switch and a computerized drum beat filled the air. Another song began to a smattering of applause. Mantana took a deep breath, sucked in her gut, and followed Ning onto the stage.

It was show time. The girls found their positions and began to dance as the song began. It was a love song that Mantana hadn't heard before. The woman at the microphone had a rather flat voice and when she received her first wreath of the night, Mantana suspected it was for something other than her singing ability. Next to her, Ning shook her tambourine and Mantana turned with the rest of the girls.

Once my heart was captured by you
Now it's only free

Free heart! Oh, my free heart!
Floating in an unhappy sea

The girls in line clutched their hearts and turned their smiling faces toward the audience. It was at that moment the woman at the microphone turned and looked at Mantana. Fortunately, she only turned for a second or two. Any longer, and she surely would have noticed the new girl fall clumsily out of line.

"Joy!" whispered Ning. "What are you doing?"

At first, Mantana thought she would faint. A sudden dimming of the lights and music and a feeling that she was standing on wet rice only added to her suspicions. Instead of fainting, she tripped forward and backed up into Peung when she attempted to take her place again. Peung pushed her sideways with a hard elbow and she might have gone down if Ning hadn't caught her. Mantana faltered for another moment before finding the balance that was needed to dance even these uncomplicated steps. She shook her hands in the air as she clumsily tried to mimic the girls' movements beside her.

"Spin!" said Ning, banging on her tambourine twice.

Everyone spun in a clockwise motion. Mantana went the wrong way and nearly collided with Peung again.

"Joy!" said Ning.

"Sorry!"

The woman at the microphone turned suddenly and met Mantana's eyes for the second time. She had a doll-like face with ruby lips and long, dark lashes. She wore the kind of expression one could trust with everything and nothing. Mantana felt her heart pound in her breast as the woman narrowed her eyes and focused on her. *She knows me*, she thought and felt like fainting again. The woman went back to her song, allowing Mantana to find her moves and finish the set without another error.

"What happened out there?" asked Ning, once the line had cleared the stage.

"It was that woman," said Mantana. "That woman at the microphone."

"Phii Aor? What about her?"

Mantana took a deep breath as Peung moved past her with a scowl on her face.

"She looks just like my mother."

*

It happened during the show's intermission that Mantana was called into the office of Khun Rangsan. She put on a robe and excused herself through the sticky bodies and cigarette smoke of the dressing room. The office door was ajar; only Khun Rangsan's owlish face was nowhere to be seen. It was his wife who now sat behind the desk. The woman's hair, the woman's eyes, the woman's nose, and the woman's mouth, even under the brightness of fluorescent lights, proved Mantana's first impression to be more accurate than she had imagined. The woman bore a startling resemblance to her long deceased mother. On stage, the idea of her mother actually paying witness to Mantana dancing in lipstick and miniskirt struck her so severely, that she did indeed, nearly faint. Here in the office, with the singer's age and social position and breast size in full view, Mantana could see how wrong she had been to mistake her for someone who had been dead for eleven years. Still, the woman's hair, the woman's eyes, the woman's nose, and the woman's mouth had a calming effect on her nerves, like a familiar song coming from the corner pocket of some long, dark market. She even had to wonder about Ning's warning, *Don't make her mad*. Don't make who mad? This woman? Ning was probably not the best judge of character.

"Come in," she said. "Sit down."

Mantana did as she was told. The closer she came to the woman, the more difficult it was to look away and stop studying her face.

"Why are you looking at me like that?" she said suddenly.

Mantana lowered her eyes, embarrassed, then stole another glance when her boss spoke again.

"What's your name?" she asked.

"Joy."

"Nice to meet you, Joy. You can call me Phii Aor. Do you smoke?"

"No, ma'am."

Phii Aor lit a cigarette. Her lips made a slight pop when she drew it from her mouth.

"Joy, I realize this is your first night on stage so I'm going to tell you how things work around here. On any given night, a dancer receives anywhere from zero to five wreaths of flowers. A singer, twice that number. Customers buy them for twenty, fifty, sometimes hundreds of baht and the performer who receives one is allowed to trade it in for half the amount in cash. The restaurant keeps the rest."

Mantana knew how the system worked, but felt it was wiser to play ignorant.

"How many wreaths have you received so far this evening, Nong Joy?"

"Twenty-six, ma'am. Seventeen twenty-baht wreaths, seven fifty-baht wreaths, and two one-hundred-baht ones."

Aor took another drag from her cigarette.

"Twenty-six," she said. "That's a lot of wreaths. How many have you given to the other dancers?"

Mantana smiled nervously. "None, ma'am."

"You kept them all for yourself?"

"I thought -"

"Yes, I know what you thought. That's why we're having this little chat. Joy, every girl receives an unusual amount of wreaths on her first night. It's sort of a welcoming gesture from our regular customers. In two or three nights, you'll be taking home an extra twenty or thirty baht just like the rest of the girls. So don't let a seven-hundred-baht night cause you to think you're any better than the others."

"No, ma'am. I'd never -"

"Good. Now, since our customers and employees have given you such a friendly welcome, it's keeping with tradition that you pay them back."

"Pay them back?" said Mantana. "You want me to give away my wreaths?"

"You want the girls to like you, don't you, Nong Joy?"

Mantana bit down on her lip. Khun Nemit had said almost the same words to her. Still, maybe Phii Aor spoke the truth. None of the other dancers had acted jealous or angry, but those kind of emotions would only cause a loss of face. If anything negative were said about her, it would be done behind her back. Ill will would be buried beneath a smile.

"Yes, ma'am," said Mantana.

"Only for tonight, Joy. Tomorrow, you can keep what you earn."

Phii Aor smiled. She had very white teeth.

"Oh, one more thing, Joy. I've heard you have quite a voice. You wouldn't mind starting off the second half of tonight's show with a song, would you?"

"Well, actually, ma'am -"

"Good. And I think it would be better if you stayed off the floor tonight. You're not too tired to dance a little more after your set, are you?"

"No, ma'am."

"Good, good. You can go now, Nong Joy."

Mantana sat there for a moment, unsure of what to do or say or feel. She hadn't realized she had been dismissed and looked at her boss, waiting for something more. When she saw that Phii Aor had gone back to her bookkeeping, she quietly stood and walked out of the office. It wasn't going to be easy, she thought, but she would have to try. Phii Aor was her boss and it was childish and silly to think of her as anyone else.

*

And so Mantana sang. She passed over the making up and breaking up love songs that came and went with each passing year and sang the *Luk Thung* songs she remembered from her childhood. Once again, she closed her eyes and imagined that she was back in her village, where the only sound that interrupted the melody of her voice was the bamboo trees rubbing in the wind. There was no audience. The men and women had all left to work the fields and factories and construction sites and mini-marts. Now, there was only the yellow dust of the road to hear her voice. And when she opened her eyes in the rainbow of stage lights, the faces peering out of the dark did not frighten her. How could they? Their eyes only saw so much make-up and so little of an outfit. Mantana, the real Mantana, stayed well out of sight.

After a thirty-minute set, she was allowed fifteen minutes before she had to join the dancing queue again.

"That was wonderful!" said Ning, with a smile on her face.

The rest of the girls agreed. The new employee could sing.

She had collected another thirty-four wreaths to give away.

9

The Cowboy Rodeo Night was closed on Sundays. Mantana had danced and sang for six consecutive nights. Her feet hurt from the new pair of boots she bought with her garland money, her face hurt from smiling all the time. Ning told her not to worry.

"I once knew a dancer who tried to widen her smile by using two plastic hooks and a rubber band. She put the hooks here, at the corners of her mouth, and stretched the rubber band around the back of her head."

"Did it work?"

"No. It looked like small birds had made nests in her cheeks for three months after she stopped wearing it."

There were money problems too. Ning didn't mind Mantana sleeping on the floor, but her roommate, Peung, was not as easy going. Mantana often found the few toiletries she owned knocked about and left open on the bathroom floor. Also, Peung always managed to kick her sometime during the night when she got up to pee. Not just on the way to, but coming back as well. Mantana knew she had to find a place of her own, only it was eight more days before she'd receive her half months salary and Phii Aor had already subtracted seven hundred baht to pay for a photograph that needed to be taken for the "Superstar Portrait Gallery" that hung in the entranceway of the restaurant.

"Why doesn't Peung like me?" she asked Ning as they strolled through the Maboonkhrong Shopping Plaza, looking at purses and jewelry and other things that neither of them could afford to buy.

"Because you're younger and prettier than she is."

"I'd leave today if I could afford a place of my own," she sighed. "If only there was a way to make extra money."

"You need to flirt with more customers."

Mantana screwed up her face at Ning's advice. "You mean let some drunk old man put his hand up my skirt for an extra fifty baht wreath? No thanks."

Ning took out a brush and ran it through her hair as they walked. A pack of children riding mechanical dinosaurs and panda bears rolled past them.

"Have you spoken with Phii Aor?"

"I don't think Phii Aor likes me either," she said with a hint of loneliness.

"Phii Aor doesn't like anyone. That woman has a heart of ice."

"Maybe I'll go to see Phii Rangsan instead. He's much friendlier."

"Just remember, Joy. If you start taking advances from next month's salary, you're going to have to take an advance from the month after that just to live. You could go into debt for a long, long time. Trust me. I know."

"But I'm broke!" said Mantana. "I spent all my money on

these boots."

She kicked the floor as if it were her boots' fault for eating up all her money.

"They are nice boots," said Ning.

Mantana looked down to decide again whether she still liked them or not. The boots were white with a black heel that made her four inches taller than she normally stood. They came up past her knee, with the backsides trimmed low to allow her to walk. Black fringe hung from three diamond studded squares stitched in the front. Her legs were terribly hot inside them, but she supposed Ning was right. They were nice. She thought of the two thousand eight hundred baht price tag and became frustrated again.

"I guess I'll just have to beg for money on the street."

"You'd rather beg than go back to your village?"

Mantana didn't answer. Of course she wasn't serious, but Ning seemed to think she was. They moved past a crowd of people standing in front of an electronics store, staring dull-eyed at an action movie playing on a big screen television. The sound of gunfire and explosions could be heard all the way down the escalator.

"If you're really in trouble," said Ning. "You should talk to Phii Aor."

"But you just said an advance would put me in debt."

"I didn't say you should ask for an advance. Phii Aor can arrange extra work for you. It's not nice work, but you won't go into debt. And you won't have to beg."

"What kind of work?"

"There's an awful lot of customers who like you. Some of them are very rich. If you were to entertain them for an evening, *outside the restaurant*, you'd come home with a lot more than what you make from twenty-baht wreaths."

The escalator reached the ground floor. Mantana forgot to step. She tripped and nearly fell on her face.

"Careful!" said Ning.

"What do you mean 'entertain'?"

"I mean show them a good time."

Mantana stopped walking and looked at her friend.

"How does a beautiful young starlet in long white boots show a rich and horny businessman a good time, Joy?" asked Ning.

"I don't know."

"Think about it."

"You mean sex?"

"Shh! Not so loud! Walk."

They walked. There were people on all sides. Families, couples, even a foreigner with bright red hair. No one was interested in the girls's conversation. There were just too many eyes, mouths, ideas, and lack of ideas.

"Ning," said Mantana, "Have you ever entertained a customer?"

"Once," she replied. "A long time ago when I first started working, a man used to come and buy wreaths just for me. I sat with him, but he never flirted or became rude. He only smiled and said, "*Kraap phom!*" whenever I asked for anything. A cocktail, a plate of fruit, anything at all. "*Kraap phom!* Yes, ma'am!" And when it was my turn on stage, he'd call a waitress to his table and begin sending wreaths. For every song I sang, no matter if it were *Luk Thung* or love, I'd receive a one-hundred-baht wreath from him. Once, there was a poem clipped to the flowers. At first, I thought he had written the poem, but I later found out that it was a song he had copied down. Anyway, it was around this time that I got sick with a bladder infection and had to stay in a hospital for two days. The bill was over ten thousand baht. Where was I going to get ten thousand baht? I pawned my gold bracelet, but it still wasn't enough. That's when I went to see Phii Aor. I said, "There's a man out there who loves me." Phii Aor said, "Take his money before he loves someone else." I decided that if this wealthy man wanted to sleep with me and help to pay my hospital bill, why should I say no? Because the Buddha says that I should say no? What about the doctors and the nurses? Do you think they looked into their hearts before giving me a bill for ten thousand baht?"

"What happened next?"

"I slept with the man. Phii Aor arranged everything. She told me not to become his girlfriend until the hospital bill was paid in full. I took her advice. I slept with the man and took his money and gave it to the doctors and nurses. I even managed to buy my gold bracelet back from the pawn shop. But I was never his girlfriend."

"Did he ask you to be?"

"Yes. He asked me. But he was married. I would have been his *mia nawy*, his minor wife. So I listened to Phii Aor and took his money until all my bills were paid."

"And do you still see him?"

Ning shook her head. Mantana had a dozen more questions to ask. Did any of the others sleep with customers? How often? Ning was no longer in the mood to answer her questions.

"Well, I certainly couldn't do it," said Mantana. "I couldn't take my clothes off in front of a complete stranger. I couldn't pretend to like it when he touched me."

"You'd be surprised at the things you can do. Wasn't it just last week that you were convinced you couldn't learn the dance routines? And what about singing?"

"Sex is different!"

"Sex isn't so different from singing and dancing. It's a performance, just like what you do on stage."

"You mean it's love that's different?"

Ning stopped walking and held out her right arm. "That's sex," she said, showing off a gold bracelet around her wrist. She then held out her left arm and pointed to two parallel scars that lay like thin pink crayons embedded in her skin. "That's love."

"Didn't you get those from a motorcycle accident?" Mantana whispered.

Ning traced the lines with two fingers from her right hand. A melancholy smile played upon her lips.

They went back to their aimless shopping and spoke no more about love or sex or money.

*

If it were a thin string that held the stars in the sky, then it unraveled and snapped the following day. Peung wanted her out. She made a secret of it no longer. Mantana had to pack her things and take them with her to work that evening. She had nowhere to stay.

And then there was the stage. Mantana danced in her outfits and boots and sang her songs with the feeling that time was running in slow motion. The faces of the crowd looked hostile and dangerous, and the constant chatter disrupted the peace she normally felt. At one point during her set, a table of drunk men began singing their own songs. Phii Aor walked over and said something to the men. They didn't sing again for the rest of the night. Mantana was grateful, but still couldn't shake the feeling that the world was spinning in odd directions. Even Bew noticed her strange frailty.

"Nong Joy, what you do?" he asked. "You sing a song not beautiful."

"I know."

"I think maybe you red light."

"I don't understand."

"Red light. *Fai daeng*. I think you blood come."

"No, Bew, no," she said.

During the first break of the evening, a customer requested her to sit at his table. He was a silver-haired man who smoked cigars and wore gold rings on four fingers of each hand. There were five other men at the table, each wearing only one or two gold rings, and smoking cigarettes. No one seemed to notice Mantana when she appeared. She even began to wonder if she was at the right table until the silver-haired man snapped his fingers and told her to massage his neck and shoulders. Mantana looked at the man's face. His mouth was turned down in permanent displeasure, and his eyes remained half closed to the world, as if there were nothing of value around him worth opening them for. Mantana slowly moved behind him and raised her fingers to the back of his neck. She held them there for a long time, until finally she muttered something even she didn't understand and rushed away from the silver-haired man's table. She hid behind a pillar, while the stage lights flashed around the restaurant like a prison break. It was then that she noticed a run in her stockings, clearly visible from where her boots ended and her miniskirt began. They were her last pair of the evening. She slumped down against the pillar and examined the damage for a long time. Then she stood and went to see Phii Aor. Her brain felt numb and useless.

Phii Aor was sitting in her husband's office, smoking as usual. Oddly enough, Mantana was glad to see her boss smoking. She looked less like her mother with a cigarette between her lips.

"Yes?" she asked, seeing Mantana standing in the doorway.

"I've got a run in my stocking."

"Don't you have another pair?"

"No," she said, and the word was a giant wave knocking her over. The word was a malicious insect stinging her from the inside. The word was the green soup of her soul, just before throwing up, and then it was throwing up. NO, she didn't have another pair of stockings! NO, she couldn't afford to buy one. Strange that it was not starvation or homelessness or the other demons of poverty that drove her to a pathetic admission of her helplessness, but a simple run in her stockings. She felt stupid; beaten and stupid. For shame, Mantana! What would her father think? Or her mother, if it were possible? What happened to the girl who bet all the village children she could catch a snake with her bare hands, and then caught one? Or the girl who chased mad dogs away from her father's shop, armed with nothing more than a broom? She stepped into the office and spoke again, quickly, before Phii Aor had a chance to think of her as someone who couldn't take care of herself.

"Phii Aor, ma'am, I heard that -"

"What?"

"I heard that I can entertain customers and make money that way. By entertaining customers."

Phii Aor looked at her sternly. "Who told you that? Did Ning tell you that? That girl can't even look after herself. She has no business -"

She stopped and closed her eyes for a moment. When she spoke again, her tone of voice was much more gentle.

"Close the door," she said. "Sit down. And don't start crying. You'll only ruin your make-up."

Mantana didn't feel as if she were going to cry and wondered why Phii Aor had said not to. She closed the door and took a seat facing her boss as told.

"Nong Joy, have you ever kissed a boy?"

"You mean on the lips?"

"On the lips."

Mantana ran through the scrapbook of her memory and lit upon the page highlighted by a boy in math class of her last year at school. Aze was his name, the younger of the Jerriporn boys, and a day wouldn't pass when he didn't walk her home or offer to carry her books. He once went so far as to hold her hand. After graduation, Aze followed his brother to a university in Chiang Mai and she never heard from him again. Mantana cried for a week straight. Then stopped thinking about him altogether.

"I've never kissed a boy, ma'am."

"Have you ever taken your clothes off for one?"

"I was swimming once and my -" Mantana looked down at

her hands. "No, ma'am, I've never done that."

"So, of course, you've never had sex with a boy."

Mantana pressed her eyes shut and felt her lips curl. Her nose tingled; her throat became hot and dry.

"Don't cry!" ordered Phii Aor.

"I'm sorry," said Mantana, swallowing her sudden tears. "No, I've never had sex with a boy. Although -"

"What?"

Mantana thought of Aze again. "I might have been in love once."

"What does love have to do with anything?"

Phii Aor took out a pen and paper and began to write.

"I like you, Nong Joy. And I don't like too many people. I'm going to give you an address. You go there tomorrow and find a man named Chainoi. I don't trust him any more than I would a sleeping tiger, but he'll give you something to do in the afternoon, and he'll pay you a daily wage. You won't have to have sex with anyone."

Mantana looked at her in disbelief.

"I won't?"

"No. And if you need a place to stay, there's a storage room in back. There's no shower, but you can use the restaurant bathroom to wash in."

"Here?"

"Don't think that I'm doing this because I like you or because I feel sorry for you. I never let my feelings get in the way of business. You're bringing in new customers and keeping the old ones coming back. We've had three bookings for private parties in the past week. It may be a coincidence; it may not. Whatever the case, I want to keep you young and fresh for as long as I can."

Phii Aor leaned down and fiddled with a lock behind the desk. Mantana heard the click of a safe's door open and close again. Phii Aor folded the address around another piece of paper and slid it across the desk. Mantana reached for it slowly. She could clearly see a five-hundred-baht note folded inside the address. With the gift in hand, she waiied and thanked her benefactor.

"Consider that a personal loan," said Phii Aor. "And until you can pay it back, I don't want to hear of you drinking, gambling, or falling in love. Do you understand?"

"Yes, ma'am."

She then opened a side drawer of the desk and took out a pair of black stockings, still wrapped in plastic. She tossed them to Mantana, who caught them in the air.

"And Joy," she said, "let's keep this between you and me."

Mantana stood and quickly moved to the door. She was about to wai her boss again when another thought suddenly struck her.

"Excuse me, ma'am. I was wondering; what did you say to those drunk men who were singing in the restaurant?"

Phii Aor smiled a nasty smile. "I told them that if they weren't quiet for the rest of the evening, I'd see to it that cement blocks were tied to their feet and their bodies thrown into the *Chao Phraya* River."

Mantana stared silently for a moment, then cleared her throat. "Would you?" she asked.

"Of course not, Nong Joy. Bad for business."

Mantana waiied awkwardly and left to change into her new stockings.

10

Who could tell what was inside a person? One smiling and pleasant boss had tried to rape her, while another, cold and unfriendly, had saved her life. Mantana had read somewhere that everything there was to know about a person could be revealed by reading his or her face. Only now that she thought about it, the article had been written by a foreigner and translated for a popular woman's magazine that sat in the waiting area of Nongluck's beauty parlor. Mantana imagined that the person who wrote it had never tried to guess a Thai person's secrets simply by looking at his or her face. That would be like absorbing the teachings of the Buddha by staring long and hard at a statue's eyes. Thai faces would have screwed up his method, disproved his theory. The writer might have unlocked the secrets of individuals in a land where everyone was so desperate to be one, but Thailand was a land of conformity. Its people, for the most part, remained hidden. What there was to reveal lay beneath so many layers of shared skin that outsiders usually gave up the search, or summed up the Thai Nation in a synthetic observation to keep the tourists coming back. The man in the magazine had wisely steered clear of Thailand, but for Mantana, there was very little world outside its borders. And as for Thai faces, she would just have to become a better judge of character.

Mantana thought about it as she went to sleep in the dark storage room of the restaurant that night.

*

The address that Phii Aor had given her was only a short distance from her new home. It took a cab ride to discover this. To Mantana, Bangkok was still twelve different pairs of black and white shoelaces, all knotted together and given a different name at each twist. She had never learned to read a map, nor could she figure out which way was north. Up and down were the only things she knew for certain.

"This is it," said the cab driver.

"Are you sure?" asked Mantana.

"This is what's written on your piece of paper."

Mantana looked out the cab window. "So you're sure."

She got out, paid, and started to walk. Before her was a carnival. It sat in the parking lot of a shopping mall behind a row of sales booths that took up more space than the games and rides. Mantana walked through the crowd, moving from vendor to vendor at a snail's pace. Beggars with missing arms, missing legs, or appendages twisted beyond repair sat in the walkway, bowing and begging for coins. She finally made it to the other side and went to a shooting gallery where a group of children, still dressed in their school uniforms, shot plastic caps at cans, bottles, and rubber dinosaurs set up behind the booth. One boy, wearing dirty shorts and a Mighty Rangers T-shirt knocked a brontosaurus off a bottle of whiskey. The boys shouted and danced until the carney awarded him the bottle. When the children dispersed, Mantana stepped up to the wooden panel.

"Twenty baht," said the weathered man working the shooting gallery.

"I'm looking for Khun Chainoi. Do you know where I might find him?"

"*Rot bump*," he said, and a plastic cap shot from the rifle of a newcomer ricocheted off his head.

The bumper cars were located just past the Ferris wheel. There was another crowd of children and teenagers waiting on a platform, poised to dash for the next available car. Music blared from four large speakers set one on top of the other. The air smelled like burning tires. A man sat in a booth, staring listlessly into space and turning the electricity on and off. Mantana walked over and knocked on the plastic.

"Khun Chainoi?" she yelled. "Are you Khun Chainoi?"

The man screwed up his eyes, nodded, shook his head, then pointed to the left. There was a ticket booth, hardly visible behind the swarm of people crowded before it. Mantana moved to the side and edged her way in.

"Excuse me, Khun Chainoi?"

"What?"

"I'm here about a job."

"You've heard of the IMF?"

"Yes."

"No jobs."

"Phii Aor sent me."

The man selling tickets stopped passing the slips of paper into outstretched hands and lowered his eyes to her boots. He kept them there for some time before raising his head to see the rest of her. He had a thin, somewhat fleshless face and his hair lay slicked back, already showing traces of gray.

"Rangsan's wife?" he asked.

"Yes, sir."

"Wait a moment." Khun Chainoi called to another man standing behind him, smoking a cigarette. The two exchanged places, and Khun Chainoi motioned for Mantana to follow him.

"You must be Nong Joy," he said, slowing down his pace to walk alongside her.

"Yes, sir."

"Aor phoned me this morning. She told me all about you. She says you need to make some money."

"Yes, sir."

"I've got just the job for you. You make fifteen percent of the earnings and all you have to do is sit. You can sit, can't you?"

"I think so, sir."

"Good. Come with me."

Past the bumper cars, past another shooting gallery, past a plastic duck pond and a ring toss game sat a poorly constructed shack with a black curtained entrance. Painted on the side was a collage of atrocious sights. There was a vampire, a demon, and a set of human limbs that had been torn from their sockets. A woman sat at a table outside, collecting ten-baht coins from people who wished to go in.

"This is the House of Horrors. You're going to work here," said Khun Chainoi. "Go in and have a look."

Mantana nodded and approached the curtained doorway. The woman at the table took hold of her arm. "Ten baht!" she said.

"I'm with Khun Chainoi."

"Ten baht!"

The woman had a very strong grip. Her face had seen many years in the sun and resembled a well-tanned piece of leather. Her gums were black from the betelnut she chewed and her lips were two thin strips of bacon. Mantana knew that the woman had been given a simple instruction, ten baht a head, twenty for foreigners, and she would follow it until the man in charge told her differently. Which is just what happened.

"It's all right, Na," said Khun Chainoi, stepping forward. "This is Joy. She's going to work here."

Na released her iron grip and let Mantana go about her business. She parted the curtain and entered the dark shack. It took only a moment for her eyes to adjust. She was in a single room crowded with bodies. A rope ran through the center, cutting the space into two halves. A tape of ghostly moans and banshee wails was playing from somewhere in back. Mantana made her way through the crowd to see what everyone was gawking at.

Three displays sat on a platform in the back half of the room. Each was lit by red and purple spotlights nailed to the walls. The first was a girl, no older than Mantana, sitting next to a wooden chair. She had long straight hair and a look of infinite boredom in her eyes. The girl's arm lay stretched across the seat of the chair, and a large knife stuck out of her wrist, just below the elbow. There was a pool of blood on the chair.

"Ooh," said Mantana.

The second display was a standing cage with a will o' wisp trapped inside. The will o' wisp had a woman's head, severed at the neck with only the esophagus, heart, and intestines still attached. The heart beat with an eerie red light, but the face of the monster, like the face of the girl with the knife in her arm, did not convey the message "Run! Run before I eat you!" but something more like "Does anyone have a cigarette?"

It was only on the third and most elaborate display that Mantana experienced what could only be described as a shock to her system. A man wearing a white T-shirt and jeans sat on a table, propped up by his arms. His legs ended an inch above his knees and the remains, two tennis-shoed stumps, lay at the opposite end of the table. A blood-soaked saw was at his side. But it wasn't the legs, which were obviously plastic, nor the blood, too red to be real, that surprised her the most. It was the man.

"Jakkrit?" she said aloud.

The man looked up at the sound of his name. When he saw Mantana, pushing to the front of the crowd, his surprise was equally great.

"Nong Joy! Nong Joy from the village! What are you doing here?"

"I'm going to work here. Jakkrit, is it really you?"

It was. Though from one look, Mantana could see that the man on the table was not the same man who came to bother her in her father's shop and woke the village up at night with his singing. That man was a drunk! This one was clean shaven and didn't reek of alcohol. Still, despite the fact that the dark circles had faded from around his eyes and the whiskey babble absent from his lips, there was something amiss. Like a light bulb with a bent and broken wire behind the glass.

"I've stopped drinking, Nong Joy. I joined the carnival when it came to town three weeks ago and stayed on when it moved to Bangkok. It's good here. Khun Chainoi takes care of me."

Jakkrit tipped a jar of red paint that sat behind him. Mantana watched the liquid ooze across the table.

"Sometimes I wear a pair of rubber legs that I tie into a knot. Then I'm The Rubber Man."

"What are you today?"

"Today I'm The Man With The Sawed-Off Legs."

Mantana laughed. A pair of children made vomiting noises beside her.

"Are there holes in the table where your legs go?"

Jakkrit cocked his head and looked at her with a mischievous grin. He then moved his legs to show their actual length. They ended an inch above his knees. Mantana couldn't believe what she was seeing.

"Didn't you know?" asked Jakkrit.

"No," she whispered.

"I could have stayed and gone from being the village drunk to the village cripple, ha ha. Do you think anyone would have shown pity on me? No. They'd say I got what I deserved."

"Nong Joy," said a voice from behind. It was Khun Chainoi.

"We'll have a chance to talk, won't we?" she said to Jakkrit.

"I'm not going anywhere."

Mantana took a last look at the place where his legs used to be, then, poor Jakkrit, she left the shack of horrors.

She was to begin work as the will o' wisp just as soon as she got into make-up.

*

Jakkrit didn't know just how he had lost his legs. The doctor told him they had been crushed, probably by a car. He told her of the old hag he had seen, and how she laughed as she gathered the wreckage of him like so much firewood before disappearing again.

"Of course," he added. "That must sound crazy to you."

Mantana shifted uncomfortably in the will o' wisp's cage. She had to kneel on a wooden bench behind a black screen that hid her body. She then leaned forward, and rested her chin on a piece of velvet. The plastic innards hung from the headrest on the other side of the screen. Mantana wanted to yawn, but held back for terror's sake. An old man and three children stood watching her. The children kept asking the old man if she were a real live ghost or not. "No, no," said the old man. "*Real* ghosts don't get caught."

The spectators left without so much as a gasp. The shack was clear. Mantana removed her head from the will o' wisp's body and stood to stretch her legs. She rubbed her sore neck and winced at the thin layer of dust she felt, kicked up by the boys and girls and stuck tight from the heat. The heat, the heat, if it wasn't the heat it was the lack of air. The shack was like a magnet for the sun. Next to her, the girl with the knife in her arm was fast asleep and the sound effects tape had run out long ago. Only Jakkrit, still faithfully bloodying his stumps, carried on the conversation Mantana had promised. The one she was simply too tired for.

"The strange thing," said Jakkrit, "is that I forget that they're gone. Sometimes, I'll try to stand up and suddenly, there's nothing down there for me to stand on. And then, ha ha, I put on a pair of rubber legs. Then I'm The Rubber Man."

He looked up, as if noticing where he was for the first time that day.

"There will be more people this evening," he said.

"I'm sorry, Jakkrit. I won't be here. I've got another job."

"You have two jobs? You must be very rich."

Mantana smiled. She had wanted to tell him about everything when she first saw him; the department store, the restaurant, all the people, both good and evil, but now, maybe it was best if he didn't know.

"Do you believe in fate, Jakkrit?"

"You mean the kind that fortune-tellers predict?"

"I mean this. Do you think our lives are already planned out for us? The people we'll meet, the things we'll see; accidents like yours - or even the day we die?"

"I don't know what good it does thinking about it."

Mantana sighed. It was quiet for a moment, then she spoke again. "How about this. You said that the people of our village would say that you deserved to have your legs cut off. Do you agree with them?"

"No," he said in an unfamiliar tone of voice.

"But some good came of it. You stopped drinking."

"If I'd found that I had golden leg bones that I could sell for twenty million baht, then I'd say that some good came of it."

It was useless. Mantana stopped asking questions. Jakkrit sensed her disappointment and ran his finger along the edge of the saw.

"I suppose," he said, "Things could always be worse."

"Worse than losing your legs?"

"I could lose my arms. My eyes. My tongue. Then where would I be? A ghost, I suppose, only not a very good one. I'd probably kill myself."

Mantana spoke without thinking. "Didn't you think about that when you woke up and found your legs missing?"

"Of course I did. Death has got to be easier than a life like this. But -"

Another silence.

"But what?"

Their eyes met in the murky shadows. "I'm afraid of dying."

"Me too," said Mantana.

The entranceway curtains parted and Mantana quickly resumed her position on the bench. It was a young couple, holding hands tightly as they approached. The girl was thin, but pretty, dressed in a black and white school uniform. Her boyfriend wore the same color combination, with the addition of a red necktie, pulled loose around his neck. They seemed to be having an awful lot of fun. Mantana watched them giggle and fall into each other and generally act like a pair of idiots.

Then she closed her eyes. There was no rule that said the will o' wisp had to look at everyone who entered the shack. She shut them tight and waited for the couple to leave before she opened them again.

"I guess they were in love," said Jakkrit.

"Yes," said Mantana. "I guess so."

*

At six p.m., Mantana was free. Instead of going directly to the restaurant, she went back to the hotel coffee shop where Ning and she ate at that hour. She was glad to see her in their usual booth, with cigarettes and coffee set out on the table like a petrol pump, fueling her for the evening.

"Nong Joy! I'm so glad you're here. I just had an argument with Peung over you. Did you find a place to stay?"

"Yes. And I found a second job, too. Only I'm not supposed to tell you about it. Phii Aor asked me to keep it a secret."

"Oh, come on, Joy. I'm your only friend."

Mantana quickly filled her in on her day job and lodgings. Ning sipped her coffee and seemed to grow agitated listening to the story.

"Don't tell the other girls, all right? Phii Aor has been so kind. She even loaned me five hundred baht and said that I could pay her back whenever I could. You were wrong about her, Ning."

Ning raised one of her penciled-in eyebrows and reached for her green and white pack of cigarettes. Mantana took one too.

"Quit," she said.

Mantana looked at the cigarette. "But I haven't even started."

"Not smoking. Quit the job. Quit both of your jobs and go back to your village before something terrible happens."

"What are you talking about?"

"Phii Aor has never done anything nice for anyone. Especially for a singer who receives three times the number of wreaths she does."

"She told me that was the reason. She said I'm bringing in new customers and keeping the old ones coming back."

"Joy -"

"Ning! You're the one who told me to go to her. When I did, I went to offer myself to any customer that would have me. If she wanted to watch me suffer, I gave her the perfect opportunity. Instead, she offered me a job and money."

"Only because she has something else in mind for you. I

don't know what, but I can promise you that it's something bad. If she had taken you up on your offer, there wouldn't be anything to worry about. But now -"

Ning's right hand suddenly covered the two thin scars that ran along her opposite wrist. Mantana pretended not to notice, and gazed out the window instead.

"I won't go back to my village," said Mantana.

Both girls lit their cigarettes and drew heavily from them.

11

Backstage was more chaotic than usual that night. Khun Rangsan, who was rarely seen in the restaurant past six, stayed through the afternoon and into the evening. His wife was in a bad temper, quite likely because he hadn't gone home yet, and continued to belittle him in front of the stage performers. Mantana overheard some of their conversation.· ·

"Did you get my note yesterday about the cleaning woman?" asked Khun Rangsan.

"Yes," snapped Phii Aor. "I got your note and I think it's a terrible idea. We don't need to hire another cleaning woman."

"But we don't have a choice. The law says that women are only allowed to work eight-hour days. Our cleaning woman works from four p.m. until three a.m. on weekdays, and even longer on weekends."

"So what? We pay her, don't we?"

"Yes, but the law,"

"What law? I've never heard of this law! I know what happened! You can't keep secrets from me! You met some poor old lady who can't afford to feed her kids and couldn't say no when she asked you for a job. Isn't that right?"

"No, dear, not at all."

"Policemen are treated well here. You don't need to start worrying about policemen. And I don't hear our cleaning woman complaining. Besides, what would she do with an extra four or five hours each day? I'll tell you what. She'd drink and gamble. She'd get sick and not be able to work at all. If you have any trouble with policemen trying to enforce the law, you tell me, right away. Until then, we don't need another cleaning woman."

"Yes, dear."

"Now go away. I want to be happy."

Mantana and Bew traded eyeliner and lipstick back and forth in the dressing room mirror, not daring to speak as Phii Aor came storming through the narrow space. She wore a long red dress that glittered in the fluorescent light. Phii Aor's face was red too, but it didn't glitter.

"Bew!" she said.

"Wah!"

"Don't wear so much lipstick. If I can't tell whether you're a man or a woman, how is the audience supposed to know?"

Bew just stared at her in astonishment.

"And Joy!" she continued in her red dress, face, fury.

"Yes, ma'am?"

Phii Aor's anger took a sudden turn. The corners of her mouth turned up, and her voice assumed a sickly sweetness.

"How was your day?" she asked, and it almost carried a tune.

"Fine, ma'am."

"Good. I'm glad to hear it."

She sneered one last time at Bew, then marched out of the dressing room.

"I'm sick of this place," said Bew, dropping his English. "They hired me to be a woman but now they only want me to be a man."

He pursed his lips and drew on a thick coat of red in defiance.

For the rest of the evening, Mantana had a sneaking suspicion that Ning's warning had some truth to it. But nothing happened. And on the following day, when she reported for work at the parking lot fairgrounds, nothing happened. In fact, for the next week and a half, the days passed by, each one exactly like the day before, with only a restless night of sleep to separate them.

Then, like a rainstorm from a cloudless sky, something happened.

It was during the second half of a Wednesday night show. Mantana had already sung two sets and it was Bew's third time at the microphone. He had opened with *Mai Tammada*, one of his personal favorites, yet sang with a detachment that seemed unusual for him. Applause was sparse, and he went into the next song without any wreaths. Mantana could make out the dark outlines of heads and bodies, but faces were difficult to see. This one might have been smiling, that one probably wasn't paying attention; anything beyond that was guesswork. So when a dozen red roses snaked through the restaurant towards the stage, there was no telling which table, which silhouette, they were from. Bew stepped forward to receive them but the flower girl, whose name was Nui, nodded for Mantana to step forward. There was laughter as Bew returned to the microphone playing the part of a scorned woman. Mantana took the roses, inhaled their fragrance, and set them down beside her. Roses were nice, but she couldn't sell them back to the shop across the street. They brought nothing but an edge of strange emotions. Someone out there in the darklands had his eye on her.

Mantana rejoined the dancing line and tried not to look at

the others.

Five minutes later, another bouquet of red roses arrived for her. Bew made a joke into the microphone and drew some laughs by shaking his finger and scolding her for taking all the roses that were meant for him. Mantana wished he would stop clowning. She didn't want to draw any more attention to herself than necessary. It was giving her a bad feeling in her stomach, like the spirits of misfortune were being shaken from their slumber and ordered to get back to their jobs.

In the middle of Bew's monologue, two more bouquets of roses were handed up to the stage.

"Nui!" she whispered, doing her best to keep the phony smile plastered to her face. "Who is sending these to me?"

But Nui only smiled and nodded because she wasn't terribly bright, nor could she hear too well.

Mantana had a pile of forty-eight long-stemmed roses laying at her side. She scanned the restaurant, though the spotlights prevented her from seeing. It was then she noticed the silence. Everyone was looking at the young and pretty dancing girl and her stage garden of roses.

"Sing!" she said to Bew. "Sing something!"

Bew turned back to the microphone. But before the music could start up again, a terrible cry came from Out There.

"Another! Another! Give her another bouquet!"

Mantana felt her legs turn to ice. The shadows and the outlines started to move, rise to their feet and dart about. A glass fell. A chair overturned. One of the dark figures, a man, was rushing forward, rushing toward her. Mantana put her hands over her heart but couldn't move from her spot. The man made it to the stage, and a half dozen hands grabbed hold of him, preventing him from climbing up. He had the look of a wild animal being administered electric shocks. Mantana instantly recognized him.

It was Khun Nemit.

"My love!" he hollered. "My only love!"

Mantana was too stunned to take in his words and consider them. Her eyes connected with his and a feeling of mad dogs fighting in a black stone alley raced through her.

"More roses! A hundred thousand more!"

The same hands that had stopped Khun Nemit from leaping to the stage pulled him backward, into the darkness. A cold set of fingers touched Mantana's shoulder and she screamed.

"It's OK, Joy!" said Ning. "It's OK."

"It's not O.K!" she said frantically. "It's him!"

Ning set a hand upon her waist and led her off-stage. Phii Aor rushed past them to take Bew's place at the microphone. She had to stop the singer from calling a grand assault down upon the rabid customer.

Backstage, Mantana collapsed in a chair.

"Don't move," said Ning. "I'll get you some water."

"It's him!" Mantana grasped Ning's arm before she could leave her. "Don't you understand? It's him!"

"Who?"

"Khun Nemit! From the department store! The man I killed!"

"You didn't kill anyone."

"He's back! Back from the dead! He wants my blood!"

"Joy, he just bought four dozen roses for you."

"He's crazy! Dying made him crazy!" Mantana bit her lip and heard the things she was saying. "What's he doing now?"

"I don't know."

"Go find out, will you?"

"You'll have to let go of me first."

Mantana released her grip and watched her friend disappear from the dressing room. She searched the table for a pack of cigarettes, found one, and lit up. Then she gagged.

"Nong Joy, what happened?"

It was Khun Rangsan. He still wasn't going home when he was supposed to and spent his evenings wandering about, trying to make himself useful. What he succeeded in doing was to drive his wife crazy, which, in turn, put all the employees on edge dealing with her temper tantrums. He wore a brown suit this night, and, as always, his round spectacles.

"Who was that man?" he asked.

"I don't know, sir."

"He's out there demanding to know your name."

"*What?*"

"He says it's urgent that he know who you are."

Mantana shook her head in bewilderment.

"There, there, it's all right. I'm sure he's just drunk."

"Yes," said Mantana. "That must be it." She took a drag off the cigarette, then snubbed it out in an ashtray already overflowing with lipstick-stained butts. "Excuse me, sir, I have to go to the toilet."

Mantana stood and walked slowly from the room. When she was sure that Khun Rangsan wasn't looking, she dashed to the backstage curtain that Ning was peering out from.

"Is he still there?" she asked.

"Yes, he's still there. It looks like his friends have calmed him down. Here, take a look."

Ning pulled back the curtain enough for both girls to see. The house lights had gone up, and the restaurant was visible to all. Khun Nemit sat at a table with four men who watched him with anger and confusion. The little manager held his head in his hands and cringed as if he were in a great deal of pain. Red roses lay scattered on the floor around him. Mantana watched the man sitting closest to Khun Nemit lean over and whisper something in his ear. He must have understood, despite his condition, because he shook his head with such fury, Mantana thought it would snap from his shoulders.

"He recognizes me," she said. "But he doesn't remember me."

"You must have knocked out part of his brain when you hit him."

Mantana took a last look at the crowd. Khun Nemit lowered his hands but didn't look up. The house lights went down again and the man on the synthesizer cued up another song. Bew was performing without any back-up. Mantana wiped her eyes and followed Ning to the dressing room. Phii Aor came rushing in moments later.

"Nong Joy! Are you in shock?"

"No, ma'am."

"Good. Both of you are on as soon as Bew finishes this number."

"Phii Aor, ma'am," said Ning. "Joy is afraid that man will try to attack her if he sees her on stage again."

"Do you know that man, Nong Joy?"

Mantana swallowed. "No, ma'am."

"He doesn't know you either. He's already been given a warning. One more disruption and I'll personally throw him out of this restaurant. His business associates don't know what's the matter with him but they've promised to make him behave. So you see," she said cheerily, "Nong Joy has nothing to worry about. Let's all get into costume and pretend that nothing has happened."

She smiled the work of two forklifts, and her nostrils flared as if something not entirely human was at work behind her decisions. Fortunately, Khun Rangsan appeared in the doorway and gave Phii Aor a reason and an outlet for her indignation. Without so much as a word, she picked up a Chinese fan laying on the dressing room table and closed it with a snap. Then she whacked her husband on the shoulder and walked out.

The discussion was over.

*

The lone stage musician was playing an electronic version of a traditional Thai song when Mantana returned to the microphone. She sang off-key and mixed up the first and second verses, though no one seemed to notice. Everyone was waiting to see whether the crazy little man suffering from a terrible headache would have to be restrained again.

Mantana finished one song, then another. The songs seemed to go on forever. Ning shook her tambourine and the line of dancing girls spun around her. Nui, the flower girl, handed up a twenty-baht string of garlands. Another arrived for Peung, who spun to her left. During the third song of Mantana's set, Khun Nemit pushed his chair out and stood up. Others at his table readied themselves to do whatever was necessary. Mantana squinted her eyes and tried to see what was happening. Then she kneeled down and turned one of the stage lights onto the audience.

Khun Nemit had climbed onto his chair, unbuttoned his trousers, and allowed them to drop to his knees. His all was visible for as long as it took one of his business associates to pull the chair out from beneath him.

"A million roses!" he cried, and crashed to the floor.

*

Everyone understood when Mantana said that she couldn't finish her set. She didn't have to resort to tears. "Get some rest," was Phii Aor's advice, and Ning's too, but once she was out of her dancing costume, Mantana sneaked out the back exit and hailed a cab at the curbside. She gave the driver an address and watched the digital meter come to life. Streetlights flashed in her eyes and neon advertisements painted the upholstery as she recalled Ning's words. Quit. Quit both jobs. Mantana rubbed her tired eyes. Was

Phii Aor somehow responsible for what happened that evening? Did she bring Khun Nemit to the restaurant, or did he just happen to show up? And why did his penis look so strange?

The ride to her old dormitory took all the money she had earned that day. The trip back would take yesterday's wages. She paid the driver and walked up the steps to her old room. Luck. Darunee was right where she had left her.

"Joy!" she said, and rushed to give her friend a hug. Darunee was dressed in a pink nightie with rabbits sewn into the breast. She smelled clean. Mantana realized she hadn't showered, and probably reeked of cigarette smoke.

"Can I come in, Darunee?"

"Yes. Do you remember Pusadee? She's my roommate now, but she's down the hall watching TV. She moved in right after you -" Darunee released her hold and stepped back. "Left."

Mantana entered the room and closed the door. Then she locked it.

"Joy, where have you been? What happened to you?"

"You have to tell me everything that's happened since I left the department store, Som."

"Well," said Darunee. "I was moved to the grocery check-out and trained to use a cash register. I make deposits and -"

"Som!"

"What?"

"I don't want to know about you! I mean, I do, of course I do, but later, OK? I want to know about Khun Nemit."

"Khun Nemit?"

"Has he been looking for me?"

"You mean after he got out of the hospital?"

"He was in the hospital?"

"Joy, you know about it better than anyone. You were there in the office with him when it happened."

"What happened?"

"I heard he had an epileptic seizure while he was talking to you. I heard you got scared and ran out."

"Where did you hear I went?"

"Home. To the village."

"Keep talking. What happened then?"

"Well, the assistant manager took over while Khun Nemit was in the hospital. He came back after a week, though no one sees much of him these days. He comes in early and stays late and rarely comes out of his office."

"Is there anything else?"

"No," she said, then; "Wait, there is something. I don't know if it matters, but after he came back from the hospital, I thought I'd ask about your wages. I wondered if he had your father's address. Only, when I finally cornered him to ask, he got this strange look on his face like he didn't know whom I was talking about."

"Is that all?"

"I said your name, a couple of times, to try and help him remember, you know, and he - he did this."

Darunee put her hands to her head and staggered back a couple of steps. She twisted her lips and crossed her eyes and made a grunting noise like some kind of hungry sow.

"His face turned red," she said, quitting her impersonation. "For a minute, I thought his whole head was going to explode. I never did find out about your wages."

"It doesn't matter."

"Then why are you so interested in Khun Nemit?"

Mantana looked out of the corners of her eyes. She saw no reason for Darunee to know more than she had to. "It's not important," she said. "I just wondered if he survived his - seizure."

"Joy, you didn't go back to the village, did you?"

Mantana shook her head.

"What are you still doing in Bangkok? Did you find another job?"

Mantana tried to smile. "I wash dishes at a *gooey teeo* restaurant," she said.

12

The next day, Jakkrit wore his rubber legs. He could bend them backwards and sideways, and crisscross them at angles that ordinary legs couldn't go. Mantana's display had changed too. She was no longer a will o' wisp, but a crazy bride. She wore a white gown, splattered with red paint, and held an axe in her hands. There were fake body parts and a large pool of fake blood that she was forced to stand in. She kept the veil down so that onlookers wouldn't see the black eyeliner and purple lipstick that coated her face. She thought she looked more silly than scary.

"Change is good, don't you think?" said Jakkrit.

"Jakkrit, can I ask you something?"

"Yes."

"Why is it you've never asked what my other job is?"

Jakkrit didn't answer. Mantana sensed something uncomfortable in the air, like the moment after a pair of black helicopters passed by overhead.

"Jakkrit? What do you think my other job is?" asked Mantana.

"Aren't you a prostitute?"

Mantana lifted her veil. "Who told you that? Did someone tell you that or did you decide it for yourself?"

"No, Joy, really. Khun Chainoi told me."

"That -" Mantana bit her lip. The girl with the knife in her arm had removed the plastic blade and stood on a black-clothed table that onlookers couldn't see. A rope hung from the ceiling that ended in a noose around her neck. When the girl stood on her toes and let her head fall to the side, it appeared she had hung herself. At the moment, however, she was filing her nails. Mantana had to be careful of what she said.

"Joy, I don't care if you're a prostitute or not," said Jakkrit. "I never did."

"I'm not."

"Say, I've got something for you to see. Here, take a look at that!"

Jakkrit passed her a crumpled photograph that he had dug from his shirt pocket. In it were three barefoot boys, smiling, with their arms slung over each other's shoulders. They stood on a dirt path with the edge of a pond visible behind them. Mantana looked at the photo, then handed it back.

"Who are they?"

"I don't know."

"Why do you carry it around with you?"

"I don't know," he said. "Then again, maybe I do. Whenever I want a bottle, I take out this picture and look at it. This was me once. This boy in the middle. This was Jakkrit. I mean, not really, but -" Jakkrit sighed and returned the photo to his shirt pocket. "You must think I'm crazy."

"No," she said, leaning her bloody axe against the back wall. "I don't think you're crazy."

"Sometimes," he went on, "I want to drink so badly, that the only thing that keeps me from going out to buy a bottle is that I don't have the legs to take me to a store. Even in the pouring rain, I'd go if I could. Even in the pouring rain."

Mantana looked again at the line that divided his real legs from the rubber ones. "Why did you ever start?"

Jakkrit shook his head slowly. "I can't remember."

A pair of teenage girls entered the shack. They observed each of them in turn, with little expression in their eyes, and walked out again.

"Joy, if I ask you something, will you promise not to answer right away?"

"Oh, Jakkrit, please don't ask me to buy liquor for you. I can't do it."

"That's not what I was going to ask." Jakkrit cleared his throat and set his hands upon the knees of his fake legs. "Will you marry me, Nong Joy?"

"No."

"Don't answer now. Think about it."

"All right. When should I answer?"

"Wait ten minutes."

They waited. The girl in the noose went outside to smoke a cigarette. A cat poked its head in and mewed.

"Has it been ten minutes?" asked Mantana.

"I don't know. I don't own a watch. It's OK. You can tell me your answer now."

"No."

"All right," said Jakkrit. "Thank you for thinking about it."

*

The afternoon went by slower than most. When her six hours had ended, Mantana found Khun Chainoi attending the bumper cars. She asked for a moment to speak with him. It was the moment she had been turning over in her mind since Jakkrit told her what the carnival boss said. Now, she was all nervous anger and determination.

"Khun Chainoi, sir, I want you to know that I'm not, nor have I ever been, a prostitute. I'm a singer at Phii Aor's restaurant. I thought she would have told you that when she spoke to you about me."

Khun Chainoi looked at her blankly. "Phii Aor told me that you were a singer and a prostitute."

"What did you say?"

"I said Phii Aor told me that -"

Mantana made two fists and lowered her head. She felt stupid and small. But there was something else as well. Something she couldn't put a name to but caused her a greater shame than being looked upon as a *sopaynee* by Khun Chainoi and Jakkrit. A tear rolled down her cheek, only to make her feel worse.

"Oho!" said Khun Chainoi. "Come here. Maybe I heard wrong."

"How could you have heard wrong? Either she said it or she didn't."

"Nong Joy, if you don't mind my asking, why is a young and pretty girl like you working in a restaurant? That kind of work can't pay well if you have to work here as well."

"I don't know how to do anything else."

"You don't have to know a thing. Just because you're the way you are doesn't mean you have to be a prostitute."

"I'm NOT a prostitute!"

"Your boss seems to think you are."

Mantana clenched her teeth. "I have to go now, sir."

"Joy, wait. I have a friend who produces karaoke videos. His office is in Taiwan, but he frequently travels to Bangkok to look for girls to star in his videos. There's no nudity. The police wouldn't let him in or out of the country if there was."

"Why are you telling me this?"

"These girls make a lot of money for a day's work, Joy. If you're interested, I could introduce you to him as soon as tomorrow. There's a two thousand five hundred baht placement fee, but the money you make on the videos -"

Mantana interrupted. "I haven't got two thousand five hundred baht."

Khun Chainoi took out a pack of cigarettes and offered her one.

"Do you know where you are, Nong Joy?"

"Of course I do."

"Tell me. Where are you?"

"I'm in Bangkok."

Khun Chainoi shook his head. "No. You're wrong. Look around you. There's nothing but automobiles and people and dogs and pollution. The air is so thick, you'll be able to walk on it in another few years. You don't live in Bangkok, Joy. You live *under* Bangkok. Ground level is actually about four or five meters above our heads. Don't believe me? Give it some thought. The only real jobs are above the second floor of office buildings. The only real places to live are in condominiums, high in the sky. Smell the air. Is it fresh? Look at the faces of the people. Are they happy? Just you wait and see, Joy. Bangkok won't ever fall. Its underbelly, where we stand now, will simply harden, like rice burned onto the bottom of a pan. And the survivors will be up there in their office buildings and condos, waiting to lay fresh concrete on all of this, all of us."

Mantana looked at Khun Chainoi with a growing sense of horror.

"I have to go now," she said.

"Look around, Nong Joy," he said. "Use what you've got before you turn into a piece of burnt rice that's of no use to anyone."

Mantana backed away from the carnival boss, turned, and walked quickly towards the street. The air stank and the people weren't smiling. Here was a cripple; here was a harelip. Here was make-up and here was poverty. Had this too been orchestrated for her or was this the way it was, the way it would always be?

The world has gone mad, she thought, and hurried away from Khun Chainoi's carnival.

*

The late afternoon sun had expended all its fuel, and it was now the sidewalks and buildings that trapped the remaining heat and refused to let go. Maybe that was the reason for everyone's strange behavior. Everyone but Phii Aor, who had air conditioning and couldn't be affected by the heat. No, she was something else altogether. Mantana thought of her face as she walked and wanted to hit, slap, scream. Forget the fact that she looked like her mother in the prime of her beauty. Just forget it! Even with all her anger, she knew that a confrontation was out of the question. Aor was a *phii*. Mantana was a *nong*. One did not show such disrespect to one's elders. A confrontation was out of the question.

She crossed the street to a line of rowshop awnings that provided some relief from the stagnant sunlight. Her mind stumbled from one scene to another. There she was, singing karaoke on a tropical island with a dozen cameras pointing at her. There she was, watching her father open an envelope that contained more money than he'd ever held before. There she was, standing at the window of her high-rise apartment, watching the cars and air and people below start to mold and rot until there was nothing left of the original. And then snow.

"*Will you marry me, Nong Joy?*"

What was that? What had he said? Mantana stopped walking to sift through her troubles and dreams until she came to Jakkrit.

It was as if she were hearing his words for the first time that day. Was he joking? No, he wasn't joking. Did he really think? Yes, he really thought. It wasn't the first time he had asked her to marry him. Back in the village, he'd get drunk and ask everyone to marry him. Only now, he wasn't drunk. And Mantana had treated him as if he were.

The world and everything in it seemed suddenly cruel to her, but only for a moment. Mantana had a difficult time holding on to thoughts like these. It was too small of a voice, always drowned out by other, louder voices within her. The loud voices didn't ease any of her gloom, nor did they provide an answer for the odd questions that often crossed her mind. They were just loud. Teachers, singers, politicians, and TV celebrities. Like standing in traffic; loud.

By the time she reached the restaurant, her anger was nearly overcome by nerves. Still, she was determined to find out the truth. She tried to think of a way to approach the subject without asking any direct questions. She washed, dressed, and with her hair still wet, went to see Phii Aor. She found her in the restaurant kitchen making coffee and setting up a serving tray. She looked more beautiful than ever, dressed in black pants and a white blouse laced with violet.

"*Sa wat dee ka* Nong Joy," said Phii Aor. "You're just in time."

"*Sa wat dee ka*. Time for what, ma'am?"

"There's someone I want you to meet."

Mantana cleared her throat. "Could I ask you something, ma'am?"

Phii Aor looked up from the hot water pot and smiled with the corners of her mouth. Mantana knew that smile. It sent shivers down her spine.

"Certainly."

"It's about something Khun Chainoi said."

"And what was that?"

"He said - he said there's a man in Taiwan who makes

karaoke videos and comes to Bangkok every now and then looking for girls."

"And he discovered you."

"No, not exactly, ma'am. It's two thousand five hundred baht to apply, but if I'm accepted, Khun Chainoi says I can make a lot of money and not turn into a piece of burnt rice at the bottom of a saucepan."

"Chainoi said that?"

"Yes, ma'am. And something else, too. What I mean is, he thought I was something else, besides a singer."

"Nong Joy, I know you have more self-respect than to ask for another loan, so I'll assume you've come to ask my opinion. My advice to you is forget it. Forget Taiwan and forget dreams of stardom. You're young and you're pretty and you're poor. Everyone, Nong Joy, and I do mean everyone, will want to take advantage of you. Especially a snake like Chainoi."

"Yes, but -"

"Bring the sugar, will you?"

Phii Aor placed the two cups on a tray and carried it to her office. Mantana followed, sugar in hand. Phii Aor fixed the usual smile upon her face and opened the door.

"Please," said a man's voice. "Let me help."

Mantana didn't want to go in. The stranger's voice was like an orange wind blowing her backward. It took a second clenched tooth invitation from Phii Aor to remind her that she didn't have a choice. Mantana kept her eyes down and only looked up when she had to.

"*Sa wat dee krap*," said the man.

Mantana waiied shyly. The man was old, older than her father, and had lost most of the hair on his head. The skin underneath was covered in small bumps and laced with intricate veins. His small face was wrinkled, like a bullet hole in a pane of glass, with a pair of shining black eyes to keep it from being dead. He was dressed in gray slacks and a short-sleeved shirt. An emblem of a man swinging a golf club was sewn into the breast pocket. When he took a step toward Mantana, Mantana stepped back. Phii Aor chuckled to prevent a loss of face.

"What's the matter with you?" she asked.

Mantana looked at her boss's red lips. "*Sopaynee*," they said. "*Prostitute*." Or had she just imagined it?

"Nong Joy, this is Phii Wen," she said, no doubt about it this time. "Joy is the one I told you about."

"Yes," said the old man, moving his charcoal eyes up and down her body. "I understand why. Come here, my dear."

Why oh why had she not gone straight to her room? She took a feeble step towards him and felt her heart pound as his old legs covered the rest of the distance. The smell of cheap cologne and tobacco filled her nostrils.

"*Prostitute*."

"Lovely!" whispered Phii Wen. "Would you mind turning around?"

Mantana looked into his black little eyes and thought, there's a black little mind behind those eyes. Then, still holding the plastic dish of sugar, she turned around and faced the door. No sooner had she taken a breath, a pair of large and spotted hands rested themselves upon her shoulders. How dare he! How dare she! What was it that made Phii Aor save her for this old turtle with the head of a snake? Money? Maybe she owed him a favor and Mantana was the payback. Was that why she had been so nice? Was that why she wanted to keep her young and pretty until this moment?

"Stop moving, Joy," said Phii Aor. "Phii Wen wants to get a good look at you."

Her words nearly made her cry. But then Phii Wen spoke and the blue tears were choked by his orange wind.

"That's fine," he said. "You're wearing an undershirt, aren't you?

Could you take your blouse off for me, dear?"

It happened in a heartbeat. The dish hit the floor and a hundred sugar cubes shot in every direction. Phii Aor shouted her name, but she was already gone. Out the door, gone. Divorced from all doubt, gone. Free of Phii Aor and her smiling turtle, gone.

On her way out, she nearly collided with Ning and Peung, smoking cigarettes in the shade of the entranceway.

"Joy! Where are you going?" asked Ning.

"I don't know."

"You're shaking! What happened now?"

"I don't know."

"Well, let's go in and -"

"No!"

Mantana took her friend's hand and pulled her aside. She tried to catch her breath while Ning continued to ask meaningless questions.

"Phii Aor," she finally spit out.

"What about Phii Aor?"

"She tried to sell me to a horrible old man."

"No!"

"Yes. He's in there right now."

Hot tears ran down her cheeks. She wiped them away with the back of her hand. "You were right. She's an awful, evil woman."

"What are you going to do?"

"I don't know. I don't know."

"Listen. Here's a spare key to my room. I'll talk to Peung and convince her to let you stay just for tonight. There's some instant soup packets on the shelf if you get hungry."

Mantana took the key and held it in her hand.

"This is the second job in two months that I've had to run from."

"You need to find a boss that appreciates your beauty and doesn't take advantage of it."

Mantana gave her a funny look. That's just what Phii Aor had said, or something close to it. She wiped her nose and shook off the rest of her tears.

"What do you know about karaoke videos?" she asked.

"You mean starring in them? I've heard it's a good way to make money. You have to be careful though. I once knew a girl—"

A public bus went by, its horn shrieking in the air. Mantana didn't get to hear about Ning's friend, though judging from the expression on her face, the girl obviously came to a bad end.

"It's just an idea," said Mantana. "Like robbing banks is an idea."

"Watch TV and eat some soup," said Ning. "You'll feel better."

Mantana said good-bye and walked disdainfully along the sidewalk. She tried to concentrate on one thing and stick with it until some kind of resolution. Her mind refused to co-operate. All she knew was that something completely unfair was happening to her, be it the spirits of misfortune at work or a rottenness brought on by real human beings. She wanted to make merit at a temple and shake the sticks and read her fortune, but all the temple gates were locked for the evening. Maybe she wouldn't even believe what the sticks had to say, but it would have been something, a piece of evidence to give her hope or make her feel justified in her lack of it.

She kept going until she came to a market, flooded with dirty umbrellas propped on metal poles. Women with their heads wrapped in cloth sat behind grills smoking with chicken and fish. Others waved plastic bags tied to sticks over their dozen steel pots of soups and curries to keep the flies away. The air was pungent with laughter and food and bickering and sweat, a general feeling of madness, but an insanity that was at least familiar to her. Mantana thought of Mr. Chai and his daughter Newt and wondered how she would have fared washing dishes at their *gooey teeo* stand.

There was no need to wonder. She already knew. She was pretty, she was young, she was poor. Until one of these factors changed, she was ultimately doomed.

A hand laid itself upon her shoulder. Mantana turned and gasped. That is, she *gasped*. There stood Khun Nemit, holding a dozen red roses still wrapped in plastic. A piercing NO shot through her brain and she tried to run. Only the little man had grabbed hold of her wrist and held on tight.

"Let go!" she cried.

"Wait! Please! I've been following you!"

Mantana pushed her arm forward, then snapped it back. Khun Nemit couldn't hold on. He dropped his roses and reeled backwards, that old expression of agony entering his eyes.

"Don't go!" he said, and there was pain in that, too.

There were too many people around for Mantana to feel as if she were in danger. And she was sick of running.

"What do you want?" she asked.

Khun Nemit backed against the blackened wall of a building and leaned against it for support. He lowered his hands and slowly opened his eyes.

"I don't know," he said.

"Do you know who I am? Do you know what you tried to do to me?"

"No."

He was helpless. Mantana took a step towards him and crushed a rose beneath her foot. "My name is Joy. I was an employee of yours. You accused me of stealing, and then you tried to rape me."

"I did?"

Khun Nemit fumbled in his coat pocket. He pulled out a wrinkled handkerchief and mopped his forehead.

"I - I don't remember," he said. "I see your face in my dreams and it hurts. It hurts my head."

Mantana stood looking at him for almost a full minute. It was suddenly difficult to feel anything at all for him: hate, anger, pity. He was just a small man with a wrinkled handkerchief, standing there in pain.

"Say you're sorry."

"Wh-what?"

"Apologize to me. Say that you're sorry."

Khun Nemit straightened himself and pushed a piece of well-oiled hair back in its place.

"I'm sorry."

"Now say you're sorry for last night."

"What did I do last night?"

"You tried to attack me on stage. Then you stood on a chair and pulled your pants down."

Another attack. Another round of pain. "I'm sorry for that, too."

"Now go away. Don't ever bother me again. If you do, I'll go to the police and tell them what you did."

Mantana turned away and started to walk. She knew, somewhere deep down, that she wouldn't get far.

"Joy, please wait! I can't sleep at night. I have such terrible headaches. Sometimes I black out and - and I can't remember what I've done. Before last night, I thought I'd kill myself. But then - then I saw you and -"

Khun Nemit winced again and covered his face with his hands.

Mantana felt a surge of electricity shoot through her veins. Her heart thumped against her chest, and the idea that popped into her head was enough to make her nauseous. It was time to speak or forever hold her peace. She spoke.

"Two thousand five hundred," she said.

"What?"

The sounds came from a dark and waterless place inside her.

She wished she hadn't said it, only she did, and said it again.

"One night, two thousand five hundred. Then you must promise never to think about me again."

Khun Nemit looked at her in astonishment. He didn't seem to be in so much pain now.

"Yes," he whispered. "Yes."

Mantana closed her eyes, and held out her hand for him to take.

Together, they walked out of the market.

*

Later on, she wondered why she was not so shocked at the bargain she made in the dirty corner of the market, the name of which she didn't even know. But if one can say she "looked within herself" for an answer, then she was met only by a blank stare, like that of a corpse. Yet there was no one, living or dead, to watch Khun Nemit escort her to the nearest hotel. There was no one to witness him kneel and kiss her feet once she removed her shoes. There was no one to demand an explanation of her because there was no one there. And two thousand five hundred was a lot of money for a "poor farmer's daughter from the North."

The pain was unlike anything she had felt before, and she was thankful for it. With the pain, she did not have to see or feel or touch the man on top of her. There was only lightning bolts and fire down below. Smashing stars and static behind her eyes. And when it was over, Khun Nemit fell into a sleep so deep, Mantana thought he had died for a second time on her.

The bathroom shower was cold. She stood beneath the water and remembered the promise she had made to herself while walking up the hotel steps. She refused to cry about what she had done, and only little girls cried over pain. She wouldn't break her word. The tears that came now were for nothing and something else altogether.

And there were a lot of them.

It was two hours before she came out of the bathroom. The bed was empty. Khun Nemit was gone. The sleep had been fake, but the deathly look of peace in his face couldn't have been. Mantana walked over to the bed and looked at the space where he had laid. On his pillow was a crumpled envelope. There were five one thousand baht bills inside. Khun Nemit had kept his word, too.

Mantana sat down and counted the money half a dozen times. Then the tears returned, and she had never felt more alone in all her life than she did in that wretched hotel room at two a.m.

*

At sunrise the next morning, Mantana walked the streets and passed by orange-robed monks with their alms bowls in hand. She bought a basket of offerings and gave out bars of soap, instant soup, laundry detergent, and drink boxes to eight different monks. When the basket was empty, she walked to the hotel where Ning and Peung lived and sat staring at her coffee in the downstairs restaurant until she was certain they were awake.

They were. Ning was drying herself from a morning shower while Peung sat lost in a Japanese program dubbed in Thai on a black and white television set.

"Can we go somewhere and talk?" asked Mantana.

"Sure," said Ning, who watched her with a certain uneasiness. "Just let me get dressed."

Mantana sat down on the bed and waited. Peung spoke without taking her eyes from the screen.

"Phii Aor is furious."

"I don't care," said Mantana.

"You should care. You'll probably have to beg if you want your job back."

Mantana didn't answer. During a commercial break, Peung

glanced in her direction. Her eyes grew wide as if she caught a glimpse of Mantana's crime against herself, then narrowed again in an "I thought as much" manner. Did she know? How could she know? Mantana felt sick inside.

"You know who that old man was in the office yesterday, don't you?" said Peung.

"No."

A wicked smile crossed her face. "That was Phii Wen. He's our costume designer. What did he do to frighten you? Ask you to take your shirt off? He just wanted your measurements, silly girl."

Ning came out of the bathroom dressed in imitation designer jeans and a T-shirt.

"I'm ready, Joy," she said.

"The man in the office was a costume designer?"

"You mean Phii Wen? Yes. After Aor told us what happened, Peung and I nearly fell over laughing."

"Aor didn't find it so funny," said Peung.

"I was really worried about you, Joy," said Ning. "You never showed up here last night."

Mantana stared vacantly at the TV set. A group of Japanese teenagers dressed in robot suits were doing battle with an orange dragon with seven heads.

"Joy, are you all right?"

"It hurt so much," whispered Mantana.

Ning folded her arms across her breast and leaned against the wall. "Oh, Joy," she said.

13

If the day before had been hot, the one after it was hell. The afternoon sun blazed in an otherwise empty sky, apparently trying to outdo all the other afternoon suns in the history of hot days. It was the unbearable ferocity of the heat that made Khun Chainoi decide to shut down his carnival in the daytime rather than pay his employees to stand around and fight to stay awake. He was figuring out a new rotation schedule in the shade of the shooting gallery when Mantana approached him.

"Khun Chainoi, sir."

"Nong Joy. I have good news and I have bad news. Which do you want first?"

"I don't know. It's been so long since I've heard good news, I probably wouldn't recognize it."

"The good news is that you don't have to sit in that hot shack all day. The bad news is that you no longer have a job."

Khun Chainoi laughed. Mantana wondered how long he had been waiting to use that joke on her. He stopped when he noticed that she wasn't joining in his mirth.

"I'm sorry, Nong Joy."

"Khun Chainoi, sir, I'm ready to meet your friend."

"What friend?"

"The man from Taiwan. The one who makes karaoke videos."

"Oh!" said Khun Chainoi with a peculiar look on his face. "That friend."

"I have the placement fee, but I'd like to see some of his work first, if that's possible."

"Sure, sure."

"You said he's in town?"

"Ah - yes. He's in town. He's in town right now. I just have to give him a call and - say, are you here alone?"

"Sir?"

"I mean, I'd like to introduce my friend to as many girls as possible. With you at the top of the list, of course."

"There's just me."

"That's fine too! I have to make some phone calls, so why don't you come back at, say, eight o'clock tonight. Can you do that?"

"Yes, sir."

"And you've got the money?"

"Yes, sir."

"Good. Good, good, good. You're going to be a very rich girl, Joy. Just you wait and see!"

*

Jakkrit lived on the carnival grounds in the last of four metal shacks. The shacks stood in a row, out of sight, along a foul-smelling ditch that marked the boundaries of the parking lot.

They tilted at an odd level and sheets of steel had already fallen from parts of the walls. Mantana stood looking at them and wondered how anyone could survive inside without going mad. She approached the door of Jakkrit's shack and knocked. Then she listened. There was no one home. She was about to leave when she noticed a trail of black smoke rising from the far side of the row. She moved slowly along the front of the shacks. A rotten stench hung in the air as if it were nailed there. Mantana covered her nose and mouth and peered around the corner. Jakkrit was there, sitting in a red wheelbarrow and holding onto the sides for support. Two other men she didn't recognize squatted over a bonfire, too involved with whatever they were doing to notice her watching. One of the men had his hand wrapped in a dirty rag and held a long rod attached to a small, wire cage. This he dangled over the flames. Through clouds of smoke, Mantana could see something, black and burning, yet still alive inside the cage. It ran in circles around the bottom and leaped against the sides in a horrifying death frenzy.

The thing was a rat.

Mantana ducked out of sight and rushed from the line of shacks before her stomach refused to hold up against the sight and the smell any longer.

Perhaps a farewell note would be better for the legless man.

*

There was no way on earth Mantana could hide what she had done from Phii Aor. One breath, one look, would have given her away. And she so, so wanted to hide what she had done from Phii Aor.

Fortunately, it wasn't difficult. Phii Aor never worked during the day and Khun Rangsan rarely left his office. Even if he did, there would be nothing extraordinary about seeing Mantana return to her room after lunchtime. She quietly packed her things and wrote upon an envelope that she was leaving to make karaoke videos in Taiwan. Then she enclosed the five hundred baht that Phii Aor had lent her and left it on the dressing room table.

She was almost clear.

Just as she was exiting the dressing room, she ran smack into a body that was hanging about outside. The surprise took another in a series of years off her life, but she regained it again when she saw who it was - none other than Bew Beautiful.

"Bad girl!" he shrieked in English. "Where you going last night? I singing all alone."

"Shh! Quiet, Bew! I'm sorry about last night. I shouldn't have done that to you. I made a mistake."

Bew took a step back and raised his hands to his shoulders. There wasn't any meaning behind this pose, he just thought it looked feminine.

"Phii Aor looking for you. She worry you have trouble."

"You mean she's not angry with me?"

"Bew don't know!" he said, raising his voice again.

"Well tell her - tell her I'm sorry."

He arced an eyebrow and looked down at her bag.

"You go now?" he asked.

"Yes, Bew."

"You have new job? Good job?"

"I hope so."

"And you no say good-bye?"

Mantana smiled and held her hand out for him to shake or kiss or do whatever he wanted with. He clasped her pinkie with his thumb and index finger and gave it a small tug.

"Good bye, Bew," she said.

"Bew have a feeling we meet again in a future."

"I hope you're right."

Bew placed his hands together and bowed. "*Sa wat dee ka,*" he said.

"*Sa wat dee ka*," said Mantana.

*

No one at the post office looked at her differently when she handed over two thousand baht to be sent to her father. No one at the hotel in which she earned the money seemed to care that she was staying for the afternoon. The world might have changed, but Mantana was the only one who noticed it.

She sat on the bed, the scene of the crime, staring at the gray and yellow walls, ceiling, and floor. Watermarks had formed monstrous faces that stared back at her. Various thoughts passed through her head. Some that were dark became light while others remained in the shadowy recesses of her mind, growing teeth and claws. At five o'clock, she hid the remainder of her money under the worn mattress and went to meet Ning for dinner.

"It's done," said Mantana. "Now I just have to get the job."

"What if you don't?"

"If I don't, I don't."

"Well, what will you do?"

Mantana looked at her from across the table. Tiny pimples had broken out across the dancing girl's forehead and an extra layer of make-up had been applied in an attempt to conceal them.

"I don't know."

"I think you should -"

"Stop," said Mantana. "Don't speak. I'd rather you didn't give me any more advice."

Ning sat back in her chair. Her lips formed an O the size of a ten baht coin.

"What did I do?"

"Nothing."

"I must have done something. Tell me."

Mantana lit a cigarette and blew the smoke to the side.

"Ning, I just spent the afternoon sitting in a hotel room thinking about these past few weeks. Thinking about Phii Aor. She was a real friend to me. She set me straight at every wrong turn I was about to make. Only I couldn't see it. Why couldn't I see it? Because you, Ning, you whom I trusted, told me over and over that she was only out to ruin me. Now, I know that you were in love once and I know it didn't turn out the way you wanted it to, but Phii Aor isn't the reason behind your broken heart. And if I hadn't been so filled with your bitterness towards her when she called me into her office yesterday, maybe none of this would have happened."

The ten-baht width of Ning's shock grew more and more expensive. Her right hand moved once again to cover the attempted bloodletting of her left wrist, as it did each time this bleak corner of her past was called to mind.

"I can't believe I'm hearing this from you!" she said. "If you had listened to me in the first place and gone home to your village like I told you to, then and only then would last night never have happened. You said yourself that Phii Aor told your carnival boss that you were a prostitute."

"She never sold me off to fuck anyone."

"Listen to you! You're even beginning to talk like a prostitute!"

Mantana brought a hand down hard upon the table, rattling the silverware and causing the water in their glasses to sway to and fro.

"I'll tell you what I am, Ning. I'm poor. Do you understand? And when a person is poor, the only thing that's good is money. The only thing bad is a lack of it."

"Is that the conclusion you came to in your hotel room today?"

"Maybe someday I'll change my mind."

"So it's OK to sleep with someone who tried to rape you just so you can take his money."

"No," said Mantana. "Yes. I don't know."

"But you just said -"

"I'm not going to eat rats!" she snapped.

Ning furrowed her brow. The make-up on her forehead broke into horizontal cracks.

"What did you say?" she asked.

Mantana shook her head and took a drag on her cigarette. She let the smoke out slowly and watched it hang in the air between them. For an odd, brief moment, she thought she saw a reflection in the smoke cloud, a face that looked at her and disappeared.

"I said nobody suffers like the poor."

Ning took a cigarette from the pack and lit it.

Neither of them was feeling very hungry anymore.

14

The carnival was like a different world at night. Everything and everyone were lit up in a rainbow of light. Even the concrete of the parking lot appeared fluorescent and store-bought. Mantana wore a short black skirt and a sleeveless white blouse. The stares and whistles she drew from groups of boys didn't bother her as it normally would. Tonight their rude behavior only reassured her they might someday buy her video and help make her a superstar.

It was a pleasant surprise to find that she didn't have to wait for Khun Chainoi or hunt him down in the crowd. He was right where he said he'd be, free from any carnival business and waiting for her.

"You're right on time," he said. "Did you come alone?"

"Yes."

Khun Chainoi looked around as if he didn't believe her. "Aor didn't follow you?"

"Phii Aor? Why would she -"

"Forget it. Do you have the money?"

Mantana handed him an envelope with the requested amount inside. Except for three hundred baht in fifties and twenties, tucked inside her purse, it was the last of her money. Khun Chainoi counted the bills, then pocketed them, obviously satisfied.

"Are you ready?" he asked.

"Ready for what?"

"I'm going to take you to meet my friend. He has an office in Pornping Tower."

Mantana had never heard of Pornping Tower. "All right," she said, warily.

She followed him to his car and got in the passenger's side. Khun Chainoi started the engine and a seat belt slid back to lock her in place. The carnival boss seemed a little bit nervous, a little bit excited, to her. He backed out of his parking spot, and sped from the lot.

"Khun Chainoi, sir, I wanted to ask you something. A favor, actually."

"What's that?"

"If it's not too much trouble, could you look in on Jakkrit from time to time? I'm worried he doesn't have enough to eat."

"Who's Jakkrit?"

"The legless man."

"Oh! The cripple! He left today."

"What?"

"Yes, he found another job. Better pay. It was a surprise to me, too."

"But that's impossible. I just saw him today."

"What time did you see him?"

"Around three."

"He left at four," said Khun Chainoi, nodding. "Yes, he found a job as a window cleaner."

"A legless window cleaner?"

"You've never seen one? They're everywhere. What happens is, a crew of men strap him to a plank and hoist him up the side of a tall building. Whenever he reaches a dirty window, the men stop the plank and allow him to clean it. It's perfectly safe. The men are very strong. And the man washing windows certainly doesn't need legs. In fact, legs are the main cause of accidents in the window cleaning business. I don't know if you knew that."

"I didn't know that."

"It's a fact," Khun Chainoi nodded.

Mantana decided not to ask any more questions for the rest of the ride.

*

Pornping Tower was a tall, gloomy building with a FOR SALE banner flapping across the fourth, fifth, sixth, and part of the seventh floors. Despite the city in plain view, the building sat on a desolate stretch of land, surrounded by wire fences and piles of rotting garbage. Giant cranes stood pointing upwards at the sky as though they were frozen in the middle of a howl. Mantana imagined that's what the dinosaurs must have looked like on their last night on earth.

"There's no one here," said Mantana.

Khun Chainoi drove to the side of the building that did not directly face the road. She saw a pair of vehicles parked in a dirt lot, along with the dark silhouettes of men lingering outside.

"Nong Joy, I have something to tell you," said Khun Chainoi. "My friend doesn't make karaoke videos. He doesn't even enjoy singing."

"What do you mean?"

The vehicles entered the beam of the car headlights. One was a van. The windows in back had been replaced with metal plates. The feeling of fear that she hadn't been able to name suddenly seized her like a hungry tiger. A tiger that had woken from its sleep.

"Don't be afraid," said Khun Chainoi. "Please, just do whatever these men ask you to do and nothing bad will happen."

Khun Chainoi pulled his car next to the van and turned the engine off. Mantana's door opened, and a pair of hands pulled her from the car. Her purse fell from her lap and landed in the dirt. The hands held her from behind and turned her to face two men with rotten fruit faces, both puffing on cigarettes. One of the men wore a mustache and sunglasses. The other had thick lips and a mess of hair that fell into his eyes. She couldn't see the face of the one holding her but could tell by the size of his hands that the rest of him must be equally large. Khun Chainoi got out of the car and went to stand with them.

"Pretty girl," said the man with the thick lips. "Did she bring any friends?"

"No," said Khun Chainoi. "She doesn't have any friends. She works day and night."

"That's a pity."

"Yes."

"Pretty girl like this. Ought to be a law."

Everyone nodded in agreement.

"Has she got any diseases?" asked the one with the mustache, who had a voice like the evil scientist in a Japanese monster movie.

Mantana spoke up. "I have AIDS!"

The men laughed. Khun Chainoi smiled and shook his head.

"Put her in the van," said the lips.

Mantana squirmed in the grip of the one holding her.

"What's her name?"

"Joy."

"Joy. Nice boots. Look at what I have here, Joy."

The piece of rotten fruit with the falling hair and heavy mouth reached in his jacket and stepped towards her. When his hand appeared again, it was holding a device that resembled an electric razor with a missing blade. He turned it over in his hands until he was sure she had gotten a good look at it. Then he pressed a button and a blue spark of electricity shot from two silver prongs at its metallic end.

"We can do this the hard way," he said. "Or you can get in the van."

The man brought the gun so close that her eyes crossed looking at it. She felt the heat from the silver prongs and stopped struggling. The man kneeled and picked up her purse.

"You dropped this," he said, and tossed it to the man with the mustache. His sunglasses prevented him from seeing, and he could only hold out his hands as the purse smacked against his belly. The man holding her got a laugh out of that.

"Let's finish this," said Khun Chainoi.

She was led to the rear end of the vehicle and told not to think about running. The one holding her let go long enough to unlock the back doors. They creaked as they opened. It was dark inside, though the thin light of the moon made it clear that there were others, at least half a dozen, sitting on the floor of the van. They were women, young women, some crying, others staring hopelessly from the shadows.

"Wait a minute," said the man with the electric stun gun. "Find out if any of them have to pee."

"Do any of you have to pee?" said the lackey, placing his large hands back upon her shoulders.

"Yes!"

"How many?"

"We all have to pee!"

"All right," he said, "One at a time. You first."

A girl no older than Mantana, dressed in shorts and a T-shirt with a pair of dancing bananas sewn onto it emerged from the van. She looked at Mantana, then at the man holding the stun gun.

"Where?" she asked.

"Here."

"I can't pee here."

"Then get back in the van."

The girl climbed back in.

"Who's next?"

None of the girls had to pee anymore. The man looked at Mantana and flicked his hair from his eyes.

"What about you?"

"I don't have to pee."

"Are you sure?" he laughed. "It's going to be a long ride."

Mantana got into the back of the van. It smelled of perfume and fear. The floor was crowded, but some of the girls slid down to make room for her.

"Watch your feet," said the ugly voice of the giant, and his large hands closed the van doors. Mantana could hear the jingle of keys in the lock, then nothing.

Five minutes later, the engine started, and they were moving.

Part Two

1

When Mantana was eight years old, there was Khun Amnuay and her daughter, Kwan. Khun Amnuay's husband had been killed in an automobile accident some years back, leaving the two of them to fend for themselves. What did she do? She did what any resourceful widow would do. She collected what she could and opened a magazine stand so she and her daughter wouldn't have to worry about where their next meal was coming from. All through the day, Khun Amnuay would sit with her magazines in the hot sun, staring out from her booth like a criminal locked in as punishment. On weekends, it was her daughter in the booth, and the number of boys stopping by for a car magazine suddenly doubled. Kwan was very pretty. And she was at that age...

The magazines were delivered each week by a man in a gray truck. Mantana and Darunee and some of the other neighborhood kids gathered to watch them arrive. Sometimes, if a magazine were torn or wet, the delivery man would tear off the cover and give it to the children. Sometimes that happened, or maybe it was just a story one of the Jerriporn boys had made up to keep them all in suspense. Mantana had never seen any free magazines.

One day, the delivery man brought another man in his truck. This one wore a suit. He spoke with Khun Amnuay for a long time. When the driver finished unloading the magazines, Mantana and Darunee were the only ones left watching. They were about to go play elsewhere when Khun Amnuay called to them.

"Girls," she said. "I want you to go find Kwan and bring her here right away."

The man in the suit smiled at them. Mantana didn't like his smile. Nevertheless, she and Darunee went to find Kwan. The Amnuays lived close to Darunee, so they didn't have to go far. They found her at home, reading a comic book on the front porch. She was wearing a white T-shirt and shorts. And she was at that age...

"Your mother asked us to come get you," said Mantana.

"Why?"

"We don't know."

Kwan walked with the girls to the magazine stand. Khun Amnuay smiled when she saw her daughter, then petted her hair and told her how beautiful she looked. Weird! But Mantana and Darunee played along and agreed, yes indeed, that Kwan looked particularly radiant that day.

"You girls run along now," said Khun Amnuay. "Go on!"

Hmf!

The next day, Darunee had stories to tell. The night before had not been a peaceful one. From her bedroom window, Darunee had heard Khun Amnuay yelling at her daughter, calling her all sorts of names. Of course, there was crying late into the night, but the real awfulness came at what must have been three or four o'clock in the morning. A bright light flashing across the walls of her room had woken Darunee and when she looked out the window, she could see the magazine truck, parked in front of Khun Amnuay's house. The engine was still running, and two men were standing alongside it. One of the men was wearing a suit. Uh-huh, you guessed it - the same man who came to talk to Khun Amnuay that very afternoon. What happened next was the stuff of little girl nightmares, but Darunee swore that it was true. Khun Amnuay waved to the men and it took all three of them to carry Kwan to the truck and make her get inside. Did she scream? Did she ever! But no one came to her rescue. The men gave something to Khun Amnuay, an envelope, then got into the truck and sped off into the night. Khun Amnuay stood outside for a while longer, perhaps thinking the men would come back. But they didn't, so she took her envelope and went back into her house.

Darunee was dreaming. She never saw such things. And if she went around telling people she did, then Khun Amnuay just might tell the magazine men to come and take her away in the middle. of the night! That's what Khun Amnuay said to Darunee and Mantana when they went to call on Kwan at the magazine stand that afternoon. Well, if she weren't here, then where was she? She was at home, of course. But she wasn't there either. Then she's gone to town to look for a job.

This was the tale that Khun Amnuay told, and this was what people believed - at least until she was far out of sight. Then and only then did the half truths and rumors rise to contradict the magazine woman's record of events. Mantana wondered if the widow was aware that people were talking about her. If that were the case, she didn't seem to care.

It was a long time before people stopped talking. And when they did, things started happening to make them whisper all over again.

The first thing that happened was this. Khun Amnuay bought a refrigerator. A couple of weeks later, she bought a television. There wasn't a face in the village that didn't scowl and sniff the air as if one's nose smelled something funny at the mention of her name. When she had a swimming pool dug and filled, people stopped buying magazines from her altogether. Mantana and Darunee looked at that pool, sitting so out of place in a field of dirt, and watched the water turn black and sink beneath the weight of insects and trash over the next few weeks.

Eventually, Khun Amnuay was forced to close her magazine stand and all but disappear inside her house. The only times she was spotted were the times she was out buying food at the market or receiving new home appliances and furniture from a delivery truck.

Mantana never saw Kwan again. As far as she knew, no one else from the village did either.

*

The men had not lied. Wherever they were going was far from where they started. Mantana sat in back with the rest of the girls, feeling sore from having to sit cross-legged for the past two hours. None of the girls spoke. When the van hit a bump, they all said "Oi!" and when the van stopped, probably for a red light or traffic jam, everyone held their breath in fear. Everyone but Mantana.

At first, she was stunned. Then scared. Now, with her dream of becoming a karaoke star trampled in the dust, Mantana's head felt heavy with rage. But she knew that her anger would just get her into more trouble, if not zapped with a bolt of electricity. She had to act smart. She had to think. And she had to remain tough, like Phii Aor in the face of rowdy customers. Like her mother in the face of death.

She started by speaking.

"My name is Joy," she said, and her words cut like a scalpel through the dark. "I was tricked into believing I was going to star in karaoke videos. I gave a man named Chainoi a two-thousand-five-hundred-baht placement fee. He handed me over to these men."

She waited.

"My name is Tan," said a voice, no louder than a bird's. "My friend and I were told there were jobs for berry pickers in France. We each paid one thousand baht to apply."

"I'm Nat," said another. "I paid three thousand to apply to an international modeling agency. The man with the gun told me he knew Kate Moss."

"My name is Nong."

"I'm Goong."

"I'm Neung and this is Yim."

"Dao."

The voices came from all directions, soft at first, but growing louder as their fear abated.

"I paid two thousand baht."

"We each paid one thousand five."

"They took my purse."

"Wait," said Mantana. "One at a time."

"My boss at the shoe factory -"

"A pair of men who said they worked for the government -"

"A policeman -"

"My mother -"

It was no use. Mantana sat and waited for the bottled-up horror stories to be released. Nong was going to be a maid for a rich family in Switzerland. Goong was selected to work as a perfume tester in Tokyo. Neung and Yim were to be room service girls in a Moscow hotel. And poor Dao was told by her mother that the men in the van were her uncles who wanted to take her out for ice cream.

"What are you?" said a voice. "An idiot?"

"Are you any smarter?" asked another. "Miss Perfume Tester!"

"At least I didn't offer my sister in my place!"

"You're lucky I can't scc you!"

Mantana clapped her hands until there was silence again.

"Does anyone know where they're taking us? We can't be in Bangkok anymore. We're going too fast and haven't turned in hours."

"We're going to Pattaya," someone said. "Didn't you read about the eleven girls from Khorat the police found locked up in the back of a Pattaya restaurant? The men who kidnapped them charged them rent and said that they'd be shot in the face if they didn't pay each week. The girls had to fuck Japanese men to make money and two of them became infected with the AIDS virus."

Someone else: "I heard of a group of girls who had signed on to be factory workers and were locked up in cells instead. The men who took them put heroin in their rice and kept giving it to them until they became addicted. After that, the only way they could get more of the drug was by fucking Japanese men."

And yet another: "That's nothing. I heard of a secret Japanese cult whose members only have sex with the bodies of freshly killed -"

"Enough!" cried Mantana. "This isn't helping! We have to figure a way out of here before we get to wherever it is they're taking us. Now there were two vehicles in the parking lot. Two vehicles and three men. That means there's only two of them up front."

"With the other one close behind."

"Maybe," said Mantana. "Maybe not. Is there anything back here we can use as a weapon?"

"There's a toilet plunger."

"Good. We can use that. We have to create a diversion.

If they pull over and let two of us out, then those two can jump on them and give the rest of us time to climb out and help."

"That's your plan?"

"Yes."

"It won't work. When they open the doors, they let only one of us out at a time."

"Who said that?" asked Mantana.

"Neung."

"All right, Neung, this is Joy. If that's the way they do it, then we have to give them a reason to let two of us out."

"This is Goong. Suppose two of us pretend that we're sick?"

"They'll just shut the door," said Neung.

"Has anyone got something sharp? Something that will cut?"

"I've got a hair clip," said a voice. "I can run it against the van floor to sharpen it."

"All right," said Mantana. "I've got an idea."

2

Up front, where the girls couldn't see, the man with the stun·
gun drove, while the man with the mustache slept. A light rain was
falling outside. It had been a good haul this time, and at five
thousand baht a head, minus the one thousand baht finder's fee, the
man with the gun and his partner with the mustache would do all
right. Some of the girls were even good-looking this time.
Especially that last one they picked up. The one from the carnival.
Now she was something to look at. The man behind the wheel was
sure he could get ten thousand for her. And maybe his partner
didn't have to know.

Then came the pounding. Normally, the man at the wheel
would ignore any noises that came from the back. Let them pound!
Only there was a muffled scream that accompanied the beat. The
man with the mustache opened his eyes.

"What are you doing?" he asked.

"I'm pulling over. The rabbits are jumping. One of them probably has to shit."

"Make it fast," he said. "We don't want to attract any attention out here."

He parked the van along the edge of the highway and switched his flashers on. The pounding stopped. The man with the mustache opened the door and got out of the van. The other took his gun from the dashboard, a flashlight from the glove compartment.

"What is it?" yelled the man with the mustache through the van doors. He was answered with a cacophony of shrieks and squeals. The man with the gun joined him.

"I'm going to open the doors," he shouted. "No one leaves the van until I say."

He tucked the flashlight in his armpit and unlocked the doors. His hand and face glowed red every other second in the emergency lights of the van. He then stood back, gun in hand, and nodded to his partner. The man with the mustache opened the heavy doors.

"What's going on back here?"

He shone the light into the back and saw the frightened girls shield their eyes from the sudden brightness.

"This one!" said the girl named Yim. "And this one! They were talking about killing themselves, and then they did! They killed themselves! One of them had a vial of poison and - and -"

"They each drank half!" said Nong. "Then they went into convulsions and started to spit up blood."

The light shined down upon two bodies lying side by side on the van floor. Their eyes were shut. There was blood around their mouths.

"Damn," said the man with the gun. "It's the pretty one."

The man with the mustache stepped forward. "This one's not dead. She's still breathing."

"Forget it. We don't have time to worry about them. Close the doors."

The man ignored the protests of his captives and swung the heavy doors shut. In the back of the van, everything was quiet again. The girls were jerked back, and the van was in motion.

"It didn't work," said Neung, who lay on the van floor, playing dead with Mantana.

"Give them time to think it over. I bet they'll get off the highway and dump our bodies."

"How do you know what they'll do?"

Mantana didn't answer. Everyone waited. Some of them held hands. Mantana didn't hold anyone's hand. They seemed to be driving straight on through the night, until suddenly the van slowed down and turned. There was an exhalation of fear and relief among the girls. Mantana pressed the cut she had made in her hand and wiped more blood upon her face. She told Neung to do the same.

"I've stopped bleeding," she said.

"Then cut yourself again. It has to look real."

The sharpened hair clip was passed to her.

"I can't do it," she said, but that was only talk. She didn't have to be reminded what was at stake. She uttered a cry of pain and did it.

"We're slowing down again. Let's get into our positions. And remember, keep your eyes shut tight. If we wince when they shine that light in our faces, it's all over."

The van pulled over and stopped again. This time, the engine was turned off. No one made a sound. The front doors opened and closed. Mantana's heart was beating so loud she thought the sound was sure to give her away. There was the familiar, terrifying rattle of the metal handles, and a small lifetime of silence before the doors finally opened. Mantana could hear crickets chirping close by and had a fleeting vision of herself lying face down in some ditch, dead for real.

"No one moves," said the man with the gun.

Mantana kept her eyes closed and waited. Neung was

unloaded first. She heard the girl's body being slid out beside her. Then a pair of hands took her under the arms and pulled.

"This one's still warm."

"Doesn't matter. They're damaged goods. Better to drop them here than in the city."

Mantana was laid down on the wet gravel at the side of a road. She opened her eyes a crack and saw Neung watching her in the flashing red lights. The blood on her face formed a maniacal ring around her mouth, like some absurd clown's grin.

"Is there any of that poison left?" said the man with the gun.

"No," said Yim.

"Where's the vial?"

No one answered.

"I said, where's the vial?"

"She swallowed it. The pretty one swallowed it."

"Hm," said the man with the mustache. "You've got to admire her determination."

Now! screamed a voice in Mantana's head. *Quickly! Before they close the doors!*

All reflex and fear, Mantana scrambled to her feet and jumped on the back of the nearest standing man. He spun around and yelled and came this close to knocking her into the open van door. She had gotten the right one. The man shot a spark of electricity in the air, temporarily lighting up the chaos. Now, thought Mantana, he would be aiming for her.

Neung, meanwhile, had chosen to kick from where she lay, which proved to have less of an effect than she counted on. The mustache man went down on the leg she had struck, then, with the speed of a tiger but none of its grace, leapt at her.

"You bitch!"

A blue spark burned the air next to Mantana's face. The gun made a terrible noise, like a snake fighting for its breath. The man she clung to was trying to find her with the metal prongs of his gun.

Mantana clenched her fist and punched him as hard as she could. The metal prongs swung in the air, creating a beautiful blue lasso for only a second. They swung outward and they swung back again. Mantana felt them, hot against her bare shoulder, and screamed.

BZZZRT!

The electricity sparked close to, but not through, her body. Mantana looked up and saw one - two - three girls from the van, kicking and punching. She saw the silver prongs come round again. She saw a girl's orange-shoed foot fly to the space between the man's legs. There were sparks, bzzrt, only this time, they came from the gunman's eyes.

The man fell. Mantana fell with him.

The mustache man had the sharpened hair clip stuck in his backside and was bleeding from the head when they rolled him off Neung. He was still breathing, still fighting, but the onslaught of Nat's fists and Tan's heels and the hard end of a toilet plunger wielded by skinny little Goong had knocked him senseless. Neung got to her feet and kicked him twice in the ribs.

"Where's Joy?" she said.

The gun and the flashlight and a few other items lay scattered about as Mantana struggled with the man she attacked, who had quickly become her attacker. He was on top, then rolled for some reason, and let her be on top. Yim and Nong and Dao tried to get a kick in, but they didn't want to miss and accidentally hit Mantana. So they stood back and screamed for her to kill him. The man rolled again, and it became obvious to her what he was doing.

"Get the gun!" cried Mantana.

It must have been close because the man on top of her was trying to reach it. Mantana raked her nails across his face and stretched her arm out for it as well. It was close all right, so close she could feel it with her fingertips. The man rolled. This time, he took hold of her shoulders and threw her off him. She skidded across the gravel and fell off the edge of the road, into some weeds.

Something hard dug into her back, causing her to see stars. The girls on the road let out a collective scream. It could only mean one thing. The man had his gun.

"Was that fun?" he shouted.

Dao sank to her knees and started to weep. The man pointed his weapon at each of them in turn. He was wild-eyed, out of breath, and when he saw his partner, lying in the road, he looked mad enough to zap everything in sight.

"Don't even think of running," he ordered. "If just one of you decides to run, I'll kill all of you. Now slowly, slowly, get back into the van."

Mantana lay staring at the stars. They were quite lovely that evening. She sat up, felt a scratch on her forehead, and saw the girls lining up to get back into the van. The man with the gun had his back to her. There was a chance she could slip away. Her hand found the object in the weeds that had stuck her in the back. She picked it up and looked at it.

Oh yes, the stars certainly were lovely that night.

Mantana got to her feet and stepped out of the weeds.

"Excuse me," she said.

The man swung around and pointed his gun arm at her. There were a few cries of dismay as the girls turned to look.

"You!" said the man.

The device in his hand suddenly rang. He extended the silver antenna and brought it close to his ear.

"Hello?" he said.

His eyes widened into two full moons a moment before the spark of electricity shot from the gun in Mantana's hand. His body flew back as if an invisible hand had reached down to lift him, shake him and discard him once his bones had turned to shrimp paste. He hit the ground with a dull thud, his arms and legs twisted in unlikely positions, his hair and clothes smoking like grilled chicken. A cell phone sat beeping in his hand.

"You dropped this," said Mantana.

"Joy!" said Neung, staring in disbelief. "You got him!"

"Is he dead?" she asked quietly.

Yim walked over and tapped his arm with the toe of her orange shoe. Then she hauled off and kicked him. The man groaned.

"He's not dead."

Neung walked to where Mantana was standing and took her hand.

"You were so brave!" she said. "Are you hurt?"

"I'll live."

Nong and Goong joined Yim at the side of the smoking driver. They each laid into him with kicks of their own.

"Neung," said Mantana, "Tell the girls not to kill them."

"Why?"

"Because maybe they've got children."

Neung squeezed her hand and went back to the crowd of angry women. She told them to take their money and leave them alone. She said it was an order from Joy. Her words seemed to carry weight. Mantana walked to the van and leaned against the side. She closed her eyes and wished for a bed, any bed. She was so tired.

"Joy!" said Neung. "Look at the money we found!"

Mantana nodded. Goong, Nong, Nat, and Tan had joined hands and danced in a circle around the men's bodies. Yim was trying to comfort Dao, who still lay weeping at the side of the road. Neung called out her name again, but it was the sound of a dream. She sighed blue and rubbed her tired eyes. To sit! She walked to the driver's side of the van and got in. An amulet with the photo of a widely revered monk hung from the rear view mirror. A small statue of a reclining Buddha sat upon the dash. And something else - a small stack of identity cards bound by a rubber band. Mantana found hers and tucked the rest in the pocket of her blouse. The girl's purses were jammed beneath the passenger's seat.

Her money was still there. Her hand jingled a set of keys in the ignition, then took hold of them and turned. The engine started.

"Let's go!" she hollered from the open window.

Neung and Yim were the first to get in front with her. The others were less enthusiastic about climbing in back.

"Can either of you drive?" she asked.

"I can drive," said Yim.

"All right. You drive. I'll ride in back with the rest. We'll turn the flashlight on to keep from being scared."

"You're not scared," said Neung. "Are you, Joy?"

"Just follow this road back to the main highway and take us to the first hotel you see."

"I'll ride with you, Joy," said Neung. "We can sing!"

Mantana got out of the van and went around to the back.

"Listen," she told the group of girls. "Don't be afraid. Just think of a place, a safe place where you've always been happy to go and keep it in your mind."

"You mean a shopping mall?" asked Goong.

Nong and Dao would ride up front. The rest of the girls got in back.

"Tell Yim not to stop for anyone," said Mantana.

"OK."

Mantana was about to get in when she noticed the man she had zapped begin to stir. She thought of the Buddha and the amulet and walked over to where he lay.

"Do you want to apologize?" she asked.

The man opened an eye and looked at her.

"I think you should say that you're sorry," she said. "You may not get another chance."

"Ooh," said the man, and didn't, quite possibly couldn't, say anything else.

"If you're sorry for what you did, blink twice."

The man closed his eyes and didn't open them again. Mantana

watched for a moment, just to be sure, then turned and got into the van.

"All right," she said in the sudden darkness after the doors were closed. "No one is afraid."

There was a grinding of tires in the dirt, and they were off.

3

Fifteen minutes later, the van pulled over and stopped. Mantana had her gun ready. She held her breath and shone the flashlight upon the door handles. Everyone jumped as they swung open. It was Yim. There was no danger. She only wanted to show them where they were: an all-night rest stop. There was food. There were toilets. The girls got out of the van and walked like zombies across the parking lot. They were dirty and sweaty and some of their clothes were stained with blood. In front of the restaurant was a rack of tourist-oriented T-shirts that said things like "Amazing Thailand" and "Scenic Pattaya." Mantana bought one with a drawing of two sailboats. Neung picked out a cartoon frog with the words "Sa wat dee" written over its head. They went into the women's room to wash and change. With her face clean, Mantana saw that Neung was the same age, if not a little younger than she. She had long, frizzy hair that she had never bothered to straighten. Her face was small, her eyes narrow. The most distinguishing feature had to be her eyebrows, thick and not altogether unattractive. She unconsciously manipulated them into a look of worry or confusion, and it was only when she smiled that they rested in place and were pleasant to look at.

"What are you doing tomorrow, Joy?" she asked, over the bathroom sinks.

"I haven't really thought about it."

"Will you stay in Pattaya or go back to Bangkok?"

"Ask me in the morning."

"Because I have a friend in Pattaya. She's a caddy."

"A what?"

"A caddy. She carries golf clubs at a country club. I don't think she makes much, but the tips are good. She told me to come down and apply if I ever needed a job."

"I don't know," said Mantana, rubbing her arms with cold water. "It doesn't sound like much fun, walking around in the sun all day with a bag of golf clubs."

"Yes," Neung agreed. "Plus my friend has to work naked."

Mantana turned off the water and looked at Neung in the spotted mirror.

"Maybe not completely naked," she said. "I think she wears a cap."

*

The only food available at three in the morning was rice soup with bits of dried pork added in by hand. The girls sat at a long table, eating from pink and blue bowls under fluorescent lights. It was the first time Mantana really saw any of the girls's faces, and she wondered what they would do now. Was it back to night shifts at a garment factory? Back to salesgirl behind the counter of a mini-mart? Or back to no job at all, like Mantana?

The party finished their meals and got back in the van. They rode for another ten or twenty minutes when the vehicle slowed down and stopped again. "Are we there?" asked some of the girls. Mantana hushed them and waited for the doors to open.

They opened.

Two men in brown uniforms stood shining their flashlights upon them. It was hard to make out their faces but obvious from their boots and holsters that they were police officers.

"Is everyone all right?" asked one.

"Yes!"

"Stay put. You're going to follow us to the police station."

The beam of light hit Mantana square in the eyes and blinded her. She held up a hand and spoke.

"We're exhausted," she said. "Could we just go to a hotel?"

"No," said the police officer.

The light remained upon her longer than she thought necessary. Then the men stepped back and closed the doors.

"We're saved!" said Goong.

"The cell phone," said Mantana. "I should have taken the cell phone."

"You don't think?" The question thinned and vanished in the dark.

At the next stop, the doors opened and Yim, Dao and Nong were made to climb in with the rest. Again, Mantana couldn't see the faces of the policemen, only a hand holding a gun, a real one this time, with real bullets instead of blue sparks.

"Where are we?" asked Neung, when the doors were shut.

"Pattaya," said Yim. "But I don't know where."

"I don't understand," said Dao. "Those men are policemen."

"What part don't you understand?" asked Neung.

Dao didn't speak again. The van rumbled on, most likely through the city due to the numerous stops and turns. Mantana knew they were close. Close to what? Mantana knew that too. They were close to the place where Kwan lived, and close to the place where the doctors were keeping Jakkrit's mangled legs. They were close to her mother's cancer, her father's poverty, and every rotten ghost that ever looked her in the eye and smiled before she had a chance to turn away. They were so close, she felt a chill along her spine. Mantana tucked the stun gun in the front of her skirt and pulled her shirt down to cover the bulge it made.

The van stopped and stayed parked for an hour before the doors opened again. The sun was coming up, and the air smelled strange. They appeared to be in another parking lot, behind a low standing brick building. The policeman flashed his gun and spoke. His voice sounded shot full of cigarette burns.

"Exit the van slowly. Walk to the gray doors. Keep your eyes forward and don't talk. If any of you try to escape, you will be shot."

The warning caused a few of the girls to gasp. The few that still believed they had a chance. Mantana stepped out of the van just after Neung. She heard a policeman tell a girl not to look at him. Mantana kept her eyes on the back of Neung's shirt as she made her way across the empty lot. One of the policemen walked ahead of the line and knocked upon the doors. Each girl harbored a suspicion of what lay beyond them, but none knew for sure. Torture chamber? Rat-infested cell? Gang of Japanese men? Maybe all this and more lie waiting for them behind the gray doors.

The policeman spoke with someone inside, then told everyone to take off their shoes. The girls did as they were told. Neung entered, Mantana followed. There were no rats, nor were there any Japanese men. There was orange carpet. When all the girls were inside, a pair of hands closed the doors. With the policemen outside, it was finally safe to look around.

They were in a room, air-conditioned, and quite big. There was a door on the opposite side, though no one was brave enough to see whether it was locked or not. At the front of the room was a slide projector sitting on a metal table. A white screen stood on a tripod facing a semi-circle of about a dozen folding chairs. Neung sat down at the far curve of the seats and Mantana took the seat next to her. The gun in her skirt had been slipping, and a few more steps would have loosened it altogether. Around the room, girls took to the seats in bewilderment and despair.

"Where are we?"

"What are they going to do to us?"

"Shh! Do you hear that?"

There was nothing for a moment, then a small squeak that started faintly and became louder by the second. Mantana thought of the rat she had seen jumping around in the cage. Now she was the rat. And this room was the cage.

The door on the opposite side of the room opened. A skinny boy, with a bowl-shaped haircut and ears fastened perpendicularly to the side of his head came in pushing a metal serving cart. The wheels went squeak, squeak. On top of the cart was a silver pitcher, a row of white cups, and a tall hot pot filled with water. He maintained a wide, silly grin on his face and became embarrassed each time his eyes met the stare of a girl. He pushed the cart to the front of the room and stopped.

"*Sa wat dee krap*," he said. "Coffee or milk?"

Everyone sat looking at him. He lost a little bit of his smile and pushed the cart into the semi-circle.

"Coffee or milk?" he asked the first girl, who happened to be Goong. Her mouth twitched a little.

"Coffee," she said.

The boy spooned a heaping of instant coffee into a cup and ran the hot water over it. He set a small packet of cream, two cubes of sugar, and two round cookies on the saucer before presenting it to her. Then he moved to the next girl and asked again. When all the girls had a beverage, he stood at the front of the room and performed magic tricks. He performed one involving two metal hoops that appeared inseparable. He separated them. He did another where he turned a black wand into a bouquet of flowers. Next, he took three red balls out of his pocket. He was about to make them disappear or levitate or turn into pigeons when he noticed that none of the audience members were drinking their coffee or eating their cookies.

"Do you need more sugar?" he asked.

The far door opened again, and eight cups rattled loudly in their saucers. Some of the cookies fell to the floor.

"Good morning! Good morning!"

A man moved along the edge of the chairs and stood before them. He wasn't Thai, he wasn't Japanese. He was *farang*.

"Sorry to keep you waiting," he said. "I wasn't expecting you in so early in the morning. Did everyone have a nice trip?"

The man stood about six feet tall. He was dressed in brown pants and a long sleeved shirt with the cuffs buttoned at the wrists. A badly knotted tie hung at an awkward length from his collar and rested upon a round, pot belly. He had a nest of brown curls on his head and a pair of eyes that squinted behind a pair of thick glasses. Also, the man had no neck. His chin just dropped off into a fleshy, stubble-ridden spare tire that his head swiveled upon.

The boy with the ears pulled at the man's arm.

"Oh, all right," he said. "Get on with it."

The boy took out a deck of playing cards and held them out for the man to choose from. He drew one and leaned forward to show the girls. It was the three of clubs. He then returned the card to the deck. The boy shuffled and pressed the cards together in his hands. Poof, the cards disappeared. He showed off his empty mitts, then crossed the room to where Mantana was sitting. His foot crushed a cookie.

"Do you have his card?" asked the boy.

"No."

He reached behind her ear. When his thin fingers emerged

again, it was holding an egg. A black three and a black club was drawn upon it. The boy displayed the egg for all to see, then took a bow. The foreigner clapped his hands several times.

"Bravo!" he said.

No one else applauded. The boy set the egg upon the serving tray and wheeled it around to collect the untouched coffee and cookies.

"My name," said the man in English, "is Mr. Simmons. And our young magician is my wife's younger brother, Wit. This room is on loan from a friend who runs an English language school."

A scream came from the left side of the semi-circle. It was Nong. She leaped to her feet, knocking her chair over as she did. Her face was all panic and terror.

"I'm not going to fuck any Japanese men!" she yelled, and ran for the gray doors. The gray doors were locked. She beat upon them with her fists and cried for help.

"Miss?" said the foreigner. "Do you have to use the toilet, miss?"

Now Neung was on her feet.

"What do you want?" she cried. "What are you going to do with us?"

Mr. Simmons looked to Wit, who dutifully translated what she said.

"She say, what you do to they?"

"Well, I'm going to give them jobs! That's what they came for, isn't it?"

Wit translated. This brought Goong and Yim to their feet. There was much yelling. The girls's voices could have shattered windows, if there had been any. The foreign man looked awfully confused. Wit did the best he could to throw some light on the situation.

"They say two man take them from Bangkok. Put in car long time."

"Not car!" said Yim. "Van!"

Mr. Simmons wrinkled his nose. "What?"

Over by the doors, Nong let out another wail and resumed her pounding. More chairs were overturned as the girls shouted their protests and moved forward with clenched teeth and clenched fists. The deck of cards fell from Wit's backside and scattered upon the floor. Mantana removed the stun gun from her shirt and stood up. The mob of girls had nearly reached Mr. Simmons, who had taken to hiding behind the movie screen. Mantana held up her electric pistol, closed her eyes, and whip cracked the air with a jolt of blue and white.

Everyone turned to look at her.

"Shh," she said, with a finger to her lips.

Mr. Simmons poked his head out from behind the screen. "You've got a gun!" he said.

Mantana understood. The girl with the gun was the girl with the voice, even if she didn't speak his language. She waved for him to come out. He did so slowly, with his hands in the air. Wit stood at his side, reluctantly.

"Now, now," said Mr. Simmons. "There's no need for violence, ha ha. I'm on your side."

The girls continued to glare at him.

"If you let me turn on the slide projector, I think everything will be cleared up."

Wit explained his intentions. Neung and Yim looked to Mantana, then stepped back to let him switch on the machine. A white square of light flashed upon the screen.

"I'm opening a club," said Mr. Simmons. "A nightclub, do you understand? Not a loud and sleazy go-go bar, but a classy sort of place where a gentleman can come to relax. I've even ordered an espresso machine."

No response. Mr. Simmons cleared his throat and continued.

"You girls are the young and beautiful hostesses that I

ordered."

"No understand!" said Yim in English.

Wit stepped up and tried to explain. "This is Uncle Ray. Uncle Ray is a good man. Uncle Ray is a generous man. Uncle Ray loves children and animals."

Mr. Simmons advanced the frames until he came to a slide. The white light was now the picture of a smiling Thai girl in a red bathing suit. The girls looked at the screen, then at Mr. Simmons. Mr. Simmons looked at the screen, then at the girls.

"This is Miss - ah, Wit, who is this?"

Wit picked up a clipboard from the lower shelf of the cart and read in English.

"Miss Pumpuang. She twenty-six year old. Her hobby: watching a TV, read a cartoon book, and sleeping."

Wit put down the list and scanned the faces of the girls around the room.

"Where is Miss Pumpuang?"

Mr. Simmons moved to the next photo. Another girl, this time in a black mini-skirt and halter. She had a wide mouth, almost overflowing with teeth. Once again, the face of the girl on-screen did not match the face of Neung, Goong, Yim, Dao, Nong, Tan, Nat, or Mantana.

Nor did the next, or the one after that.

"You're not the girls I hired!" said Mr. Simmons, frantically clicking through a photo gallery of women. "*These* are the girls I hired! This one and this one and this one!"

Wit translated, although most of them, Mantana included, had figured things out for themselves. Neung snatched the clipboard from his hands and read.

"Prakanom Modeling Agency. Experienced and beautiful hostesses fluent in English, German, and French. Available for short or long term employment."

"Fluent in three languages," said Yim. "Ha!"

"There's an amount next to each girl's name. It ranges from two to four thousand baht. Wait, this one is more but she can speak Czech."

"How much do you think we cost?" asked Nong.

All eyes went to the foreigner. Wit was doing his best to explain that these were not the girls from the Prakanom Modeling Agency. These girls were from somewhere else.

"Are you telling me that I just paid fifty thousand baht for eight girls who can't speak a lick of English?"

Wit nodded, pleased that his boss finally understood. Mr. Simmons's ears turned a bright shade of pink and a patchwork of creases broke out across his forehead. He turned to the girls and spoke through clenched teeth.

"How," he said, "did you get here?"

*

The men who had kidnapped them were ballpoint pens from Mr. Simmons's shirt pocket. The girls were cigarettes, the van, the green and white cigarette pack. Wit's jack of clubs was laid down to represent Bangkok and the queen of diamonds was of course Pattaya. Yim gathered the cigarettes around the jack and introduced the ball-point pens in a deep, frog like voice.

"You! You! Want you money?"

"Yes! Yes!" said the cigarettes in falsetto. "Money good!"

Mantana drove the empty pack with her right hand and parked it near the cigarettes.

"In!" said the ballpoint pens. "I take you to a job!"

The cigarettes danced in Yim's fingers as she said "Hooray, hooray." Then, naming them off one by one, she returned them to the pack.

"Joy, Nong, Goong ..."

When all the cigarettes were back in the pack, Mantana

steered it across the carpet to the queen of diamonds.

"I think Taiwan," she said. "But no Taiwan."

"France," said Tan.

"Ice cream," said Dao.

Mr. Simmons removed his thick-lensed glasses and pressed his thumb and forefinger into his eyes. He rubbed them hard, then pinched the nerve in between. It somehow caused his lower lip to stick out and twitch. He stayed that way for some time, pinching and twitching. Until finally, he put his glasses back on and spoke.

"So the bottom line is, you were tricked and I was tricked and someone's come out fifty thousand baht richer. That explains why you all look like scared mice."

The girls looked to Wit for a translation.

"The line beneath you is the explanation for fifty thousand mice," he said.

Neung approached the boy and gave him a mean look. The oversized, somewhat stupid grin flashed across his face, then disappeared just as quickly.

"What kind of job were we supposed to have applied for?"

"A good job! You get to wear pretty clothes."

"How much does it pay?"

"Uncle Ray is a very nice man. He bought my mother and father a house. And he teaches me English. If you work for Mr. Ray, you won't be sorry."

"How much?"

"I don't know. I think three thousand a month."

"Where will we stay?"

"I'll find rooms. Cheap rooms. I was born in Pattaya. I know this city better than the rats."

"What are you two talking about?" asked Mr. Simmons.

"Lady want know about job," said Wit.

Mr. Simmons rubbed his unshaven chin. "I can't give anyone a job until I've spoken with my wife."

He looked down at the pack of cigarettes and the ballpoint pens and the playing cards still lying on the carpet. A silence had taken root around the room, and the only smile came from the face of the Prakanom Model still looking out from the movie screen.

"Wit," said Mr. Simmons. "Why don't you run to my car and see whether there's any application forms in the back seat."

Wit nodded and disappeared through the door he came in.

"What did he say?" asked Neung.

"I think he wants to give us jobs," said Mantana.

"Is he crazy?"

The girls stood quietly, as if waiting for Mantana or Neung or anyone with a voice to decide upon their next move. Only they were beyond all that, now. There were no more threats, no more guns. When Mr. Simmons came back with the applications, some took from the pile, some didn't.

"Joy?" said Neung. "You didn't take one."

Mantana smiled wearily. "It's been a long day," she said.

4

The truth was, Mantana had never considered going back to her village. Not when she said good bye to Neung, not when she took a motorcycle taxi to the Pattaya bus station. It was only after she had purchased her ticket and sat on the hard, wooden benches that it occurred to her just what she was doing.

She was admitting defeat.

The bus to the North did not pass through Bangkok. Instead, it circled the city, past long stretches of roadwork and construction. Then came the traffic. For thirty minutes she sat staring at a billboard for Clean and Happy Soap. The bus moved, and for another long while the view was brick walled by an advertisement for Dreamland condominiums. Dreamland offered green grass, blue skies, everyone happy, and even wild animals like deer and rabbit poking their heads out of a nearby forest. The condo itself was big and white, shaped like a castle with its very own flag waving from the top.

The construction workers would have to be magicians, like Wit, she thought, to bring life back to the patch of ruin they worked in. Mantana didn't know what it looked like back when people traveled by ox cart, but she knew that it wasn't like this. Did the man who painted the billboard advertisement really believe - ? No, he couldn't have. Mantana rested her head against the bus window. Man would never be reduced to absolutely nothing in the world. For when they were close, he'd call his nothingness SOMETHING and try to sell it to the first fool who believed him. The longer she looked out the window, the more everything looked like nothing to her.

Once out of the Bangkok area, traffic was not as congested and the flat, grassy plains of central Thailand provided her with hours of unchanging scenery. Several times, she was close to falling asleep, only to be awakened by a cassette tape of loud pop songs that the driver plugged in for everyone's enjoyment. Four more hours passed before Mantana asked to be let off at the side of the road. She walked to the shade of a road sign and waited for a motorcycle taxi to drive by. She waited a long time. She was about to start walking when a passing car suddenly blew its horn and veered to the side of the road.

"Joy? Is that you?"

It was Nongluck. Nongluck, her friend, who had gone to work and laughed and eaten three meals a day while Mantana slept with her former boss for money and held her pee in the back of a dark van. She walked to the car and did her best to smile. Nongluck's pretty face smiled back.

"What are you doing here?" she said. "Get in, I'll take you back to the village."

Nongluck opened the door for her.

"Don't you have a bag?"

"No," said Mantana.

"But all you have is a purse. And look at those boots! Where did you get them? Joy, are you in trouble?"

"I'm fine," she said, and her voice choked. "Please, just drive me home."

Nongluck switched gears and stepped on the gas. Another car honked and swerved to avoid hitting her as she pulled back onto the highway.

"Does your father know that you're coming?"

"No," said Mantana, wiping her eyes.

"Hm," said Nongluck. "There's something you should know."

"What?"

"You remember the widow Amnuay?"

"How could I forget?"

"She moved in with your father. She's living with him now."

They rode for a while in silence. Then Mantana asked her to stop the car. Nongluck pulled to the side of the road. Mantana opened the car door and tried to throw up. There was nothing in her stomach. Nongluck patted her back affectionately.

"You should be happy, Nong Joy," she said. "Amnuay has money. And your father needs someone to look after the shop while he's at work."

"I want to die," said Mantana.

"Don't speak like that! Everyone knows you tried your best. Times are tough, Joy. Even the Jerriporn boys are out of work. The government decided to close thirteen banks last week. Both of them came home with empty pockets. It's worse for them because they'd gotten used to being rich! People like us have always had to struggle. We wouldn't know what to do with ourselves if we suddenly had it easy. So stop feeling sorry for yourself. Let's stop and eat some *gooey teeo* before I take you home."

Mantana closed the car door and laid her head back.

"No more tears," said Nongluck, and spun her tires in the dirt before jerking the car back onto the pavement.

*

Khun Apichak's *gooey teeo* stand stood among a row of fried rice, fried noodle, and more *gooey teeo* stands in a market just before the village. His wife sold sweet rice wrapped in banana leaves at a table opposite her husband. They were both very happy to see Mantana.

"Where did you go for so long?" asked Khun Apichak.

Nongluck answered for her. "Joy found a job in Bangkok. She's come home to give money to her father."

"And a day off too! I haven't had a holiday for seventeen years. Maybe I should go to Bangkok along with everyone else."

"Everyone else?" said Mantana.

"Everyone! Even that drunken no-good who used to roam the streets at night. He got tired of begging for whiskey so he took an axe and chop! chop! cut off his legs and crawled to Bangkok. I'll bet he's a rich man by now. People always give money to cripples."

Mantana and Nongluck took their bowls of soup to a table in the shade and sat down. Mantana lifted a pair of chopsticks and stirred the thin noodles without eating.

"My father and the widow Amnuay," she said. "It doesn't make sense."

"I always thought she was crazy," said Nongluck. "Ever since her daughter was taken from her."

"No one took Kwan from her. Amnuay sold her to a pair of men who put her in the back seat of a car and drove away in the middle of the night. That's how she became rich. Off her daughter."

"I've heard that story. But who knows what to believe when the facts aren't given on TV? Do you know that some people even say I was the one who caused Jakkrit to lose his legs? Phii Ouen, that fat bastard, says that he saw my car pass by just before Jakkrit started yelling his head off."

Nongluck stabbed a pork ball with her chopsticks and lifted it from the broth.

"I wasn't even outside at the time. I was home in bed."

"Jakkrit doesn't blame anybody," said Mantana. "Except maybe himself."

Nongluck looked at her, somewhat taken aback.

"How would you know?"

Mantana avoided her eyes.

"I don't. I'm just guessing. Nongluck, I need to ask you a favor."

Nongluck's chopsticks froze midway between the broth and her mouth.

"I'm not going to ask for money. It's something else. I don't want to go home looking like this. Can I take a shower at your place?"

"Of course you can."

"And," Mantana pressed her lips together and waited before speaking again. "Could I borrow something to wear?"

Nongluck smiled and reached across the table to squeeze her hand.

"I'll even do your hair for you."

*

The village looked exactly as she remembered. There were Phii Gaa's chickens strutting about their bamboo cage. There were Phii Kum's cannas growing in a line next to her front porch. There were the earthen red water urns that survived the Duangdao fire and there were the charred remains of the house that didn't. Mangy dogs, with or without names, continued to roam the streets looking for something to eat. The village looked exactly as she remembered. Only everything was different now.

Mantana showered and sat in a chair while Nongluck cut her

hair. Then she went to a sofa and found that she couldn't get up again. Nongluck moved a fan from her bedroom and positioned it to blow upon her.

"Go to sleep, Nong Joy. You can go home tomorrow."

"Nongluck," she said, already waist deep in a dream, "it all went so terribly wrong."

"Don't worry. You'll find a way to make things better."

Nongluck disappeared onto the small balcony and came back with a broom to sweep hair clippings off the tiled floor.

"Why is it you never remarried?" asked Mantana.

She stopped sweeping and smiled without looking up. "When I was your age, finding a man was the most important thing in my life. Well, I found a man and spent the next year of my life feeling worse than I ever felt before. He cheated on me, he lied to me, and I'm sure if I would have stayed with him, he would have eventually begun to beat me. I suppose you could say I made the wrong choice, and you'd be absolutely right. But after I left him, love wasn't so essential to my existence anymore. The old ladies think it's a crime that I choose to remain single. They think I should be fulfilling my role as a wife and mother. I'm not saying they're wrong, but I do know this; I'm much happier being alone than I ever was with a man."

She propped the broom against the wall and adjusted the fan to blow on Mantana.

"You've got a lot more time ahead of you than I have," she said. "You're still young and pretty. Who knows? Anything could happen."

Mantana tried to protest, but laid her head back and closed her eyes instead. She didn't want to be young and pretty. Young and pretty had brought her nothing but trouble. Why couldn't she have been born with fish scales for skin or eyelids that didn't blink in unison? Maybe then people wouldn't lie to her, unless they said things like "My, how lovely you look today, Miss Fish Skin," or "Gosh,

I didn't notice that your eyes don't blink in unison," because people could never tell the complete truth, no matter how honest they were.

It was her last thought before drifting off to sleep.

*

When Mantana awoke, she didn't know what time it was, what day it was, and, for a moment, where she was at all. She sat upright on the sofa and waited for it all to come back to her. There was that, that happened, then, oh, yes, then that. Mantana saw a note sticking out from underneath the fan. She picked it up and read. Nongluck invited her to make herself at home. And there was a special outfit hanging in the bathroom for Mantana to wear. She put the note down and walked lazily to the bathroom. Nongluck's choice of outfit was a purple skirt and jacket over a white blouse. There was even a pair of shoes for her. They would do.

Mantana switched on the television before going back into the bathroom for a shower. The water was cold and made her dance. When she finished, she heard a strange report being given in a referee's voice. Mantana looked out of the bathroom to see whether it wasn't just a comedy show. No, it wasn't a comedy show. Still dripping, she wrapped a towel around her and moved close to the set. What she saw made her smile. Two Thai girls were squaring off against each other in a boxing ring. Girls! When the bell rang, they moved towards each other, throwing punches and kicks. For ten minutes, Mantana stood staring at the TV set, until the match ended, blue trunks victorious over red, and a pair of teenaged boys was introduced for the next fight. She switched it off and dressed. Then and there, it struck her that Thailand was on a strange road into the future, and its anchor into the past was slipping faster and faster every day. What it all meant, she couldn't say. She had always been taught that tradition was sacred and made life pleasant and safe; and she believed it. But how exciting it had been to see those girls, skinny-legged and ordinary like herself, trying to knock each other out! Mantana bet they would have the same ferocity with Thai husbands who kept mistresses behind their backs. Pow! Lights out!

It gave her something to think about.

*

It was well past noon when Mantana returned home. A half dozen unfinished projects still lay scattered around front. Mantana went to the door and found it locked. She had to go around back and crawl through an open window. *Tch-haw!* What she saw inside was nothing short of astounding. Amnuay had not only moved in, she had brought all of her "stuff" along too. The dull green refrigerator they had owned since Mantana was a little girl had been replaced by a deluxe model with an automatic defroster. There was a microwave oven, a blender, a coffee maker, and enough plates, cups, saucers and utensils to set a table for three families. There was a sofa, a coffee table, and Oho! A twenty-inch television sitting on an oaken shelf with a stereo system and speakers beneath it. The explosion of furniture and appliances made the room cramped and not at all like a home, no matter who lived there.

Mantana was afraid to look farther, but looked anyway. It was just as she thought. Her father's bedroom had been completely redone, redecorated, removed. A strange bed with pink sheets now lay in place of his familiar, worn-out mattress. Everything old, everything she knew, had been boxed up and placed, where else, in her old room. Even the color photograph of her mother that used to sit on her bedside table was gone. Mantana tried to remember the face in the picture, the one she had woken up to and went to sleep with year after year, and was dismayed that the only face she could see was that of Phii Aor. Where was her mother? Her mother whom she loved and missed.

With the former inglorious arrangements just a memory, an emptiness crept into her stomach that had nothing to do with the fact that she hadn't eaten breakfast. Then she heard the front door open and close.

"Father?" she said.

"Who's there?"

The voice was one she knew from somewhere far away, in a place she visited only in nightmares, or when locked in the back of a van. Mantana counted to three, then walked out of the bedroom that wasn't hers anymore.

"Joy!" said Amnuay. "What are you doing here?"

Amnuay had gotten old. Old and fat. Her mole had not stopped sprouting gray hairs, and the darkness that encircled her eyes was now an unhealthy shade of red. She wore her hair pulled back and tied in a short, knotted pony-tail. A long, flower print dress, common among housewives, caused Mantana to wonder where the widow was spending her money these days.

"Where's my father?" she said.

"Working. Where else? He's laying bricks for an apartment that's being built in town. J.V., J.B., oh, I forget now. Started just last week, he did, and it's a good thing, too. What with the way your father throws his dice!"

"Who's minding the store?"

"It's closed for today. There's never more than a few customers past noon. Everyone goes to work during the day. Not worth the trouble if you ask me. Still, there's no reason to tell Prapeut. Does he know that you're back? And what about dinner? Will you be staying for dinner?"

Mantana walked past the woman and out the door. Another minute with her and she might not have been able to control herself any longer. She had to get to town. She had to see her father.

Amnuay had spoken correctly about one thing; at one p.m. in

the midday sun, there was no one around to give her a ride. Then she remembered the boys on the corner. Surely they would still be there. Once there were four, but their number must have dropped since Jakkrit left. The boys on the corner were jobless, lazy, sometimes drunk, but hardly dangerous, though Mantana had always been told not to speak with them. They just hung out or played chess or smoked cigarettes or talked about the mechanical problems of their motorcycles. Sometimes, one of them had something to do at four o'clock. They were all Mantana's age or older. And none of them had a girl of his own.

"*Sa wat dee ka,*" said Mantana, approaching the wooden platform with a thatched roof that the corner boys had built for no other reason than to sit about and lie about and continue to be called "the Corner Boys."

"*Sa wat dee krap.*"

There were only two that afternoon. Mantana didn't know their names. One had yellow teeth and pockmarked skin. The other had long hair, with thin eyebrows that met on the bridge of his nose. They watched her with their tiny eyes and toothpick grins.

"Still sitting in the sun, are you?" she said. "Why don't you go help Khun Surimon build her bird feeder?"

"She never asked us to," said the one with the long hair.

"Hmf!" said Mantana, then took off her jacket and slung it over her shoulder. Her new haircut made her look less like a teenager and more like a young woman. "So I suppose you're just going to sit here all day."

"Why? Do you have a better idea?"

"Well, you could give me a ride into town."

"O.K!" said the one with the yellow teeth.

He climbed down from the platform and onto an old red motorbike. It started on the third try. Mantana tied the jacket sleeves around her waist and rode sidesaddle on back.

"Where to?" he asked.

"I'll tell you when you get there."

*

J.V. Apartment was a five-story structure built on a soi close to the main market. The boy with the yellow teeth let his passenger off at the mouth of the narrow lane and asked whether he should wait. Mantana told him not to bother.

"The next time you want a ride," said the boy, but didn't finish his sentence.

Mantana walked toward the construction site without giving him a second glance. The building was nothing but a skeletal frame of bamboo with a concrete foundation. The foundation was enclosed in brick. Two dozen men and women, some unrecognizable in sun hats and face masks, hammered, shoveled, and smoked cigarettes around the site. Another ten or eleven formed a human chain along the side of the structure and passed buckets of concrete up with their right hands, down to fill again with their left.

"Excuse me," Mantana said to a man sawing what looked like steel beams. "I'm looking for Khun Prapeut."

The man stood and removed his cap. His face was sun beaten and bore deep crevices that collected sweat and dust. He scratched his forehead, then called out to another worker.

"Hey! Where's Prapeut?"

The second worker waved an arm towards the other side of the construction site. Mantana placed a handkerchief over her mouth and moved further into the dust and noise. Then she saw him. He was squatting next to a pile of bricks, examining the front wheel of a wheelbarrow. A cigarette hung from the side of his mouth. Mantana walked closer and stood behind him.

"Hey!" she said, then louder, "Hey!"

Her father turned his head and looked at her. A sudden animation seemed to slap him across both of his baked brown cheeks, but he was quick as ever to stifle it. Mantana placed her hands together and waiied. She too was happy to see him, but didn't want to make her emotions overly apparent. It was this way with them.

"How are you?" she asked.

"This wheelbarrow," he said. "I'm thinking about switching the front wheel with the one out back of the house."

"Father, I've been home."

She searched for a reaction among his crow's feet and worry lines. He seemed more concerned about the wheelbarrow.

"How could you let that woman move in?" said Mantana. "All that stuff! I didn't even recognize the place! And do you know that she already closed the store for the day? She's horrible!"

Prapeut stood and tossed the cigarette from his lips.

"She's helping to pay off the mortgage on the house."

He still wouldn't admit that the debts he accumulated were from gambling.

"But you know where she gets her money! Everybody knows! Kwan sends it to her from - from who knows where! Some filthy place with men and rats and -"

"That's just gossip. You never really believed that. Here, now, take a look at this wheel and tell me if you think it's the same size."

Mantana walked to the wheelbarrow and turned it upright. Then she pushed it, hard as she could, away from where they stood. It rolled about ten feet, and fell over on its side. Her father's lips formed a small, dry circle, but didn't make a sound. Some of the other workers had witnessed the show of disrespect and leaned against their shovels to watch. Now if that were their daughter, some of them thought...

"That's *our* house!" said Mantana.

Prapeut turned and saw the other workers watching them. His emotionless front was broken, and his voice cracked with anger.

"Walls and floors belong to us, sure. But what good is living in a house if there's nothing to put inside? Now, go on back and help Amnuay make dinner. Unless you've got to be somewhere in those clothes of yours."

Mantana swallowed and tasted the dust around her. It was a mistake to have come home empty-handed. A bigger mistake than she first imagined. When she looked at her father again, it was like seeing him for the first time through adult eyes, and she saw something that she hadn't seen before. She had left him, almost as her mother had left him, stranded in the house he had built to raise a family in. Although her intentions were good, her father was no longer young. And, like most people left holding the short end of the candle, he wanted things. Things he'd never use, things he didn't even understand, but things, just the same. Shiny, expensive things that he could look at and that could look back at him with a wink and a nod and a plastic smile that said "Prapeut, good man, you are one piece closer to having more and having it better than everyone else." It was in this light that the promise she made to her mother made more sense than ever. Mantana couldn't be upset with him for this attitude. In fact, he had every right to it. He probably didn't give two spits for Amnuay. She was just a cloud that drifted in, dropping her things all around the house. She was a cloud, maybe so, but she wasn't going to leave him like his wife and daughter had.

"I'm sorry," said Mantana, and kneeled down on one knee as she waiied him.

His fingers touched the top of her head and she got up again.

"I have to go."

Her father frowned, but made no attempt to stop her. Instead, he took out his wallet and drew three one-thousand-baht bills from it.

"I can't," she said.

"Yes, you can," said her father. "It's yours. You earned it. The department store sent it to the house some two weeks ago. It's all right. You don't have to tell me where you're working. That cheap outfit and the fact that you don't have any money to give me says that it can't be very much."

Mantana was stunned. She took the money and crumpled it in her fist.

"I'll find a way," she said, but the machine gun rattle of a nearby jackhammer pushed her words from the air. She wanted him to hear; she wanted him to know. Someday he would have his things. And he wouldn't have to ask the widow Amnuay for them. She yelled again.

"I'll find a way!"

"Sure you will," said Prapeut. "Just walk down this alley and take a right at the next soi."

Mantana watched him wave to the construction crew who had stopped to look. Then he closed the invisible door between them and went back to work.

Nongluck sold her the purple outfit and shoes for one hundred and fifty baht, minus the belt. Mantana broke one of her thousand-baht notes to buy another one at the market. Then she walked to the bus station and boarded the three o'clock special, Pattaya bound.

5

It would be another two weeks before Mr. Simmons could open his club. After the fiasco with the bogus employment agency, he had to cancel the order for his espresso machine and do what every other bar, nightclub, and discotheque was already doing: stick a help wanted sign in the window and hope for the best. Neungruethai, or Neung, was the first of the kidnapped girls to agree to stay on. Goong and Yim were the next. Mantana, the last.

Neung was overjoyed at her friend's return. She immediately wanted to find a room for the two of them. Mantana had to decline. She no longer trusted her judgment of people and decided against placing herself in a position of relying on, or being relied upon. From now on, misfortune would be of her own making. She wanted no one to blame but herself.

Instead of being offended, Mantana's resolution only seemed to increase Neung's admiration of her. And when Mantana rented a room above a mini-mart across from the bar, Neung was quick to find one on the same soi, so they would always be within a stone's throw of each other. A distance that became shorter each time Neung showed up at her door. Reluctantly, Mantana agreed to eat breakfast with her, then lunch, then dinner. Then whatever else Neung had in mind, which usually meant shopping for clothes they both sorely needed, or simply walking the streets, exploring their new home. They had two weeks to kill. Mantana had her department store money. Neung somehow got by.

They talked.

They talked about the foreigners they saw. They talked about which go-go bars had the most colorful neon display. They talked about how dirty the sea was and how beautiful it looked at night. The one thing they didn't speak of was opening night.

They each slept with spiders on the ceilings above their beds.

In the last week of September, a knock came on Mantana's door. It was Wit with a message from his Uncle Ray. Rehearsal was to begin that afternoon at two. Rehearsal? Wit gave her a flower from a bunch he held under his arm and a card with the name and address of the place where she would be working. There was a cartoon drawing of a woman in a bikini holding the neck of a champagne glass that was twice her size. In bold letters were the lines **Sexy Girls, Exotic Dancing, Happy Hour 6-8,** and **Special Shows Nightly**. Wit smiled, then went off to find Neung. It had to start sometime, she thought.

The name of the "club," as Mr. Simmons called it, was the Cherry Bar. It was a medium-sized space that only looked big on account of the mirrors that covered the walls. A catwalk ran through the center of the bar, with stools like centipede legs running alongside it. There were also cushioned seats against the walls, and tables big enough for a bottle, an ashtray, and an elbow, nailed to the floor in front of them. At the far end, to the right of the catwalk, was the bar. To the left, the entranceway to the toilets and dressing room. The ceiling was loaded with the usual array of spotlights and sirens, with the addition of a giant disco ball hanging motionless above the center of the stage. Girls wandered in quietly and sat as far from the catwalk as possible. Some checked and double-checked the address on the card, as if ashamed to admit that this was the place they had applied and been hired to work.

Of the twenty girls Mr. Simmons had hired, only eight showed up for rehearsal. This was bad. This wouldn't do. Mantana and Neung sat uncomfortably in one of the cushioned seats. Before them, Mr. Simmons seemed to be throwing a temper tantrum of sorts. He walked the length of the bar, mumbling to himself, chuckling, then cursing with words they knew like "shit!" and "damn!" Wit explained to them in Thai that more than half the girls scheduled for rehearsal had changed their minds or found other work. Poor Mr. Simmons, thought Mantana. His luck appeared to be just as bad as hers.

Then another woman, a Thai woman, entered the room. She wasn't old, maybe only thirty or thirty-two, but it seemed she had inadvertently banished her youth by the very means she attempted to preserve it. Everything about her had been done too many times, her hair, her face, even her body. Done, done, and then undone by the rays of the sun. She wore her hair in two short braids that curved outward from the sides of her head and just barely touched her shoulders, a look that was popular among young girls and women trying to appear young. But it wasn't just the hair. Everything from her meticulously plucked eyebrows to her violet painted fingernails reminded Mantana of a long morning spent in front of a full-length mirror to achieve - *what?* Still, hadn't Phii Aor once told her that girls in their youth always think this way, and it was best not to judge others in their struggle with time? Either Phii Aor or her mother, one of them had said this to her.

The woman walked to the front of the room and stood next

to the frustrated Mr. Simmons. The smell of her perfume followed after.

"Eight!" he said.

She spoke with him in English. "There will be more girls when the club is open. You go get the light balls now."

"Light balls? Ah hee hee hee! Ah ha ha ha!"

That was how Mr. Simmons laughed. Ah hee hee hee, ah ha ha ha.

"You mean the light bulbs!"

Mr. Simmons turned to the girls. For a moment, everyone thought he was about to do something, quite possibly say something, until the woman took his arm and led him to the exit.

"Well then, I'll just go and get those light bulbs," said Mr. Simmons, and walked out the door.

The woman turned to her audience. "My name," she said, "is Anchulee. You can call me Buoy. I believe I'm a *Phii* to all of you. First, I'll tell you a little bit about myself."

Everyone waited. The woman's eyes went from one girl to the other. She wore an expression of such obvious disappointment on her face, the girls squirmed in their seats as if looking for a place to hide. No, these weren't the beautiful and intelligent models her husband had ordered to entertain sophisticated and worldly gentlemen. No, these weren't the girls that were fluent in English and French and had an education that would make them lively conversationalists. These were just skinny Thai girls with crooked teeth who were aware that Hitler was bad and Antarctica was cold and dinosaurs roamed the planet a long, long time ago. Beyond that, well... Phii Buoy sighed heavily and continued.

"Now, I'd like to know who each of you are."

Neung whispered into Mantana's ear. "I thought she was going to tell us about herself."

"I think she just did," whispered Mantana.

Phii Buoy turned to the girl sitting nearest to her and asked her name.

"Kay."

"Where are you from, Kay?"

"Chiang Rai."

"How old are you?"

"Twenty."

"What's your favorite kind of ice cream?"

Kay looked around nervously. She had a wide, flat face and pale skin. There was a black and white tattoo of a butterfly on her left wrist, only the ink had not been stitched deep enough to last, and the lines of the wings were already beginning to fade.

"Vanilla?" she said.

Phii Buoy repeated the word and moved to the next girl seated against the wall. This one had a round face and short, brownish orange hair. Her eyebrows were severely arched, making her look angry when she wasn't smiling, devilish when she did. Phii Buoy asked her all but the ice cream question. This girl's name was Pen, and she came from Hat Yai. She was twenty-three years old.

"If you could keep one animal from the zoo as a pet, which animal would you choose?"

Pen thought. The questions were probably meant to lighten the tension, but were somehow only making it worse.

"An ostrich," said Pen, and a couple of girls laughed.

When Phii Buoy got around to Mantana, the question was this: "If you could travel back in time to any year, which year would you choose?"

Mantana responded without blinking. "The future."

"I said back, back in time."

"I wouldn't go."

Phii Buoy set her hands upon her hips. "Why, dear girl?"

Mantana tightened her lips, aware that she had become the focus of everyone's attention. "Because, ma'am, my mother died when I was a little girl."

"Wouldn't you like to visit her?"

"Not," said Mantana, and stopped. "Not like I am today."

Neung was the last. She'd only eat hot dogs if she could only eat one food for the rest of her life. That ended the question and answer part of rehearsal. Wit came in on cue with his metal cart full of coffee mugs and cookies, and passed them out among the girls. He did more magic tricks, this time pulling a multi-colored stream of handkerchiefs from his balled-up fist and producing a baby chick from underneath a coconut shell. Then he collected the empty mugs and left the room.

"All right then," said Phii Buoy. "Now that we've gotten to know each other, I'd like to see the hands of our first timers. Who has never danced topless before an audience?"

Six of the eight girls, Mantana and Neung included, raised their hands. Tattooed Kay and a girl from Nakorn Sawan named Ale, did not.

"You can put your hands down. I can see that many of you are new to this line of work. Well, don't worry. Over the course of the next week, I'm going to hold your hands and guide you through everything you'll need to know. I'll explain the rules of the bar, demonstrate ways to keep our customers happy, and pass along advice to keep you out of danger. But before we begin, I must tell you right away. My number one rule is *smile*. Leave your troubles at home. I only want to see girls that love their job. Happy girls. Happy *happy* girls. Can you all smile for me now? Smile and show me how pretty you are."

The girls smiled. The look of disgust returned to the woman's face and Mantana could swear that a shudder passed through her body.

"Good!" said Phii Buoy, with some effort. "Now, let's all take our clothes off!"

*

There was a total of five rehearsal sessions. On the first day, Phii Buoy wanted to look at everyone's body. She wanted to see scars, moles, hidden tattoos, or any other mark of suspicious origin. She gave advice on shaving, make-up, and dental hygiene. Fresh breath was very important, she told them.

On the second day, the girls were given a lesson on how to talk to customers. Each girl was given a list of questions with appropriate answers prepared by Phii Buoy and Mr. Simmons. The list was in English. The girls were to memorize the questions and be able to answer in whatever order they were asked. Phii Buoy read through the questions and translated them into Thai. The girls took notes. The list read:

1. **What is your name?** My name is _____.
   "Always give your nickname," Phii Buoy advised. "It's much easier for a foreigner to remember a girl named Yim than a girl named Attitaya."
2. **Where are you from?** I'm from _____.
3. **How old are you?** I'm _____ years old.
   "Any girl over thirty should answer 'I'm twenty-nine years old.'"
4. **How long have you been a bar girl?** Two months.
   "Two months is a good length of time. A customer will think you have experience, but not too much experience."
5. **Why did you choose to be a go-go dancer?** Money.
   "Don't ever tell a customer that you love sex. Don't ever tell one that you hate sex. This job isn't about sex; it's about service. A waitress's job at a restaurant has nothing to do with the way a customer cuts his steak. A waitress's only concern is that the customer gets what he orders."
6. **Do you have a boyfriend?** No.
7. **Why don't you have a boyfriend?** A boyfriend wouldn't let

me work here.

8. **Do you like working here?**   It's OK.

"Same as with sex. Don't ever say you like or don't like what you do."

9. **What do you want to do whcn you finish working here?**

I want to go to school and learn to be a nurse.

10. **Have you had an AIDS test?**   Yes.

There was a nervous whisper around the room.

"Are there any questions?"

A hand went up. It was Ale.

"I don't understand number eight, ma'am. Why shouldn't I be able to tell a customer that I like my job?"

Phii Buoy nodded as she listened. "Most of the questions I asked while I was learning your names yesterday told me nothing about the kind of person you are. Kay likes vanilla ice cream, Pen would like to take care of an ostrich, Neung likes eating hot dogs. That's the level you want to be on with customers. You never know how a man might judge you, so keep your opinions to yourself. Better yet, have no opinions. That way you can say whatever you think the customer wants to hear. If a customer is wearing green, your favorite color is green. If a customer is fat, you're sick of skinny boys. And if a customer says he loves you, you love him too."

"So we should lie?" asked Yim.

"Don't think of it as lying," said Phii Buoy. "Look at it like this. Who is your favorite cartoon character?"

Yim smiled. "Chin Jung," she said.   Chin Jung was a mischievous little boy who lived in Japan.

"Right. He's very funny, isn't he?"

Everyone agreed. Chin Jung was funny.

"Now suppose Chin Jung stepped out of your television set one day and into your room."

A childish giggle went around the room.

"That's right," Phii Buoy continued. "You'd laugh because Chin Jung is funny and you'd expect him to make you laugh wherever he is. But suppose for a moment that when Chin Jung wasn't on television, he wasn't funny. Suppose he turned out to be a boring little brat who picked his nose and whined until he got on your nerves."

"But Chin Jung isn't real," said Yim.

"And neither are you," said Phii Buoy. "You're nothing but a plaything in the minds of our customers. And the more real you become with your opinions and ideas and likes and dislikes, the more a customer will want to find another girl that subscribes to his fantasy. Just like Chin Jung is better off as a cartoon, you'll find work a lot more profitable if you leave your personalities at home."

Another silence followed, as if Phii Buoy's words carried a weight that would sink any bathtub toy a kid would want to play with. Mantana had the feeling none of the girls were happy being compared to a cartoon character, let alone called a plaything. Phii Buoy asked again if there were any more questions. This time, there weren't.

That afternoon, the girls got their first AIDS test.

*

The third day was dancing. Phii Buoy mounted the catwalk and told the girls she wanted to see energy on stage. No shuffling back and forth. Phii Buoy grasped one of the steel poles, one hand over the other, and straightened her arms. She bent her knees and slowly parted them as she lowered herself, down, down, until her body was shaped like an arrow pointing to the underworld. Mantana noticed Mr. Simmons looking on, nodding to himself as if lost in memory.

"Now up," said Phii Buoy.

Catwalk rotation was explained, and a list was drawn up

detailing who was to dance in which order.

"And ladies," said Phii Buoy, "friendliness is permitted, but never try to steal another girl's customer."

Plastic tags were handed out. The tags had numbers on them. The girls were to wear the numbers when dancing. If they were bought from the bar, they were to give their number to Buoy.

"Many men will want to keep your number as a souvenir," she told them. "They cannot."

Mantana got number thirty. Neung got sixty-nine and complained. She traded it for number twenty-seven which she was happy with because it was only three away from Mantana's number.

On the fourth day, there was a special guest. An old friend of Phii Buoy's. The woman's name was Miss Gigi and she had platinum blond hair. Mantana had never seen a Thai woman with blond hair before. This was really an event. Miss Gigi had something she wanted to show the girls. She was going to need Mr. Simmons's help. Mr. Simmons wasn't hard to find. He always seemed to be waiting just outside the door. He entered smiling, dressed in a red shirt and brown slacks. Then the three of them, Miss Gigi, Phii Buoy, and Mr. Simmons, blew up balloons. They tied the ends tightly and gave them all to Mr. Simmons, who was breathing hard, but still smiling.

"Oh, is it my birthday?" he asked.

"Yess!"

Miss Gigi pinched his rubbery cheek and climbed the catwalk steps. She lifted her skirt and wiggled out of a pair of blue lace panties. Mr. Simmons pretended to admire his big balloons. Miss Gigi lay down on her back and opened her knees in his direction. Then she pulled a long thin tube from a hiding place in her blouse. The tube was silver, with "GIGI" painted on in red. It was her own personalized tube. Whatever she is going to do, thought Mantana, she's been doing for a long time.

Miss Gigi inserted a small black pellet into one end of the tube and tapped the opposite end against the orange carpet.

"Are you ready?" she asked.

"Yes, Miss Gigi."

The woman with the platinum blond hair slid the silver tube into the dark spot between her legs. Maybe two inches, give or take half an inch. She aimed, and with the effort one might exert blowing a fly from one's hand, contracted her stomach muscles and fired.

Bang, went the balloon in Mr. Simmons's hand.

The girls applauded. Some of them had seen this trick before. It was a first for Mantana.

Miss Gigi removed the tube from her middle.

"Does anyone else want to try?"

"I've got a clean tube," said Phii Buoy. "Never been used before. This act will be part of our special show."

Special show. The girls all knew what that meant. Dancing on the catwalk paid forty baht an hour, the same as not dancing on the catwalk. *Gooey teeo.* Dancing topless paid one hundred baht an hour. Fried fish. Dancing naked was two hundred baht an hour. Steak and wine. And the special show? Three hundred per act. Acts lasted the length of whatever song the DJ happened to select. Short song, short act, three hundred baht. Down payment on a *gooey teeo* stand of one's own.

A girl sitting near the bar asked, "Is it dangerous?"

"Only if you have a bad aim," said Miss Gigi.

The girl stood. She had a thin, skeletal face and large features. Her hair was long and flowed in a nicely sculpted wave across her forehead. A foreign hairstyle, it saved her from being plain.

"What is your name, dear?"

"Sai."

"Come on up, Sai."

Sai climbed the steps and stood next to Miss Gigi. She was dressed in black jeans and a tank top. Miss Gigi told her to take off her pants. The girl wasn't shy even before Mr. Simmons who stood holding his balloons, looking on. Phii Buoy handed her the tube and watched her measure it in her long-fingered hands.

"Have you ever done this before, Sai?"

"No."

There was a moment where Miss Gigi and Sai just looked at each other. Everyone was holding her breath, waiting. Then Sai smiled awkwardly and took off her jeans and panties. The two women standing half-naked on stage seemed perfectly natural to Mantana, and she wondered if Mr. Simmons were having Man Thoughts.

"First," said Miss Gigi, "you want to load your weapon. Put the pellet in this end and pack it down by tapping it two or three times. There's a wire at this end to keep the pellet from falling out or getting sucked up inside you. Now, just before you're about to perform, it's a good idea to grease yourself with lubricant. You don't want to dry up in front of an audience. Here, sweetie, you can use some of mine."

Miss Gigi held out a small white jar in her hand.

"If you'd like my husband to leave," said Phii Buoy.

"He's not bothering me," said Miss Gigi. "And in three days, you're all going to be doing a lot more before a bigger audience than Mr. Simmons."

"That's right, Miss Gigi."

Mantana looked at the floor and wondered if the two women had planned some of their dialogue beforehand.

When Sai finished with the lotion, Miss Gigi told her to lie down on her back. She spread her legs, and the fresh tube was inserted. Mr. Simmons held up another balloon. A blue one, this time.

"Take aim and push with your diaphragm. Don't push with your stomach or you'll fart."

Sai positioned the tube and moved her stomach up and down.

"It's not working."

"Take it easy," said Miss Gigi. "Concentrate."

Sai pushed again.

Nothing.

"Try it at home tonight," said Miss Gigi.

Sai sucked in all her breath for one more try. There was a sudden, audible puff of air and *zing-bang-wow*; the balloon exploded in Mr. Simmons's hand.

"You did it!"

Everyone applauded.

"She did more than that!" said Phii Buoy. "Look at the wall!"

The clapping stopped. Sai's pellet had flown through the balloon and lodged itself in the wall three feet behind a stunned Mr. Simmons. Pieces of concrete and paint fell from the indentation, and a crack indicated that more would be coming down soon.

Mr. Simmons moved to inspect the damage. "That's uncanny!" he said. "You could kill somebody with that!"

Sai removed the tube and slipped back into her jeans. She climbed down from the narrow stage and walked proudly back to her seat.

There were no more volunteers that day.

*

The final day of rehearsal was more of a pep talk than anything else. The group of girls had reached thirteen, and even the newcomers had become a part of the strange bond that formed among them. Mantana learned some of their names. She didn't learn them all. They all sat quietly while Phii Buoy spoke.

"It's no secret," she began, "that we're here to make money. It's also no secret that the things you do may cause you to feel afraid, sad, even hateful of yourself and others. There's going to be a lot of ugly old men who will want to kiss you and lot of handsome princes who will fall in love with you for a night. All I can say to you is, don't forget why you're here."

The AIDS results were handed out with the costumes and everyone was told to show up the next night at six p.m.

"Get a good night's sleep," said Phii Buoy.

"It could be your last," said orange-haired Pen, though no one thought her joke was very funny.

*

Neung and Sai and some of the other girls were planning to get drunk that evening, their last before joining the ranks of full-fledged working girls, but Mantana didn't want to leave her room. Neung offered to stay with her but Mantana told her to go, have fun, and they'd meet again tomorrow.

"It's not good to be alone," said Neung. "Especially tonight when you can still change your mind."

"What's wrong with changing my mind?" asked Mantana.

"Nothing. If you can afford to change it."

It was a long sleepless night that followed. With her eyes wide open, Mantana would become lost in some vivid dream of home. In one version, she returned to find that every wrong had been miraculously righted, and it had all been done by Mantana's hand. But every miracle had a price tag on it, and the part of her that couldn't sleep refused to let this fantasy continue without an explanation as to where the money had come from.

She turned over and tried again.

In another of her waking dreams, she stood in a field of tall grass without a house or advertisement for as far as she could see. The clouds above shifted and turned and first appeared to be one thing, then another. She could hear a girl weeping, but the wind, blowing from all directions, made it impossible to tell where the sobs were coming from. Mantana moved through the grass, thinking that the girl lay in front of her, only to realize she was somewhere far behind.

It was this particularly maddening vision that made her get out of bed and light a cigarette in her only chair near the window. The menthol tasted good in her mouth. She watched the smoke rise in a neat funnel and thought about Phii Buoy's time travel question. Mantana had meant it when she said she wouldn't venture into the past. Only the future, to see what lay ahead. What was there in the past? Only pain. What was she in the past? Just a foolish little girl who counted her toes and pretended to have conversations with insects to pass the time, time until now, this day, this night, when she was a grown-up making grown-up decisions. But what about her safe place? The one she had invented for herself when she stood on stage, singing in Phii Aor's restaurant or trapped in the back of a van? How could she explain the feeling of serenity it gave her when it was nothing but - gone?

Oh, headache!

Oh, bigger headache when she thought of what the foolish little girl who talked to bugs would be doing the very next night and all the nights that followed. Mantana closed her eyes and pressed her knuckles in the sockets. Deep within her, she knew that the spirits of misfortune were gearing up for war. She could hear the battle song they sang as they marched.

Burn that village to the ground!
Hand over old man Prapeut to the whore Amnuay!
And say nasty things about that wife of his! The one who died!

The past could no longer be a refuge for her.

She was all grown up.

Part Three

1

The first time Mantana took her top off in front of an audience... The first time she danced against a steel pole... The first time she let a man feel her breasts... The first time she said "I love you"... The first time she was bought from the bar... The first time she went to bed with a man from Switzerland... The first time she walked home at four in the morning... The first time she was drunk in the afternoon... The first time she was hung-over in the evening... The first time she went to bed with a man from Germany... The first time she thought about killing herself... The first time she went to bed with two men from America, both in the same night... The first time a condom broke inside her... The first time she put a man's thing in her mouth... The first time a customer told her that he loved her... The first time she went to bed with a man from who knew where... The first time she lost count...

The first time she sent money home to her father.

They were the strangest six weeks of her life.

*

It was a Saturday night, two weeks after the *songkran* festival that marked the Thai new year.

"Hello! What you name?"

"Jack."

"Hello, Jack. My name Joy."

"I like your boots."

"Yes. I like too."

Mantana sat down next to the foreigner. He was seated in one of the stools that surrounded the catwalk. Mantana had noticed him watching her in a mirror as she danced. Everyone had a reflection somewhere in the room, and it was a cinch to see who had their eyes on her and who didn't. Some men simply stared, but others, like this one, tried to act disinterested and watched her reflection instead. Mantana considered it both amusing and ridiculous to see a line of eight or ten men with their heads all turned in different directions, still trying to get a glimpse of her.

"Where are you come from?"

"New York."

The foreigner finished his drink and avoided her smile. He was handsome, thought Mantana. Handsome like a movie star. He had longish brown hair that hung in thick strands over his forehead, and a jaw that stuck out, almost to the same length as his nose. Also, his chin had a vertical indentation that marked him as handsome, though Mantana didn't know why.

"You a movie star?" she asked.

"A movie star? Ha ha. No, I'm not a movie star. But I do a lot of acting. Right now, as a matter of fact, I'm considering whether I should fall in love with you or not."

Mantana laughed too, though she didn't understand what he was talking about.

He sighed and shook his head. "I'd better not," he said, "You're too sweet. I can tell just by looking at you."

She wanted to ask what was the matter, why he looked so sad, but he removed his check from the plastic cup before she got a chance to sort the words out in her mind.

"I'd like to pay," he said.

She took the check from Jack's fingers and stood in her tight-fitting skirt. There was no sense in feeling slighted. Phii Buoy had told her once that men didn't come to go-go bars looking for a beauty pageant. Each customer had his own taste. Some desired fat girls, others sought out the grotesque and scarred. For a working girl to be shunned meant nothing, said Phii Buoy. Mantana knew in her head that Phii Buoy was right. Still, it was disappointing to find a man as young and handsome as Jack, only to watch him walk out the door. If she could just talk to him. Maybe then things could be different.

She carried the check to the bar, where a couple of girls stood eating watermelon seeds. They cracked the shells with their back teeth and spit them into their hands. Then they ate the seeds.

"Number forty-seven wants to pay," she said to the short-haired girl from Nakorn Sawan named Ale. Ale didn't want to put on the bikini for men. Ale didn't want to take off the bikini for men. Ale had been pregnant once and suffered a miscarriage when a former employer insisted she go on lifting heavy boxes, no matter how pregnant she was. So Ale hid her scars and worked the bar.

"Can you get it for me, Joy? I've got to make three different drinks for the men at seats six, seven and eight."

The girls with the watermelon seeds looked at her. One was tall and skinny with a face nearly wider than the head it was attached to. A white cotton square was taped over her right eye. The other was short and dumpy, covered in black make-up that made her look like a witch. On one of the short girl's arms was a tattoo of a butterfly, "BUTTERFFAE" stitched in above it. On her other arm was a pair of wings and "SOFT LOVE." There were others on her legs. All the girl's tattoos looked as if an artist drunk on whiskey had done them.

"Excuse me," said Mantana, rudely.

The girls parted, a handful of shells falling to the floor.

"Say, Ale, how do you ask "Why are you sad?" in English?"

Ale thought for a moment. Then she brought out a small blue notebook with a picture of a silver moon on the front. She opened the notebook and scanned a list of English phrases she had been keeping track of. Mantana leaned sideways to get a look at the sentences. They went:

I work here first time.
Are you boring with me?
Can you remember me?
I think. You not to miss me.
What you think of Thai lady?
Do you love me?

And so on. Mantana didn't see anything that would help her.

"Try *why you no have happy*," said Ale.

"Why you no have happy?" said Mantana. "Thanks, Ale."

She picked up a small, silver tray and carried it to the man at the catwalk. "Why you no have happy?" she said along the way. "Why you no have happy?" Only when she felt confident enough to use it on Jack, she found that he was no longer in such a hurry to leave. Orange-haired Pen had found him and was currently engaging him in her own brand of charm. Mantana had seen her at work many times. Even when she wasn't on the clock, she practiced perfecting her methods by doing crab-like aerobics where she sat. Pen didn't bother with any "Hello's" or "Where you come from's." She placed her hands upon the shoulders of an able-bodied customer and jumped into his lap. From there, she proceeded to bounce, twist, rub, and gyrate until her victim was reduced to the state of a drooling monkey. Pen often claimed that men had made offers to marry her while in this position. Marry and take her away to whatever land they were from. The problem was, it didn't last. It couldn't last. Once she stopped moving long enough to let the poor monkey man go to the bathroom, smoke a cigarette, or simply breathe, the customer lost interest, nine times out of ten, and Pen would return to the stage with little more than a hundred baht tip and a hearty thank you.

This time was only slightly different.

The foreigner Jack appeared well on his way to falling under the spell of Pen's lap-dance, and she seemed to be working extra hard to get him there. She had reached the part of her charm in which she held her face steady before the customer's and emulated the expressions of a woman about to climax. Jack averted his eyes for a moment, just a moment, and caught sight of Mantana. The intensity with which he watched her on stage returned to his eyes as he locked them upon her. Close like this, without the separation of music and lights, his gaze made her feel strange, as though he were searching for someone else that was alive inside her. Maybe he saw a sister or an ex-girlfriend the same way Mantana used to see her mother in Phii Aor.

That was all Pen could take. As soon as she noticed that she was no longer the object of Jack's desire, she bounced from his lap and walked away, turning only to shoot a pair of hissing snake eyes at her rival.

Mantana didn't know what to say. She presented the check to him on her silver tray and waited as the man from New York pulled out a leather wallet from his back pocket.

"Are you here every night?" he asked, avoiding her eyes as if afraid to look again.

"Sunday no."

He laid two one-hundred-baht bills on the one-hundred-eighty baht tab, then another hundred on top of that. It was only when he stood that she could tell he was drunk.

"You can keep that," he said. "Or split it with your friend, I don't care."

Mantana swallowed. It was now or never. "Why happy you no have?"

A small, unnecessary smile flashed across his face. "I guess I just haven't met the right girl," he said, and walked out of the bar. Mantana watched him go, wondering if she had spoken correctly. The sound of her name snapped her back into the here and now.

"Joy!" called the voice again from the far end of the stage. It was Neung. She was dancing in a pair of neon green bikini underwear. "Tell Sai she's up after this song."

Someone was always having to tell Sai she was up. Mantana took the silver tray to the bar and slid the hundred-baht note into her own bikini top. Fifty belonged to Pen. She'd give it to her as soon as she cooled down.

The shells of watermelon seeds crunched beneath her feet. The girls were still standing there, cracking them with their teeth.

"Do you work somewhere?" Mantana asked the one with the tattoos.

The woman looked at her but didn't answer. Ale took the silver tray and exchanged glances with her.

"These girls shouldn't be here," said Mantana.

"I know," said Ale. "Did you find out why your customer was sad?"

"No," she said. "But I have the feeling that he's always sad."

"Why do you think that?"

"It's in his eyes."

*

When Mantana saw that Sai was in the arms of a sailor, she

was more forgiving of her for missing her cue. Sailors were the worst. They usually haunted the larger, fast food style places like Lana A-Go-Go and Homework, though they occasionally found their way to the smaller sois and darker doorways. The sailors were young. They roamed in packs. Where there was one, four or five others could not be far behind. They were the most impolite of all their customers and seemed incapable of exiting the bar without leaving their mark, either with some wild and offensive gesture towards the girls, or a drunken act of violence toward an employee or another customer. Nevertheless, until they gave themselves a reason to be thrown out, they were paying customers, and had to be treated as such.

This one sat against the wall in one of the two-person sofas, his shirt open and lack of sobriety apparent. Sai looked at Mantana and raised her eyebrows. She knew, she knew, but what could she do? The sailor's arm was locked tightly around her and his face pushed against her small breasts. Mantana tapped him on the shoulder, once, twice, and a third time. The sailor raised his head and looked at her, angrily.

"She must go to dancing!" said Mantana.

All he had to do was tell her to fuck off or try to push her away. Then she could get Ad to "escort" him out. Ad was the bouncer. He was the biggest Thai man Mantana had ever seen. Ad had a receding hairline and a face like a pouting baby. It was probably due to this that his toughness was often called into question. She once saw him take a punch from a sailor, laugh, and punch back. That was the end of the sailor. This one wasn't as stupid. He wiped the angry look from his face and removed his arm from Sai.

"I come back," she said, and ran off to get ready for her show.

The sailor took hold of Mantana's hand and belched out a *sit down*, or something to that extent. Mantana sat. Maybe she could get a lady drink out of him before he got too rude.

"What you name?" she asked.

"Jerry."

Jerry had fat, ugly lips and eyes drawn too dark upon his face. He reminded her of a *likay* performer, made up to look like someone both real and unreal.

"Where you come from?"

"You see," said Jerry, "I've got this friend, lived in Bangkok for three years and he's never paid for it once."

Mantana looked at her knees. He wasn't answering her questions.

"He says -" the sailor hiccupped, "he says donut shops and public buses are better than any whore bar."

The song that had been playing ended and another, romantic one began. The stage lights dimmed as Neung and two other dancers walked off and Sai, alone, walked on. The first thing she did was sit down, then roll back to remove her bikini bottoms without bending a knee. It was an indication that she had something hidden inside her. She took off her top and started to dance. She danced by holding onto a steel pole and twirling herself around it. After three or four twirls, she reached between her legs and pinched the end of a pink ribbon with her fingertips. The ribbon unfurled from within her as she pulled. She tied the end to one of the silver poles and danced to the next. The ribbon changed colors as it slid out of her.

"I ain't looking for no dumb whore," said Jerry the sailor. "I'm on the make for an educated girl. And I don't need to pay for it, no way."

He spat as he said the word "pay." Mantana felt it against her shoulder.

"My friend in Bangkok, he says all the really hot college babes hang out in donut shops, like I was just saying. They go there to meet foreigners and hope that they'll get hit on. Plus, they're in a donut shop. You know, it's so much more natural than a go-go bar. I mean, these girls are *real*. They're like *real* Thai girls. So what you do is, go to a donut shop and pick one out. Smile, maybe say hello. Then when she's all done drinking her soda pop and chit chatting with her friends, BAM! You follow her out the door, onto a bus. Those buses in Bangkok are crowded, right? So all you gotta do is inch your way through the crowd until you're stuck tight against the babe of your dreams. Then let nature do the rest. Woo! Ha ha!"

The sailor leaned back in the sofa and yelled "Woo!" again. He was very excited. He wiped his nose with the back of his hand and reached for his beer.

"So," he said. "Do you ever go to donut shops?"

On stage, the ribbon was almost completely unraveled. It formed a multi-colored zigzag along the six steel poles and glowed eerily in the black lights. Across the bar, she noticed Pen watching her with a wicked smile on her lips. Pen knew all about sailors, probably better than any of them. When the song ended, three hundred baht, so did the dance, and Mantana applauded as Sai loosened a knot and the colorful pattern fluttered from the poles. Sai wrapped a towel around herself, and left the stage.

"I go dancing," said Mantana.

"No, wait a minute," said the sailor. "Touch me here, just once, will you?"

"Dancing."

Mantana stood. The sailor didn't try to stop her. She went in back, past the toilets, to a tiny dressing room with only a blue curtain for privacy. Sai moved down to let her in.

"Did you get a drink off the sailor?" she asked.

"No," said Mantana. "He just talked. I didn't understand a word he said."

"Well, I'm not sitting with him anymore. He kept asking me to feel his *koey*. And when I did, there was nothing there!"

They both giggled at this.

2

Neung was doing well. She had herself an old fellow with a hearing aid who seemed to be giving her no trouble at all. When she asked for a lady drink, he bought her one. When she asked for another, he bought her another. All the while watching her like a dish of ice cream that lay just beyond his reach. In a little while, he would most likely buy her out and take her to his hotel room and give her a relatively painless fucking. Mantana was glad to see that she had found someone of a less brutal nature than her past few customers had displayed. Still, one never knew. The smiling old man might just want to put his thing in her behind like her Tuesday night, or throw a fit when he couldn't ejaculate like her Thursday night. One never knew.

It was Mantana's turn on stage. She was one of four girls in a line. In the beginning, dancing was the easy part. Dancing meant she wouldn't have to sit with a customer. She wouldn't have to smile and hold his sweaty hand and listen to his voice grow louder in an attempt to make her understand what he was saying. Only now, with money no longer a dream but genuine and real, things were different. The job was the job was the job, and dancing on the catwalk was a waste of time. What, with all those men out there! All those fat wallets! *Don't forget why you're here*. Phii Buoy was right. It was better to be on the floor, on the hustle. Besides, she sometimes thought that showing off her breasts worked against, rather than for her. It killed the mystery of what lay behind her bikini. And Mantana knew, as any working girl with half a brain knew; mystery, lies, fake orgasm, and the bizarre idea of love were all that a girl had to keep a man coming back for more. The rest was just push there, jerk here, hair, sweat and semen.

When her three songs were up, Mantana returned to the dressing room. Phii Buoy was there waiting for her. She was dressed in a tight red dress with matching lipstick. Phii Buoy wasn't available to customers. She only looked that way.

"The man you were sitting with wants to buy you out."

"Jack?" she asked, with a hope that made her wonder about her attraction to the handsome Romeo.

"The sailor."

Mantana sighed. The sailor. He would paw her, try to kiss her on the mouth, knock over the bedside lamp on his way to the toilet, then pass out five minutes before or after sticking his thing in her. And when he awoke the next morning, he'd refuse to pay. Mantana had been with four sailors. They were all the same.

"I don't want to take any chances getting my money from him," said Mantana. "Tell him it's one thousand baht to buy me out."

"That's a pretty big bar fee."

"If he doesn't like it, tell him those girls at the bar will go for a bag of watermelon seeds."

"They've already been told to leave," said Phii Buoy. "They weren't ours."

Mantana nodded. They frequently got girls off the street that came in and tried to hustle customers. Their trick was to pretend they were bar girls, and collect the three-hundred baht fee for buying them out. They then disappeared with the money, leaving the customer waiting. And waiting. And waiting.

Mantana finished dressing and opened the curtain.

"Then tell him I've got AIDS. Tell him anything. I'm sick of sailors."

"Fine. I'll send Pen over to keep him company."

Mantana froze. She was about to give in and agree to go with the sailor, really she was, only Phii Buoy was a little bit angry with Mantana's stubborn behavior and turned her back on her just as soon as the words had left her mouth. Mantana rushed to stop her and nearly crashed into Neung coming out of the women's toilet.

"Joy! The old man is buying me out! And guess which hotel he's at."

"Which hotel?"

"The Pattaya Somersinn!"

Neung clapped her hands, then gave her a big hug. Mantana groaned as Neung squeezed her in her arms.

"Not now!" said Mantana. "Let go of me!"

Neung released her and looked questioningly into her eyes.

"Are you all right?" she asked.

"I'm so stupid," said Mantana. "I told Phii Buoy that I wouldn't go with that drunk sailor out there and now she's going to send Pen over to take care of him."

"So what's the problem? Pen certainly doesn't care. She'll sleep with Arabs and Indians as long as they pay. Look."

Neung stepped aside to allow Mantana to gaze through the smoke and the lights. Pen was standing before the sailor, rubbing her legs together like a boy scout trying to light a fire. The sailor lay sprawled out on the sofa as if dropped there from a great height. His arm moved, his head turned, and Pen was on him. A fly in the web of a hungry spider had a better chance of survival.

Mantana twirled a strand of hair around her finger.

"*Dham jai bhak bhen moo,*" said Neung. "*Dham jai joo bhen Aids.*"

She was referring to the sailor. Do as the mouth pleases, you're a pig. Do as the cock wishes, you're AIDS. Mantana didn't believe that Pen was sick. Phii Buoy wouldn't have allowed her to work if she was.

"She's going to think I did it on purpose. She's going to think I told Phii Buoy to send her over to him."

"Why would she think that?" asked Neung. "And besides, what does it matter?"

Another smile lit up Neung's face. Joy's story was over and hers had begun again. She had to go. Mantana wished her luck and watched her rush off to change into her street clothes. What could she do? She didn't want to make an enemy of Pen, but she had a feeling the damage was beyond repair.

Then she had an idea.

What if she found the most heinous, fat, and despicable foreigner in the bar and threw herself at him? Not for long, just until Pen was bought out for the night. If Pen saw her sitting in the lap of someone worse than the sailor, wouldn't that make up for things a little? It was worth a try. Mantana excused herself through the bar, carefully staying out of the sailor's.line of sight, and searched for a grotesque to flirt with. It was still early, not even ten o'clock, and most of the sofas and stools were still waiting to be filled.

She found one.

He was about fifty, oversized, and wet with sweat. A regular. He sat in the corner, drinking soda pop from a straw, watching, nodding, waiting for a heart attack for all anyone knew. He came about twice a week, always paying his bill with the right amount, and never spending more than one hundred baht. The girls had given up on him. They just let him sit. An identification tag that he wore around his neck said that his name was "Kevin." One night when he called out for a soda pop, the nearest girl said to a waitress, "Crazy Kevin wants another," and the name stuck. At least until a short, muscular man with a face like a burnt brick came in and announced to everyone that he was indeed "Crazy" Kevin McCormick. This Crazy Kevin drank beers straight from the pitcher while his friends cheered him on. This Crazy Kevin took his shirt off and got up on stage to dance with some of the girls. Mantana left with another man before she got to see Ad walk him to the exit, but after that, no one referred to the fat and sweaty man in the corner as "Crazy Kevin" anymore. They just called him "Kevin."

Disco lights and disco music ricocheted off the walls and ceiling and floor as Mantana made her way to the man in the corner. It wouldn't be the first time she had sat with him. Many girls abided by the "creepy but paying" customer rule and gave him at least one chance to change their minds about him. Kevin had yet to change a single mind in the bar.

"Hello, what you name?" said Mantana, sitting down beside him.

Kevin shrugged his shoulders once, twice, and a third time. He spoke without looking at her. "Bed's not made," he said. "Sergeant says bed's not made."

Mantana sniffed and turned away. Kevin stank. She took a deep breath and tried again.

"My name Joy. Where are you come from?"

"Sergeant says I have to bounce a case quarter. Bed's not made until you can bounce a case quarter. That's what the sergeant says."

The man's hands played some wild game in his lap. He was rapidly touching his fingertips together in different combinations - thumb to forefinger, pinkie to ring, middle to thumb. What first seemed like a series of random movements soon revealed itself to have a definite pattern. It was hypnotizing, in a way.

"Sheets have to be tight."

Beads of perspiration appeared on his forehead. The faster he went, the more he sweated. Some of the beads started to roll down his cheeks.

"Do you like to buy me some drink?" said Mantana, nervously.

"SODA POP!"

Kevin's hands came to a sudden stop upon his knees. It was only a moment before a young waitress brought a soda pop to him on a tray and exchanged it for the empty one on the table. She slid another bill into the plastic cup, looked at Mantana, and walked away. Kevin's next round of concentration went into drinking the soda pop.

Mantana looked toward the sofa where the sailor lay. He was alone again, with his elbows on his knees and his shoulders slumped low. A white sailor's cap sat crooked on his head. He seemed to be trying to remember something. Where he was. What happened to his friends. Why he wasn't at sea. Then he raised his eyes, saw the topless bodies on stage, saw the flashing lights, saw the three Japanese men who had just come in, and lowered them again.

"Are you looking for me?"

Mantana turned her head. Pen stood before her in street clothes. She wore a pink miniskirt and a tight black pullover with a cartoon kitten's face upon it. A small, plastic purse was slung over her shoulder. Mantana couldn't tell whether there was a sneer across her face or it was just the way she had applied her lipstick.

"I've got someone for you," said Pen.

"I'm with someone already."

The man sitting next to her had begun his finger game again. He muttered to himself about bed sheets and case quarters as a new coat of sweat broke out upon his face.

"This is someone special," said Pen, with a sarcasm that

indicated that she had the upper hand in whatever game that she was playing. "You've never seen him before. In fact, no one has."

Pen held out a business card. It was from the Prince Hotel. She turned it around to show Mantana the back. *Room 515, 11:00* was written there in red ink. Mantana knew what it meant. Mr. Simmons had some kind of deal with the owners of the Prince Hotel. Whenever a guest requested a woman sent to his room, the hotel manager telephoned the Cherry Bar. The prices for a room service girl were double what they were in the bar and girls were only allowed three hours, which meant customers often skimped on the tip. In the month and a half that Mantana had been working, she had only been called once. It was by a Thai businessman who had to catch a plane the next morning and didn't want to waste time socializing. He was rough and cheap, but she walked away undamaged. Other girls had not been so lucky and returned with stories of handcuffs, three on one sessions, and outright refusals to pay. There was nothing more dangerous than walking into a hotel room blind. All the girls had developed a sixth sense of reading customers. Without this unique foresight, walking into the Prince was like throwing oneself into a river before checking to see how deep the water ran.

"I don't want it," said Mantana.

"Well, you'd better take it. Phii Buoy herself told me to give it to you."

"That's a lie!"

"You go and ask her, Nong Joy."

Mantana snatched the card from her hand and got to her feet. She moved past Pen and walked to the DJ's booth where Phii Buoy stood talking to a young man in sunglasses. She didn't have to say a word. She just held up the card and waited for an answer. Phii Buoy looked at her, still a little peeved.

"It's The Prince or the sailor," she said. "I can't let you wait for a movie star to come strolling in."

"Why did Pen have to give it to me?"

"Because my husband gave it to her an hour ago. When the sailor wanted to buy her out, she wanted to know what to do about her eleven o'clock appointment. I told her to give it to you. I think that's fair, don't you?"

Eleven o'clock. That was less than an hour away. Phii Buoy told her she could get dressed and take a shower first. Then she was off to the bar where Mr. Simmons stood punching receipt totals into an adding machine, a pair of reading glasses perched on the end of his nose. From the raised platform of the DJ's booth, Mantana's eyes went from one scene to another. It all looked like a bad soap opera she was forced to play a part in. In one of the sofas sat Neung, dressed in her street clothes and wearing a frown upon her face. She held the old man's hearing aid in her hand and spoke into it like a microphone. "We go now!" she told him. The old man looked at her as if he didn't know what she was talking about. Go? Go where?

Against the opposite wall, Pen's sailor had woken up and exploded, as sailors were known to do. Over the check, over his missing shipmates, over anything and everything that came to mind, boom. A hand job was quieting him down, though the expression in his eyes was ugly drunken rage. Mantana's anger fell back into pity as she saw what Pen had to deal with.

Meanwhile, the Japanese men along the catwalk had all found - or been found by - girls. One of the girls was tattooed Kay with her wide, flat face. Mantana didn't recognize the other. The Japanese men were very serious looking. They kept one hand around their beer glasses and one hand on their knees. No speaking, just sitting. The girls smiled and petted their shoulders and waited for a loving response. Then another girl, a girl named Pookie from somewhere in the South, walked by and ran a fingernail across everyone's back. Pookie didn't have to sit with a Japanese man. She had gotten lucky in the hand throw. Scissors cut paper, rock broke scissors, paper covered rock. Pookie didn't have to sit with a Japanese man.

On stage, the second act was about to begin. This girl was called Wan. She was a small, sickly thing with a lazy eye and a pierced nipple. She kept her shoulder length hair over as much of her face as was possible. Wan removed her panties and set a tall drinking glass down on the catwalk. A girl on the floor handed her a small bucket filled with ping pong balls, and the boy in the DJ booth turned down the heavy disco beat. Wan loaded, then stood over the glass. She spread her legs as far as they would go and loosened her stomach muscles. Some of the balls made it into the glass, others hit the rim and bounced around the stage. All the men in the bar, dark slacks, brown belts, button-down shirts, expensive wristwatches, gray-be-gone hair, and cigarette-stained everything, watched the pussy of the girl on stage. Neung's old man, yet to get out of his seat, watched the pussy of the girl on stage. Pen's angry sailor, reverting back into the dopey-eyed kid that he was, watched the pussy of the girl on stage. Even sweaty Kevin had stopped playing his finger game long enough to watch the pussy of the girl on stage.

Wan dropped twelve balls in all, reloading only three times. When she finished, she wrapped a towel around her middle and carried her glass and her bucket and her panties off the stage. The Japanese businessmen applauded. The music went up again.

There is a pla-ace
A place we can go
A place called hea-ven
I think you should know

Mantana watched another pair of dancers take to the catwalk, each holding a piece of fruit in her hand. This was the Lady Love Banana show. Mantana chose not to watch. She stepped down from the DJ's booth and moved to the back of the bar. Mr. Simmons stood blocking the entrance to the dressing rooms with a dazed expression on his face.

"Excuse me," said Mantana.

He snapped back to the here and now and stepped aside to let her pass.

"Mr. Simmons *sabai dee mai*?"

"I've got a girl on stage shooting bananas across my sophisticated gentlemen's club," he said. "Of course I'm not *sabai*."

Mantana's clothes were kept in a locker just past the dressing room. She took them out, and went behind the blue curtains to get ready for her next appointment. Skirt, top, lipstick, she was almost finished when Neung appeared.

"Come in," said Mantana. "Close the curtain."

There was a beaten and weary look in her eyes. She entered the dressing room and collapsed on a hard wooden stool.

"I'm back to work," she said.

"What happened to the Somersinn?"

Neung shook her head. "The old fucker had no idea I wanted money from him. He thought I was just being nice."

"I didn't think people like that existed anymore."

"He said I could come to his room for tea in the morning with his wife and fourteen-year old daughter."

Mantana sighed. Neung cracked a smile and the two of them couldn't help giggling over the thought of Neung sitting down for tea with a foreign family.

"How are you doing?" she asked.

Mantana showed her the card.

"Aw, Joy, not the Prince!"

"Phii Buoy's angry that I turned down the sailor. I think she's letting Pen get a little revenge, too."

"But The Prince! The Prince is awful!"

Mantana shrugged her shoulders. There wasn't anything she could do.

"I'll be back by closing. We'll go have a drink if you're still here."

"Just hope you don't get the Frenchman," said Neung.

3

The man in room 515 was named Gilbert, and he came from Paris. He was in his forties, black hair, black mustache, and eyes so blue, Mantana wondered if they were real. He answered the door wearing a dress shirt and necktie, pulled loose around the collar. And he smelled good. Too good, thought Mantana. Too polite. The stories must be true.

"But you're so beautiful!" said Gilbert, welcoming her in. "*Tres belle!* They never send girls as beautiful as you!"

Mantana walked cautiously to the bed and sat down. The room was nicer than many hotel rooms she had been in, with carpeted floors and pictures of Phang-Nga Bay nailed to the wall. There was a small refrigerator and a television near the window.

"Would you care for a beer?" asked Gilbert. "Or a wine cooler? My God, woman, you are absolutely gorgeous!"

"Water," said Mantana.

"Of course!"

Gilbert opened the refrigerator and took out a bottle of water. He was so excited, he fumbled the glass in his hands and nearly dropped it.

"You must excuse me," he said. "This is my Christmas morning. My wedding night. This is the highlight of my life. I loved you the moment I ordered you. This is the only time I am truly happy."

He poured the water into the glass and handed it to her.

"Back in Paris, things are much different. I have my job, my books, I even have women, but nothing compares to the joy of being locked in a hotel room with a girl such as yourself. A gold-skinned maiden who doesn't understand a word I'm saying."

Mantana sipped her water. If talking was the worst of his faults, the next three hours wouldn't be so terrible.

"I have a little friend," he continued, pacing the room now. "He lives here, behind my ear. I haven't seen the little dickens's face, so I can't tell you whether he's an angel or a devil. My *petit ami* speaks on behalf of what you might call my conscience. He tells me things like 'Gilbert! Sleeping with prostitutes is wrong! You must stop!' ha ha. He asks 'Why don't you settle down with a nice French girl and stop taking all these trips to Pattaya?' And do you know what I say to my little friend? I say 'Anyone can get married! Anyone can have a family!' I sincerely believe that it takes a man to discover his pleasure in life and pursue this happiness for as long as he is able! Until there is nothing left to do but die! Die with a big fucking smile on his face!"

The Frenchman stood before her with a big smile on his face. His eyes went up and down her body like a tailor measuring her for a suit of clothes.

"You poor thing. This can't be enjoyable for you," he said. "But let's not think about that part."

He kneeled down and looked her in the eye.

"Have you had an AIDS test?"

"I no AIDS," said Mantana. At last, something she understood.

"Because I don't like to wear a condom. Do you understand? No condom."

Mantana felt a knot tighten in her stomach.

"You no have condom," she said, trying to get the words to come out right, "I no sex you."

"Ha!" said the Frenchman. "You passed!"

He took a small box of condoms out of his shirt pocket and set it on the bedside table.

"You're so lovely," he said, getting to his feet again. "You make me wish I could say something to you. But no! No, no, no! Communication only leads to misunderstanding and there must be no misunderstanding between us. Misunderstanding leads to jealousy... distrust... dishonesty. And at its worst -"

Gilbert paused and looked at her from the corners of his eyes.

"Nuclear war!"

Mantana took another drink of water.

"Do you know the story of the Tower of Babel? No, probably not. But I'll tell you something. The Lord God was doing those idiots a favor by tying their tongues and scattering them around the world. Just think of the gift he had bestowed upon his creation! The inability to communicate! Allowing each and every one of us to decide on our own what is beautiful and what is not. What constitutes music and art. What makes up love and happiness. Then we had to go and ruin it by inventing languages. Common tongues - *ack!* Now it's television and textbooks and thousands upon thousands of brainwashed zombies that make our minds up for us. I won't have it! I'm at home with my own reasoning. I trust my own judgment. If I say the earth is flat, it's flat, end of story. *Fini.* And what's all this fuss over nature? I abhor nature! Give me a good city block any day of the week. I suppose I've got a little of Baudelaire in my soul. But you wouldn't know about such matters, would you? You, you... My God I want to kiss you!"

The Frenchman moved close and puckered his lips to kiss her. He undid them suddenly and pulled back to look at her.

"We live in such a terribly unimaginative world," he said.

Mantana assumed it was time. Gilbert gave her a towel and robe and let her shower alone. When she came out again, he instructed her to sit on the bed and please don't turn on the TV and wait just a moment while he too, showered. Mantana sat. Gilbert went into the bathroom and closed the door. Then he began to sing.

There was a glass bowl on the bedside table that the condoms lay next to. It didn't look as though it belonged to the hotel. Mantana leaned over and looked inside. A dark red powder covered the bottom of the bowl, like ground chilies, only finer. Mantana sniffed. The powder had no smell. A knock upon the door startled her.

"Gee-bert!"

"What?"

"People come visiting you!"

"Oh no, no, no," said Gilbert. "That's just room service. I told them to come fifteen minutes after you arrived. Could you get it for me, please?"

Another knock.

"*Gok gok*," said Mantana.

"What?"

"*Gok gok* on a door."

The bathroom door opened. A cloud of steam and the Frenchman's wet head and mustache appeared.

"It's room service, do you understand? It's all right. Just open the door. Open the door."

Mantana nodded. She went to the door and opened it. A hotel attendant stood in the hallway holding a silver pitcher and a wooden spoon on a tray. The attendant was in his early twenties and regarded her as most Thai men regarded her while she was on the clock - as if they too could have her if they so wanted, but didn't, of course, because they had better things to do. Mantana took the silver pitcher from the tray. It was hot. The attendant nodded his head in a reverse direction to indicate that he had performed his duties, then closed the door. Mantana set the pitcher and the spoon next to the bowl. She had a feeling they went together.

Gilbert finished showering, and came out of the bathroom.

"Excellent!" he said. "Everything's in order. And you're even more stunning out of those silly clothes."

Wearing a white hotel robe, Gilbert walked to the bedside table and tested the water in the pitcher by inserting his index finger. He then poured the contents of the pitcher into the bowl and stirred.

"This should be cooled by the time we - ah, by the time I'm ready. You see, I'm not the type that simply gets what he pays for. When I purchase a toaster, I want that toaster to sing opera while it's browning my bread. When I buy an electric can opener, I insist upon one that can vacuum my carpet as well. And you, you ode on a Grecian urn, you're going to give me pleasure beyond whatever price tag is attached to you."

Gilbert held the bowl before her. The powder had dissolved into a thick red liquid that still gave off wisps of steam in the air-conditioned room.

"This is where I gag the angel or devil behind my ear and have so much fun, it's going to feel like crazy monkeys are bursting from my head!"

Gilbert set down the bowl and kneeled before Mantana. He lifted a hand and stroked her face.

"For the next two hours and twenty minutes, I am Gilbert the Gypsy and you are Esmerelda, my virgin queen."

He screwed up his face and shook his head violently.

"No, no. You're too young to be a queen. You're a princess! A virgin princess. *Ack!* to hell with royalty. Royalty would know how to speak English. All right, I'm a pirate and you're a native from Tahiti. You've been out gathering coconuts all morning and I'm the dirty, unshaven pirate man with scurvy and dysentery and pieces of eight. No? No. Never mind the pirate routine. Let's try this. You come from the Planet of Love located in the Galaxy of Passion. Yes? Of course, there's no men on your world, everyone reproduces by - oh, how should I know? The point is, you're here now. You've come seeking..."

Gilbert stroked his mustache as his eyes darted wildly in their sockets.

"Sex!" he said.

"Sex," said Mantana.

Sex, they agreed.

*

With a series of elaborate hand gestures, Mantana finally understood what she was supposed to do with the red stuff in the bowl. And when the talking Frenchman on top of her raised the upper part of his body and yelled "Now!" she followed his instructions and poured the warm goo on her stomach.

"Oh!" he said, pressing himself upon her. "Look at that! I'm making love to a virgin! Look at all the blood! You naughty girl, why didn't you tell me that you were a virgin? Be careful that you don't get any on the walls!"

*

Mantana's three hours were up. She showered and dressed and smoked a cigarette while the Frenchman lay in bed, staring up at the ceiling. The sheets were ruined.

"I'm so depressed!" said Gilbert. "The first girl I ever made love to was a virgin. Beatrice. Bloody Beatrice. I never knew a human being could lose so much blood and still be home by ten. It was on the sheets, on the floor, on our shoes. It was everywhere! It was glorious!"

"I must to -"

"Shh!" he said. "Don't speak."

He sat up slowly and wrapped the scarlet-stained sheet around his middle.

"Pants," he said.

Mantana handed him his pants. He removed a thousand baht note, then another, and gave them to her. Mantana looked at the money, stunned.

"It's a lot," said Gilbert. "I don't usually give out so much. Girls might take me for an cash machine. But I have a feeling about you. You're good. Not at what you do, you're just good."

They sat looking at each other until the Frenchman's lower lip trembled and his voice broke.

"Go! Before I ask for your name!"

Mantana put out her cigarette and picked up her purse on the way to the door.

"I should have been born a pirate!" cried the Frenchman. "At least then I'd have a fucking parrot to keep me company!"

Mantana closed the door behind her. She took the elevator down and got off on the ground floor. The hotel attendant who had delivered the hot water was manning the front doors.

"How's the room?" he asked.

"It's fine."

"That's good. Last week we had to repaint the walls."

Mantana left the Prince Hotel. It was two a.m.

4

Fucking customers was not the worst part about being a prostitute, Mantana decided one afternoon, over a gin and tonic in her apartment. Fucking customers was the worst part about *becoming* a prostitute. But now that she was one, the worst parts were the memories, definitely the memories of fucking customers. It was not a hundred and one play-by-plays that attacked her mind, it was more like the Funniest Home Videos TV show she sometimes watched, with the Thai voices dubbed over the English. The show often had three to five-minute segments of different scenes spliced together from tapes sent in by viewers. And something went wrong in every scene. Sometimes it was a little thing, like a man answering a telephone the wrong way and placing the mouthpiece against his ear. Other times, people fell into lakes or drove their cars into mailboxes. These were things that probably weren't so funny at the time, but suddenly hilarious when looked back upon. That's how Mantana saw her hotel room nights - in bits and pieces that at the time meant nothing to her, but seen from afar, spliced together scene after scene, made her want to run to the bathroom and wash herself, no matter how clean she already was. There was the time an old man's teeth fell out of his mouth when he came. The time a customer asked her to swing a big pink hula hoop around her hips as he masturbated. The time a man got a bloody nose, the time she noticed shit stains on the sheets, the time a customer asked if his girlfriend could watch. It was all there without music or laughter or fade-out to commercial.

So were the depressing butts, the hairy backs, the animal noises, the alien nipples, the accidental farts, and the Oh My God look on the customers's faces when they shot their loads into the condom inside her. It was a look that reminded her of a blind fool named Worapoch that the monks used to care for at a temple outside her village. At least until he threw himself off the roof of a house, holding only a broken fan and his pants.

"It's yellow!" he used to cry, and pulled out a tooth when no one agreed with him.

Worapoch's joyous non-joy was in the customers's faces, and it was in her ugly memories as well. Mantana had enough rotten hotel room clips to fill a thirty-minute television program. In another six weeks, she'd be able to run a full hour's worth through her head. She thought about the girls who had been prostitutes for years and years. Did new scenes replace the old ones? Did one hanging bag of balls become the sight of all hanging bags of balls? Or did they pile up like garbage?

"Think of the money, Joy," she said to herself when the gloom threatened to obliterate her. "Think of the money."

The money was good. There was no question about it. In the mere nine weeks that she had been working, she had been able to send her father nearly ten thousand baht. More than enough to buy a few things to show for himself, and hopefully replace the junk that Amnuay moved in with. She was keeping the promise that she made to her mother, and that was reason enough to go on.

She mixed herself another gin and tonic.

The next day, she turned twenty.

*

About a week after Mantana had received her windfall from the Frenchman, the handsome movie star Jack showed his face in the bar again. The sight of him made her smile, although she knew it was foolish to develop crushes on customers. And besides, she was already sitting with one. It was bad form to just up and leave. She looked around to see who would take him. She didn't look long. Pen came in from outside and flew to the seat next to his like the butterfly girl that she was. Their silly feud had been over and done with for a week, but the score had obviously yet to be settled for Pen. This seemed to be the opportunity she was waiting for. Against her wishes, Neung had gone and told everyone about Mantana's two thousand baht night with the Frenchman Gilbert. Two thousand baht that "would have been Pen's" if Mantana hadn't "stolen" her customer away that night and left her to a drunk sailor. Or so Pen said. If being bought out by Jack was her way of getting back at Mantana, so be it. Let her go with him every night of the week! What did it matter to her?

Mantana cursed the butterfly girl under her breath and crossed her legs on the barstool.

The man she sat with had yet to buy her a drink. He was American with a horseshoe of hair fitted around his head and long black hairs sprouting from his nose. His eyes were round like buttons. He drank orange juice and looked up words in a dictionary to use in questions for her. He had a lot of questions. His questions didn't make any sense. Mantana wished he'd lean back so she could get a better view of Jack and Pen.

"*Mee pop mai?*" said the American.

Mantana looked at the word in the dictionary. *Baap.* Sin. Do you have sin? Mantana shook her head. Next word. *Na-rok.*

Hell. Mantana pointed to herself and said;

"Buddha."

"Buddhist," he repeated, and quickly looked up another word. It was one she already knew. *Sopaynee.* Prostitute. The man looked at her as though he were waiting for an answer.

"You *farang*," said Mantana, growing tired of his questions. "I am Thai. Not same same."

The man pointed to the word again and looked at her. Normally, she would have excused herself for the bathroom and waited for another girl to take her place before coming out again. Only she didn't want to make herself available with Jack at the bar and Pen in his lap. She might be tempted to run a fingernail across his back or smile in his direction. She might be tempted to steal him away. Cheap Charlie with the eyes like buttons asked another question from his dictionary. Mantana overheard Phii Buoy's voice behind her and turned to get her attention. Phii Buoy had once told the girls that she would help with whatever language problems they had, so long as they tried to work them out on their own first.

"What is it, Joy?" she said in English.

"This man wants to know -"

"In English, Joy."

Mantana screwed up her face and flattened her tongue. "He wanting know why I am Thai girl."

Phii Buoy looked at the American. "What is your question?"

"This girl claims to be a Buddhist, but she's a prostitute. And everyone knows prostitution is a sin. That's a fact of life, no matter which religion you belong to."

"I am Thai," said Mantana.

"That's the answer she gave me," said the man. "Which isn't really an answer at all now, is it?"

Phii Buoy spoke slowly and politely. "When Joy says that she is Thai, it is not the same as when you call yourself American. I have been to your country and wondered why people called themselves

American when everyone was so different. Not just color of skin, but customs and beliefs too. Then my husband told me that these differences are what makes America strong. He said America is like a big shouting competition, and the winners are the ones whose voices are heard above all the rest. In Thailand, it is not the same. We are joined by our King, our religion, our culture, and our rice. It is our common bonds that keep us gentle and unified. It's true, Joy is what you say she is, but she will continue to love the King, make merit at the temple, and eat rice. She will still be Thai. Does that answer your question?"

"Partly," said the American. "Would you mind doing me a favor? Would you translate what I say from English into Thai for this young lady?"

"Certainly."

"Could you tell her that, despite what you said about how un-Thai it is to step out of each other's footsteps, I have some very good news for her."

Phii Buoy turned to Mantana and translated. "Joy, I have some news for you."

"There's a man named Jesus Christ who loves her so much that he once gave his life for her on the cross so that she would never have to feel alone or misunderstood or sinful again."

Mantana looked at Phii Buoy. She translated;

"Joy, when you're finished here, I want you to go outside and try to bring customers in. The Titan Bar has some kind of dog show that's taking a lot of our business."

The American continued, "Tell her that no matter how far down she sinks, this man will be there to lift her up and let her know that she is one of God's special children."

"Also," said Phii Buoy, "the Love Me bar on Soi Pattaya One just got a fish tank. They're advertising a real live mermaid."

"Finally, tell her that if she does not accept the love that Christ offers, she'll be spending an eternity in hell, where the devil lives, instead of in heaven with all God's angels."

"Go as soon as he gives you his book," said Phii Buoy. "You're wasting your time sitting here with him."

"He's going to give me a book?"

"I think she understands," Phii Buoy told the American. Then she nodded to Mantana and walked away.

As if on cue, the American reached into a green knapsack and pulled out a book.

"Let me give you this," he said. "It's printed in English and Thai. Read it in your spare time. There's a phone number in back."

Mantana took the blue, plastic-bound book from his hands and looked at it. A real live mermaid, she thought. Wow!

Mantana said good night and walked away from the man at the bar.

*

Mantana took the long way around the catwalk on her way to the velvet curtains. Pen and Jack were still together. She could see Pen laughing and running her fingernails across his shoulders. She could see Jack with his eternal look of contemplation. Pen raised her arms in a cat-like stretch and lowered them around his neck. Jack kept his eyes upon Pen's lipstick lips and orange bangs and glistening skin. This time, he didn't bother to shift his gaze when Mantana passed by. Just another customer, she decided. Just like all the rest. This thought only made her angrier for some reason.

Outside the air felt hot and sticky. Two girls from the Cherry, Yim and Pookie, sat on stools cooing and calling to passing tourists. Their voices were fishing poles, their bodies were the bait. Across the narrow soi, girls from the Titan were doing the same. Only one of the Titan girls, a short, wiry-haired thing dressed in a white swimsuit, kept running out from the boundaries of the bar to attach herself to men's arms. She pulled neckties and slapped bottoms and danced in the soi as if she were drunk. She wasn't just fishing. She was fishing with dynamite.

"She's taken in five men since we've been out here," said Yim.

"She's letting men feel her up right on the street," said Pookie.

Mantana caught the girl's narrow eyes from across the soi. She had a small, upturned nose and puckered lips. She had the face of a rat. Mantana averted her eyes, though she still felt the girl watching her.

"Hello! Handsome man!" called girls from both sides as a pair of tall, blond men appeared from around the corner. "Sex-ee man!" The cries and whistles started with the Cherry and Titan girls and followed the men as they passed the Wildflower, the Bronco, and the Happy Beat Beat Bar. They could be heard all the way to the opposite corner, ending in the call of an Indian man in a turban who stood outside his shop yelling "Handsome suits, *for you!*"

"I'll be right back."

Mantana disappeared into the bar and came out with a fistful of candy striped pencils, so new, that the writing end was still unsharpened and flat.

"I remember seeing Mr. Simmons put these in a cup behind the bar. I'm certain he'll never get around to sharpening them."

She broke the erasers off two of the pencils and asked Pookie to hold the rest. She slid the erasers, one at a time, into her bathing suit, then displayed her special effects for both girls to see.

"Oho!" said Pookie.

"Wow!" said Yim.

"Now you."

The girls each broke off a pair of erasers and fitted them into their tops as Mantana had done. Pookie's erasers were pointing in different directions, one up, one down. Mantana straightened them and took a step back for a second look.

"Perfect," she said.

"Now what?" asked Pookie.

"We wait," said Mantana, and pulled up a stool to sit on.

*

By half past eleven, the Cherry Bar was as full as any Saturday night of the month, thanks to Mantana and her magic erasers. The clientele was strictly Wednesday night, however - loners, drunks, and backpackers as opposed to single men, alcoholics, and tourists. A Wednesday night customer did not have a wife at home that he pleasantly lied about. A Wednesday night man was divorced. Often more than once. They carried scars and deformities and sweat-stained shirts around like luggage. Most of the time, they didn't know whether they wanted to get laid or go back to their hotel room and take a bath. They seemed to have an equal passion for both. They were rarely dangerous, although they were probably considered a part of the "criminal element" in their own societies. A girl never knew what to expect with a Wednesday night man, any more than she did with a Friday or Saturday night man. But the Thursday morning statistics all pointed to a feeling strangely similar to biting into a moldy piece of fruit.

Of course, there was always the exception.

Mantana waited outside until Jack left with Pen. She had done it, thought Mantana. Good for her. She looked away as Pen led her man to the curb. Tuk-tuks roamed the sois all night. It wasn't long before one pulled over. That should have been the end of it. Pen's silly sex tricks had worked and off they would go to fuck and count money. That should have been the end of it, and would have too, if Mantana hadn't taken one last look to see Jack watching her with that same, strange plea for help he seemed to hold in reserve just for her. It was then that she knew - he wished it was her sitting next to him in the back of the tuk-tuk rather than Pen. Rather than

Pen. A long-fingered hand turned his face away suddenly. Pen's eyes burned with jealousy, but they soon vanished in a cloud of white smoke. The tuk-tuk sped off. When the air cleared, Mantana could see the rat faced girl in the white swimsuit, spinning through the soup of car exhaust and neon. She was desperate now, probably coming down from whatever high she was on, and looked more like a sweaty beggar crying "*Kor dtaang!*" than an object of anyone's desire.

Mantana loosened her top and let the erasers fall from her breasts.

"I'm going back in," she said.

"Are you sure?" said Yim. "It's Wednesday night, you know."

"I know."

Mantana stood and moved to the curtains.

"Thanks, Joy," said Pookie.

"Thanks for what?"

Pookie smiled, revealing a row of crooked teeth. "You know," she said. "For thinking."

Mantana parted the curtains and disappeared inside.

*

The night went on.

Mantana did her time on stage, ate *som tam* with Neung, flirted with a British man, and clipped her toenails while Sai performed the Pussy Smoke Cigarette show on the catwalk. She had been bought out enough times in the past few weeks to keep any black check marks off her page in the bargirl notebook, but knew she should be hustling. The money she sent her father every other week was enough to buy two or three things with, but that was all. She imagined it was a paltry sum compared to what he had racked up in gambling debts. Nevertheless, it was more than her father ever brought home from his construction work and, unlike him, Mantana was never in danger of a lack of work. She imagined the widow Amnuay offering money of her own, but this too was an amount that would someday run out. The widow had a pile. Mantana had a *steady income*. And when the widow's money was gone, so, she imagined, was the widow.

With this in mind, she put away the toenail clippers, reapplied her make-up for the thousandth time, and went back out on the floor. The stools along the catwalk were full of aging foreigners with their butts overflowing on the red cushions. Most had already been found by bargirls. Mantana passed by, listening, not listening; understanding, not caring.

"I'll tell you what I miss most. Two pieces of white bread, a big slice of lunchmeat, lettuce, tomato, and mayonnaise. We call it a lunchmeat sandwich."

"So I said to the driver, I don't want to go to a jewelry store, I want to go to the place I told you to go. Eighty baht he says. Another fucking thief!"

"I'm sorry, luv, I've been throwing up all day."

She finally settled next to a man with dark, shoulder-length hair and a T-shirt with the sleeves cut off. His arms were muscular and covered in tattoos. The tattoos were pictures of women on skeletons and skeletons on motorcycles. Also, the man was cursed with a speech impediment that prevented him from being too loud or obnoxious. Everything he said came out in a high-pitched voice, as though he were imitating his favorite cartoon character or sucking on helium. Wes? Was that his name? Ways? Mantana couldn't understand a word. There was only that sound, that comical siren, whenever he opened his mouth. The man bought her a ladydrink, however, and made a You and Me motion between them when it was time to pay the check. He was no movie star like Jack, but it was better that way. Hope in a go-go, even the slightest trace, always led to disappointment.

Mantana let Phii Buoy know that she was going with a customer and went in back to change outfits. She realized she hadn't bothered to ask which hotel he was staying at. Then again, would she understand him if he told her? Better if Phii Buoy found out for herself. Wherever it was, she hoped it had a refrigerator stocked with booze. Girls weren't allowed to drink while they were working but what they did on their own time was between them and their customers. Perhaps after a few drinks, the man's speech would make a bit more sense to her.

In back, past the toilets and the dressing room, sat a fire door at the end of the corridor. It was open, but no alarm was sounding. Normally, there was a red light and a *whee whee whee* to let everyone know that a customer was trying to escape without paying his check. Where was the light and the noise now? Mantana walked down the corridor and looked outside. There was a man on his knees, throwing up in the dark alleyway. He wiped his mouth, then turned to look at Mantana.

"Sorry, luv," he said. "The loo was occupied. My stomach couldn't hold it."

The man got to his feet, staggered back a step, then excused himself past Mantana.

Wednesday night, she thought.

She gripped the steel handle, and swung the fire door shut.

*

There were small ones and there were big ones and then there were the kind like the man with the bird's wail voice had. It was the size of an eggplant. Mantana closed her eyes and clenched her teeth as the man entered her. Salty tears came with the pain of her customer's wild joy. His squeals echoed around the room, and bounced off the walls, no longer comical or cartoonish, but pig-like and terrifying, like something primitive gaining access to his blood.

"Ow," she whispered through her sobs. "Ow, ow."

The burn between her legs lasted long after the two hundred baht tip he gave her.

5

The afternoons had become the time to drink and one of Mantana's favorite drinking games was called Leave Town. In this game, Mantana packed her bag and looked all around her room for anything she might have left behind. Then she'd look at her watch, always five minutes behind, cheap piece of crap, and realize she'd have to stop drinking if she wanted to be sober by 6 p.m. Being sober was no problem. Never being drunk enough, that was the seemingly impossible part.

The streets of Pattaya were always a little bit strange in the space of time before nightfall. The sun didn't set on its own, but was pushed out of the sky by sidewalk vendors and mama-sans anxious to begin their business. Inside the bars and go-gos, time sat lifeless, waiting for the moon to give the OK for one hundred DJs to crank the volume, ten thousand women to begin their dance, and one hundred thousand foreigners to fall in love, whether it be hungry rat alleyway lust or rose garden fairy sweetness. Mantana and Neung sat eating stale peanuts, waiting for the dead time to end.

"Has Pen showed up?" asked Mantana.

"I don't think so."

"She's going to say something, you know. Something about Jack. She won't be able to resist."

"I don't know what you're talking about," said Neung.

"Just wait and see," she said, and bit her lip at the thought of the man she had been with last night compared to the man that had taken Pen home.

Pen was twenty minutes late. Mantana turned around and faced her as she approached. Here it comes, she thought. Only there was no comment.. Pen passed by without even looking up and went quietly to the dressing room. When she came out again, she found a seat against the wall and sat by herself. Her face looked like a cloud in the yellow stage lights. A cloud wearing too much rouge.

"What's wrong with her?"

"Maybe she's in love," said Neung.

"Is that a joke?"

Neung shrugged her shoulders and ate another peanut. In love! Girls like Pen didn't fall in love, did they? Mantana slid off the barstool and brushed crumbs from her skirt.

"Where are you going?" asked Neung.

"Over there."

And she went. She passed the stage and stood before Pen, waiting for a reaction. Where were the eyes burning with jealousy now? Pen looked at her with cloud-eyes and appeared not to recognize her. This was not the look of someone in love, thought Mantana. This was much more serious.

"Are you all right?" asked Mantana, feeling her own jealousy soften.

"Yes."

"Do you want to talk?"

"No."

"I had a rotten night last night," she said. "There was this customer -"

Pen's eyes drifted across Mantana's face and didn't settle again until the rotten night story was removed from her immediate span of attention. Mantana saw that she was suddenly made invisible and halted her attempt at communication. She nodded and looked around and gave up and walked away because there was nothing left she could do.

"Well?" asked Neung upon her friend's return.

"She's a ghost," said Mantana.

*

A new batch of girls was starting work that evening and each of the Cherry Bar bargirls had been instructed to pair up with a first-nighter to show her how things worked. The new girls were across town, probably watching some of Wit's magic tricks in the orange-carpeted room, and would be arriving with Mr. Simmons shortly. Mantana tried to put herself in a good mood, but there were too many things bothering her. Pen's silence was bothering her. The anxiety that her last customer had infected her with sickness was bothering her. And what about that list of rules that Phii Buoy had stuck to the dressing room wall? Certainly, something like that couldn't be passed over with a shrug. According to the "new guidelines," the girls could be fined fifty baht for smoking, one hundred baht for missing their turn on stage, and another hundred for failing to keep customers entertained. Yim said the list was for the new girls and didn't apply to them. Mantana knew, however, that in two or three weeks, the new girls would be the old girls and the rules would apply to everyone.

Mr. Simmons led the parade of new girls into the bar at a quarter past seven. Phii Buoy had gone out to buy candles and eggs and wasn't there to greet them. Instead, Mantana, Sai, Yim, and a half dozen other girls moved to the front of the bar to say hello and introduce themselves. Pen didn't move. She kept to her seat against the wall and gave dirty looks to anyone who turned their eyes in her direction.

"Where's Neung?" asked Mantana.

"I saw her go into the bathroom about ten minutes ago," said Yim.

"Is she all right?"

Yim didn't know. Mantana was about to go back when her friend suddenly appeared, smiling a forced, plastic smile. Maybe she was used to seeing Neung in her fixed state of worry. Maybe it was the bad feeling she had all day. Then again, maybe it was Neung's smile that sent a chill through Mantana, one so obvious that Neung turned to a barroom mirror to see what could cause such a shock.

"What?" said Neung, the familiar panic returning to her eyes and eyebrows.

Mantana couldn't explain it, but Neung's unusual grin somehow reminded her of the days when her mother's illness first began to manifest itself. It came through a darkness around the eyes, through a weakness when she tried to climb the stairs. And yet her mother smiled through it all. Mantana recalled watching her and believing that whatever was wrong would soon go away, like the toothache she once had from eating so much ice cream. After a while, her convictions were reduced to hope, hope constricted to fear. The smiles disappeared. And everything got terribly lonely.

"Joy?" said Neung.

"It's nothing," said Mantana. "You look different, that's all."

"Neung and Joy, would you please come over here?" said Mr. Simmons. He had shaved recently and his thick, spare tire of a neck showed traces of razor burn.

"Ladies," said Mr. Simmons. "I want you to give a warm welcome to our new employees."

"*Sa wat dee ka*. My name is Pear."

"Hello. I'm Pim."

"Look-Gayt."

There were eight new employees in all. Eight women, hired by Mr. Simmons, and they were wrong. They were all wrong. Imagine buying a kilo of sweet oranges, only to find their insides white and dry. Imagine seawater polluted by a nearby pig farm. Imagine swallowing a bug and wondering if it would bite from the inside. Mantana looked at Neung and saw the disbelief in her face as well. It took little Sai, with her air cannon of a sex organ, to blurt out what was on everyone's mind.

"They're old!"

They weren't just old. They were used. Ex-prostitutes whose every inch of flesh bore some mark of bad sunlight. Their hair hung in strands of blue cigarette smoke; their eyes sat like burnt neon in the eye sockets. And there were scars, both visible and invisible. Scars of unwanted childbirth, unwanted years, unwanted unwantedness. The women made Mantana a little bit afraid when she looked at them, like that spider on the ceiling she didn't know whether to kill or let live to eat the other bugs. She just couldn't imagine these women were going to be Cherry Bar girls.

And she wasn't alone.

"Find a partner," said Mr. Simmons, in a weary voice. "Sai, why don't you take Miss Pim here?"

Miss Pim had short black hair and a face like an overripe mango. She kept sticking a plastic menthol inhalant up her nostrils, first the right, then the left.

"Sai," repeated Mr. Simmons.

Sai turned her back on the group and walked away. So did Neung. So did Mantana. Soon, there was no one left to be partners with the new women. The girls regrouped in back.

"I'm not working with those old whores," said Sai. "They

stink!"

"I say we make them choose - us or them!" said Yim.

Kay and Pookie agreed. Just then, Phii Buoy entered the bar carrying a shopping bag of supplies. Mr. Simmons explained what had happened and pointed to the back of the bar. Phii Buoy handed him the shopping bag and walked back herself.

"That's enough," she said. "Now listen to me. The new employees have arrived, and I want you to be friendly to them."

"They're old!" Sai pointed out once again. "And they're dirty. They belong in some brothel where the lights are low so that customers can't see their faces."

"Nong Sai," she said with an angry impatience. "Do you remember last Friday when you were the only girl available to do a show? Do you remember how you had cramps and couldn't pop any balloons? Now Raymond and I know that you're all good workers and we appreciate your efforts, but we don't want to lose any more customers because there's only one girl on stage when they peek in from outside or no one to sit with them after they've ordered a drink."

The girls bowed their heads and felt ashamed. All but Sai, who was still fuming.

"Did you have to hire so many witches?" she asked.

"In one week, half of those women will have quit. If my husband and I really wanted eight girls, we would have hired sixteen. So if there aren't any more comments, I'd like everyone to go back and *wai* them."

There weren't any more comments. The girls dispersed and slowly made their way back to where the new women stood waiting. A few took to the stage. Mantana stayed behind.

"Phii Buoy, ma'am, do you know what's the matter with Pen? She looks like she's sick."

"She came back from her trick at 4 a.m. I was up doing paperwork when I heard her come in through the back and up to her room. That's all I know."

"Neung says she might have fallen in love."

Phii Buoy laughed. "Pen's too smart for that."

Mantana moved away from her boss, somewhat distressed at this last statement. Distressed because she had allowed herself the beginnings of a crush and she wouldn't want Phii Buoy to think of her as stupid. But if it weren't a broken heart eating at Pen, what was it? She watched Phii Buoy say a few words to her and she watched Pen get to her feet and return to the floor.

She sighed, still feeling a little drunk, and went off to find a customer to sit with.

*

Like it or not, the women went to work. Mantana paired with one named Ay, but lost sight of her as soon as the Friday night crowd filled the barstools. No matter. Yim and Neung had forsaken their chaperone duties as well. And Sai? Sai hadn't even made an effort.

The special show that night involved one of the hard-to-look-at ladies, Pear, and a shallow pan of live eels. The first thing the performer did was empty the eels onto the stage and let them wiggle around for a few minutes, most likely to wake them up. The animals looked like thin streaks of oil rolling down the side of a hill. Customers along the catwalk grimaced in anticipation as the showgirl straightened their rubbery bodies and guided the fleeing ones to the center of the stage. Then she took off her clothes. A soft pink spotlight enveloped Pear's round tummy, barely masking the blue-green bruises that spotted her abdomen. The boy in the booth played a popular and slow love song about how nights are so long after the one you love loves someone else.

"It was good, Joy."

Mantana had been in a trance watching the pink lights turn the air into cotton candy. It was indeed quite common among the staff to space out and forget just where they were. Some of the girls even enjoyed the fact that time went faster under the hypnotic spell of the lights and music. Hearing her name snapped Mantana back into reality. It was Pen, standing next to her with a sort of crooked smile on her face.

"Buoy said you were asking about my health," she said. "But isn't that what you really want to know?"

"What?" said Mantana, still somewhat dazed.

"He thinks I'm beautiful. He might even want me to be his girlfriend."

She was talking as though she were out of her mind. She held onto the bar and cackled as she swung her head down. Her orange bangs fell like a shredded curtain in front of her eyes. Mantana set a hand upon her shoulder. It felt cold. Pen looked up at her with a sarcastic sneer.

"I'm beautiful!" she spat.

Anything else out of her mouth was drowned out by a sudden round of applause. On stage, Pear lay on her back and raised her legs into a perfect though somewhat veiny V formation. She held an eel in each hand. Like some bizarre carnival ride, the animals were guided through the pink haze into her. When these two were in, she cupped a hand over her opening and carefully pushed in two more. Whether the creatures went in for lack of a better instinct or sucked in as if through a vacuum cleaner was a mystery to all but the woman on stage.

Pen had disappeared in all the excitement and Mantana suddenly felt sick. She backed up toward the exit and bumped into Wit, holding a pad of paper and a pencil.

"*Som tam?*" he said.

"What?"

"Yim and Kay want me to go out for *som tam*. Do you want some too?"

"No."

Another round of applause moved like a wave across the bar. Pear was on her feet now. She moved like an overweight, uncooked noodle, twisted and crossed and freakish. She was struggling from one end of the stage to the other, where a large glass fishbowl sat waiting for her. The fishbowl was about half full of yellow water. The woman couldn't take a full step. At one point, she doubled over, apparently in agony, and continued on by inching her feet sideways, still clutching at her blue-green middle, smothered in pink.

The audience started to chant.

"GO! GO! GO!"

The woman was almost to the opposite side of the stage. She stopped and hunched down and held herself as if to keep from exploding. Then she clenched her teeth and stretched her arm out for the fishbowl. It was just out of reach. The woman's eyes rolled back in her head, and her arm fell limp. Wit the magician rushed in to move it closer to her.

"Say, I'm going out for *som tam*."

The woman shook her head violently. She sucked a lungful of air in through her teeth and turned her back to the fishbowl. Then she bounced, once, twice, until she was high enough to squat over the glass rim.

"GO! GO!"

The first eel shot from her body like champagne, shaken up and popped. The others followed in a single file line. Their keeper seemed to be doing all that she could to stay conscious. Most of the eels made it into the fishbowl. Some didn't, and dropped to the stage. The creatures moved much slowly now, even the ones who had a taste of freedom. Like they were drunk or something.

When all the eels were released, the woman sat down, exhausted, while the audience gave her another round of applause. She wrapped herself in a towel and went slowly down the steps while

Wit gathered the escaping eels and Ad the Bouncer mopped the stage. She stopped suddenly and turned back around.

"Nong Wit," she said.

"Yes?"

"I'll take that *som tam* now. Extra spicy."

Enough. Mantana pushed aside the velvet curtains and stepped outside for some air. Neung and Sai were out there already.

"You look pale," said Neung. "Eel show?"

Mantana nodded and drank from a bottle of water that Neung held out to her.

"You know what this means, don't you?" said Sai. "This means our scale of income will change completely."

"How so?"

"Right now it's three hundred baht for special shows. Just watch. Pretty soon Phii Buoy's going to begin wondering why she should pay me three hundred baht for shooting balloons when her buffalo whores can stick live animals into their cunts for the same amount."

Mantana was about to calm her by saying that Phii Buoy wouldn't do such a thing but she held her tongue instead. The truth was, she didn't know what Phii Buoy was capable of any more than she had known what Khun Nemit, Phii Chainoi, or even she, herself, was capable of.

"A girl at the Honey Bar told me the U.S.S. something or other is coming into port next week and all the bars are hiring new girls," said Neung.

"Oh no," groaned Sai. "Not more sailors."

"Have either of you spoken with Pen tonight?" asked Mantana.

"Forget about Pen," said Neung. "She's crazy."

The girls across the soi called out to a pair of passing tourists. Sai cupped a hand to her mouth and added her voice to the discount siren song.

"Hey you! Woo-hoo! Come inside please!"

The men passed by without looking.

"Good for you," said Sai. "There's no one here but old buffaloes."

6

Things got worse for Pen. When she wasn't sitting in the corner, staring into the lights like a mesmerized chicken, she was out on the floor, flirting from man to man like a wild woman, like a swing pulled back and let go to fly too high. And once she peaked, her viciousness returned with a vengeance.

The first time she was caught yelling at a customer, Phii Buoy deducted one hundred baht from her salary. The second time, she was fined another hundred and given a warning that if she was caught yelling again, she would be fired. Phii Buoy's words had an effect on her. The next time she lost her temper, she kept her mouth shut and broke a bottle over her customer's head instead.

Two things saved her from losing her job and going to jail. The first thing was this. When Pen picked up the bottle, she did it blindly, while it was still in the foam holder that kept it cold. The glass broke inside the foam and saved the customer's head from any serious damage.

Now for the second thing.

Mantana was dancing on stage when the "event" occurred. Kay

and Wan and the buffalo named Look-Gayt danced with her. Mantana and her boots held the audience's attention, but she was watching Pen, and could clearly see her anger building as the man groped her breasts and tried to stick his tongue in her ear. The man was a lizard, to be sure, a lizard in gray shorts and a pink shirt, but he was no worse than the other customers who wanted to kiss / suck / touch without paying for anything more than their bar tab. There was no reason for Pen to pick up the bottle and do what she did, but she did, and it would have been the end of her if Mantana didn't give everyone reason to believe that it was something that had to be done.

"Knife!" she screamed, and screamed again.

The girls on stage shrieked and ducked.

Ad the doorman was the only other person that was immediately capable of movement. He rushed over to where the two sat and looked from one to the other. It was obvious he didn't know which one to grab first, Pen, holding the neck of a broken beer bottle, or the foreigner next to her, holding his forehead and moaning. Mantana helped in his decision-making process by pointing at the foreigner.

"He's got a knife! I saw it!"

"A knife!" said Ad, and held up his heavy forearms for protection.

"He tried to cut her!"

"*Ai heea!*" Ad grabbed the man from behind and squeezed. The foreigner's eyes bugged in their sockets as he was lifted from his seat, carried out, and deposited on the sidewalk.

Phii Buoy was quick on the scene. Pen had slipped back into the casual indifference that followed her outbursts, and left Mantana as the sole eyewitness. She told Phii Buoy everything, about how the foreigner was sliding a hand up Pen's skirt and how he was trying to kiss her on the mouth. Yes, and that's not all. He had a knife too. Mantana saw it with her own eyes, even if the other girls didn't.

"Pen?" asked Phii Buoy.

"What she said," said Pen.

There were police. The foreigner returned with his head bandaged and pointed out the woman who had assaulted him. Mr. Simmons was nowhere to be found. Phii Buoy came to her defense. She didn't employ criminals. Only good girls. The two police officers stopped listening to Phii Buoy and looked at the girls on stage instead. The foreigner demanded that something be done. One of the police officers told him he could fill out a complaint form and if the same thing happened again...

"You mean I have to stay and wait to get hit with another beer bottle before you'll do anything?"

The policemen looked at each other. One of them said something that made the other laugh. Phii Buoy signed her name on some form or other, and waited for them to leave before telling her husband that it was safe to come out. Mr. Simmons broke no laws, but the less available English in a situation such as this, the better.

And so, Pen was given another chance. Whether or not she would take advantage of the kindness shown to her was impossible to tell. She closed up like a book written in an ancient language once the ordeal was over and refused to say another word. Phii Buoy took it as a momentary trauma and sent her home for the evening. Mantana watched her leave from a seat at the bar.

"Could I have a glass of water with one ice cube?" she said to Ale, serving drinks. Water with one ice cube was a secret code among the working girls and bartenders that meant a shot of vodka would be added to their drink. Coke with one ice cube was the code for whiskey. The girls brought in cheap brands to add to the bottles of expensive liquor to prevent Mr. Simmons from becoming suspicious. Nevertheless, he was suspicious. Someday, someone would be fired, but at the moment, Mantana didn't give a damn.

"I saw what happened," said a voice next to her. It was Ay, the woman she had partnered up with a couple of nights ago. Ay wore a scar around her neck that Sai liked to joke about. She said that a lover had once tried to saw her head off to make her more attractive. In truth, it was painful and sad to look at and Mantana wished Sai wouldn't make jokes about such tragic features.

"You'd be wise not to get involved," said Ay.

"I don't know what you're talking about," said Mantana.

"I've seen this happen to dozens of girls. It's always the same. A nice girl comes to work in a not so nice place and finds she has to invent a new personality to charm the customers. If she wants to make money, that is."

"What's wrong with that?"

"There's nothing wrong with it, if she can live and work without thinking about what she does. Once a girl starts to feel bad about herself, it's all over."

"What do you mean?"

"I mean there comes a time in every prostitute's career when she sees herself in some dirty hotel mirror and despises the person she's become. So, after work, she'll go home and try to figure out what to do with this new personality. A lot of them try to kill it with booze or drugs. Others go crazy, like your friend."

"She's not crazy."

"Maybe not. But she's dangerous. Dangerous to herself and her customers and anyone who tries to help her. If I was the mama-san, I would have fired her a long time ago. And I'd put out word to as many bars as I could not to hire her. She needs to go home. She needs a long rest. That's the only way she'll remember who she once was."

Mantana didn't say anything for a long while. Then she asked:

"And what about you? What happened when you saw your new self in a dirty hotel mirror?"

"Some of us can die, but keep on working." She reflected for a moment and scratched the place that was so sad and painful to look at. She scratched it so hard, Mantana had to look away, fearful that it might burst open. "It's difficult at first, but essential in the long run."

Mantana looked back and met the old prostitute's eyes for a moment. It felt as if she were looking into a pair of dark and empty skeleton's eyes.

"I've got to get back to work."

The woman moved away from the bar, leaving Mantana with her watered down vodka, one ice cube. Flee from the tiger, meet the crocodile; with Ay out of sight, a new face could be seen entering the bar.

It was Jack.

*

He was alone, as usual, and his eyes lit upon the catwalk girls before he even sat down. Handsome as ever, thought Mantana, especially in his cowboy boots and dark blue shirt. She fixed her face in a compact mirror and finished her drink. Then she went into action.

Too late.

One of Sai's aptly named buffalo whores had gotten to him faster than Mantana. This one suffered from acne scars and a thin black mustache that men couldn't see when she buried her face in their laps. Damn her and her filthy whore ways!

With Pen sent home for the night, it was up to those available to fill in for her on the catwalk. Mantana saw that a turn was almost up, and volunteered herself for the next song. She hurried into a two-piece bikini, then onto the stage. Then she took it off again.

It was the first time that she had danced completely nude. Of course she had danced topless, and often flashed her lower half for a hundred baht tip from some outstretched hand. But dancing naked, along with special shows, was something that was decided in the first week of employment. Simply stated, there were those who did, and those who didn't. Those who didn't were the ones who were bought out on a regular basis, tipped, and treated to a hotel room breakfast. Those who did, did it for the money they didn't make from customers. Maybe it was their looks, maybe it was their personality. More often than not, it was their looks. Sadly enough, it was the girls who danced naked who usually ate *gooey teeo* on every next morning of their working life.

When Neung and Yim and Sai saw Mantana, dancing naked on stage, they assumed it was a twenty-year-old pie in the face for those forty-four and fifty-one year-old buffalo whores who kept trying to steal their customers. And they cheered. They cheered so loudly that Mr. Simmons came running out from his back office to see whether his bar had exploded or not. They cheered so loudly that passers-by on the street had to stop and wonder what kind of world lay beyond those mysterious velvet curtains. Most important of all, they cheered so loudly that Jack turned away from his buffalo whore and didn't turn back again.

She had him.

Her song ended. Mantana changed into her bargirl outfit and took the seat next to him. After the way she had singled him out and flirted with him from the stage, none of the old women dared to move in on him again.

"Hello!" she said.

Jack didn't speak. He only looked at her. Was this the look that turned Pen's mind inside out? No, it couldn't be. Jack's eyes were like a child's eyes looking in the window of an ice-cream store, with only a couple of baht in his fist. It was something else. It had to be something else.

"Would you go home with me tonight?" he asked.

"Where you stay? Which hotel?"

"I have an apartment."

"Five hundred baht for bar. I go with you."

Jack took out his wallet and gave her a thousand baht bill.
Whatever the source of his sadness was, it certainly wasn't a lack of
money for ice cream.

"Wait a minute," she said. "I go to change. You no butterfly
another girl."

"I'm not a butterfly," said Jack.

Hmf! thought Mantana. A liar too. How this *jao choo* could
have any effect on Pen at all was beyond her. She smiled as she
wondered if her crush on the man had turned to anger. Bah! What
did it matter? Whatever feelings lay in her heart were secondary
to the hard-earned awareness that was stored in her brain. The
only weapon a prostitute had against handsome men with sad eyes.
It was just hard to believe that Pen's awareness was made of a
softer stone than hers.

Mantana found Phii Buoy outside, of all places, scolding
Neung for spending too much time fishing and not enough time
entertaining. She noticed Mantana motioning to her from the curtains
and stepped back inside.

"A customer wants to go with me," she said, and held out
the money to show she was serious.

"I've never seen you dance naked before, Nong Joy. Did
that man with the brown hair have something to do with it?"

"No, ma'am."

"He was one of Pen's customers, wasn't he?"

"I don't know, ma'am."

Phii Buoy took the bill and counted out seven hundred in
change from her money belt. Mantana felt a little better knowing
she had taken him for an extra two hundred. She grasped the money
with her fingers, but her boss didn't let go.

"Don't forget what you're paid for, Joy. You're here to entertain,
not to seek revenge."

Phii Buoy released her grip on the bill.

"Go," she said.
Mantana turned, and went.

7

Mantana would not allow herself to become stupid with love. She was under no illusions. Jack was a customer and she was his girlfriend for the night. Once he handed over the money, once she acted out her role, there were no more reasons for hanging around than there would be after buying a pack of cigarettes at the mini-mart check-out counter. Nor did she want revenge. Perhaps the illness that Pen was suffering from was one that had its roots deep inside her. She couldn't blame Jack for bringing it on. So what if he were handsome, sad, even rich! So what if he were all these things and so what if he were nothing at all. Mantana tried to keep these thoughts in mind as she rode next to him in the back of a taxicab. She tried, only she failed. She liked this man so much, she hated him. Maybe Pen did too, and ended up hating herself. Mantana couldn't let that happen to her.

Jack lived on the seventh floor of a beach-side condominium. There was a revolving door and a real, working fountain on the way to the elevators. Two Thai girls sitting behind a receptionist's desk looked at her but didn't smile. Three thousand per month? Four thousand and a boss who patted their bottoms every chance he got? Mantana wouldn't smile either if she were sitting behind that receptionist's desk.

Jack pressed the UP arrow and they stepped into the elevator. The sides were mirrored, and it seemed she could see Jack watching her from a multitude of angles, just like in the bar. His hand disappeared into his shirt pocket, then held something before her. It looked like a gold bracelet. Mantana took it from him and examined it closely. It was beautiful.

"It's yours," he said. "But you have to do something for me first."

There was no music to shout above now, and the sound of his voice was slow and smooth. The gold caught the light and flickered like stars in the mirrors around her. Was it the same bracelet he had offered to Pen? Mantana handed it back to him and nodded that she understood.

The elevator stopped. The doors opened. They walked down the carpeted hallway and stood before room number 703. Jack unlocked the door and looked into her eyes.

"I'm never quite sure how to do this," he said, shyly. "So I usually just do it."

For a moment, she thought he would say something else, or maybe kiss her, which she would let him do, on the lips if he wanted. Only he turned and opened the door of his apartment instead. It was dark inside.

"Please."

Mantana entered the room and Jack followed behind her. He closed the door and locked it. Then he switched on the light. The room was spacious with marble floors and a bay window that overlooked the sea. A raised wooden platform lay at the far end of the room. In front of the platform was a chair, a tripod, and the morning newspaper spread out to cover the floor below. A pair of tall spotlights, the kind that television film crews used, stood at the front corners of the makeshift stage.

And then she noticed the walls.

Her first reaction was to run, run away, run fast, but she found herself moving further in, closer, like an invisible hand was pushing her from behind. The walls of Jack's room were covered in crudely framed canvas paintings that hung next to and above one another. The canvases were approximately the same size, and filled with the most bizarre witches brew of colors that Mantana had ever seen. But they weren't just meaningless swirls of paint. Each one contained a person that became a woman that became a nude the longer she looked at it. Some of the women were beautiful, as if inspired by a sunset on Ko Samui or a rainbow that appeared deep inside some caves of the North. Others were not so beautiful. These resembled the statues of demons she had once seen at a temple in Ang Tong rather than -

prostitutes.

They were portraits of bargirls, every one of them. Mantana's eyes searched the canvases, mystified, repulsed, amazed. She didn't know how long she spent gazing upon all the faces and bodies but when she reached the end of one wall, she moved immediately to the next and began again. At one point, her foot bumped into something. There were four more stacks of portraits propped against the wall she was examining. Each stack held six or eight more paintings. Mantana looked at the stacks, then flashed her eyes at Jack.

"The walls were full," he explained. "I had nowhere else to put them."

Unmoved, her eyes returned to the portraits. Yes, indeed, he had gotten them right. He had looked and he had seen. The lipstick, the moles, the wrinkles, the loneliness, the silliness, the self-importance, the child at home, the husband long gone, the boredom, the desperation, the addictions, the sadness, the indifference, the suffering. He had looked with those sad eyes of his, and he had seen.

"Where is Pen?" she asked.

Jack took a ballpoint from a cup and held it out to her.

"No pen! Girl Pen. Girl friend me you buy from bar."

"Oh," he said, apologetically. "She's here in my pile of unfinished works. She wouldn't sit still for me. And she wasn't happy with the result."

Jack held up a canvas for Mantana to see. Upon it was Pen's mousy face in all its little-girl sensuality and panic. Panic? Mantana had never noticed it before, but there it was in brilliant oranges and blues - panic. It was in her eyes and in the curve of her mouth. It even reached down into her arms and breasts, panic. Jack had depicted it like a deformity one's eyes are immediately drawn to. Only Pen's deformity was of a type that couldn't be covered over with make-up. It was one of the soul, all-encompassing, and it made her look like something she never resembled in real life, a frightened bat ricocheting off the walls of an all too lit-up world. Was *this* Pen? Was *this* who she was?

Mantana angrily flashed her eyes at Jack, then stepped closer to examine the details. As if adding insult to injury, Jack had spared her nothing. Pen's make-up had been drawn in like a clown's. Her nose was that of a pig. The nipples of her breasts reminded Mantana of fat raisins. Anything and everything that one should remain silent about blared from the canvas like a man with a megaphone announcing Pen's defects, Pen's faults, Pen's grotesqueness. Mantana lowered her eyes and tried to think of Pen as she was. As she really was.

"It's not how I wanted it to be," said Jack, quietly. "But like I said, she wouldn't sit still."

He set the work down and buried it behind two other canvases.

"Let's hope this one turns out better. We'll do two sittings, if things go well. I need you to pose for both. The first may take three or four hours, but the second will be short. In between sittings, I want to have sex with you. Actually, I want to have sex with you right now, but it's essential to the painting that we wait. I've got a television in the bedroom. I'll plug it in out here so you can watch it while you sit."

A strange fear gripped Mantana. She closed her eyes and imagined Pen, up there on the platform, trying to look her most exquisite. Smiling, flirting, revealing herself in ways completely unknown to her. Then coming around to see the work of art Jack had made of her. A horror show. She thought about what might have gone on behind Pen's eyes as she saw herself, perhaps for the very first time, more clearly and more distorted than any mirror would ever show. And surrounded by the ghosts of all those other girls, gazing down from the walls, silently whispering what no prostitute would ever dare admit to herself:

This is how you are. This is how you'll stay.

Jack set a freshly stretched canvas upon the easel, then brought a small television out of the bedroom. This he placed upon a chair close to an electrical outlet and plugged it in. He asked her which channel she liked, and she said seven.

"Are you sure? There's Thai boxing on seven."

"Three OK," she said blankly.

"If you want to take a shower first, the bathroom is right through there."

"Thank you," she said and continued to stand in the center of the room, unable to pull herself from her thoughts.

"What I mean is, if you want to get undressed, I'm ready to begin."

Begin. Mantana understood that word. He wanted to paint her now. The fear grew worse.

"Pen, she very sad," she said.

"Some girls are better off not looking at the pictures I paint. But I have to paint them." Jack cleared his throat and took a step towards her. "It's my way of loving you. *All* of you."

If there were ever a time when she wished she couldn't understand what was being said to her, she wished it had been the moment Jack spoke. But she understood. The words made Mantana feel cold, or at least the part of her that once wondered if he could love only her. The words turned her love sour. Jack took the gold bracelet out of his pocket and fastened it around her wrist. As disturbed as she felt, the grown-up, money-wise, no-fool-for-love Mantana could not find a reason to leave. Phii Buoy's words echoed in her mind. *Don't forget why you're here.* Mantana closed her eyes and counted to ten. Customers had called her worse things than "whore," in the past. Why should this man's judgment make her feel any different from the hundreds of others who had seen her, on stage and off? Mantana already knew the answer. Jack's verdict would last, long after the others had faded from memory. Still, she couldn't say that she wasn't curious. Would she be beautiful or hideous? Worth hanging on the wall or forgotten behind a stack of rejects?

"I take a shower," said Mantana. "I sit for you."

Jack nodded. "There's something about you," he said.

Mantana bowed her head, then went into the bathroom and closed the door. As she looked in the mirror, she imagined Pen, no more than a week ago, standing in that very same spot and seeing her reflection for the very last time. Before the vision of herself was replaced by the whore in the portrait.

"I'll survive this," said Mantana, "and I'll be richer for it."

The gold bracelet sparkled upon her wrist.

*

It went like this. Mantana lay naked on the stage for two and a half hours while Jack painted. She lay on her side, her head propped up on her right elbow, her left arm lifted unnaturally over her head. It was terribly uncomfortable. Television helped. She watched a talk show, a game show, a half-hour music video program and, when there was nothing else to watch, boxing. Sometimes, Jack asked questions. He pointed out a scar on her right knee, hardly noticeable, and asked how she got it. Mantana didn't know. It happened when she was very young. He wasn't going to paint that, was he? Yes, he was going to paint everything. Mantana clenched her teeth and bore her discomfort in silence.

Shortly before the station signed off for the evening, Jack laid down his brushes and spoke.

"I'm ready."

Mantana sat up and wrapped a towel around her middle. The left side of her body was sore, and her arms had lost all feeling. Slowly, slowly, she stepped down from the platform and walked to the other side of the canvas. She had been waiting too long and felt too tired to be hateful or afraid. And what she saw did little to bring those emotions back to her.

The painting was - well, it was - OK.

She smiled through her pain and told Jack it was very beautiful. Inside, she was let down. The painting contained neither beauty nor ugliness, neither sorrow nor joy. Wasn't she, as a working girl, entitled to these things too? This was just a picture, like a nine-year-old who can color the monkey chief Hanuman without slipping outside the lines. Jack had stayed in the lines and he had created a market seller's picture. He had created nothing.

"It's not finished," he told her.

Mantana looked at him, then the painting. What was left? He had gotten her lips right. He had fixed her navel in its proper place. She even noticed the scar he had painstakingly hinted at upon her knee. Mantana stopped looking at the painting. Another fight had begun on television. Jack didn't want to watch. He wanted sex. They went into the bedroom and got undressed. Seeing him naked and feeling his hands upon her did nothing to influence or deflate her feelings for him. Love had nothing to do with sex. She understood that now. Fucking was part of the nighttime ritual just like brushing her teeth was part of the morning ritual. It was a dullness that still required her attention, with no point in feeling happy or sad or anything at all. She wanted clean teeth, she wanted the tip, so Jack the painter fucked away while Mantana wondered what he *really* did for a living.

Ten minutes, and he came.

"*Aawuuy!*"

He rolled off after a few seconds and lay at her side. Mantana was relieved. She didn't like her customers to linger inside her, even handsome ones. She once told Neung that if she were a hotel, check-out time was noon, not 12:05.

"We have to go," said Jack, taking her hand.

"Go?"

"I have to finish my painting."

Jack got out of bed and slid into a pair of green boxer shorts while Mantana searched for her towel. "Forget it." He led her back to the stage and helped her assume the original pose. Mantana didn't need any help. When it hurt, she knew she was in position.

Then he went at it again. He painted more haphazardly this time, grabbing brushes at random and throwing paint upon the canvas instead of applying the gentle strokes he had used before. Brushes fell, paint splattered, curses flew. At one point, he became so angry, Mantana thought he would fly into a rage and break everything in sight.

"No!" he yelled at the canvas. "Christ! What are you *thinking*?"

He frightened her when he was like this. Like a demon had taken control of his body.

At 3:20 in the morning, he spoke. It was the first time he addressed her since they began the second sitting.

"That's enough. I can finish without you. Take a shower." He waved a yellow-and-blue-smeared hand in the air. "Go to sleep. Or if you'd like to go back to the bar, I can pay you now."

Mantana moved her aching limbs and waited for the blood to begin flowing again. She went into the bedroom and wrapped a sheet around herself as Jack continued painting. Then she fell on the bed, exhausted.

What a night! She never dreamed she could be so tired from sitting. She forced herself into an upright position and looked around the tiny bedroom. There was nothing to give her a clue as to what kind of man had painted, fucked, and painted her again. She saw no indication of where he was from, or how he spent his days. She couldn't even say whether he liked the colors yellow and blue.

She heard a noise. It was Jack.

"That's enough," he said through a yawn. "That's enough."

He left his paints and his canvas and shambled into the bedroom. The colors of the rainbow dotted his arms, chest, and face. His hair was a mess. He patted her on the shoulder, then collapsed on the bed.

"Don't steal anything," he mumbled, then closed his eyes and began to snore.

Mantana wanted a shower. She wanted to be home. She wanted what she always wanted following a trick. Money and peace, in that order. No matter how soft the mattress and pillow was, she wanted to be somewhere she knew, and knew her too. She stood and walked out of the bedroom. Jack's work space was a disaster area of spilled paint and balled up newspaper. Mantana shook her head. What was the point of it all? With his money and looks, he could afford to fill his room with girls, real flesh-and-blood girls, every night of the week. Why make such a mess?

Mantana stepped up to the canvas and looked at what Jack had done to her.

Wow.

Things had changed in the four-by-six world of the painting. A dozen different flowers had been added to the colors, each one performing its own kind of magic. The intricate details were still there, but they seemed so much more real now. Maybe even bigger than real, because the details in the painting weren't going to change or fade with time. They were stuck there forever, and it was beautiful. She was beautiful, as beautiful as Pen was hideous.

It wasn't right.

She turned around and looked again at the women hanging on the wall. All the faces and colors. It was all a lie. Mantana rubbed her eyes with the knuckles of her index fingers. He almost had her. Almost. But it would take more than flowers in the paint to hide the truth from her. And when she opened her eyes again, she no longer saw beauty or sorrow or any of the things she had seen before. She saw a great big lie.

This is how you are.

The girls were painted as Jack felt they deserved. He painted the girls as he *thought* they should be, probably depending on the sex they had given him. If she were really as beautiful as he depicted her, then Pen would have to be just as horrible as he made her out to be. And Pen wasn't horrible. Scared, confused, bitter, and angry, yes. But horrible? Jack had no right to do that to her, or to any of them for that matter. He had no right to cheat them that way.

This is how you'll stay.

She turned away, unable to look anymore. After the smiles, the sex, the shower, and the promises, none of it had anything to do with her. The girl that he saw was a ghost filling a bikini, filling a fantasy. And for a bar fee and a tip, the ghost would come to life. The ghost would smile, fuck, pretend to enjoy it all, and fade away. Where was *she*? Where was *Mantana*? Jack couldn't capture her in a single night any more than he could purchase her love. He couldn't define her in a portrait any more than a curious tourist, peeping through the barroom curtains, could write her biography.

She had escaped his trick. Pen hadn't.

Mantana showered and got into bed next to him. There was nothing to do but wait for the morning, when she could collect her money and gold bracelet and get out of that beach-side apartment.

*

That night, she dreamed of Jakkrit. Why Jakkrit, she didn't know, but there he was, smiling and waving to her from behind a tree. A tree in a field. The only tree in sight.

"Nong Joy! Come quickly!"

Mantana crossed the field. The faster she walked, the further away he seemed to become. So she ran. At last, she was making some progress.

"Nong Joy, I thought I'd never see you again! So many things have happened. You must listen, Nong Joy!"

"I'm listening," she said.

"The village is gone!"

"Gone? What do you mean gone?"

"The Clean and Happy Company decided to run a pipeline through the village shortly after you left to become a prostitute. Everyone was evicted from their homes. Oh, Joy, bulldozers and wrecking balls have torn down everything, even the trees! And to top it off, they insist on burning tires day and night. A great big pile of burning tires!"

"But why?"

"Who knows!"

The field flattened out around her, as if a strong wind were blowing. The clouds shifted. The sky turned a synthetic orange.

"I thought the Clean and Happy Company made soap," said Mantana.

"They make everything. Soap, constitutions, pop songs, auto safety manuals, sidewalks, shopping malls, you name it! They also produce ninety percent of the shows you see on television. They've only recently branched out into laying pipelines."

"But they can't just destroy an entire village! People will hear of it! People will know!"

Jakkrit shook his head.

"They own the newspapers too."

"Jakkrit, you could get into a lot of trouble talking like this."

"Only if they catch me, Nong Joy!"

Jakkrit stepped out from behind the tree. Mantana gasped. It was Jakkrit, the man she knew, from the waist up only. His lower half was that of a giant spider, with eight hairy legs all moving in sync. He scuttled close to her and placed his hands on her shoulders. Mantana stood frozen with fear.

"I went to bed with a spider. I know it's horrible, Nong Joy, but it was the only way."

"The only way?" she whispered.

Jakkrit nodded. "The only way I could walk again. You of all people ought to understand that."

She looked into his eyes and saw for the first time how dark they were.

*

Mantana was quiet as she accepted the gold bracelet from Jack the next morning. She drank a cup of coffee and watched a pair of Thai celebrities make *tom yam goong* on television. And then it was time to leave. She hadn't rushed, nor had she taken her time. It was all by the book; it was all routine.

"Joy, I'm sorry to see you go," said Jack.. "I think we've done some wonderful work together."

Mantana put her shoes on and tried not to look at the walls. When she did, they seemed to grow higher and close in on her. All through the morning, the feeling that she was in a man's apartment had left her. This place was more like a prison, with all the inmates stacked in cells, looking out at the new arrival. A dirty prison, with a warden who claimed to love his prisoners, but never remembered their names.

"At least tell me whether you like it."

"What?"

"The painting," said Jack. "Your painting. Do you like it?"

"Joy no like," she replied. "Good-bye."

"Wait a minute!"

Jack rushed to stop her from leaving.

"Really?" he asked in the voice of a fourteen-year-old child-man. "You really don't like it?"

She knew that a lie would make him feel better and ease him enough to let her leave, but she didn't want to do it. She didn't want to lie. She felt dirty enough as it was.

"Joy no have happy," she said.

Jack's mouth hung open as he gazed into her eyes. He seemed to understand, maybe just a little, and stepped back apologetically.

"I want to give you something," he said, "before you go."

He went back into his bedroom and came out again holding a pair of name cards. He examined them both, then handed her one. Mantana took it without attempting to read it.

"Some of my work will be on display at an art gallery here in Pattaya. That's an invitation to the show. The opening isn't for a couple of months, but if you're free, maybe you could come and " Jack laughed without humor and threw his arms up. "And have a glass of wine."

He turned back towards his painting and folded his arms across his chest. Mantana slid the cards into her purse and opened the door without any opposition. She looked back once and saw his arms fall to his side like a defeated boxer. Then she closed the door and left as quickly as she could.

8

During her afternoons, Mantana rarely did more than eat, sleep, and clean her tiny room. Sometimes, in her remaining hour before work, she walked to the thin strip of beach that lined the coast and watched the sun sink into the horizon. The sky never failed to provide her with a dazzling display of reds and violets. On these occasions, she dressed in regular clothes and wore only a touch of make-up. She sat on her favorite stone bench and tried not to meet the stares of passing men. There were some girls who used their every waking moment to sell themselves for a little extra on the side. Time off to them was money going into some other girl's purse. Mantana often wondered how long it would be before watching sunsets didn't matter anymore, and life became one long fucksearch for money.

There were days.

There were days.

"The thing is," she told Neung during one of their afternoon breakfasts, "there will never be enough."

"Enough what?"

"Money."

"As long as you don't know what you want, there will never be enough. Me, I know what I want. I have a goal."

"Which is?"

"I want enough to take care of my baby until the child is sixteen years old."

"What baby?"

"The baby I'll have when I retire."

"And the father?"

"I'd rather not know."

"Neung! Besides being an absolutely crazy idea, you're talking about an impossible amount of money. Even the highest paid working girl in Pattaya couldn't retire before she's thirty. And you know what happens when you reach that age. You turn into one of those buffaloes that Phii Buoy hired."

"What happens to me doesn't matter, just as long as my child is beautiful. And it's not impossible. I have an exact amount in mind. If I eat only once a day for the next eighteen years, I'll be able to retire when I'm forty-two. Women can still have babies when they're forty-two."

"Do you really think you're going to work at the Cherry for another eighteen years?"

"There's always the chance that some foreigner will ask me to be his girlfriend. If that happens, I bet I could cut those eighteen years in half."

"You're crazy, Neung."

"I'm realistic. You should open your eyes a little bit more too, Joy. Start thinking about your future. There's a million foreigners out there who would love to have you for a girlfriend. Just pick out a rich one who's not deformed or sick and don't be in such a hurry to leave the next morning. Stick around. Wash his clothes. Clean his room. Be his sexy little maid. Better yet, find some crazy old man who doesn't have much time left to live. Get him to change his will so that he leaves his fortune to you."

"Neung!"

Neung looked at her, quite innocently.

"What?" she said. "It's them or us, isn't it?"

*

The following Monday was a Buddhist holiday. Bars were not allowed to sell beer. Prostitutes were not allowed to be prostitutes. All the bar owners had to play a game with the law enforcement officers. The game went like this. The bars opened around nine or ten o'clock, allowing customers to come in and suck on soda pop or coffee. Lights were kept on; music was kept low. None of the girls danced. Dancing was against the law. A girl could go to jail for dancing. So customers and bar owners sat around and waited for midnight, when the game was over, the holiday was over, and everyone could get back to work.

Mantana and Neung and Sai put in a request for the day off. Sai had an idea that the three of them should go to Samet Island and play in the sand and sea. There were enough girls now to cover for the sick and vacationing, she argued. Phii Buoy let them go.

"Just make sure you're back on Tuesday," she told them.

So, early that morning the girls met in front of the bar to give food and flowers to passing monks and be blessed in return. It was the only time of day when the streets were clear of tourists and hustlers. The neon fixtures could have just as easily been bamboo. Afterwards, they got into a tuk-tuk and rode to the bus station. There were two buses leaving for Rayong. Sai refused to get on the fan cooled, orange line, remarking that it was a chicken coop on wheels. She insisted that they take the more comfortable air-conditioned blue line. Why not? From Rayong, they rode a passenger truck to the pier at Ban Dai. A boat was about to leave for the island. They boarded, fifty baht a head, and held on as the boat rocked in the salty waves. Watching the mainland disappear was one of the greatest thrills Mantana had experienced in a long time.

They made it to the island and checked into a guesthouse twenty minutes before the noon hour. From then on, they did exactly as they said and played in the sea. The water was far from still, and big waves occasionally swept in, throwing them off their feet to a cacophony of laughter and screams and rushing water. And once they recovered, another would be fast approaching, rising higher and higher until the crest broke and came crashing down in a wonderful chaos. The sky was blue and clear.

It was perfect.

"I'm so happy that we came!" Mantana called to Neung, who was trying to regain her balance in the surf. "I don't want to go back!"

"I saw an a-go-go bar about fifty meters past the pier. Maybe you should be an island prostitute."

Mantana shielded her eyes and looked at the palm trees growing at the edge of where white sand became Someone's Property.

"It wouldn't be like it is today," she hollered back.

Neung couldn't reply. A strong rush of water pushed her over just as she had managed to stand. Mantana and Sai laughed. Neung decided it was time to get out of the water.

*

It had only been a day that had gone by, but to Mantana, it was the first memory of her second life that was worth hanging onto. In the evening, they ate to the accompaniment of the surf, then drank cocktails at a seaside bar. Money was no object. Not when life was this good. They had each declared not to talk about work, but somehow, the conversation always drifted back to the Cherry Bar and beyond. Sai had only just discovered that Mantana was once a singer and wanted to know what it was like.

"My face hurt from smiling all the time."

"Still," said Sai, "wasn't it better than being a bargirl?"

"In the nightclub, I always had the opportunity to close my eyes and lose myself in a song," she said. "That's something I can't do at the Cherry Bar. I can never forget where I am, no matter how hard I try."

"You're always so serious, Joy. You need to lighten up and have fun."

Mantana looked her square in the eye. "Don't you feel sick about what you've become?" she asked. "Doesn't it hit you as you're going to sleep or eating your lunch or looking to see what time it is?"

"I haven't become anything," said Sai.

"You're right. We haven't become anything. We've become less of what we used to be."

There was a sharp BANG that jolted her in her seat. Neung had slapped her hand on the table.

"The only thing you've become is richer!" she said. "You haven't grown a third eye and you don't stink like shit when you walk down the street. You have a job, you have an apartment, and you have friends. How is that different from a secretary or a waitress or a telephone operator? It's not different! It's not different at all!"

Neung's eyes were alight with anger. She lowered them and continued in an uncertain voice.

"I'm tired of listening to you talk about yourself as though you've turned into - into some kind of monster. Because when you do, you're not just talking about yourself. You're talking about me and Sai and every other working girl who's trying to make a living."

There was a long, uncomfortable silence.

"You're right," said Mantana. "I'm sorry. I know there are girls who live with this like a telephone operator lives with being a telephone operator." She looked at Neung and gave her a half-hearted smile. "I just don't think I'm one of them."

"Give it time, Joy."

Her voice was different now. The anger was gone, and she seemed to be pleading with Mantana to agree with her. Like she was looking at those eighteen years before her as a jail sentence she didn't want to spend in solitary confinement.

"Are you OK, Neung?" asked Sai.

"I'm fine. Why?"

"Because you're acting drunk but you're still on your first cocktail."

Mantana looked at Neung's eyes and waited for her friend's reaction.

"I'm fine," she said, and glanced at Sai with noticeable resentment.

Sai nodded, and cracked a piece of ice between her teeth. "Do you know why I hate those buffalo whores so much?" she said. "They didn't die when they were supposed to. They managed to outlive the pussy sickness and psycho customers, and they still didn't kill themselves."

"They're survivors," said Mantana.

"My grandmother is a survivor. She's the only woman I know to have lost her house nine times to floods. Can you believe it? Nine houses in sixty years swept away by the river. Those buffalo whores aren't survivors. They're lucky, that's all. Me, I don't want to be lucky like that. I'm going to kill myself on my twenty-seventh birthday."

"That's in six years!"

"Twenty-six if I get any fatter."

Mantana knew that Sai was oblivious to Neung's eighteen-year declaration. She tried to change the subject, only now the two girls were arguing over a prostitute's time limit and there was little to do but wait it out. Sai was rigid on her five or six more years of fading beauty. Neung was determined to see it through until middle age.

"What do you think, Joy?"

"I was just wondering if Pen has a time limit."

They ignored her comment and continued their debate.

The next day, they all got on a bus back to Pattaya.

9

Mantana's room had not moved. Everything sat right where she remembered leaving it. There were no red roses on her gray sheets, no gift wrapped boxes of chocolates, no balloons tied to the neck of her rotating fan. Still, over one hundred men would be happy to see her that night. Mantana could no longer see the irony. She felt only the loneliness.

Her overnight bag could wait. Other things were more important. She found a clean glass and sat down to drink what was left of the vodka. The first sip didn't make her feel any better about being back. But feeling better wasn't the point. Not feeling anything at all - *that's* what she was aiming for.

There was a knock. Mantana hid the bottle and put her eye to the peephole. Then she opened the door.

It was Yim. She was dressed in green pants and an oversized black T-shirt that said "Aloha Hawaii." Her face was suffering from an outbreak of pimples, and she had applied a cream meant to blend in with one's skin tone. Only Yim's skin tone was a few shades off.

"Phii Buoy wants us all in an hour early tonight," she said.

"Why?"

Yim didn't know. Mantana invited her in for a drink. OK, but she could only stay for one. Phii Buoy was giving her a hundred baht to give everyone the message. Mantana fixed a drink and handed it to her.

"What's in it?"

"Vodka."

"Vodka and what?"

"More vodka. It must be important, whatever Phii Buoy has to tell us."

"She told me not to bother with Pen. She was acting crazy again last night. I bet Phii Buoy fired her."

"Aw, no. What did she do now?"

Yim drank some of her vodka, gagged, and wiped her mouth with the back of her hand.

"Don't you have any ice?"

"Keep drinking. You'll get used to it. Tell me about last night."

"Pen was exposing herself to customers. All the customers. Then she started jumping on their laps and kissing them on the mouth. She even knocked a glass out of a man's hand and broke it on the floor."

"She was fired for breaking a glass?"

"This was at ten o'clock, when it was still illegal to be hustling. We all tried to warn her, but there was this look in her eye like she couldn't understand what we were saying. Phii Buoy finally had to tell her to leave."

"Damn" said Mantana. "Damn! Damn!"

"There wasn't anything you could have done, Joy."

Yim set her drink on the table and hiccupped.

"I've got to go tell the rest of the girls," she said.

Mantana saw her to the door. Before she left, Mantana took

her hand and squeezed it tight.

"What were you doing," she asked, "before you were kidnapped?"

"I was studying to be a lawyer in Bangkok, only I ran out of money after my first year."

"You want to be a lawyer?"

"Sure! I'm smart enough. I'm just not rich enough. I'll see you in a few hours," said Yim.

The room was quiet again.

*

"*Clean and Happy! Bye Bye Bac-tee-ree-aah!*"

Neung was in a good mood. She sang and danced a pair of chopsticks through her bowl of *gooey teeo*, tilting them to the left, the right, and straight up in the air like a pair of legs in a line dance.

"Why are you so happy?" asked Mantana.

"No more Pen."

"You don't know that for sure."

"*Bye bye cra-zee Pen!*"

"Eat," said Mantana, annoyed with her friend. "We're going to be late."

The girls sat in the shade of a soup stand on South Pattaya Road. The family that owned the restaurant had served them many times in the past. That didn't make them any friendlier. The old hen of a cook, for example, insisted upon sprinkling garlic in Mantana's soup when she specifically asked her not to. These days, she waited until the soup was in the bowl and called out from her table "No garlic!" which elicited a dirty look from everyone who worked there. Only today, her thoughts were on Pen and she had forgotten to yell.

"She did it again," she said, looking at her soup. "She put

garlic in my soup. I swear, if I ever own a *gooey teeo* stand -"

Neung let out a loud, sarcastic laugh and pretended to choke on a *look chin* ball of pork and other ingredients.

"Now that's moving up in the world, Joy!"

"I didn't say I was going to do it. I was just imagining."

"You'd be better off..."

Her words trailed off into a meaningless mumble, and she lowered her face to shovel in more noodles with her chopsticks.

"Mm," she said. "Mm."

Mantana watched her. "Neung," she said.

"What?"

"Is there anything you want to tell me?"

"Not that I can think of. Why?"

Mantana shrugged off the question. Neung didn't press it. She ate the rest of her soup while Mantana fished the garlic out of hers. When it was finally edible, she had lost her appetite. *I could use a drink*, she thought, and would have said it out loud and unashamed on any other day but this one. Instead, she sat stringing together Neung's outbursts and odd behavior over the past few weeks and wondered where she was putting the needle since the crooks of both her arms were clean. Back of the leg? Ass?

"Why are you looking at me like that?" said Neung, suddenly.

"We should go," said Mantana.

They paid for their meals and walked back to the bar, each holding her own suspicion of the other.

*

Pen was not fired. Pen was dead. It happened some time in the early morning hours. She had tied one end of an electrical cord around the headstand of her bed, the other around her neck. Then she lay down and rolled off the edge. Her face was only four inches from the floor when the police found her. How did they know to come looking? Pen phoned them moments before to say that her body would be waiting.

The girls of the Cherry Bar sat along the wall and looked at the floor. No one cried. No one felt anything except a little bit surprised that she had the courtesy to telephone the police first. Even Mantana, who had sneaked in the remainder of her vodka before the meeting, took the news as if she were reading the warning label on a pack of cigarettes. Pen was dead. Smoking caused cancer. Neung was high on drugs. Mantana was probably an alcoholic. And here it was only Tuesday. Everything was as real as it wasn't real. Some peanuts would be nice, she thought.

Then it was Mr. Simmons who stood before them. After that first meeting where his future employees cornered him behind a movie screen, Mr. Simmons rarely communicated with the girls. He usually sat in his office, sulking over the fate of his "gentlemen's club," or dreaming up new and different ways to become more organized and efficient. He spent so much time wondering where the past had gone and where the future was headed that he hardly got any real work done. Of course, all his breakthrough ideas were immediately implemented and quickly forgotten. Mr. Simmons obviously regarded Pen's suicide as a serious matter. This time he had an idea and he was bringing it to them directly. Even Phii Buoy appeared to be in the dark. She translated as he spoke.

"When I was a Boy Scout some forty odd years ago, our scoutmaster took us to Lake Wadhams and made us all pick a buddy before we went swimming. That meant each of us was responsible for someone else. If the boy I chose as my buddy started having trouble, or looked as though he were about to drown, I was to holler for help, and not try to save him myself. That way, I wasn't in danger of going under with him. I don't know why Pen did what she did, but I suspect that some of you do. Maybe it could have been prevented had Buoy or I known. Maybe not. Nevertheless, we're going to try the buddy system here, in this bar. We're going to look out for one another, just like boy scouts, ah, *girl* scouts. Now, if I leave the choice up to you, you'll just pick a girl who is already your buddy and continue to keep secrets from us. So I've written up this list of who will be buddies with who."

Mr. Simmons removed a folded piece of yellow paper from his shirt pocket and read off the pairs of "buddies." As everyone expected, the young were paired with the old, the "babies" with the "buffaloes." No one was fooled. Mr. Simmons was using Pen's death to try to force everyone to get along. Sai was teamed with the woman who smoked cigarettes with her pussy and Neung got the one who worked with frogs and eels and baby chicks. Mantana's buddy had yet to arrive.

"She's new," said Phii Buoy.

When Mr. Simmons finished reading the list, he told all the girls to sit with their partners and get to know each other. Become friends. Cake and coffee would be provided.

No one moved.

"Any questions?" he asked.

The girls looked around as if they had been told to assemble a car out of rubber bands and old shoes.

"I have a question," said Sai. "Suppose my buddy kills herself. Does that mean my pay gets cut?"

Mr. Simmons looked at his wife. She didn't bother to translate.

"We haven't discussed that yet, but it's a good point. You can be certain there will be repercussions for the loss of a buddy."

Another question, this time from Yim.

"Are we getting paid for coming in early tonight?"

"No."

"We're out of candles," said the woman who dripped wax on her tongue and breasts. "And the ones that you've been buying burn too slowly."

"I'll look into it," said Phii Buoy. "Are there any questions about my husband's idea?"

"Yes," said Neung. "Is he serious?"

The room fell uncomfortably silent. Mantana shook her head as if emerging from a deep sleep. Pen was dead. The widow Amnuay was living with her father. Jakkrit asked to marry her. What was everyone talking about?

"Excuse me," she said. "I want to know when the funeral will be."

Phii Buoy looked surprised. "You mean Pen's funeral? There won't be one. She wrote down phony telephone numbers and addresses on her personal data sheet. If she has any relatives, I don't know how to contact them."

"What about her identity card?" asked the prostitute Ay. "You should be able to track someone down with that."

"It's in police hands now," said Phii Buoy, obviously annoyed.

Mantana closed her eyes. The police might try. They might not. How important was a dead prostitute? Her body would most likely be handed over to a foundation that dealt with the unknowns of society. The foundation would bury her in a grave along with all the other unidentified, unclaimed corpses that week. There she would lie for a period of no less than one year. After that, the bones would be dug up, washed in a chemical solution, and burned, the end.

"If there are no further questions, we'll bring out the cake and coffee," said Mr. Simmons, who had been listening without a clue as to what was being said.

"Nong Joy," said Phii Buoy, "Can I see you for a moment?"

Mantana stood as the rest of the girls broke into nervous chatter. She moved to where Phii Buoy was standing and waited as she gave final instructions to "do as my husband says."

"Let's go in back," she said. "You know I had no idea what my husband was going to propose just now, but it actually fits in with my plan rather well."

The office door opened. Ad the doorman came out with a tray of chocolate cake cut into two-inch squares. White frosting over a pink and smiling rabbit spelled out the words "Happy Tugboat." Wit stood alongside him with plates and forks. The door swung shut behind them.

"Is Mr. Simmons ready?" asked Ad.

"Maybe we should have bought fruit. Cake is so - fattening." Phii Buoy dipped a finger into the frosting and stuck it in her mouth. With her other hand, she waved the pair on. She removed her finger with a smack of the lips.

"Are you all right, Nong Joy?"

"Yes, ma'am."

"Is there anything you're not telling me?"

Mantana wondered if she could smell the alcohol on her breath. She swallowed and spoke.

"I think that we should hold a funeral ceremony for Pen."

"I thought you didn't like Pen."

"She was one of us."

"Funerals are expensive, Joy."

"Then we should at least have her body cremated at a temple."

"I'll make a deal with you, Joy. I'll put up half the money for a funeral, a cremation, whatever you want, if you can raise the other half. Then we'll talk. Right now, there's someone waiting that I want you to meet."

"Oh, ma'am, I haven't looked at myself in the mirror."

"It's not a customer. It's a new employee. Sort of a new employee. I already decided to entrust her to your care before this whole buddy thing was ever mentioned. You seem to be the most mature of all the girls working here."

"I don't understand."

Phii Buoy smiled and opened the office door. The girl who

was to be Mantana's buddy had apparently been waiting since the start of the meeting. She stood upon their arrival and waiied. Mantana returned the greeting. The girl wasn't like any prostitute she had ever seen. Mantana looked at Phii Buoy, looked at the girl, then looked at Phii Buoy again.

"She's seventeen," said Phii Buoy, anticipating her question. "She only looks twelve. She won't be dancing; she won't even start work until after ten, when there's less chance of a police inspection. She'll stay in back and only come out for interested customers."

"Seventeen?" said Mantana.

"Your job will be to set her up. You'll check customers out before introducing her and make sure she's not going home with a lunatic. I trust your judgment, Joy, which is why I selected you."

Mantana gazed at the girl, standing nervous and awkward in the center of the room. She had shoulder-length hair and dark brown skin. Probably from the Northeast. It would be another year before the girl could be legally employed. Until then she would have to make a living under the table. Slipped out of back rooms and put away quietly before anyone caught on.

"You want me to be her pimp?"

"I want you to look after her. You'll receive ten percent of whatever she makes and a five hundred baht bonus after every ten customers. All I ask is that you find someone for her before making yourself available."

Phii Buoy paused and waited for a response. A question, a nod of the head, anything. Mantana just stared at the girl.

"Well?" she asked. "Aren't you going to ask her name?"

"Excuse me," said Mantana. "I haven't eaten yet today. I'm going to get some cake before it's all gone."

She opened the door and walked out. Phii Buoy didn't call after her. Back in the bar, Mr. Simmons was still trying to coordinate the scene. He wasn't having much luck.

"Sai! Neung is not your buddy! Who's your buddy? Go

find your buddy! You too, Neung. You two can chit chat later. Right now we're mingling. Like at a party!"

It's a madhouse, thought Mantana.

*

The hardest part about cremating Pen wasn't finding a coffin for under a thousand baht or locating nine monks who would pray at the burning of her body. The hardest part was convincing the police that she was actually going to go through with it and not sell the internal organs to the Koreans or the Chinese. The ceremony would take place on the following Sunday. Mantana asked all the girls to attend though she had not asked them to help with the cost. Everyone told her they would come. Everyone stayed home. Mantana went alone to listen to the monks chant and watch the smoke rise from the top of the chedi-shaped crematorium. She sat alone, and she went home alone. And the next morning she returned with a basket of food to make merit and collect the remains. These were stored in an urn that she also paid for with the money she was saving for her father. She placed it on the small table near the window of her apartment and decided that whenever visitors came by and asked "What's that?" she'd answer "That's Pen," and that would be the end of it.

10

The hot season was over, said all the newspapers, and the rainy season had begun. The storms seemed less frequent but more violent than the years before. There was a flood. The flood lasted for several days. People waded through the streets on their way to work while vendors sold *som tam* from flat-bottomed boats. Children played on the curb, waiting for waves made by passing buses. Through a window above a mini-mart, sitting with a glass of vodka and Pen's ashes, Mantana looked down upon the quiet chaos. With the coming of the rain, she no longer bothered with sunsets and stone benches. She only left her room twice a day, once for food, once for work. She had heard that the bigger go-gos were losing business due to a lack of tourists. Bar owners were complaining about the dirty water and dead animals floating by. *Som num na*. Mantana didn't feel sorry for them. She had heard stories of these two and three level go-gos with their multi-platform catwalks and special effects. Drinks were expensive, the girls were unfriendly, and security was always watching. Tourists were lured in with the promise of something grand and sent out again drunk, broke, sexually aroused, and mad as cobras. One good thing about the rain was that it taught these thieves and vamps to be a little more respectful of their profession.

Respectful? Mantana traced the water ring left by her glass and wondered if her trial by fire were over. Maybe it was Pen's death, maybe it was something else, but somewhere in the midst of all that rain, her working life had become, well, *easier*. A month ago, she would say that insanity had finally set in, only she didn't feel insane. Nor did she feel hopeless to the point of despair. What was, was, and it seemed like an awful waste of time and energy feeling terrible about it. It was from this perspective that Neung's eighteen-year contract with herself no longer seemed so impossible. Mantana figured with pencil and paper that she could reach her own goal in no more than six or seven. What was her goal? A big number with lots of zeros after it. That much.

She made flowers out of her zeros and blackened the middles as the rain tapped against her window.

*

The days became weeks became months. Mantana still checked the expiration date on the milk she bought but, for the life of her, didn't know whether it was September or October. Though a splinter of ice in her heart might have helped her accept the reality of her days and nights, there was never an assurance that trouble had passed.

Take the buffaloes.

Mr. Simmons's buddy system only served to make enemies of the girls who didn't much like each other anyway, and the rift between the original girls and their older co-workers had grown wider than the catwalk they all had to share. Words were rarely spoken, but the undercurrent of animosity caused tempers to flare and often provided entertainment for customers that couldn't be found on any special show list in town.

For Sai, every night was the last straw.

"I can't work like this anymore," she threatened. "As far as I'm concerned, it's them or us."

"What are you going to do?" asked Neung.

"I'm going to talk to Phii Buoy. Tomorrow, before work. Do you know what I'm going to say?"

Mantana and Neung knew perfectly well what she would say. They had listened to her complaints daily, and had given up disputing her various facts and fictions. There was no proof, for example, that the buffalo whores performed their own abortions. Nor was it true that they had surgically implanted an instrument that allowed them to open bottles with their vaginas. There was validity, however, to the obvious annoyances such as the way the older women regarded them. Mantana and Sai and Neung were "babies" though they had been there since the opening of the bar. The word was thrown around in English by the women until it was impossible to be buddies with them. There were also the nights when stage dancing turned into a raucous display at their instigation, forcing half of the girls to wait outside while customers were invited to strip down to their underwear and dance alongside the old maids. In the end, it was decided. If Sai was willing to stand up to Phii Buoy and launch into one of her now famous tirades against these women, Mantana and Neung agreed to lend their names to the cause.

Both Mantana and Neung showed up earlier than usual on the day of Sai's meeting with Phii Buoy. The office door was closed and a DO NOT DISTURB sign, stolen from a hotel, hung on the doorknob. There was a crazy feeling between them. Maybe this was it. Maybe Phii Buoy would fire them all for their lack of cooperation and constant complaining. They agreed to take Sai out to a nice restaurant and get her drunk if that was the case. None of them wanted to think about what they'd do after that.

Five thirty, five forty-five. Yim showed up and asked what they were doing.

"We're waiting for Sai," said Neung.

"Why? Where is she?"

"She's in Phii Buoy's office telling her that we don't want to work with the buffaloes anymore."

"Really?"

"Yes. And we might all get fired," added Mantana.

"Count me in!" said Yim. "That bitch Look-Gayt tries to steal my customers every time I turn my head away."

Yim took a seat alongside them. The door to Phii Buoy's office remained closed. Neung tiptoed close to it and listened. A big smile crept across her face. She hurried back to where the girls sat.

"They're really going at it in there!" she said. "Fighting like tigers!"

Everyone jumped as the door opened. A fat man in a yellow shirt came out, followed by Mr. Simmons. It was Mr. Helmut from the Mirage Bar. He and Mr. Simmons walked to the exit, speaking to each other in loud, business-talk voices, and rattling their keys in the front pockets of their pants. As the large man pushed the curtains aside to leave, who else but Phii Buoy came strolling in, carrying a plastic bag from the grocery store.

Arai wah?

Mantana looked at Neung. Neung looked at Yim. The bosses finished their good-byes and moved away from the curtains. Phii Buoy had some new candles for the fire woman to try. She spotted the girls sitting along the catwalk and excused herself from her husband. Her lip curved into a sneer as she approached.

"Uh-oh," said Mantana.

Phii Buoy stopped before them, and folded her arms across her breasts.

"How long have you known?" she asked. The question was directed at Neung.

"Known what, ma'am?"

"How long have you known that Sai was planning to quit today?"

"Sai quit?" asked Yim.

Neung protested. "I didn't know anything about it!"

"We thought she wanted to talk to you about - something," said Mantana.

"She talked to me all right. She told me that her mother was ill, and she was needed at home."

There was a dumb silence as the girls lowered their eyes to avoid her stare.

"Is there anything else?"

"Not that I know of, ma'am," said Neung, quietly.

"Joy?"

Mantana hesitated before she spoke. "No, ma'am. Nothing else."

Phii Buoy sighed dramatically, turned on her heels, and disappeared into the back. The girls looked from one to the other in bewilderment.

"She quit," said Yim. "I can't believe she - *quit.*"

"She didn't have the guts to stand up to Phii Buoy," said Neung. "She was a coward."

"Actually," Mantana said quietly, "I'd say she's just the opposite."

*

Tai was the name of the seventeen-year-old girl who waited in the back office and played a hand-held video game while the rest of the girls hustled for her. Since Mantana refused to take on the responsibility by herself, the task of finding a man for Tai was split among all the bargirls with a two-hundred-baht bonus thrown in as an incentive. For the first few nights, it was hard to remember that she was back there. She was a shy, quiet thing who jumped at the sound of her own name. Phii Buoy gave the details. Tai's parents died when she was little. She went to live with her uncle, who abused and raped her. There was more to the story, and Phii Buoy told it very well. Around the part where she was forced to work in a sweat shop for fourteen hours a day, the story began to grow dull. It was tragedy upon tragedy, and they had heard it, if not lived it, all before. The innocent were punished, puppies were kicked, pink dresses were torn to shreds, candy was murdered. Meanwhile, the guilty smoked cigars and had their nose hairs trimmed. Phii Buoy could speak with a voice full of emotion and even throw in a few tears. Everyone already knew how the story ended. Tai went to work in a broken-down brothel full of stains on the walls and sheets and ceiling and floor, while the ones responsible were home watching game shows on television. She was forced to take on two, sometimes three men at a time. The nightmare ended when she ran away in the middle of the night. Phii Buoy honestly believed she was doing her best to help the poor girl, and hoped everyone would lend a hand in finding her a decent customer.

The buffalo whore named Pear was the first to collect the two-hundred-baht finder's fee. The customer she happened upon was a businessman from Alaska, bald, with a mousy face and wire-rimmed glasses. Name: Lloyd. Lloyd was interested in young girls. Lloyd was in luck. Word got around fast. Tai had a customer! Phii Buoy nodded to Mantana, who was in the middle of a stage set. It was now her job to see that she was ready. Mantana waited for the song to end, then climbed down and went in back.

"Tai," she said, "you've got one."

Tai sat in a chair hunched over her video game. It was a Japanese game in which a tiny computer chicken had to be fed, played with, and allowed to sleep. The chicken also crapped tiny computer blips that had to be cleaned up to keep the minuscule barnyard smelling fresh. Failure to respond to the beeps and whines that indicated hunger, playtime, or make poop time meant that the chicken would become depressed and die, and the game would be over. The team of Japanese scientists who designed the game obviously gave no thought to a prostitute's work schedule when they allowed the fate of a nonexistent chicken to be placed in her hands.

"Tai," Mantana said again.

"My chicken's been alive for two weeks," she said. "It's almost feeding time. If he doesn't eat, he'll be cranky."

"If the customer waiting for you doesn't get laid soon, I think he'll be crankier."

Tai let out a long breath. "All right," she said. "But I'm bringing it with me."

*

The cost of buying young Tai from the bar was double that of the regular workers. Mantana escorted her out the back, down an alley, and into the street. Mr. Lloyd was waiting in front of the mini-mart, just as he had been told to do. Mantana turned to the girl and wiped a smudge of lipstick from her cheek.

"You have condoms, don't you?"

"No."

"Here. Take some of mine."

"Phii Joy, if I ask you something, will you tell me the truth?"

"Yes."

"Will it hurt?"

"Will what hurt?"

"You know - sex."

"Hello again!" said Mr. Lloyd, tired of waiting. He smiled and nodded, and his face looked like a squashed durian. "Shall I get a cab or do you want to take a tuk-tuk?"

The choice was made for him even as he spoke. A yellow cab pulled to the curb, and the passenger side window came rolling down.

"You!" said the driver, leaning over in his seat. "Where

you go?"

Mantana grasped Tai's skinny arm.

"Are you saying that this is your first time?"

"I've kissed boys before."

"What about your uncle?"

"I don't have an uncle."

"Then who abused and raped you after your parents died? Who made you work in a sweat shop for fourteen hours a day? Tai! What about the brothel you ran away from?"

Tai raised her eyebrows and smiled with the corners of her mouth. Mantana was dumbstruck. Every flashing light became a poison-tipped arrow streaking in some random direction. Every car horn and catcall was a fleeting spirit, out for blood. And the crazy thing was, only Mantana could see it.

Mr. Lloyd got into the cab and left the door open for her.

"Sweetheart!" he called. "The night's not getting any younger. And neither am I!"

"I have to go, Phii Joy."

Mantana let her arms drop. Tai turned, and disappeared into the back of the cab. Mantana watched the cab pull away from the curb and into traffic. All she could think of was her own first time and how awful it had been. Were all fates entered into so blindly? Mantana sighed and felt her new-found indifference crack. What could she do? What could anyone do? She had not been able to help Pen, and there was nothing she could do for Tai. All she seemed fit to do was look on helplessly and collect the ashes when it came time to die.

Mantana took the long way back to the bar. The alleyway gave her the chills. She returned just as the Fire Show was about to begin. Mantana hated the Fire Show more than the Pussy Open Bottle Show and thought about spending the next half hour fishing instead of hustling. Only four girls had already taken up the seats. Disappointed, she went back inside the bar.

The woman who performed the Fire Show was nicknamed Fai, or Fire, because everyone had forgotten what her real nickname was and started to call her by her talent instead. She liked it, apparently, because this was the name she used with customers. Her English was bad, however, and her introductions always came out "I a Fai, I a Fire." To which Mantana had heard three different customers reply "You're five?"

Fai began her show by holding a pair of burning torches and swinging them around until red and orange circles appeared at her sides. Next, she held the flames close to her legs, arms, and breasts. The fire woman never caught on fire, although a drunken Englishman once burned his hand trying to prove that the whole thing was a sham. That was the first and last time anyone questioned the authenticity of the Fire Show.

Mantana changed back into her bikini and came out just as Fai was putting the torches in her mouth. It was time for the second act of her show. The D.J. slowed down the music, and Ad the doorman handed up a pair of burning candles. This part of the show lasted about five minutes and earned her five hundred baht. When it was over, her legs, stomach, breasts, arms, face, and tongue would be coated in hot wax. Then she wouldn't be the fire woman anymore. She would be painful to look at.

Mantana found Phii Buoy adding receipts at the bar.

"I'm back, ma'am," she said.

"Any trouble?"

It was probably better, Mantana decided, if Phii Buoy didn't know that Tai was a virgin. "No," she said, "no trouble at all."

"There's a *farang* sitting by the wall over there that's been asking for you. Why don't you go keep him company?"

Mantana took her boss's suggestion and made her way to the man against the wall. The smoke from Fai's burning torches had temporarily replaced the stink of ashtrays and sweat, and soon the candles would make the place smell like an Indian restaurant.

Mantana sat down next to a young man with a small pony-tail and sleep-ridden eyes. She set a hand on his knee.

"Hello what you name?"

"Oh wow!" said the young man. "You're wearing a number. Just what does that mean?"

A waitress knocked upon their table and pointed. Mantana looked in the direction indicated and saw Phii Buoy motioning to her right and mouthing something. *Mai chai kon nee!* Not that one.

"Oh, accuse me," said Mantana and moved to the next foreigner seated against the wall.

"Hello what you name?"

The man turned and looked at her. He had white hair and a white mustache, though he really wasn't that old. His face lit up when he saw her.

"Joy! You're here! I asked the mama-san to send you over, but she said you were out. I thought I'd missed you!"

"Hi!" said Mantana. Who was this man and how did he know her name?

"I was so afraid on the plane ride over that you'd quit working or found someone to take care of you. Of course, that's just what you need, isn't it? Someone to take care of you."

The man with the white mustache took her hand in both of his. Mantana looked hard at his face. Searching, searching. She put a pair of black-framed glasses on his nose and took away his mustache. *Na lae!* She had him. Four months ago, maybe three. He once bought her out and took her to a nice hotel. The sex was quick and clean, the tip above average. Just a minute, she'd have his name. It began with a W. Water... Waller...

"Wall-ter!"

"You remember!" He was so happy. "I didn't think you would."

Of course she remembered. Prostitutes and elephants never forget. But elephants didn't get ladydrinks for their talent.

"Can I buy you a soda, Joy?"

"Yes."

Mantana excused herself and went to the bar to claim her first drink of the evening. She'd probably be able to get two more off him before he bought her out. Maybe it was only ninety baht extra in her purse but Mantana had trained herself to think in two sets of numbers. One set for herself, and one for her father. Three ladydrinks would be enough for her to live on for one day. A generous tip went home to her father and might someday be enough to drive the widow Amnuay from her house.

There was a short burst of applause as the fire woman exited the stage. Sure enough, her skin was suffocated and senseless under trails of different colored waxes. Mantana stood at the bar and waited for Sai to appear with her balloons and blowgun. Only the music started again and three girls whose names she didn't know took to the stage in neon bikinis. Sai wasn't going to shoot balloons or play the bugle or blow out birthday candles on a plastic cake that said "Cherry Bar" anymore. Sai had quit.

It would take a while to get used to that.

For the next hour and a half, Mantana drank her ladydrink, excused herself to dance and returned again to listen to Walter talk. Walter liked to talk. He told her about the farm he owned in Idaho and all the fresh potatoes and carrots he grew there. Walter said she'd find it very peaceful. Mantana nodded and smiled, but really didn't know what he was going on about. And it was difficult to pay attention when thoughts of Tai clutching the bedsheets under bald-headed Lloyd stuck needles in her mind.

"Would you like another drink?" asked Walter.

Mantana shook her head. Walter took out his wallet and handed her a five-hundred-baht bill. He said something in English, but Mantana neither heard nor cared. The language of money spoke loud and clear. She could do her job blindfolded if only men didn't like to look at her eyes. She took the money and motioned to a waitress for the check.

"I go put on clothes," she said.

Walter smiled and assured her that he wouldn't move. She already knew he wouldn't. As she made her way to the back, a small figure brushed against her shoulder and went speeding ahead. Mantana stopped, not believing her eyes for a moment.

It was Tai.

Mantana turned to see whether anyone was chasing her. There didn't appear to be anyone in sight. She quickened her pace to the back, only to find the office door shut and locked from the inside.

Mantana knocked. "Tai! Tai, it's Joy. Open the door!"

She jiggled the doorknob. Nothing. Mr. Simmons was out making his rounds of everyone else's bars, but Phii Buoy would have a key. She smiled at Walter as she passed by and held up a finger that meant one minute. Then she stopped again. Tai's customer, Mr. Lloyd, was standing at the entrance way shouting at Phii Buoy. His face was no longer squashed like a durian but crumpled up, sort of like a paper bag. She moved closer to hear.

"Look at my hand! Look! I tried to get the little bitch to put down her video game for thirty seconds, and she bit me! The little whore bit me!"

"I'm sorry, sir," said Phii Buoy, using her best calm-down voice. "Would you like another girl?"

"I don't want another girl! I want my money back! And you'd better hope that I don't have rabies!"

Phii Buoy refunded his money and added an extra five hundred baht for any inconveniences. She tried to get him out as quickly and quietly as possible, but he was set on playing out his role of the victim. He broke away from Phii Buoy and began to display his right hand to other customers in the bar.

"See that?" he said, raising his thumb before a foreigner's eyes. "Whore bit me."

"Yeh, that's some souvenir."

After three more strangers paid witness to the offense, Mr. Lloyd took his money, took his thumb, and stormed out of the Cherry Bar.

"Where is she?" said Phii Buoy in a voice that would frighten children and small animals.

"Ma'am," said Mantana. "There's something you should know."

"*Where is she?*"

Mantana bit her tongue. "She's in your office."

Mantana watched her boss's mouth twitch, then followed her as she cut a line through girls and customers. Another smile for Walter, another "just a minute," and she was back listening to angry knuckles against the door of the office.

"Tai! You open this door right now!"

Mantana had never seen Phii Buoy this angry before.

"Ma'am, you really should listen to what I have to say."

Phii Buoy stopped rapping the door and glared at Mantana. "What?"

"Tai's a virgin."

Her reaction was visible. The anger that had been propping her up and making her seem physically bigger than she really was vanished in an instant. Her eyes softened and became almost motherly. She leaned against the door as if she were going to faint.

"A virgin," she said. "I almost sold a seventeen-year-old virgin for one thousand baht."

"You didn't know," said Mantana, feeling a certain sympathy for her boss.

"Of course not. If I did, do you think I'd have let her go for only a thousand? Virgins are an endangered species in this town, if you haven't noticed. I've heard some foreigners will pay up to ten thousand for one."

Mantana backed away from the office door. Her sympathy had done a back flip. Phii Buoy was... Well, she was nothing but...

Just a pile of... There wasn't a word for what Phii Buoy was.

Meanwhile, a handful of girls had gathered to watch. Neung was among them.

"What happened, Joy? Why did Tai attack that man?"

"He tried to take her chicken away."

Mantana turned her back on the crowd and went to gather her clothes and purse from the small metal locker near the rear exit. Tai had given in, given up, and let Phii Buoy in. There was a scream, a slap, then no sound at all, except for the office door clicking shut. Mantana moved to the dressing room and changed outfits. She polished her face, reapplied her lips, and shook some powder onto the palms of her hands. What she saw in the mirror had ceased to be a disguise she wore while she was on the clock. Now, it was all her. When she came out, Neung and an even bigger crowd were loitering in the hallway.

"Oho!" she said. "This isn't a car crash! Get back to work!"

Surprisingly, they scattered, back to their stools and customers. Even Neung didn't hang about to ask questions. She stopped and wondered where this voice came from. Certainly, it wasn't from strength like that of Phii Aor. Nor was it from authority like that of Phii Buoy. No, she thought, this was the voice of something that was feared. Something ugly that threatened to get uglier if its demands weren't met. How much more of her, she wondered, had gone rotten inside?

Mantana lifted a strand of hair that had become glued to her lips and went out to meet her man for the evening.

11

Walter stayed in the same hotel, quite possibly the same room in which he stayed before. Mantana went through her shy motions, knowing when to keep him in suspense and when to give him what he wanted. It was a strangely regular session, over in a matter of minutes once he had found his way inside her. That didn't matter to Walter. He seemed to get a bigger thrill out of watching her and trying to communicate.

"I've missed you so much! Ever since our night together, I haven't been able to get you out of my dreams. Do you understand?"

Mantana smiled and shook her head.

"You are here," tap, tap upon the head. "And you are here," tap, tap upon the heart.

Yes, she understood. She lived in his head and his heart. This wasn't new to her. Nor was it as much of an honor as Walter apparently thought it was. Tap, tap upon the billfold, thought Mantana. That's where she really lived.

Walter talked her to sleep. He talked her awake the next morning and didn't stop over breakfast. Sometimes, he spoke very seriously. Other times, he broke up laughing and told her "I think you know what I mean." But they were only words without meaning to Mantana.

Then he asked her to marry him.

Mantana had always been told to accept a marriage proposal, so long as the customer didn't regard it as an excuse for not tipping. The chances of a customer returning to buy out his girl were better if he believed they were engaged to be married. When Walter heard her OK, he clapped his hands and said, "Oh boy!" just as if he had won a new color television. Of course, he had to hug and hold her for a long time before letting her breathe again. Mantana knew to say OK. She didn't know what would come next.

"First of all, you'll have to stop working at the go-go bar," said Walter.

"No can stop," she said in English. "Father Joy no have money. He problem very big." Then she added for effect, "About doctor."

Walter spoke in a guarded tone.

"How much does he need?"

Mantana threw out a number. It was a big number, big enough to see how much old Walter really loved her.

"If I give you that much, do you promise to stop working at the bar?"

"Joy promise."

There were questions. The questions took longer than the speeches because Mantana had to answer them as well. Did she have AIDS? No, no AIDS, no boyfriend, no children. The questions were giving her a headache. No jail, no drugs, no alcohol, no gambling. Then he asked her something that would have made her laugh out loud, if she still had laughter inside her.

"And will you love me?"

"Yes," she said. "When you give money?"

"I have to go to the bank first. How about tonight?"

"Joy working."

"You said that you were going to stop."

"Working. Then money. Then stop."

"Stop working, then money."

Mantana sat on the bed and looked down at her toes. She didn't like this game. She had heard stories of working girls marrying their customers. Some of the stories reminded her of fairy tales. All of them were too fantastic to believe. Walter brought out a dictionary and placed it in her hands. She found the word for debt and explained that she owed the manager five thousand baht. All right, said Walter. Mantana scowled and continued to thumb through the pages. When would he refuse her? When would he say no?

There was the matter of an apartment, a monthly allowance. Mantana figured out what she would need to live on and multiplied by three. All right, said Walter.

"More," she said.

"How much more?"

"More more."

"All right," said Walter. "More."

There was no longer any doubt left. Walter loved her. Walter was the one. He was a human ATM machine. All she had to do was smile and pat his belly and let him tickle her nose with his mustache in order to withdraw funds. He was the customer all the girls at the Cherry, probably all the girls in Pattaya, dreamed of landing, crazy as he was rich and so head over heels in his notion of love that he'd empty his vaults, leave his family, and travel halfway around the world to claim the object of his obsession. A girl would have to be a fool to say no to him.

No! Not that easy! Where was the money? The money was in his promises. She would have to quit the bar to have it in her hand. And then there would be Walter every day. Happy Walter, horny Walter, foreign Walter. Maybe he would ask her to live in another country. A country that was not Thailand. Would he want children? Would their children ever see their grandfather?

Mantana held out her hand.

"Money for fucking," she said.

"Sweetheart -"

"Money for fucking!"

She stamped her foot on the hotel room floor and glared at him. It had never been real. She could see that he knew. Maybe he had been playing her along too, agreeing to everything with a price tag to see what lay underneath. Walter pulled out his billfold and gave her two thousand baht bills. She walked to the door, waiting for him to stop her. If he really, really loved her, he would stop her. She opened the door, stepped into the hallway, and closed it again. He didn't stop her. It was twelve steps to the elevator, one minute or more for the doors to open. He didn't stop her. He was a liar. He didn't love her.

A boy her age was manning the buttons inside the elevator. His eyes went up and down her body in the predictable manner. He pressed the G button only after Mantana moved to press it herself.

"How much?" he asked.

Mantana didn't answer. If she had a gun, she would shoot him. If she had a knife, she would skewer him. If she had a hurricane trapped in a shoebox, she would let it loose before his eyes and show him just how she felt.

"How much?" he said again.

The elevator stopped. The doors opened. Mantana walked out and made it to the street before she broke down in tears for the first time in months.

Strangely, it felt better than the best sex she was ever paid to have.

*

It was a long time before she could stop crying. It was a long time before she wanted to stop crying. As long as she cried, she felt alive, or rather, life returning. And even when her eyes were dry, it still felt like a wonderful flood of rainwater was gathering inside her. She walked aimlessly along the crowded, afternoon sidewalks and wondered about the murky but reliable peace of mind that had vanished in the air after Walter's proposal. She didn't feel like going back to her apartment, or the bar, or to Neung's or anywhere else in the whole stinking city. So she purchased a pair of dark sunglasses and a white hat and walked down unfamiliar streets in an attempt to forget. After three or four city blocks, she wanted a drink.

Across the street was a sign painted on a bedsheet advertising free wine. It seemed too good to be true. Mantana crossed over and read the fine print. The free wine was available by invitation only. Invitations were being sold for four hundred baht per person. Mantana moved to the side and slid her glasses down to look in the window. What she saw made her shiver as if some *songkran* prankster had held an ice cube to the back of her neck and let it slide down her spine. She readjusted her dark shades, and pulled her hat down low. Then she went in.

Once again she discovered herself among old friends. There weren't as many this time, but Mantana recognized most of the faces. They had found a new home, temporarily, upon a series of white, gallery walls. Jack's whores. If only they could see themselves now.

About a half dozen men and women held expensive wine glasses and examined the paintings with untrained eyes. Some of them said "beautiful" and some said "hmm," and moved on to the next painting. They couldn't be blamed, thought Mantana. How could they know what to look for?

"Excuse me, ma'am," said a Thai man with a round head and glasses who had been watching her since she walked in. "This exhibition is by invitation only."

Mantana dug in her purse, pulling out crumpled packs of cigarettes, used lipsticks, and a broken hairbrush before she found what she was looking for. She handed over the bent name card that

Jack had given her.

"Aah," said the man. "Very good. Are you from a magazine?"

Mantana might have smiled at the man's question if a familiar painting hanging on the wall behind him hadn't caught her eye. Familiar, yes, for it was the one Jack painted of her. Not a single color or line had changed since that night she first looked at it, and for a moment, she felt the old anger return. The nerve of the man! He didn't just stop at glorifying or demonizing the women he fucked, he had to put them in frames and hang them up for all to see. Who would know that the girls in these paintings were no one but ghosts that resided in Jack's imagination? Mantana had the sudden urge to take up paint and paintbrush and show the world what customers looked like to her. *Tch!* If art was all about expressing one's emotions like Nongluck had once told her, then she wouldn't need paint. She could just stand back and throw garbage at an empty canvas. There was her beauty. There was her honor. There were her emotions.

Only now, as she moved to stand before it, something altogether different occurred to her. It was like one of Wit's optical illusions that boggled the eyes until one learned how to see. Then it all became clear.

The girl in the painting was her. Jack had looked and he had seen. There were no untruths in his vision. He saw what all men saw. She was beautiful, she was sexy, she was sweet, and she was kind. She was a temporary relief from loneliness, depression, or a troubled marriage. She was an outlet for aggression, frustration, and stress. She was the closest and the farthest thing from love. Where was *she*? Where was *Mantana*? There was no more Mantana. Now there was only the Nong Joy of the painting. Her tears of the morning had been a reminder of the girl she once was and wasn't now. That's why they felt so good. This, she knew, was what Pen had realized, and what had driven her insane. For how could one walk among the living, when one existed only in men's dreams?

Mantana turned back to the man with the round head and

glasses.

"Is the artist here?"

He looked at her, then at the painting behind her. She waited, her face like stone. The man folded his hands and smiled.

"You'll find Mr. Del Rue in the Artists Lounge. Straight through that doorway."

The Artists Lounge was a small room with people shuffling in and out. No wonder. It was here that the wine was being served. Mantana made her way through the crowd and stopped when she saw Jack. He was seated on a sofa with a cigarette dangling from his lips, listening intently to another Thai man who sat directly across from him. He was dressed in his usual cowboy boots and jeans, and a black shirt with the sleeves buttoned. His shaggy locks were combed back, and he wore a pair of wire-rimmed spectacles that reflected the light and made his eyes difficult to see.

"He's being interviewed by *Men's World* Magazine," said the round-headed fellow who had boldly followed her into the tight space.

Mantana squeezed behind a waiter frantically filling empty glasses and positioned herself at Jack's side. At that moment, he called to the man who had been breathing down her back to come and help him with the language barrier. Pong was his name. He hadn't noticed her, and round-headed Pong was now occupied as translator, leaving her free to eavesdrop.

"Mr. Del Rue," said the Thai reporter, "tell our readers about this show."

Pong translated.

"Well, technically, this is my second show in Thailand. The first took place about two years ago in Bangkok and was only allowed to open for a select group. It closed after three days. For this new show, I selected paintings that I've done since then, although my freedom of expression has been slightly limited due to the lessons I learned from the last show."

"What do you mean?"

"The censor says I can only exhibit paintings of women from the waist up, and only in Pattaya."

The reporter continued. "Mr. Del Rue, because you reside in a country with such a great variety of beautiful scenes, many people are wondering why you chose prostitutes for your subject."

Pong began to translate. Jack nodded, and broke into the question before he had a chance to finish.

"The people who wonder why I choose to paint Thai prostitutes when there's a perfectly good waterfall or sunset or golden temple right around the corner are the people who don't like to admit that life isn't always pretty. And suffering - *real* suffering - doesn't end with a *mai pen rai*. Let me put it to you this way. When I look at a mountain, I see a mountain. When you look at a mountain, you see a mountain, too. There's no question about it. But when you and I look at a girl dancing on a catwalk, laying eggs with her pussy, I'm not so sure we see the same thing. Maybe you see something sexy, something revolting, I don't know. Maybe you see something you wish you could sweep under a rug and forget about. I paint to show you - to show anyone who has the humanity to look - that these girls are human beings."

Pong translated. The Thai reporter jotted down a note. He was about to ask another question when an onlooker interrupted him. It was Mantana.

"Why you no speak true?"

The chatter around the room suddenly went silent. Jack turned to see the girl in the hat and sunglasses standing next to him and furrowed his brow. Mantana removed her disguise and looked at him.

"Joy!" he said.

Pong the translator got to his feet, clearly with the intention of removing her from the premises. Mantana took a step back, but kept her eyes locked on Jack.

"Wait, Pong," he said. "Let her speak."

Mantana repeated her question in Thai. "Why don't you tell the truth?"

"What did she say?" asked Jack.

The translator translated. Jack put a finger to his chin and looked at her. "What truth?" he asked.

"You said you paint us because you love us," said Mantana, recalling his words from their evening together. "All of us."

Jack smiled when he heard the words translated. "That's right," he said. "I said that."

The magazine reporters scribbled away.

"The truth is," she said, feeling her lower lip quiver. "We can never be loved as human beings. And you cannot be loved without your money."

The man with the round head and glasses paused before translating. It was in this instant that Mantana turned and walked away. The crowd of people parted as if afraid to have any contact with her.

"What did she say?" she heard Jack demand. "Dammit, man, tell me what she said!"

Maybe he would understand her words, maybe he would even run after her. It was no use chasing her now. Once she left the room, she faded away into the sidewalks and the streets and the pale yellow sunlight, as only real ghosts can.

12

The following afternoon, Mantana told Phii Buoy that Walter with the white hair and mustache was crazy and to inform him that she was gone if he came looking for her.

"That's the third customer this month you're not here for," said Phii Buoy. "What's wrong with *this* one?"

Mantana looked at her point-blank. "He wants me to quit work and marry him."

"Is he rich?"

"Probably."

Phii Buoy stopped what she was doing, which was adding each girl's monthly total in the bar's black book, and turned her full attention to Mantana.

"One doesn't become better with age, Nong Joy. Not at this job."

"Someday, I'll stop."

"Nong Joy," said Phii Buoy. "In fifteen years, I've seen one hundred different ways for a Thai girl to go into a go-go bar. I've only seen two ways for her to come out again. Pen's way, and mine."

Mantana looked at her boss and thought she saw something frightening in her eyes. Like a shadow in the moonlight.

"Mr. Simmons was a customer?"

Phii Buoy went back to her book, her face expressionless.

Mantana spoke without thinking. "Did you ever -"

"Love him?" said Phii Buoy. "Know him? Tell him the truth about anything? No. That's why I use a calculator and you're still opening condoms."

"I could still quit," she said. "Like Sai."

With one hand writing and one hand punching numbers, Phii Buoy slowly shook her head.

"Sai is now an employee at the Honey Bar on Soi Three."

The mama-san closed the book with a snap and excused herself. She seemed upset now, retreating in her businesswoman ways to maintain posture, to save face. Mantana watched her silently. Sai hadn't made it. Pen had made it, but Pen was dead. She saw Phii Buoy turn and look at her before disappearing in back. It was the look of someone who had revealed too much of herself, and suddenly wished for approval. Mantana had no approval for her. As far as she was concerned, Phii Buoy hadn't made it either. She simply did it with her clothes on.

Mantana turned away sharply, and walked out of the bar.

*

Then came Tai's chance to pay back some of the money she caused the bar to lose. Mantana's Frenchman had sent his card down once again, with a request for her services. Room 704, wear white.

"He'll do," she said to Neung. "He's a little weird but he's not dangerous. And he tips big."

"How do you know he'll want a virgin over you?"

"He poured fake blood on me just before he came the last

time I visited him."

"Oh," said Neung.

Phii Buoy was all for Mantana's idea. It seemed her dreams of netting a small fortune for Tai's virginity had encountered a snag. Her normal connections were either wary of the law or broke due to the recent flood. The only other offer she had on hand was from a self-proclaimed Russian count who was rumored to have slept with over five hundred virgins throughout the Kingdom. The Russian count was trying to secure his place among the great lovers of the world, even though the highest paid prostitutes in Pattaya knew that the world had no more great lovers. Bar owners were boycotting the count due to a fear that he was spreading disease. The Frenchman, Mantana assured Phii Buoy, was harmless.

So that evening, Tai's video game was locked in the top drawer of Phii Buoy's desk, and Tai was sent to meet the Frenchman. There was a five-thousand-baht price tag attached to her that night. The Frenchman could either take it or leave it.

"I wish I was still a virgin," said Neung. "Do you know I gave it away for free?"

Mantana smiled. "Boyfriend?"

"Seventeen years old. I thought he was going to marry me. Only he got another girl pregnant and didn't tell me until after the baby was born."

"That's terrible!"

"He was the first and the last to get sex from me without paying. I just wish I hadn't given him my most valuable time. It feels like losing a winning lottery ticket."

Mantana caught sight of Mr. Simmons across the bar.

"Neung," she said. "Did you know about Mr. Simmons?"

"What's to know?"

Mantana tried to imagine the man at a younger age, straddling a catwalk in some nameless go-go bar, gazing up at his future wife. Was she dancing when he decided that he loved her, or was it afterwards in bed? Or maybe it occurred on the other side of the world, standing in the shower while his long-nosed, pale- skinned American girlfriend waited to get in and use the bathroom.

"Egads! I'm in love with a Thai prostitute!"

"Joy?" said Neung.

"A foreigner asked me to marry him last night," said Mantana. "I told him I would, but then I walked out on him."

"Was he a creep?"

"He was a customer."

"I don't understand."

"He was old. He had money. He was willing to give some of his money to me if I agreed to be his wife. Maybe I should have stayed, for my father. For him, I should have said OK, foreign man, I don't understand a word out of your mouth but I understand the exchange rate of your money so I agree to be your prostitute wife from now until forever. I should have said all this, but I couldn't."

"Joy -"

"Sometimes, I can see my heart and I know that it's dead. It died here, a long time ago. I just can't stop hoping that it will come back to life."

"You're talking like a little girl," said Neung angrily. "You used to be strong, but now - now you're not thinking. This is a job, just like any job. You start out small, you behave, you follow the rules, and someday you get promoted. Only your promotion is to get married and have children."

Mantana thought of Jack's painting and her ghost existence. "How could any of us be mothers?"

"Easy! You let the customer do it without the condom."

On the other side of the bar, a strange sight was making its way around the catwalk. Two strange sights, actually, a man and a woman, both Thai, looking like tourists trying to cross a Bangkok highway. They examined the girls on stage, spoke closely into each other's ears, and moved on.

"Do you think they're lost?" asked Neung.

"Maybe they're looking for someone," said Mantana.

The couple came up from behind Yim, who was sitting next to an overweight foreigner with an even more overweight beard. They looked at the back of her head, then the woman extended a finger and tapped her on the shoulder. Yim turned around. The expression on her face showed that she was equally baffled. A middle-class, middle-aged Thai couple - *in a go-go bar?* Mantana saw everyone's lips move but couldn't make out the words they formed. Yim finally shook them off and pointed to the back.

"Maybe they have to use the toilet," said Neung.

"I don't think so."

Mantana stood and walked to the back of the bar. The couple had passed the toilets, passed the office and dressing rooms, and stood before the double row of lockers. The man put on a pair of glasses to survey the locks. He was being very thorough, like a detective searching for a strand of bad man's hair.

Mantana closed her robe and tied the sash. It was quieter in the hallway, quiet enough to speak in normal tones.

"Can I help you?"

The man stopped examining the small combination locks and turned his attention to Mantana. He didn't look like a detective. He looked like a banker. In the fluorescent light, she could see he was old enough to be her father, or any of her customers for that matter. His wife looked on from behind.

"Ma'am," he said. "Please excuse us, Ma'am."

His politeness surprised her.

"My name is Tamal. This is my wife Umphawan. We aren't from Pattaya. In fact, this is my wife's first time here."

"First time!" said Umphawan. "And last!"

"Do you need to use the toilet?" asked Mantana.

"Why?" said Tamal.

"Because - because you're back here."

"We don't need to use the toilet!" Umphawan stepped to her husband's side and grasped his arm. "We're looking for our daughter!"

Mantana swallowed. She felt a bit weak, a bit nauseous, but tried not to let it show.

Tamal spoke next. "We've been to dozens of bars today with no luck. Finally, a man at the Star Seven Club told us that a young girl from Rayong came to see him about a job some two or three weeks ago. He said he recommended her to this place."

Mantana took a deep breath. "Is her name Tai?"

The relief was so visible, it almost became a fourth person in the hallway.

"Where is she?" said Umphawan.

"Gone." Mantana took a step back and thought fast. "The manager sent her to buy *som tam*. Let me go ask when she'll be back. From her errand."

Mantana took another step back and bumped into a large customer shaped like a cowboy.

"Scuse me, little lady."

His touch affected her, almost as if it were occurring in front of her own father and long gone mother. Mantana put her hands up to block any further contact and rushed from the back hallway. Neung was no longer sitting at the bar. She had moved to a scientist with crazy ideas perched alongside a table. Mantana ran to her side and hollered in her ear:

"They're her parents!"

The scientist with crazy ideas was pleased to find two girls at his table.

"Who?" said Neung.

"That man and woman. They're not looking for a toilet. They're looking for Tai!"

Mantana grabbed her friend's shoulders and shook.

"I've - got - to - go - get - her!" she said.

Neung held her wrists until she stopped.

"Are you crazy? Send them away! Tell them you've never heard of a girl named Tai! That's what Phii Buoy would do."

"Forget Phii Buoy!"

"Then what about Tai? If she wanted to return home, don't you think she would have done so by now?"

The scientist with crazy ideas didn't understand what the girls were arguing about, but it was very exciting to watch.

"Don't you see?" said Mantana. "Tai doesn't have to be a prostitute. She has parents who care about her. She can go to school. She can have boyfriends. She doesn't have to stop -"

"Stop what?"

The words were out of her mouth before she had a chance to call them back.

"Stop being a girl."

Neung's eyes narrowed into a sneer. A short silence made it obvious that neither of them would back down.

"Go away, Joy," Neung said coldly. "I'm working."

Mantana left the table and wondered who else she could turn to. There was no one else. Past the catwalk, past the beaded curtains, stood Tamal and Umphawan, waiting. Mantana was no longer nervous or ashamed as she approached them.

"Are you going to beat her?"

"Excuse me?" asked Tamal.

"Tai. Are you going to beat Tai?"

"No," he said. "We just want her back in school."

Mantana looked from one to the other. Then she made up her mind.

"All right," she said. "I'll take you to her."

The only way Mantana could leave the bar was if she were bought out. That would have to be Tamal's job. Mantana instructed his wife to wait outside while they settled the bar fee with her boss. Umphawan didn't like the idea, but went along with it for her daughter's sake. Mantana opened the fire door exit for her and waited while Tamal escorted his wife to the street. Phii Buoy gave no thought to Mantana's choice for the evening, most likely figuring him for a businessman or a politician who would finish quickly and tip without realizing the value of his money. When the tab was settled, they rescued Umphawan from the suspicious eyes of street girls and mama-sans, and got into a taxicab.

"Prince Hotel," said Mantana.

"I thought you said she was going out for *som tam*," said Umphawan.

"That's enough," said Tamal.

She was quietly relieved that no one asked any more questions.

*

There were two receptionists working the front desk of the Prince Hotel as well as a bellboy who waited at the front entrance to greet people and carry their luggage. The bellboy's name was Dung and, like all bellboys she met, wanted to see Mantana with all of her clothes off. It took fifty baht and the vague promise of a blowjob to get him to open the back door and sneak her up to the seventh floor. Tamal and Umphawan waited in the lobby. There was no reason for them to see what their daughter was doing upstairs.

Mantana exited the elevator and walked down the hall to room 704. She adjusted her halter top and knocked. A minute passed. She knocked again, harder this time. What if she were too late? She put her ear to the door. It wasn't necessary. The commotion that suddenly broke behind the door broke loud enough to be heard down the hallway in either direction. A door slammed. A bedside table, or perhaps a chair, fell over and hit the floor. Someone yelled. Mantana grew worried and knocked again.

"Mister Gee-bert!"

The door opened. It was Gilbert. Gilbert the Frenchman. He looked at her until his eyes grew big as coconuts. Then they narrowed again and he took her by the arm.

"Come in!" he whispered. "Quickly!"

Mantana allowed herself to be pulled in. Gilbert closed the door behind her and locked it. There was no sign of Tai.

"What's going on here?" he said. "Where were you? Is this some kind of prostitute's joke?"

The Frenchman was obviously upset. He unhanded her and paced the room as if he couldn't decide where to stand.

"Your friend's locked herself in the bathroom. Do you know how old she is? She's a child! That's how old! She should be home skipping rope or making snowflakes out of construction paper. Why, I nearly jumped out of my skin when I saw her. Whose idea was it to send her here? Yours? What kind of a man do you think I am? One round of Virgin and the Gypsy doesn't make me a pederast! Do you know I could be arrested just for having her in my room?"

Mantana couldn't understand a word he was saying.

"Tai?" she said.

Gilbert stopped pacing and came closer to her.

"Die? Die? I'd die if the police arrested me. I'd die if my wife found out. I'd die if my friends and co-workers knew. I'd die if I had to explain to my daughter why Papa was caught with a teenager in his room. I'd die and I'd die and I'd die but what would really kill me is if I couldn't come back and sleep with any more real prostitutes!"

He stood only a few inches from her and gazed passionately into her eyes. For a moment, she thought he might kiss her. Instead, he screwed up his face and stamped his foot several times on the floor.

"I picked up a fungus in Indonesia," he said. "Itches like the devil!"

A slight creak was heard from across the room. The bathroom door opened enough for Mantana to see Tai peeking out. Mantana moved past the Frenchman who stood rubbing his toes into the carpet.

"Tai," she said, "What's the matter?"

Tai opened the door another inch. Half of the girl's painted face looked out from the brightly lit bathroom.

"He won't fuck me," she stated blankly. "Phii Buoy will fire me if he doesn't fuck me."

"No one is going to fire you."

"She said that this was my last chance."

"Don't worry. I've taken care of everything. There's someone waiting in the hotel lobby for you this very moment!"

"Another customer?"

"That's right. Another customer. Another chance."

Tai opened the door and came out. She looked different now, in her pink halter and black bikini. Back in the bar, she looked just like a working girl. After seeing where she got her nose and her manners and her quiet way of doing everything, she looked like a dumb kid playing dress-up. The sight of her sent Gilbert into another fit of nerves. He darted about the room, making sure the curtains were closed, the door was locked, and no policemen were waiting to jump out from behind the bed.

"You know I could go to jail for this! You know that, don't you?"

Mantana led Tai to the door and unlocked it.

"Phii Joy," she said, "how will I know whom to look for?"

"I told him what you're wearing."

"But how did you know to come?"

"I didn't. The customer downstairs made a better offer for you."

Mantana squeezed her arm and led her out into the hallway. She could have gone along, but chances were the receptionists wouldn't let her return to the seventh floor once the reunion was over. So she watched instead, at least until the young girl boarded the elevator and disappeared behind the sliding steel doors. She hoped to feel something for the good deed she had performed but sadly found nothing inside. She closed the door and locked it again. There was still a dissatisfied customer to be dealt with. And the last time she checked, she was still a prostitute.

She returned to the room, and smiled for the Frenchman. "OK, I wirgin for you."

Gilbert had stopped pacing long enough to light a cigarette from which he drew short, frantic puffs.

"I don't sleep with little girls," he said. "Uh-uh. Not me."

Mantana knew she had some work to do. She crossed the room and stood close to him. He took another puff of his cigarette and looked down at her.

"Trying to make up for your blunder, eh? I see your game plan."

Mantana tried to slip into his arms. He backed away instead. She stood there, feeling as she used to feel on stage, when a single spotlight was trained upon her. Gilbert, meanwhile, was performing his one-man talk show again.

"It's all a game to you, isn't it? A game of money. What good is love to a girl like you? What good are promises? Why, I'll bet your whole life is just one big lie!"

He started to move in a circle around her.

"Your smile is a lie. Your sex is a lie. I imagine you've got so many lies stored in that brain of yours that they've become your only truths. And now you're trying to corrupt me, isn't that so? Anything for money - that's your motto. First you send the child, then you yourself make an appearance. What's next? Have you got any barnyard animals waiting in the hallway?"

Mantana was getting dizzy. His voice reached a fever pitch. He stopped circling her and pointed accusingly.

"I, my lady, am not your puppet!"

There seemed to be no reason to stay any longer. Mantana lowered her head and moved for the door. Gilbert bolted past her and got to it first.

"Oh no you don't! I'm just getting warmed up!"

He blocked the door with his body and refused to let her pass.

He said: "You *want* me to cheat on my wife!"

He said: "You'd just *love* to take away my free will!"

He said: "You think I'm a *worm*! A *joke*!"

Then he unhitched his belt from his trousers, slid one end through the buckle, and widened the circle to fit around his neck.

"A *dog!*"

The Frenchman dropped to all fours and held up the loose end for Mantana to grasp. Once she held it in her hand, he stuck out his tongue and ran it sloppily across her toes.

It was going to be a long night, thought Mantana.

13

The next morning, Mantana collected her money and left after a hurried and unmemorable goodbye. That was how it usually went with the ones who substituted their private fantasies for sex. A customer had no problem being spanked, whipped, tied up, and called the strange words they had to teach her to say, but just try to get him to sit down for a cup of coffee the next morning. Impossible! Mantana didn't care. Dung the bellhop had promised to give her a full report on Tai's reunion with her parents, and she was anxious to hear it.

Everything had gone according to plan. The whore in the pink halter top walked into the lobby and started to cry when she saw the polite couple who was waiting. Her make-up ran. She was a mess. If she were planning to fuck any more men that night, she would have to wash her face and start all over again. It was that bad. The polite couple? Oh, they cried too. At least, the woman did. The man just stood there with his arms folded. He wasn't happy, but he knew his manners. After that, they left. Dung knew. He opened the door for them. Now about that blowjob -

"Some other time."

Mantana got into a cab and made it back to her apartment before 9 a.m. She fell asleep and dreamed that she was caught in a rainstorm. It was raining one-hundred and five-hundred and one-thousand-baht bills. Pink and violet and white; the colors of money. She tried to grab as many as she could, but the bills kept slipping from her hands. The dream progressed, and she became aware of someone in the distance, a shadowy figure who just stood and let the money fall without trying to collect it. She tried to move in the direction of this mysterious person, only the high heels she wore kept slipping upon the bills.

The figure disappeared. Buried alive by money.

That was all she could remember when she woke up.

*

It was late in the afternoon when Mantana got into a tuk-tuk and told the driver to take her to the countryside. The driver wanted an address. Mantana didn't have one.

"You're drunk," he said, and drove away before she could get into the vehicle.

She wasn't drunk. But she was feeling particularly high-strung for some reason. If only she could spend three or four days on an island to collect her thoughts and relax, maybe find herself again. She knew Phii Buoy would never grant her the time off. And there weren't any holidays for a long, long time.

A boy and a girl sat on the steps of a shopping plaza behind her, picking lice from one another's hair. They were both in the last of their teenage years, shabbily dressed and dusty. She could hear them arguing in deep, monotone voices. Mantana walked by and noticed the needle marks that dotted their ankles. There were still people lower than she was. She moved on, uncomforted by her thought. A ladyman in tight shorts and a pink shirt approached on her left. He had a girlish walk and carried a small black purse on his shoulder. Mantana met his eyes. The ladyman stopped and shrieked.

"Nong Joy!"

She shielded her eyes from the sun and looked at him.

"Bew!"

Bew wrapped his arms around her and screamed. Mantana was equally happy.

"What are you doing here?" she asked.

"I working at Sing-Sing! I a star!"

Mantana knew of Sing-Sing. It was a grand cabaret that featured nightly transvestite shows. The owners of Sing-Sing hired only the most beautiful and talented *gatuhy*s from around Thailand.

"That's wonderful," she said.

"Now you!"

Mantana continued to smile, but knew that the look in her eyes would betray her. She stepped back and allowed him to look at her.

"I work at the Cherry Bar," she said quietly.

"Oh! Oh, oh! Is good?"

"No, Bew. It's not good."

"Why you no go back to Bangkok? Phii Aor missing you."

"Really?" said Mantana, and thought she would cry.

"Everyone gone now. Ning gone, Peung gone, Bew gone. Now have a singer not so good."

"Do you want to have lunch with me, Bew?"

Bew pouted his lips. "No have time. Bew must go to practice. You come see me tonight?"

"I have to work," said Mantana. "But I'll come another time."

"Is a promise?"

"No," said Mantana. "But I'm happy for you."

Bew hugged her again. "You go back to Bangkok," he said before he left. "Is best for you."

She watched him walk away and had to restrain herself from

calling out to him.

The reunion did little to calm her nerves. She put food in her stomach at a *gooey teeo* stand and realized, as she seemed to do every afternoon, that the day had tricked her again and left her with little more than what was needed before she had to go to work. It wasn't fair. For every hour that was taken from her day, two more seemed to be added to her time at the bar. Mantana wearily made her way home to drink from her bottle and smear make-up over the inflammation that had broken out on her left cheek.

It was only Monday.

Amazingly, she was on time. She changed into a pair of blue panties and a blue nightie that laced across her breasts. Then she went into the bar and waited for Phii Buoy to interrogate her about Tai. Phii Buoy didn't even look at her as she went by. Mantana sat down at the bar and asked an unfamiliar face for a glass of water. Girls came and girls went. Who could keep track of them? Who would want to? Mantana only knew that if any more parents showed up looking for their long-lost daughter, they'd better not come to her for help. She was through being kind-hearted. She was through being anything.

Neung tapped her on the shoulder and sat down next to her. She had already forgotten Mantana's words from the night before. Mantana told her of Tai's reunion with her parents. Neung listened with an indifference that only annoyed Mantana more than she already was.

"That would never happen to me," she said. "If my mother and father ever saw me again, they'd pretend not to know me."

"But don't you think they'd be happy to know that you're alive?"

Neung thought about it.

"The first time I left home, I left too late and missed the bus to Bangkok. So I went back, planning to leave the next day. My parents had locked the door and refused to let me back in. My father told me to sleep with the chickens."

"You're their daughter. How could they be so cruel?"

"We were poor. We've always been poor. When the poor have love in their hearts, they'll only become poorer."

"You don't really believe that, do you?"

"I sure do."

Mantana sighed and rubbed her temples. "When I tried to leave, my father threw my suitcase onto the roof of our house. I had to climb up and get it."

"He must have really loved you."

"He still does!" she shot back.

Neung coughed and failed to notice that Mantana had taken offense. This passed too. Grudges could never be held for long. Like a shot on a quiet battlefield, either of their names could suddenly be called to entertain or to dance on the catwalk. There was no time for grudges. On stage, a pair of buffalo women kicked off the start of another night. The music went up; the lights went down. A group of men with black hair and black mustaches entered through the curtained door and found seats along the catwalk. Neung watched them with a projector showing some old and best forgotten memory upon the walls of her mind.

"They're Saudis," she said. "I don't want to be fucked by a Saudi."

"Oh and do you think I do?"

Neung looked at her friend, surprised. "Joy, are you all right? You're acting strange."

"I'm fine," she said. "Just a headache. Let's go for a cigarette in back. The buffaloes can take them."

That sounded good to Neung. They avoided Phii Buoy and took the long way to the beaded curtain separating the bar from the toilets and dressing rooms. Mantana stopped before a mirror to check on her skin irritation. It looked worse than it did ten minutes ago. She wondered if this was the last phase of her incompleteness. The loss of her beauty. She turned away and moved to the fire door that still needed to be fixed. The door was open and Neung stood in the alleyway looking like, well, like she had seen a ghost. It was a look that unsettled Mantana's already unsettled nerves and caused her to hesitate before scolding her about leaving the fire door wide open for Mr. Simmons to see. She walked quickly down the corridor and grew even more panicked when she saw Neung's pack of Falling Rain cigarettes lying on the ground.

"Joy," said Neung, "you're not going to believe this."

Mantana stepped past her and gazed down the alleyway.

"That's it," said Neung. "That's the van that brought us here."

Mantana stared at the vehicle wedged in tight between the walls. It certainly looked like the van they had been trapped in, but how could she be sure with only the moonlight to go by?

"Do you think there's anyone inside?" asked Neung.

"I don't know."

"What should we do?"

Mantana slowly shook her head. "I don't know."

Another voice. American and loud. "What's going on here? Why is this door open?"

It was Mr. Simmons. He wore a blue checkered shirt and brown pants.

"Well?" he said.

Mantana took him by the shirt sleeve and led him into the alley. She pointed to the van, then to Neung and herself.

"Van of bad man," she explained in English. "Take to here."

"This van?"

Mantana and Neung both nodded.

"Are you sure?"

"Sure," said Neung.

Mr. Simmons rubbed his neck. "Go back inside." He unhitched a cell phone from his side pocket and dialed a number. With his free hand, he shooed the girls inside and closed the fire door.

"How strange," said Neung. "I didn't think he would care."

"He doesn't," said Mantana. "Not about us, anyway. He's still angry over the money he lost to that phony modeling agency."

"The one that promised experienced hostesses that could suck a man's cock and moan in four different languages?"

"That's the one."

It was only a few minutes before other, more familiar faces appeared in the bar. There was Mr. Helmut, owner of the Mirage Bar, Mr. Dimitri of the Mustang, and Mr. Bruce from the Nice Tits A-Go-Go. They had all done business with the "Prakanom Modeling Agency." They had all signed a contract. They had all been had. The models turned out to be runaways, drug addicts, carnival girls, and petty criminals who, like Mantana and Neung and the rest of the girls they had been captured with, were either too afraid to seek justice, or too far down on their luck to hope for revenge. The foreign bar owners didn't feel the same. They had visa runs to make, wives to support, police to pay off. And they hated to be cheated.

Mr. Helmut, Mr. Dimitri, and Mr. Bruce all stood at the bar, watching the stage show with hairy forearms folded across their chests. Once Mr. Simmons told Phii Buoy what was happening, the role of strategic commander shifted hands and the working girl turned mama-san sent Mantana and Neung back to the fire door to keep an eye on the van. If anyone, that is, *anyone* was spotted near the vehicle, one of them was to immediately relay the information to the front. There was no way the van could make a speedy exit from the narrow alley. Whoever steered it in had done so to hide it.

They waited.

"I hope it's the one with the mustache," said Neung. "I'd really like to sock him. Or maybe it will be his friend."

Mantana didn't share in her excitement. "Maybe it will be a complete stranger," she said.

"Or that carnival owner you once told me about. The one

who sold you off in the first place. What was his name?"

"I don't remember."

Neung sighed, frustrated by her friend's strange mood.

"Don't you want to cut his dick off and stuff it in his mouth?" she asked.

"Why?"

"Because! Because of what he did to us!"

"Because of what who did to us?"

"*Him!*"

Mantana bent forward and rested her forehead on her knees. She knew what Neung was talking about. She only played ignorant. Him was the unlucky one to come out of the shadows and claim the driver's seat. Him was the main face in her revenge fantasy. Him was the reason behind it all. The question was; who was Him? Was it the carnival boss who took her money? Was it the two men who had locked her in the van? Or was it the police that escorted her the rest of the way? Mantana turned her head and looked at Neung. For the first time that evening, she saw that her face too had broken out in pimples. Only she had buried them so deep in make-up, that they looked like pieces of rice frozen in plaster. There was a word for them, and the word was *soam*. *Soam* didn't mean that one looked old. It meant that one looked as if she had snubbed her youth out on the sidewalk with the heel of her shoe. Factory workers who spent two hours commuting to a twelve-hour day and two hours coming home to a short sleep often looked *soam*. Students who were forced to study under the pressure of dishonoring their family looked *soam*. And prostitutes, no matter what their working hours consisted of, looked *soam*.

"We made a mistake," said Mantana. "This isn't the van."

"What?" said Neung.

"Look at it. It's the wrong make. The wrong color. The wrong everything."

"But you said you were sure."

She got off her feet and brushed off the back of her skirt. "I'm sure that this isn't the van. Let's go back and tell Mr. Simmons."

Neung shook her head. "I'm staying."

"I'm telling you, this isn't the same vehicle."

Neung fixed her eyes to a space in front of her and continued to wait. Someone would appear sooner or later. Someone from Mantana's past. Someone from Neung's. Someone they had never seen before. Someone they thought they knew. An ex-prime minister. The Channel Three weatherman. A singer / actor / model who was half Thai and half *farang*. Pretty Soldier Sailor Moon. A beast with a thousand faces all smiling and excusing themselves and quietly blaming the other. It was all too ridiculous. The guilty party was already assembled, and it was the world around them. And it was themselves as well.

Mantana stood in the fire door exit breathing in the stink of the alleyway garbage. She felt the writhing of a cat being strangled within her and clenched her fists so tight, her fingernails dug painfully into the palms of her hands.

"You want to put a face on the reason we're here?" she said. "I can see one now."

She marched out of the doorway, into the dirty alley. There was no fear in her. A short bamboo pole that had once been the handle of a broom lay on top of a trash can. Mantana grabbed it without stopping. She approached the van and halted before its headlight eyes and windshield hairline. Here, at last, was someone to blame. A silent culprit who offered no explanations or apologies. Mantana gritted her teeth and raised her weapon.

"Say you're sorry."

She swung it, swung it hard, and closed her eyes as it hit the windshield. It didn't break. It didn't even crack. A tough bastard. Well, Mantana was tough, too. Not the little girl who wondered what her toes would say if they could speak, but the grown woman, or whatever she was, that fucked for money. Mantana hit it again and the damn thing came to life. It cried out like the ten-faced *Tossagan* himself had come screaming down from the clouds. Eyes opened and closed, blinding her in their infernal light. The entire battlefield seemed to erupt in rat chaos around her. The bamboo pole fell to the ground as she covered her ears and staggered back. Maybe she was screaming, maybe not. The next thing she was aware of was a pair of hands taking her by the wrists and pulling her back. She was dragged by the arms along the jagged cement as the monster she had awakened continued to thunder and lightning.

And then it stopped.

Whoever had been holding her was no longer part of the picture. Mantana was released and she fell upon her hands and knees. There was grass on the ground. Green grass, the real stuff. She propped herself upright and looked around. She was back in the field of her dreams, now sprayed with flowers of every kind for as far as the eye could see. A light wind brushed against her face, and she looked up. Large white clouds floated against an ocean of blue sky. Each one in the shape of a sex organ or a foreign currency or a used rubber.

"Phii Joy?"

Someone was standing behind her. Mantana turned without rising. A teenage girl stood no more than ten feet away, though Mantana hadn't noticed anyone approach. She was at the height of her youth and beauty, white teeth and not a worry line on her. The wind sent ripples through her long, dark hair as she shifted her bird's weight from one blue-jeaned leg to the other. The girl placed her hands together and bowed.

"*Sawadee ka*," she said. "It's been a long time."

Mantana blinked twice. In between, she remembered the childhood story of how the widow Amnuay sold her daughter in the middle of the night. And how, when Mantana refused to believe it, she went to the widow's doorstep, only to be shooed away.

"*Kwan!*"

Speaking the name aloud nearly took the breath out of her and she was glad to be on the ground so she wouldn't have to fall down again.

"What happened to you?" she asked.

Kwan lifted the corner of her mouth as if the answer were obvious. Above them, a giant cock floated by.

"Here's what happened," said Kwan. "I sold myself for eight years at a go-go bar in Patpong. I don't know when I caught the AIDS virus, but as soon as it became obvious that I was sick, I was fired and had to look for work in massage parlor brothels. That didn't last long either. I died four months ago."

"I'm sorry," said Mantana.

"Here's what happened. I was taken to a brothel down south where a Swiss businessman fell in love with me. We married, and moved to Switzerland, where there's money and snow. My husband gave me enough to open my own restaurant. It's called 'Taste Of Thai.' I'm also three months pregnant with our first child."

"I'm so happy for you!" said Mantana.

"Here's what happened. I danced for a few years right here in Pattaya before I became addicted to heroin. Believe it or not, I was hooked for five years. I used to shoot up in hotel bathrooms just before a customer fucked me. At the end of it, I was down to eighty-three pounds. I lost my health and my beauty. Now, I'm one of those people you see living in metal shacks beneath the overpasses in Bangkok."

"Oh," said Mantana.

"What happened to you?" asked Kwan.

A hypodermic needle and a little bar of hotel soap passed by overhead.

"Me? Well, I let my ex-boss sleep with me. Then I was kidnapped. Since then, I've slept with many men. Some of the men were nice. Some were not so nice. One man poured red goo over my stomach and pretended he was making love to a virgin. Another time, he pretended to be my dog and asked me to spank him for being naughty. Once, a man fucked me so hard, I thought I would have to go to the hospital. Then there was the man who painted a picture of me, then fucked me, then redid the picture and showed me for what I was. He made me feel as though I didn't exist anymore, except as a ghost. Then an old man wanted to marry me. I said no to him."

"But what *happened*?"

Mantana looked into the eyes of the beautiful young girl.

"I attacked a van in the back alley with a broom handle," she said.

A cloud went by that resembled an elephant with an oversized trunk. Mantana looked at it from a different angle and realized it was something else entirely.

"Are those clouds going to pass by forever?" she asked.

"No," said Kwan. "You're going to wake up soon and all this will be gone. But you've learned an important lesson today, Joy."

"I have?" Mantana said suspiciously. "What's that?"

"You've learned there's no one but yourself to blame for your misfortunes. Whether you're sold, bought, kidnapped, tricked, or handcuffed to a bedpost, you still have a strong, wonderful NO inside you that no one can touch. Hang on to that NO and you're not what the world around you is telling you to be. I know that it's not easy to do when money is constantly whispering yes, but only you can keep it from being torn from you, Joy. And sooner or later, you'll be glad you did. You'll come to understand that NO is the only thing worth keeping in life."

"But I don't have anywhere to go."

"You're wrong, Phii Joy. You can wake up and be somewhere else. Me, I'm stuck here watching these horrible clouds go by."

Kwan looked to the horizon and sighed.

"Oh, one more thing," she said. "When you see my mother, tell her I forgive her."

"I will," said Mantana.

Kwan nodded with such peace in her eyes that Mantana found herself smiling when she awoke.

"Nong Joy?' said a voice. It was Phii Buoy. "Are you all right?"

"Yes," said Mantana. "And I quit."

*

The van, as it turned out, was not the same vehicle that had brought Mantana and the others to Pattaya. It belonged to the Saudis that Neung had wished to avoid. There was some confusion among the mustached men as to why their car alarm was performing its own light and sound show in the alleyway, but as Mantana's blows did no considerable damage, they simply switched it off and returned to finish their drinks. The bar owners returned to their bars. Mantana was sent home for the evening. Phii Buoy insisted that she was "burned out" and refused to take her resignation seriously until she had a night's sleep. Mantana agreed, and went back the next day to hand in her outfit and collect her pay.

"You make a good living here," said Phii Buoy. "Are you sure you want to throw it away like this?"

Mantana said she wasn't sure, but that she was going to try. She waiied the mama-san and asked her to tell Mr. Simmons and the others goodbye.

Neung visited as she was packing. She talked about the customer she had gone with after Mantana left the bar. He was a young man who couldn't stop licking her navel. Even after he had jerked himself off against her leg. Even after she had fallen asleep. She didn't mention Mantana's outburst and refused to believe, right up until their last moments, that her friend was leaving.

"Will you write?" she asked glumly.

"I'll write," said Mantana.

Neung gave her three different phone numbers and told her to call if she changed her mind. Mantana gave her one and told her the same.

"Well," said Neung, "I guess I'd better get ready for work."

"Work? You don't have to be at work for another four hours."

"I've got to see someone about - something."

"You mean you're going to buy drugs."

Neung looked at her, and her eyebrows displayed the fear and desperation that accompanied her habit.

"I know, Neung," said Mantana. "I've known for some time."

"It's not serious," she said, almost pleading. "It helps me get through the night."

Mantana nodded. A part of every working girl she knew had to live, and a part had to die. Figuring out which half to take to work and which to bury deep inside was the test. Neung would not see out her eighteen years. Mantana knew this as sure as two and two made four. And herself? She could only hope she was killing the right part.

It was one o'clock in the afternoon.

That was the last they ever saw of one another.

Part Four

1

The rest of the story goes like this.

Mantana rode two buses that afternoon. One into Bangkok and one out again. She only stayed for about twenty minutes this time. Instead of arriving home at a late hour, she checked into a hotel in town and slept through the night. Maybe it was the dim light of the hotel room, but Mantana could swear her face was clearing up. The next morning, a local bus took her as close to the village as it went. She had to get off at the side of the highway and walk for half a mile.

The first place she passed was her father's store, which was not only closed, but gutted as well. A few empty beer cans littered the ground out front, and a charred circle of earth showed that someone had recently held a bonfire. A scrawny dog lay on its side in the shade of the place, either too weak or too hot to get up and bark at her.

Mantana kept going. There were people now, some she knew, some she probably would have recognized if she stopped to greet them. Around the next corner was her father's house. Whatever hopes she had that things had returned to normal were dashed when she saw Khun Amnuay squatting next to a plastic tub, wringing one of her father's shirts out over soapy water. A clothesline running the length of the front porch displayed the results of her morning work. Mantana took a deep breath and approached her.

"*Sawadee ka, Na.*"

The widow looked up and dropped the shirt back into the water. She waiied and immediately began to fuss. Mantana was not expecting this.

"Child!" she said, "You look exhausted!"

"I had to walk from the highway."

"Come here... Just a moment... Sit down... It's cooler inside... Let me get you some water!"

Khun Amnuay left the clothes to soak and went into the house. Mantana set down her bag. Should she go in? Didn't she have a right? How terrible it was to have to decide. In the end, she went in.

There were still things. A variety of things. Things with plugs but no outlet to fit them in. Things that had been turned on their sides and converted into tables. Things that had been taken apart, and things that might have had some use if the instructions hadn't been lost. At least now, the things had a place. They had all been pushed against the walls to allow the room to be a room again. There was a familiar straw mat on the floor, and a television with bent aerials that appeared to be the only reason for electricity to continue flowing.

Khun Amnuay returned with her water.

"Is my father here?"

"Oh, your father. You know that job of his. He puts up buildings and houses faster than they can find people to live in them. Me, I'm old and fat. Fat and old. Still, every now and then, someone will ask how old Amnuay is today. Every now and then. Things are different now that I've moved out of that house of mine. I remember you kids used to come over and skip rope in front."

Mantana had no recollection of that. She remembered being too scared of Khun Amnuay to go anywhere near the house. Especially after Kwan disappeared:

"Child! Have you eaten yet?"

"Khun Amnuay, I have to ask you something. Is my father still in debt?"

The widow threw her arms up in the air.

"No! Child, no! His insurance covered some of the bill, and the generous sums you sent every month took care of the rest."

"What insurance?"

"Why medical insurance, of course. But not much! Five nights in the city hospital would have ruined us if you hadn't helped."

"But I thought he had a gambling debt."

"Oh, he did. I paid that for him. Of course, we had to sell many of our things. I told him that if he ever gambled again, I'd shoot him."

"So why was he in the hospital?"

"He gambled. I shot him."

"You *shot* my father?"

"Yes. And he hasn't gambled since."

Khun Amnuay came closer and touched Mantana's cheek with the back of her weathered fingers.

"You look so thin, dear."

*

Mantana's father had indeed been shot, and had the hole to prove it. The bullet had passed through his side without causing any major damage. Khun Amnuay offered no apologies and told him he was lucky that she was such a bad aim. Word got around. Instead of throwing out the crazy woman as everyone thought, he quietly married her one Sunday before going to work. He showed both acquisitions to his daughter, the wound and the ring, then casually asked what was for dinner.

Fish.

Mantana and Amnuay had spent the afternoon at the market, then home again to prepare it. The dinner conversation was kept light, with none of the questions that Mantana had prepared herself for. No one seemed the least bit interested to know where she had been or why she came back. After the meal, Amnuay insisted that Mantana spend time with her father and leave her to do the washing up.

It was a cool, starry evening. Prapeut sat on the porch smoking a cigarette. Mantana sat down beside him and stole one from his pack.

"You smoke now," he observed.

"Just a little."

Her father nodded. "I suppose you'll be leaving again tomorrow."

"Actually, I was thinking about staying for awhile."

"Did you lose another department store job?"

Mantana didn't answer.

"Your room's been cleared out," he said. "You're welcome to it for as long as you like. I've just got one rule. You don't say anything mean or bad to Amnuay."

"But she shot you!"

"She took care of me."

"And she's crazy."

"She has a good heart. And I know what you're going to

say next so let me tell you here and now. What happened between her and her daughter -"

"You can say her name."

"All right. What happened between her and Kwan happened a long time ago. She's suffered enough for it."

"I forgive her," said Mantana.

"What?"

"I forgive her. I won't mention it again."

They sat and smoked. The sounds of crickets and a far-off television program were the only sounds that broke their silence.

"I saw her," said Mantana.

"Who?"

"Kwan."

"You couldn't have."

Mantana turned to her father and waited. He blew smoke from his lungs and spoke.

"A few years ago, she married a fellow who took her back to Germany with him. I don't know why any Thai girl would go running off to Germany with a man she can't even speak with, but that's what happened. And, you know the rest, he up and left her in a foreign land where she didn't know how to tell what time of day it was, let alone survive."

"Did she die?"

"Your stepmother tried to bring her home. As soon as she had an address, she sent all the money she had in the bank. One day she got a letter in the mail. There was no return address on it, but she thinks the husband must have sent it. Inside was all the money she sent and a newspaper clipping. It was in German but Amnuay knew what it was. It was Kwan's obituary. That's the end of the story."

Mantana let her cigarette fall to the ground and started to cry. Her father put an arm around her and drew her near.

"That's the end of the story," he said again.

*

The rest of the story goes like this. With the three of them, Mantana, Prapeut, and Amnuay, working through the mornings and afternoons, it was only a matter of days before the store was open and running again. Prapeut had gone to the city and purchased a half dozen of everything they used to sell: beer, soft drinks, shampoo, laundry detergent, notebooks, candy, and cigarettes. Khun Amnuay peeled off the price stickers, and marked everything three to five baht more expensive. Mantana set things up as she remembered. Since she had been gone, a "beautification program" had been initiated in the nearby city. A fast-food chicken restaurant, a seven-story shopping plaza with an aquarium on the top floor, and four more apartment buildings were in the works. Traffic lights had been put up at six different intersections and one hundred police officers had been deployed for traffic duty. All this progress had an effect upon the village as well. For the first time ever, a road had been paved, the road that ran in front of Mantana's store.

Not everyone was thrilled.

Phii Kum said it would only bring strangers in, while Phii Gaa complained that the smell of tar was making his chickens ill. He wanted to assemble the villagers to form a human chain and block any further development. But everyone he spoke to simply said, "Times are changing," and the road-work went on. It all made Mantana a little excited. If things kept on in this manner, who says she wouldn't need a parking lot soon?

Phii Nongluck was one of her first customers. Her beauty parlor was doing well, and she could afford to take a vacation every six or eight months. She had been to Cha-am Beach the week before the store opened and showed off a necklace of seashells that she bought. Nongluck had many stories of her trip but there was one in particular that Mantana insisted she retell. It happened on her way home. She had stopped off in Bangkok and decided to go to the Chatuchak Weekend Market. As she was crossing a pedestrian bridge opposite the old Mor Chit Bus Terminal, she saw a man on the walkway begging for change. She ignored him, as she did most beggars, but unfortunately got a look at his face. Too much of a look, if you want to know the truth. It was Jakkrit.

That was all Mantana needed to hear. Good, because Nongluck didn't want to speak of it anymore. The next day, she closed the shop and took yet another trip to Bangkok. At the end of the ride, she climbed the stairs and searched the flyover that Nongluck had described. Jakkrit wasn't there. She moved down Viphawadi Road and crossed every bridge for the next half mile into the city. There were plenty of beggars. There were mothers with children and children without mothers. There were the diseased, the crippled, and the blind, all sitting in the sun with an outstretched hand or bowl or plastic soft drink cup from a nearby fast food restaurant. There was no Jakkrit. Finally, she turned around and walked back to the bus station, determined to try the bridges that lay in the opposite direction.

On the second flyover, she found him.

He was sitting on a torn square of cardboard, leaning against the concrete sidewall for support. The sun shone directly upon him as well as the wooden bowl that people stepped over to avoid kicking. Nongluck had not told her all that she had seen that day. Jakkrit's legs were still missing, sure. And now his arms were gone too.

Mantana approached and stood before him. His face was turned down, his eyes fixed on some invisible spot upon the walkway.

"Oh, Jakkrit," she said, and her voice choked with pity.

The crippled man came to life and looked up. His face was coated in sweat and dirt, and it looked as though he hadn't washed his hair in ages. Nevertheless, a brightness flashed in his eyes and he smiled awkwardly, as if he were still learning how.

"Nong Joy!" he said. "It's really you!"

"What happened to you?"

Jakkrit turned his head to regard each of his shoulders. The stumps of his arms were just visible sticking out of the sleeves of a grimy yellow T-shirt.

"They took my arms."

"Who took your arms?"

He suddenly lost his smile. "Nong Joy, you'd better not ask that. It's dangerous for you to be here. If they see you talking to me, they might try to hurt you."

Mantana sat down next to him.

"Who?"

"Bad men."

"I've had more than my fill of bad men. I'm not afraid of them anymore."

"I'm not joking. These men wouldn't think twice of doing to you what they did to me."

"Well, where are they? Can you tell me that?"

"I don't know where they are. They bring me to one of these bridges every morning and leave me here until well past dark. There's a boy they've hired to feed me and bring me water. He comes around every three or four hours to empty my begging bowl."

Mantana sighed and took a handkerchief from her purse to wipe his face.

"And, don't tell me," she said, "these men have promised you a share of whatever you make but hide it for safekeeping."

"Yes. And if I tell a policeman about what they make me do, I'll never see any of it. Ever."

"Jakkrit, do you really think you'll see any of it, ever?"

"They also said they'd kill me."

Mantana spit on the handkerchief and wiped his face.

"Well, she said, "believe it or not, a position is available in a newly remodeled store that I think you're just the man for."

"What could I do in a store?"

"You could be a cashier."

"But I don't have any hands!"

"Even better! I won't have to worry about you stealing from me!"

She got to her feet and brushed off her jeans.

"Now, don't go anywhere. I'll be right back."

Mantana walked to the stairs and down to the street. She flagged a taxicab and explained to the driver that she had a friend on the bridge who couldn't climb down the steps by himself. The driver wanted to know how he got up the steps in the first place. Mantana told him that he didn't have any arms or legs and some men had carried him up to beg for them. The driver shook his head and drove away.

She decided to be more direct in her approach.

"I'm going two blocks to the bus station," she said through the next open taxicab window. "You can charge me double and add a one-hundred-baht tip if you carry my disabled friend down from that bridge."

This time, she had a deal. Jakkrit was terrified for the entire journey. He was convinced that the men who had sawed his arms off were waiting for him at the foot of the stairs. When he was proved wrong, then they must be at the bus station. Mantana had to tell him to shut up before he spooked the cab driver into pulling over and letting them both out.

When they reached the bus terminal, Mantana found a luggage cart to push Jakkrit in. Since there were no sides to it, he had to lay flat on his back while Mantana bought tickets and hunted for the right bus. His dirty face was now a pale, frightful color, and his eyes darted in their sockets as though they were trying to find a way out.

"It'll be OK, Jakkrit."

"I'm trying, Nong Joy."

Luckily, there was not a long wait for their bus, and within the hour, they were heading out of the city. Traffic was bad around the airport and Futurepark Shopping Mall, but once the bus cleared the suburbs of Bangkok, the dirty storefronts and varicose-veined sky gave way to the greens and blues of the countryside. It was only after they passed the ancient capital of Ayutthaya, seventy kilometers to the north, that he could finally rest.

"It feels good to close my eyes," he said. "I usually sleep with them open."

"That sounds awful, Jakkrit."

Jakkrit smiled his familiar, awkward grin. "Everything's awful until you get used to it. It makes me wonder if a newborn baby's first cry isn't one of hunger, but terror."

"The sad part is, they don't have any idea how much worse it's going to get!"

There was a morose silence between them. Jakkrit's body began to shake and a low, guttural sound emerged from his lips. Mantana realized he was laughing. Her face broke into a smile.

"What's so funny?" she asked.

"I was just thinking about all those poor babies. Not a clue among them."

Mantana burst out giggling and Jakkrit laughed along with her. It was strange to hear such sounds coming from his dilapidated form. Strange but good.

"Life is terrible!" he shouted.

"Rotten!" she heartily agreed.

A couple of passengers turned to look at the odd, merry pair. Mantana ignored them and raised an imaginary glass up before her.

"To life!" she said.

"To life," said Jakkrit.

It wasn't such a bad ride home after all.

2

The cool weather was cut short faster than anyone wished for, and days of blinding light and unmerciful heat returned to the cities and villages like a fat landlord demanding payment in sweat and fatigue. Jakkrit was the only one who didn't appear bothered by it. In fact, after just a week back home, Mantana wondered if there were anything short of a plague that could bring his spirits down. She fully anticipated acting as a nurse for him, and even looked forward to devoting her time to helping a friend in need. Until Amnuay *tch-haw'd* the idea and said she'd take care of him herself. And she did, much better than Mantana ever could. She washed him and combed his hair and sang songs with him as she carried his pegged body to the toilet. Just like a mother again, thought Mantana. It was obvious that Amnuay was the one for the job. Mantana would have to find some other way to fill her time.

For a short while following her homecoming, Mantana put her energies into running the store. She meant what she said about hiring Jakkrit, and asked her father to build a special chair that allowed him to sit upright behind the counter. He was then trusted with the cash box, which lay open before him. From his seat, he added the totals of customer purchases with his eyes and told them the correct amount of change to take. No one dared to cheat. The villagers knew that one shout from Jakkrit would bring down the wrath of Amnuay, who was always known to be a little bit crazy and recently rumored to have shot her new husband, wounding but not killing him. But that wasn't the real reason customers were honest. The real reason was that Jakkrit had become so friendly and wise in the wake of his misfortune that those who once scorned him began to consider him an upstanding member of the community. Khun Apichak's warehouse of a wife even asked whether she could rub one of his stumps before buying a lottery ticket. Jakkrit consented, though neither he nor Mantana could see how losing his arms and legs could turn him into a lucky charm.

Each day, the three of them opened the store at 7 a.m. and stayed until late in the evening. Mantana and her stepmother took turns going to the market or returning home to make dinner. On some days, heavy with heat, Amnuay told her to go home and rest. She had Jakkrit to keep her company. Mantana felt guilty abandoning the store, until she returned an hour later to find that she wasn't missed at all. Soon, she saw no harm in sleeping late one or two days of the week. Or allowing herself a holiday here and there. On some days, she would simply take off on a long walk, as if sleepwalking, and snap out of her daze far from home, suddenly terrified that the afternoon had passed her by and she had only minutes before she was expected on the catwalk. It took some time before she calmed down and remembered that she didn't have to go to work. She had quit. She had escaped. She even said it out loud, "I quit. I don't work there anymore," if only to quiet the voices that followed her like a monstrous shadow. "I quit. I quit. I'm not available."

But the voices only grew louder as nighttime drew its curtain.

"Nong Joy, what are you doing?" Jakkrit said to her one

afternoon, after she had wandered in and out of the shop half a dozen times. She was about to say "working" but knew she'd never get away with it under Jakkrit's watchful eyes.

"I'm just here," she said.

"But where is your mind these days?"

It was a valid question. Mantana didn't know how to answer. That is, she didn't know the language to speak so that anyone besides herself would understand. Maybe if the ghostly old hag appeared in the fields, Mantana could sit down and ask for some advice. Tips on how to get out of bed in the morning or raise a spoonful of rice to her mouth or respond when her name was called. Because it was these things that were becoming more and more impossible to her with each passing day. Jakkrit watched her with his alert eyes.

"Joy?"

"I don't know, Jakkrit." Then, without thinking, "Maybe it was a bad idea to come back here."

"You can't run away from yourself, Nong Joy. That's something I've learned."

As she sat dreamlessly in front of the store, fearing the day drift into night, she saw a delivery truck pass by. It was the very same company that used to ship expensive new things to Amnuay's house, back when she was a lonely widow. In the flatbed of the truck was a fine new sofa. Amnuay, as if drawn by an ugly memory, stepped outside to look.

"Do you think it's going to the Jerriporn's?" asked Mantana.

"Last month it was a new refrigerator," said Amnuay with a touch of unrequited anger in her voice. "Before that, a twenty-inch television."

Mantana turned to look up at her. Her eyes seemed to blaze in their sockets.

"That's not going to the Jerriporn's," she said. "No. These things are filling your friend Darunee's house."

"Darunee?" said Mantana, suddenly feeling her own black thoughts escape from their nest and scatter like roaches. "But Darunee's in Bangkok."

Mantana watched her stepmother, waiting for an answer that made sense and would allow her to breathe again. When she saw that one wasn't coming, she spoke again, as if in protest to the woman's silence.

"Darunee works in a department store. I know because I worked with her there for a short time myself."

"Last month it was a new refrigerator," Amnuay sighed as the exhaust trail of the delivery truck faded into the air. "Now a sofa. Well, and why not?"

She turned and moved back into the store, wrestling with her own private demons.

Ten months ago, Mantana would have spent the day wondering how Darunee, who was a lovely, though somewhat naive girl, could afford to send home the kind of money that bought fine new sofas and color televisions. Now, she no longer tapped her brain with questions. She hoped the best for her childhood friend, wherever she was, whatever she was doing, before realizing that it wasn't the best that Darunee needed. Mantana looked up at the clouds, big and white against the blue sky.

"I hope I'm wrong," she said. "For your sake, Som."

*

Meanwhile, Prapeut found work in town. The long-planned shopping center was finally ready to be built. He was especially proud, considering the firm only hired seasoned construction workers. This was not a job he had to beg for; this was a job he was asked to do.

It was a wholly different man that greeted her in the morning.

"Sleep well?' he asked. "You've been lying in bed a lot

these days. And your face looks pale. You need to eat more vegetables. Tell Amnuay to put some carrots in your dinner. Good for the blood, carrots."

Who was this man and what had he done with her father?

After Prapeut went to work, she lazed through the morning, making plans for her day. She started a List Of Things To Do but didn't get past number one: eat breakfast. She considered going to the store but knew that she would be equally bored there. No, not bored. Boredom she could fight. She felt lost. If only she had someone to talk to, maybe even cry to. Perhaps then she wouldn't feel so alone.

There was no one.

Around ten in the morning, she heard a pair of motorcycle engines outside. Mantana went to the doorway and looked out. It was two boys she recognized from the corner. One, she recalled, had once given her a ride to town. Their faces were young, their skin bad, their teeth awful. And now they sat parked in front of her house.

"We're here," said the one who had driven her to town, noticing her look out the door.

"What?" shouted Mantana.

The boys switched off their bikes.

"We're here," he said again, with an ugly smile on his face.

"So?"

They both broke into trashcan giggles.

"What do you want?" she asked.

"We heard -" said the other, but only laughed for the rest of his thought.

Mantana stepped out of the doorway.

"You heard what?"

"I've got eighty baht," said the one she had ridden with. "How much are you?"

Both boys laughed like a pair of hyenas. Mantana bent down

and picked up a rock. The Corner Boys quickly started their engines and sped away. She watched them go, poised to throw it if they decided to look back.

Bastards!

Mantana went back inside and shut all the doors and windows, despite the heat. The boys's laughter echoed in her head, and she covered her ears to try to stop it. Only two sets of laughs became four, four became eight, and soon there was an entire go-go bar filled with music and cheers and words of love, the worst kind of love, spinning in her head. This wasn't what she came home for. This wasn't what she wanted.

There was an answer. There was her father's gun. She breathed heavily as she thought of placing the barrel to her temple and silencing the voices for good. A trickle of cold sweat ran down the bridge of her nose. It wasn't the first time she had considered suicide as an option. It was, however, the first time it came without the fear of dying tacked onto the end. She sat in the hot room for nearly an hour, waiting for the static of whispers and giggles and flesh to clear from her mind. Waiting for the idea to turn sour. She was still waiting when a knock came on the door.

Instead of jerking her back into a familiar frame of mind, the sudden visit by an unknown party sent a shock wave through her that made her heart race and her head feel drunk. It was one of the Corner Boys, back to see what his eighty baht would buy. It was Jack, hoping to paint her again. It was Gilbert, wishing for more abuse. It was Walter, holding a wedding ring in his sweaty palm. Mantana pressed her forearms to the sides of her head and folded her hands at the base of her skull. She felt so hot, she imagined orange flames licking her legs and arms. Hottest of all was the burn down below, the one that used to come like a last ditch protest against the approaching night.

They wouldn't get her this time. No matter how high the bar fee, no matter how rich and handsome the man. Mantana had quit.

She was no longer available. Not now, not ever again.

She lowered her arms. The pain was gone. Everything was gone. She floated to her feet like a ghost and drifted to her father's worktable. Amnuay had never bothered to sort the screws and nails that lay scattered across the surface. What did it matter now? The key was kept on a hook, hammered into the back leg of the table. Mantana ran her hand along the edge and felt the sharp pain of a splinter enter her little finger. She drew her hand back and looked at the pinprick of blood. How odd, she thought, that she could still bleed. It occurred to her that she ought to leave a note but really had no idea what to write. Strangely enough, however, she had known for some time what her last words would be. *"I'm sorry, mother."* It was all that she felt needed to be said.

Another knock echoed through the house.

"Nong Joy!"

Mantana's hand found the key and stopped.

"Hello? Are you in there, Nong Joy?"

That voice. She knew that voice. Her heart beat in her breast as she lowered her hand. This was insanity. After months of wondering, months of waiting, she had finally reached the point of madness. Wasn't it better this way? Wasn't this what she had wanted all along? There were no mirrors in madness, no disguises or second selves. In madness, all the different parts of her could come together and eat *som tam*. The horrible and the beautiful. The hooker and the little girl. The one who had failed and the one who was never meant to succeed. Mantana stood and moved slowly to the front room. Her legs felt incredibly weak, like gravity was playing some mean, practical joke. She still had a voice. She used it.

"Hello?" she said.

"Open the door, Nong Joy."

She slid the bolt from its hole and stood back. The door opened. Yes, this was exactly what she had been waiting for.

"*Mae!*"

Mantana's mother stood before her, radiating beauty and light. If it were another of insanity's tricks that brought the two of them together, then three cheers for insanity. Somewhere there were fireworks, somewhere there was an orchestra, somewhere there was an audience looking on and drying their eyes.

"I'm sorry!" she said, and fell into the woman's arms, weeping with joy.

How odd, she thought, just before fainting, that her mother should be smoking a cigarette.

3

3 weeks earlier

It was seven o'clock on a Sunday evening when the phone rang. Phii Aor recognized the voice immediately.

"Hello? Phii Aor, *ka!* I am a Bew. Can you remember me?"

"Yes, Bew, I remember. How's your new job?"

"Tonight, I am wearing a feather dress. Do you know what is feather?"

"Yes, Bew."

"*Kon nok*," said Bew, telling her anyway. "Tonight, I am a big sexy bird."

"Is that the reason you called?" asked Phii Aor.

"No is not! Bew have any news I must to give to you."

"I'm listening."

"Today, I see Nong Joy."

Phii Aor sat upright in her chair. "What did you say?"

"Nong Joy! She here in Pattaya!"

"You've spoken with her?"

"Only short time. Phii Aor, *ka*, Nong Joy is working - not good!"

"Tell me, Bew," she said, tightening her grip on the receiver. "Tell me everything."

*

Kay was in tears. She had taken up the candles of Fai the fire woman and dripped hot wax all over her body. The show went well, for a first-time performance, and a few customers clapped their hands. Afterwards though, when she stood in the shower of the ladies toilet and scrubbed the hardened wax from her body, she discovered that a mass of red pimples had broken out on her skin. The next morning, she awoke to find that the pimples were now welts, and had spread to places the wax hadn't even touched. She was covered with them. How could she work? She couldn't, not looking the way she did. All she could do was wring her fists and cry and wonder where the money would come from to pay the rent.

"Calm down," Phii Buoy told her that afternoon in the back office of the Cherry Bar. "You're just having an allergic reaction. You'll be fine in two or three days."

"But what if I'm not?"

Phii Buoy sighed. Three quick knocks, and the office door opened. Mr. Simmons poked his head in and looked at Kay.

"Jesus Christ!" he said. "What happened to you?"

Kay burst into tears.

"What do you want?" said Phii Buoy, in a clearly irritated English.

"There's a woman here looking for Joy."

"Joy doesn't work here anymore. She quit last week."

"That's what I told her. She wants to know where she went."

Phii Buoy raised an eyebrow. She looked again at Kay,

now covering her damaged face with a pair of spotted hands and shaking from the aftermath of shedding too many tears.

"Did she say what her name was?"

"Ore," said Mr. Simmons.

"*Aor,*" she corrected. The name meant nothing to her. Whether it meant anything to Joy was another question altogether.

"Kay," she said, as tenderly as her patience would allow. "Be a good girl and wait outside, would you?"

Kay uncovered her face and spat bitterly, "Why is Joy more important than me?"

Because she made it, thought Phii Buoy, but didn't dare say so.

"Raymond, please take Kay to the doctor and get some medicine for her."

"What?" said Mr. Simmons. "Now?"

"Now."

"Well," he said, knowing that arguing was out of the question. "All right. But that's not catching, is it? Whatever she's got?"

Kay stood and moved past Mr. Simmons, out of the office.

"And Raymond?"

"What?"

"Send Miss Aor in on your way out."

*

Everyone was aware that Mantana had gone home, but no one knew exactly where that was. "Somewhere in the North," was the best answer Phii Aor could get from the girls that were called into the office. Phii Buoy told her not to worry. Neung would know. Who was Neung? Neung was once her best friend.

Neung walked into the bar at a quarter past six. Less than two minutes later, she was sitting in her boss's office, figuring one of the girls had cheated a customer and this was Phii Buoy's way of finding out who. What didn't make sense was the strange but beautiful woman who also sat in their company. They waiied each other as Phii Buoy made meaningless introductions.

"This woman is looking for Joy," said Phii Buoy. "Do you know where she is?"

Neung's eyes darted to the stranger, then to her boss. "I don't know."

"Didn't she give you an address?"

"No."

"And she never once told you the name of her village?"

"No."

Phii Buoy lost her patience. She was about to speak again when Phii Aor interrupted her.

"Neung," she said calmly, "I'm not a bad woman. I'm Joy's friend, too. A long time ago, Joy was a singer at my restaurant. I knew from the moment I saw her that there was something special about her. Everyone knew it, even the audience. I've just recently learned what became of her after she disappeared from Bangkok. To tell the truth, I expected to find her doing well for herself here and was afraid that any offer I could give wouldn't be enough. But now that she's left, I'm even more afraid. I'm afraid for her."

"She's fine," said Neung. "She just needs to be left alone."

"I'm not so sure of that," said Phii Buoy. "Nong Joy didn't go home a rich girl. In a week or two, her money will be gone. What do you think she'll do then?"

"She once said she wanted to open a *gooey teeo* stand."

"Neung," Phii Buoy said, "if you had to choose between a thousand baht night at the Cherry and a two hundred baht day selling soup, which would you choose?"

"Joy doesn't want to come back!" said Neung, frustrated, sad, and a little bit confused by the line of questions. "She hated it here."

"She hated herself," said Phii Buoy. "She hated the scars she picked up here. And like Phii Aor, I can't imagine her returning to her old life and picking up where she left off. She's too sensitive and intelligent to pretend that the past eight months of her life simply didn't happen."

The mama-san surprised herself with these words and quickly looked at Phii Aor.

"Not that I care," she said, as if suddenly remembering her mantra. "It's not my job to care."

Phii Aor folded her hands in her lap. "Nong Neung, I'm going to tell you something I haven't told anyone before."

She sighed and looked into the bargirl's eyes.

"I'm partly responsible, I believe, for Nong Joy working here. She needed to make some extra money while she was employed at my restaurant, so I sent her to work for someone who couldn't be trusted. I thought it would be for a short time, no problem. I was wrong."

Phii Aor looked down at her hands and slowly shook her head.

"If Nong Joy is happy, I'll give her my regards and be on my way. But if she's in pain, I want to do everything I can to help her."

There was a half minute of silence before Neung spoke.

"You'll let her sing at the restaurant again?"

"Nothing," said Phii Aor, "would make·me happier."

"She liked singing," said Neung, wishing with the loneliness of a single star seen through a city-lit sky that someone in the world cared about her, too.

Phii Aor unfolded her hands and leaned, ever so slightly, forward.

"Where?" she said.

*

It was another murky hot afternoon in the parking lot carnival

run by Khun Chainoi. The manager sat in the shade of the House of
Horrors, jotting down ideas in a notepad and just as quickly crossing
them out. In Thai, his spelling was poor. In English, it was
atrocious. He moved his lips and sounded out words as he wrote.
So far, he had four ideas, three of which bore a heavy black line
drawn through them.

Butifel Thailand Modals
Predy Girls For U
Titanik Modal Agensee

The last one, Sexy Lady Modal, needed something more to
it. Khun Chainoi added the words "Have Many Happy" and tapped
the pencil eraser against his pockmarked chin. It had been a long
time since he used the name "Prakanom Modeling Agency." Perhaps
it was time to drag it out of the cellar. Khun Chainoi was sure he
still had some bogus cards, displaying the company name, a P.O.
box, and a small cartoon of a girl in a red bikini holding a champagne
glass and saying hello in four different languages. It was this cartoon
that spoiled it for him. Even if a foreign bar owner didn't remember
the name, he thought, he'd surely recall seeing that cartoon
somewhere before.

Khun Chainoi crossed out the Sexy Lady Modal Have Many
Happy idea, deciding it was too long to serve as a valid title. He
needed a name that said it without saying it. He put the tip of the
pencil to the notepad and wrote:

Thailand Joy

Thailand Joy. He sat looking at the words until the sound
of gravel crunching beneath a pair of shoes - two pairs of shoes -
caused him to look up. Two men wearing long pants and sandals
approached him. The larger of the two wore a plaid denim shirt
and bore a crescent-shaped scar upon his left cheek. His partner was
snake-eyed and thin, wearing a yellow T-shirt with the Clean and Happy
logo across his chest.

"*Sawadee Krap*," said Khun Chainoi.

"*Sawadee, sawadee,*" said the men.

"Hot day, isn't it?"

"Yes," said the man in the T-shirt. "Must be at least thirty degrees Celsius."

"In the shade!" said Khun Chainoi.

"Who's in there?" said the man in the denim shirt, motioning to the House of Horrors.

"Ghosts."

"Let's go in. We need to talk."

Khun Chainoi shielded his eyes from the sun. "No one can hear us. Look around. The carnival is empty this time of day." He put down his notepad and squinted to see. "Who are you?"

The man in the T-shirt took a photo out of his back pocket and held it out for the carnival boss to see. It was a picture of a girl in a miniskirt and sparkling top. Her face was made up and smiling. Down below, in gold letters, was printed

Cowboy Rodeo Superstar: Joy

Khun Chainoi didn't have to search his memory. He knew her. She was the most beautiful girl he had ever collected on.

"Phii Aor says she worked for you once. She says you tricked her into believing she would find work as a karaoke video star, then sold her into prostitution."

"I don't sell girls into prostitution!" he snapped. "That's not what I do."

"Let's go inside," said the denim shirt.

Khun Chainoi sighed. "So you can kill me?"

"We'll talk about it inside."

"For what it's worth," said the carnival boss, "it's the foreigners I cheat. They're trying to take over our country, you know. I advertise beautiful models that want to work in their whore bars down south. I send photos, resumes, even slides. I make it look completely legal. Then I round up eight or ten girls. Poor girls, abandoned girls, girls who haven't got a chance of survival in this city any more than a cockroach does trying to cross the highway. The foreigner sends me a deposit; I send the girls. Maybe it's not the job I promised, but most of them are grateful to have found work. And the foreigners won't turn them away. They'd rather have something to show for the money they've spent than admit to being robbed."

"How is it that no one's found you yet?"

Khun Chainoi shrugged his shoulders. "I change P.O. boxes. I hire anonymous drivers. I have a few friends in the police department. The girls think I'm just a link in a very long chain. Besides, most of them have led such miserable lives, they don't know who to blame for their current misfortune. And how can any of them blame me when the final choice lies with them?"

The man in the T-shirt looked at the photo of Mantana.

"This one doesn't look as though she had it so bad."

"No," he agreed. "She was something special. I should have asked for double."

"Let's go."

Khun Chainoi dropped his notepad and pencil and slowly got to his feet.

"I can give you more than whatever Aor's paying you," he said.

"I've yet to meet one who couldn't," said the man in the denim.

"I'm not afraid, you know. It's you whom I'm afraid for. Someday soon this city will rise like a dragon and breathe fire on us all. The streets are its veins. Pollution is its skin. Selfishness and greed are its blood. You can already smell it. And, if you close your eyes, you can hear it. Yes, yes, I know. Inside."

The men followed Khun Chainoi into the House of Horrors and shot him twice in the head. His body was hoisted onto the table once used by a legless employee named Jakkrit, and left there to bleed.

That evening, customers paid ten baht each to enter and look at his corpse.

4

5 weeks later

"Ladies and gentlemen, Miss Mantana Sirilaksana!"

It was an amazing thirty-five degrees Celsius on a Sunday afternoon in April, but not even the heat could dampen the spirits of Prapeut, Amnuay, Jakkrit, Nongluck, and the rest of the villagers who had closed up shop and taken the day off to watch Nong Joy make her television debut. She looked stunning in a long pink gown that glittered beneath the lights. Her hair was done up in a classical knot and the bejeweled earrings, necklace, and tiara she wore seemed fit for a princess. Behind her, a line of female dancers swayed in tune to the opening chords of music. She sang a song in the *look thung* style that had been written for her by Phii Aor and Khun Rangsan. The name of the song was "No Part Of You," and had a chorus that went

> *You can be the front*
> *of an elephant*
> *ask me*

to be your rear
but your elephant ways
only bore me
and I see you're too drunk
to steer.

The song was a hit wherever there was a television plugged in and switched on. In the dressing room of the Pattaya Sing Sing Nightclub, Bew Beautiful screamed so loud among his fellow dancers in drag, that one of the full- length mirrors shattered into a million pieces. In a tiny room on the fourth floor of an apartment building inhabited by employees of the Bangkok-Senat Industries, a factory worker named Ning looked at the set and refused to believe her eyes. Across town, the diminutive manager of the Rim Ping Department Store stopped to look at the forty or fifty screens in the electronics department of his store and suddenly felt a headache coming on. Returning to the coast, in the back room of the Cherry Bar, Phii Buoy, Mr. Simmons, Neung, Yim, and an assortment of working girls cheered so loudly, they could barely hear what Nong Joy was singing about. As different as they all were, everyone shared the idea that the girl on television must be in the middle of a grand party (for the show wasn't live), probably being showered with roses and congratulations.

They were wrong.

Mantana had turned down an invitation from Phii Aor, and checked into a nameless hotel to watch herself sing on television. It had been a stunningly quick rise to stardom since she was released from the hospital and began her second attempt at a singing career in Phii Aor's restaurant. The doctors who treated her emphasized the importance of rest after her nervous breakdown, but Mantana preferred her own therapy. What she didn't know was that a number of eyes that lay in the darklands of the audience weren't just dirty old men and bored husbands, but agents, producers, and talent scouts as well, many of whom had wanted to sign her the first time they saw her on stage. Only the beautiful girl with the lovely voice had disappeared, without leaving so much as a forwarding address. Thus, upon the night of her sudden and unexpected re-emergence, she found herself mobbed by the group of executives and hacks, all determined not to let her get away again.

Phii Aor handled most of their questions. It was a night she too had been waiting for.

"Miss Joy, where did you go for so long?"

"She went fishing," said Phii Aor.

"Fishing for a whole year?"

"Deep sea fishing."

Her answers brought more laughter than surprise.

"Say, Joy, did you catch anything?" asked another of the men hoping for a piece of her future.

"Yes," said Mantana. "But I threw them all back."

More laughter. Joy was a hit.

Her song ended with an enthusiastic round of applause and the television program cut to a commercial for new and improved Clean and Happy. Mantana didn't feel as she thought she would feel, seeing herself on television. For some reason, she hoped that this would be the event, the next really big event in her life that would allow her to step out of her skin and become someone new. As she switched off the television, however, she knew that she wasn't going anywhere.

Things weren't all gray. The love she was shown while lying in her hospital bed helped to remind her that she wasn't as alone in the world as she often feared. Nongluck did her hair. Jakkrit talked about the future. Amnuay fussed about the pillows. And her father asked whether there was anything he could do. It all meant more to Mantana than she would ever be able to explain. She felt life return to her. She felt the horrors of nights past fade from memory, the memory behind her eyes and the memory between her legs. She almost felt whole again.

Almost.

There still remained something. A sliver of bedsheet, caught beneath a fingernail. A hint of beer breath stuck in her ear. A midnight reflection that refused to go away. These things did not come to her as images from the past, but rather as reminders of some part of herself she had banished to the dark woods and desperately needed to reclaim. It was a feeling as if she had invited everyone she knew to her going away party, but forgot to ask the one who would be hurt the most by her oversight. Who was he? What was his name? She felt that she couldn't go anywhere until she knew

Mantana put on her shoes and left the hotel room. There were things to think about - her clothes, her hair, her vague but growing popularity. Mantana didn't want to think about any of these things. Not until she had an answer. Not until she knew which question to ask. She went out into the heat and walked in the direction of the market. Here, the feeling of reality merging with nightmares might provide a clue to what she was looking for. She passed a line of women sitting behind their pots and pans of curries, brushing away flies, and moved in deeper. The river of bodies became thick, as did the air she breathed. When the crowd became impassible, she closed her eyes and listened. She was surrounded by so many different sounds, it was impossible to single out one without another quickly taking its place. Here was the scratching of plastic heels against the rough concrete. Here was a maniacal laugh, followed by the pounding of a butcher's knife against a block of wood. Here were long, rusty chains, swinging back and forth in the air above her. Here was the gibberish of a foreign tongue, describing the content of a madman's dream.

She opened her eyes. There were no demons, no ghosts. Everything - everyone - was as they should be. Everyone but her. She continued on, heavy with the sensation that she was elsewhere, and her body was only moving from the routine of being part of a crowd. She might have gone on, dreaming like this, but the woman who was walking in front of her stopped suddenly and took a full step back, right into Mantana.

"Ow!" she said, then noticed it wasn't just one clumsy woman. The entire crowd had reversed direction to allow a space to open in the middle of the walkway. Mantana pushed forward to see what was going on. She squeezed in next to the one who had bumped her and turned her attention to the dirty concrete floor.

It was a cat.

A kitten, to be precise, barely old enough to walk. The thing was white with patches of black around its eyes and ears, giving it the appearance of wearing a mask. The kitten must have wandered away from the place its mother had given birth, and stood mewing its head off to the delight of all those around.

"Look at it!"

"The poor thing!"

"Give it some milk!"

Mantana waited. The tiny creature looked around, took a step, then continued its relentless crying. *This is your moment* she wanted to tell the terrified creature; *enjoy it while it lasts.* Just then, a small child came forward from the opposite side of the circle. This one too walked with the unbalanced steps of early youth. Although the child wore yellow pants and a dancing bananas T-shirt, Mantana found it impossible to tell whether it was a little boy or a little girl. The length of the hair, the shape of the mouth, nothing gave the kid away. The child's eyes were fixed upon the kitten, however, and his or her amazement brought even more joy to the faces watching.

"Awww!"

"What a sweetie!"

The child approached the kitten and stood, transfixed for a moment, observing its delicate movements. Then, with a quickness and agility well beyond the child's years, the little boy or girl lifted an orange-shoed foot and brought it down across the back of the unsuspecting creature. A collective gasp interlaced with a few screams shook the rusty chains that hung above. Mantana covered her mouth as a woman, probably the child's mother, rushed forward to scoop her son or daughter up in her arms.

"Naughty! Naughty!" she cried, and pushed her way back into the crowd of horrified onlookers.

The kitten was still alive. Its back was broken and a strange, milky froth had gathered at its nose and mouth. A hunchbacked man wearing a dirty red apron appeared as if on cue, holding a long pair of metal tongs in his veiny hands. He picked the kitten off the concrete and deposited it in a nearby garbage bag, already overflowing with banana leaves and plastic food containers.

"Good bye, kitty," he chortled, and limped back to wherever he came from.

The crowd moved on, some chattering about the sadness of life, others too stunned to say anything at all. Mantana walked with them, dazed at first, then slowly feeling that sleeping part of her awaken and throw a lump of coal into an ash-laden furnace inside her. By the time she reached the other side of the market, she was, well, smiling. *Smiling!* Her brain replayed the scene of the innocent child stamping on the even more innocent kitten, ha ha, and the horrible shock, tee hee, that followed. Horrible? Why, yes, simply awful! She covered her mouth, this time to hide the giggles that were escaping from her lips. Another moment, and she had to lean against the side of a building to prevent herself from exploding with laughter.

What a bad, bad girl she was!

Yes, perhaps, but for the first time in a long time, she felt whole again. This was the way it was for her now, and there was no sense in calling a mango blue or the moon cheese, or a rose perfect when everyone knew it had thorns that could bite.

She sang the lyrics to a popular and meaningless love song

as she hailed a taxi to take her to Phii Aor's restaurant. It would soon be the beginning of another night. Mantana felt some applause was finally due.